SWEET SEDUCTION

Colin leaned close and kissed her tenderly. Rivers of fire coursed through Meary's veins.

"Please do not be doing that," she begged.

He kissed her again. "Don't you like it?"

"Of course I like it. 'Tis why I must be insisting ye stop." It wasn't at all what she had meant to say, but she didn't know how to call the words back.

"But I don't want to stop," he breathed against her ear.

Meary felt herself melting against the strong arms embracing her, leaning closer into his broad chest. Every sense seemed multiplied tenfold. She found herself returning his gentle kisses, tentatively at first, then more boldly. It was heavenly lying here kissing him and being kissed by him. She wanted the moment to last forever. . . .

RENE J. GARROD

WILD IRISH EMBRACE

ZEBRA BOOKS
KENSINGTON PUBLISHING CORP.

ZEBRA BOOKS

are published by

Kensington Publishing Corp.
475 Park Avenue South
New York, NY 10016

First printing: June, 1992

Printed in the United States of America

To my husband Delmar,

*Because no hero of my imagination
will ever hold a candle
to the flesh and blood man I married.
Thank you for your patience.*

I love you.

Chapter 1

County Clare, Ireland
1712

Meary O'Byrne tensed, alert to the vibrations of horse hooves upon the sod. The rider, whoever he might be, was advancing at a thunderous pace. Her slender fingers tightened on the intricately carved head of her walking cane, and she made her way to the verge of the lane. The two men with her followed, pricking their ears, and within moments they too could hear the pounding approach of the steed. The three stood side by side as they waited for the rider to pass.

Seumas O'Hanlon held fast to the leads of their cart pony, alternately stroking the pony's velvety nose and his own wild mane of coarse, shoulder-length, grey hair. "In a fine hurry some fool is," he observed in his native Gaelic tongue.

"Aye," said Meary, sidling a few inches closer to him.

Flanking her left side, Brendan, the third member of their little traveling troupe, nodded and slipped a

7

protective arm around Meary's shoulders.

The drum of hoofbeats grew louder and louder, but just before the rider reached them Meary heard the pounding slow and lighten. As horse and rider came abreast of them and stopped, she could hear the blowing of the horse's lungs and smell the mingled scents of leather and sweat.

"Good day to you," a rich, baritone voice greeted in English.

Meary felt Brendan stiffen, and she patted his hand. His distrust and dislike of anything and anyone English was admirable, but he possessed not an agile mind and was wont to do and say things unwise. She held tight to his hand as she waited for Seumas to give reply to the stranger.

Lord Colin Garrick surveyed the group before him as he awaited a response to his salutation. All were dressed in a fashion several years behind that of London but current by Irish standards, the quality of their garments bespeaking neither great wealth nor penury.

Though the old man was short of stature, he being only slightly taller than his shaggy pony, and his limbs were gnarled by disease or some cruel trick of nature, he stared boldly up at him with piercing, sea-foam green eyes. There was keen intelligence in his assessing gaze, and the contrast of his savage looks made the keenness all the more evident.

The younger man stared too, with the open contempt of a willful child. His eyes were a startling emerald green. He was tall and spare, and he boasted a thick head of auburn hair cropped at the collar.

But it was the young woman with them who caught and

8

held Lord Colin's attention. Never in this life had he hoped to see such perfection in the female form. She was an angel. Pale. Ethereal. Exquisite. A cascade of waist-length, flaxen hair framed her heart-shaped face. Her eyes were the color of hyacinths, her nose small and straight, her lips the hue of a virgin's blush.

He repeated his greeting, this time in halting Gaelic.

"Ye know our tongue?" she asked.

Her voice did not disappoint. It was as lilting as her face was beautiful. "I speak a half dozen words at best. I understand a little more," Lord Colin replied. "And you? Do you speak English?"

"I speak Gaelic and Latin and Greek. English I speak only of dire necessity. 'Tis such a coarse language, don't ye think?" Meary responded to his question in Gaelic.

His saddle creaked beneath his weight. "I fear my understanding of your language is insufficient to follow your speech. Pray answer me in English, if you are able."

She repeated her answer in English.

"Had I been previously inclined to be disloyal to my mother tongue, you have dissuaded me. When you speak it, it has the sound of melody," he informed her.

"Then mayhap I shall not speak it to ye again," she retorted, secretly assigning his compliment to her voice to his own resonant tone.

"My dear lady, you must speak it. Else how shall we converse? My ignorance of your language puts me at your mercy."

Meary raised her chin a notch and cocked her head to one side. A slow, sportive, smile spread across her face. The English stranger intrigued. "An Englishman at the mercy of a poor Irish maid. Now, there's a pretty picture.

'Tis many wrongs I'm tempted to avenge for me country-men. Do not put yourself at me mercy.''

"How can I not?"

"Ye wish to trod on Irish soil, then learn to speak with an Irish tongue," she advised.

"Admirable advice." Lord Colin proclaimed as he contemplated a lively notion. His days and nights were long and lonely. The lady was lovely. Prudence and practicality demanded one day he learn the Irish language. He was of a sudden in the mood for a few days' pleasant diversion. "Will you do me the honor of becoming my tutor?" he asked.

The thus far mute old man stepped forward. "Nay, she will not! Begone with ye!" he shouted in faultless English, waving his arms at milord's steed.

Lord Colin held his horse in check. "Are you the lady's sire?"

"I am Seumas O'Hanlon, poet, weaver of tales, and gentleman of letters. Meary O'Byrne is a child of me heart not of me loins, but I guard her no less diligently had God blessed me otherwise. She does not tutor smooth-tongued, English dogs."

"Ah, you misjudge me. It is precisely because I am not well-oiled of tongue I request her tutelage."

Meary listened to the exchange, feeling a mixture of amusement and alarm. It was not like Seumas to openly taunt the English usurpers. Many was the time he had cautioned her it was imprudent to make one's private opinions public.

Seumas continued to scowl and flap his arms. "Begone or I'll put a curse upon yer head."

"I have heard of your poets' curses. Shall you raise

boils upon my brow?" Lord Colin inquired calmly.

"Likely in a more private place," Seumas rejoined.

"Indeed." Lord Colin was well used to the prejudice of the Irish against him and was tempted to be on his way, but the woman faced him unabashed and unblinking. There was a haunting quality in her deep blue eyes, an inscrutable quality about her entire person that urged him to stay and vie for the right to a few days of her company. "Mayhap a compromise is in order. I see by the contents of your cart you are musicians." He addressed his next words to Meary. "Lady, come to my household and play for me."

"Why should an angel be playing for a devil?" Seumas demanded.

"She should not," Colin quietly replied. He shifted on his mount, again giving Meary his full attention. "What say you, fair lady? Will you play for a mortal man? Will you play for a man who is guilty of no more or no less sin than the next fellow?"

"Nay," Seumas answered him.

"I asked the lady," Lord Colin rebuked.

Meary struggled within herself. She wanted to play for this man, even if he was an English devil. She liked the sound of him. He piqued her curiosity. But she could not in good conscience defy Seumas's wishes in the matter. Love and respect for her adoptive father and mentor decided her words. Drawing herself up, she resolutely replied, "I shall not be playing for ye."

"Then, I bid you good day, fair Meary," he said, his deep voice brittle with some dark emotion.

Meary fingered the ridges of the wolf head adorning her cane as she listened to the slap of leather, followed by the heavy thud of horse hooves rapidly striking the turf, fade into the distance. Her carriage lost its stiffness and she frowned.

"What 'tis it, Meary?" Brendan asked. "What 'twas it that bad man said to make ye be looking so sad?"

"'Twas nothing he said, Brendan."

Brendan hunched his shoulders and scuffed the toe of his shoe in the dirt. His voice barely above a whisper, he asked, "'Tis it me making ye frown? Are ye angry with me 'cause I be too dull-witted to be understanding what he said?"

"Nay, Brendan, nay." Meary squeezed his hand. "I'm not angry with ye. How could I be? Ye are the sweetest brother a maid could ever wish for."

"But I'm not clever like ye and Seumas."

"Ye are kind, and kindness 'tis a far greater virtue than sharp wits."

Satisfied, Brendan took the leads to the pony from Seumas's hands and coaxed the pony and cart back onto the lane. Upon hearing the rasp of the rotating wheels, Meary fell in behind the cart. Seumas shambled to Meary's side. He tucked his knotty fingers around the smooth hand holding the cane as they walked.

"So, shall ye be telling *me* what 'tis marring yer countenance?" he asked.

"I have a wish to play for the man."

"Do ye mind telling me why?"

Meary shrugged. "What harm can it do? We've played for the English before. Ye have said 'tis wise to keep our eye upon our enemy."

"Me old eyes have seen all of him they care to. I don't like the look of him, Meary. Especially the look of him

12

when his gaze be lighting upon you."

"How does he look?" she queried.

"Hungry."

Meary laughed with gay reproof. "Ye need have no fear I'll fall prey to an Englishman's blandishments."

"Have I not? Never before have ye questioned me judgment when I say where we will and will not play."

She had no ready answer to his words. They were the truth. Still, she could not slough off this odd need she had to learn more about the stranger who had crossed their path. "'Tis just I have a feeling about the man. I *feel* we should play for him."

"This feeling ye have only compounds me fear for ye," he argued.

"'Tis not an affection for him I'm feeling. 'Tis the other." Her pensive smile was as enchanting as a cherub's. "Ye have always told me I should be trusting these queer feelings I get."

"That I have," Seumas admitted, a note of resignation creeping into his voice. "But are ye sure 'tis the angels speaking to ye and not the devil himself?"

"Aye. 'Tis the same as always when I know what I should be doing without knowing the why of it." She could feel Seumas's gaze upon her, studying her intently.

"I can see ye be telling me the truth," he sighed out after a long spell of silence. "I can't be arguing with Providence. We'll find yer Englishman and play for him."

"Thank ye, Seumas."

"I'll not be accepting yer thanks. I may be willing to do this for ye, but 'tis done with a heavy heart."

Meary stroked the sleeve of his forearm. "Ye worry

13

overmuch for me."

" 'Tis worried ye'd be too if ye could see him as I do."

"Mayhap if ye tell me how ye see him, me feelings will change."

"Would that I could be believing that, but fate does not shift her will as readily as the wind changes course. If 'tis meant to be that ye play for the brute, I fear we must resign ourselves to enduring the ordeal."

"Tell me what ye think of his person just the same," she pleaded.

"I'd say he's a tall man, lean . . . and dark of hair. His head 'twas bereft of wig and powder, worn like a trades-man, tied back in a riband," Seumas began his descrip-tion, imbuing it with the rich and elaborate details of a seasoned storyteller. "His brows be straight and his eyes a deep brown. He has a small scar upon his cheek. His nose 'tis of reasonable size. His mouth wide. His jaw neither pointed nor square."

"And his garments? What have ye to say of those?"

"They be those of a gentleman of wealth. His coat 'twas pure scarlet and fine-tailored. His neckcloth and the cuffs of his sleeves stitched from good lawn and lace. His breeches be made of excellent leather. And his jack-boots fit his legs well and 'twere black as the sky on a stormy eve."

"Would ye judge him handsome?"

"Some, I'm sure, would say he's so. But me, I prefer to do me judging of a man's handsomeness by looking to the handsomeness of his deeds."

"So, I would not be far wrong if I were to be believing his face 'tis as fine as his voice," Meary spoke her thoughts out loud.

14

" 'Tis talk like that 'twill bring me to an early grave. He's not a man for ye, Meary. He's an Englishman."

" 'Tis curiosity, nothing more, I assure ye. I've no use for an Englishman no matter how fair of face," said Meary firmly rejecting the implication her interest might be more than she was professing. She gently traced the fingertips of her free hand first over her lips, then over her eyes and down her nose and cheeks. "And what if I did want him? He'd not have me if ye were to serve me up on a silver platter. . . . Or have ye forgotten that I'm blind?"

Chapter 2

If Seumas disagreed with the sentiment of Meary's last speech, he did not give voice to a contrary opinion.

Meary was grateful he didn't seek to coddle her with cajolery. Blind she was, and no amount of wishing it was otherwise would change the fact. After her accident, she had been bitter, biliously bitter, but years ago she had battled her way up from a soul-smothering morass of self-pity and had come to accept herself as she now was. Part of accepting the loss of her sight was also accepting the loss of the traditional dreams of maidenhood.

Meary did not cling to a false modesty. She knew she possessed a rare beauty. She knew because she was constantly told it was so and because she remembered her face and figure from the time before the accident. But beauty was of scant use to a blind maiden.

Men, be they Irish or English, were not eager to form attachments with maidens such as she. Especially since the flight of so many young Irishmen to the continent had left Ireland overflowing with maidens pining for mates—maidens who could tend to a man's needs far more efficiently than she was able.

Meary bore the knowledge her life would never be touched by romance with little regret or rancor. In truth, she had never met a man she desired to wed, so she counted it no great loss. She had Seumas and Brendan who loved her well. She had her music. She was given a gracious welcome, food enough to fill her belly, and shelter wherever she went. She was content. Nay, more than content. Her life was a joyous celebration of everything worth holding dear.

Her thoughts circled back to the Englishman. He hadn't even given them his name. So, why did she feel it important that they travel to his home? She pondered the question for a long while before shrugging her shoulders and abandoning the futile quest for an answer. When the time came, she would know. For the present, she would just be satisfied Seumas was willing to bend to her bidding.

They trudged along for the space of several hours, Brendan leading the pony cart, Seumas and Meary trailing behind. Conversation was spare and sporadic and concerned nothing of consequence.

At midday, they stopped. Meary helped Brendan spread a blanket on the heath while Seumas brought out the oatcakes, goat cheese, and a jug of *troander* that their most recent patron had provided them. A westerly breeze caressed Meary's face, and she paused to draw in deep breaths laden with the fragrances of sea, sod, and wild thyme before she began to apply herself to an oatcake.

"There be a cottage up ahead," Seumas commented between chews. "I suppose we ought to be stopping there to be asking after the Englishman."

"I cannot see your scowl, but I can feel it," Meary said.

"Mayhap 'twill not be as vexatious as ye fear, playing for the Englishman."

"Will it not? Mayhap 'twill be worse."

Meary laughed at his dire prediction. "I fear ye are thinking with your passions and not with the fine head ye wear upon your shoulders. A wise man once told me 'tis a dangerous thing to do."

Seumas snorted in disgust at having his own advice thrown back at him.

Meary continued, "We know nothing of this Englishman to be making us hate him above any other. In truth, ye must admit he has presented himself better. What other Englishman do we know has expressed a wish to learn to speak Irish?"

"The wish he expressed was to be having the saucy wench he met upon the road by his side. His wish to learn our language 'tis a ruse. He forsook it quickly enough when I told him nay."

Meary pursed her lips. " 'Tis true. Still, if ruse it be, 'tis an unusual one. Mayhap I shall put him to a test when we find him."

"I pray that we do not find him," Seumas grumbled. "Though in this sparse country, I fear he'll be all too easy to find."

Smiling, Meary reached for a hunk of cheese. Brendan subtly guided her fingers a few inches to the left. Her prize in hand, she brought it to her lips, testing the taste and texture with her lips and tongue before she took a bite. After chewing and swallowing a morsel of the tangy cheese, she softly queried, "Even without a name to aid our search?"

"A rich Englishman living among poor Irish doesn't go unnoticed," Seumas proclaimed. "Likely, we'll meet

18

legions ready to be telling us the tales of his theft and brutality."

"I grant ye he could not have come by Irish soil except by theft, but he did not sound like a brutal man."

"How can ye defend a man ye do not know?"

"'Tis just a feeling," she answered serenely.

"Bah! *Me feelings* be telling me ye are leading us into a kettle full of trouble."

"Seumas, ye have the gift too? Why have ye not told me before?" Meary chided impishly.

"Nay, I have not yer gift." Seumas tweaked her upturned chin. "But I have eyes and ears and a nose to smell vermin when they be sniffing about me treasures."

"If he be vermin, I'll light a torch and drive him away from our Meary," Brendan chimed in.

"Ye'll do naught unless I be telling ye to," Seumas cautioned. "I'll not see ye hanged."

"But if he tries to hurt our Meary . . ."

"I won't be letting him do that, Brendan, I assure ye. If he lays a hand upon her, I'll be taking care of him meself."

Meary shook her head and let out a long-suffering sigh. "The two of ye are worse than prattling old woman. I can be taking care of meself where the Englishman is concerned."

"Ye are too independent for yer own good, Meary O'Byrne."

"'Twas ye who taught me to be so, Seumas O'Hanlon," she retorted.

"I overdid me lessons. How was I to be knowing the weepy little blind orphan I took under me wing would grow to be so headstrong?"

Meary laughed. "Ye have known me since I was a babe.

19

Had ye not an inkling?"

"Aye, I should have seen it coming," he groaned. "I let me sorrow for ye make me as blind as thee."

"And in truth ye do not regret it."

Seumas gifted her with a discordant symphony of guttural moans and keening wails before proudly admitting, "'Tis true. I don't regret it."

Meary leaned close and kissed his weathered cheek. There was no one on this earth she loved better than Seumas, and no one with whom she found more pleasure in engaging in a game of words. Often they argued for the sheer joy of whetting the talents of their tongues and the shrewdness of their wits. Today was no different, except she sensed Seumas truly was wary for her where the Englishman was concerned. Rather than alarm her, his wariness made her that much more curious about the man they had met upon the road.

They consumed the last of their meal in compatible repartee. When she was finished, Meary stood and shook the crumbs from her skirt. "'Tis going to rain within the hour," she announced.

Seumas glanced up. Towering columns of grey-black clouds gathering in the sky supported her prediction. "Aye. We best be moving on our way if we hope to be reaching shelter in time."

They arrived at the cottage just as the first cold, fat raindrops began to fall upon their heads. A rail of a woman wearing a ragged, woolen dress stepped out the door to greet them. Reed-thin children followed at her barefoot heels.

"Good day to ye. Good day to ye," the peasant woman

greeted enthusiastically. "Come in and get yer fine selves out of the rain."

"We be thankful to ye for yer hospitality," Seumas replied.

He ushered Meary through the door of the stone cottage while Brendan made sure the instruments in the cart were completely and securely covered with a tarpaulin before following the others into the one room dwelling.

Seumas led Meary to a rough-hewn stool near the hearth, then settled himself on a bench flanking the trestle table in the middle of the room.

A few moments later the lady of the house was pressing wooden tankards of home-brewed ale into her guests' hands, apologizing as she did so. "'Tis a poor brew at best, but 'tis all I have to be offering, and 'twill take the chill out of yer bones."

"'Tis fine, generous hands that offer it, so to me 'twill taste like heavenly nectar," Seumas assured her, then took a sip and smiled convincingly despite the unappealing taste.

"Ye be a true gentleman," his hostess announced.

Meary tasted the liquid in her own cup and was inclined to agree with their hostess. The stuff was weak and flavorless, but because she knew it truly was the best the woman had to offer, she too pretended to take delight in the beverage.

The musky odor of turf smoke permeated the cottage, overlaying the stale aroma of toil-tempered bodies living in close quarters. Continuing to explore her surroundings with her finely tuned senses, Meary listened to the shuffle of feet moving about the room, trying to determine how many pairs there might be. She guessed

21

the number of people in the cottage at six, but as she was about to give voice to her conjecture, her ears picked up the sound of cooing coming from the corner. Abandoning all thought of anyone else in the room, she eagerly asked, "Please, may I hold the babe?"

"Of course ye may." Their hostess retrieved her child and settled him into Meary's waiting arms. "His name 'tis Brian," she announced proudly. "I named him after the great Brian Boru."

" 'Tis a fine name for a fine boy," Meary complimented as she cuddled him close. Stroking the silky fuzz atop his tiny head, she nuzzled her nose against his neck, reveling in the divine scent of newborn flesh.

Confident her son was in good hands, the lady turned her attention back to Seumas. "Ye all be welcome to stay here as long as ye like."

"Grateful we are for yer offer, but we won't be troubling ye longer than it takes the storm to pass."

" 'Tis no trouble. Anything Brigitte Deane can be doing for the great Seumas O'Hanlon and his friends 'tis an honor."

"Ye have heard of me?"

"Who in all Ireland has not? I recognized ye the moment I laid me eyes upon ye," she assured him. "Yer skill with words 'tis without equal."

"Do not be saying that in front of me Meary," Seumas admonished, grinning broadly.

The sound of her name caused Meary to raise her head and attend the conversation more closely.

Seumas continued without pause, "She fancies herself possessed of a more nimble tongue than I."

" 'Tis not true." Meary spoke the words to the babe in her arms, but she made sure they were loud enough for all to hear. "Me tongue may be well-honed from the years I've spent in his company, but I still lose more battles than I win."

"A piteous maid, is she not?" Seumas gleefully mourned her plight. "Twenty years of age and she has yet to achieve the wisdom of an old man."

All present joined in his mirth.

As a steady torrent of spring rain drummed upon the thatched roof of the cottage, Seumas proved their hostess's high regard well-founded by entertaining the household with enthralling tales of the daring deeds and heart-stopping adventures of Irish men and women past and present.

Meary sat, content by the hearth, rocking the babe while she listened to the familiar stories and the equally familiar gasps and squeals as his audience reacted to the vivid scenes he painted with his words.

Brendan squatted on the dirt floor at her feet, his head resting against her knee.

At length, the shadows of dusk began to fill the room, and Mrs. Deane stirred herself to begin preparing the evening meal. "It looks as though the rain 'twill not be stopping for ye this day. The saints be smiling on Brigitte Deane and her kin," she announced as she nestled a fresh piece of dried turf into the embers glowing on the hearth and hung a pot of water on the hook above the fire.

Seumas accepted the compliment to the pleasure of his company with one of his own. "In all me travels, I've never told me tales to a finer audience."

As Mrs. Deane prepared potatoes for the pot, she and Seumas continued to exchange compliments. It wasn't long before her husband and two older children entered the cottage.

After introducing himself and his progeny, Mr. Deane pronounced himself every bit as delighted as his wife to have them in his home.

Meary smiled at his warm greeting. Wherever they traveled, it was the same. No matter how poor the household, they were always welcome.

When she was younger, she had once questioned Seumas about the morality of accepting food from those who had so little for themselves. He had told her a heart full of pride was more important than a belly full of food. She hadn't completely understood his meaning that day, but over time experience had brought her enlightenment.

To refuse a family's generosity merely because they were poor would be the meanest of insults.

Tonight they would sing and play for the Deanes as sweetly as they would play for royalty. They would give them a bright memory to keep them warm on cold winter nights. Their children would tell their children of the night their house was blessed by a visit from the great Seumas O'Hanlon.

The food they consumed was insignificant when compared to the pleasure they could give to people whose pleasures were far too few.

Their supper consisted of boiled potatoes and buttermilk, the mainstay of every peasant home, but what the dinner lacked in grandeur was more than made up for by the quality of companionship. The cottage was alive with a melee of conversation as everyone happily chattered with everyone else.

The merry mood continued uninterrupted until they came to the end of the meal. As Mr. Deane urged Seumas to take the last potato on the trencher, he innocently inquired, "Where is it ye be coming from and where is it ye be traveling next?"

"Most recently we come from Castle Athenry, but 'tis a rare acre in Ireland we've never called home. As to where we be going; 'tis a mystery I'd be happy not to be solving." As he said the last, Seumas's voice rumbled with discontent.

When he refused to seize the opportunity to elicit the information they sought, Meary interjected, "We are looking for an Englishman."

A hush fell over the room. Undeterred by the stony silence round the table, Meary borrowed Seumas's words to describe the one they sought, ending with, "Have ye seen or heard of him?"

"Aye. He be living in the old tower house upon the cliffs. 'Tis an hour's hard ride from here. Half a day on foot," Mr. Deane said.

"Has he lived there long?"

"Two seasons, no more. 'Twas his uncle stole the land from the rightful Irish owner. He never set foot on it. Gave its keeping over to a manager with less brains than a sheep and a cruel streak as wide as the River Shannon."

"And the new lord?" Meary pressed.

"He inherited the land from his uncle," Mrs. Deane provided the information.

"Do ye know his name?"

"He calls himself Lord Colin Garrick. They say he be the second son of some English marquess."

"How come ye by yer information?" Seumas queried, relieving Meary of the burden of conducting the inquiry all alone.

"Me cousin Fiach and his family work his land. Fiach told me all he knew to tell when his family came to be paying us a visit last Christmastide," the lady responded.

"Did yer cousin Fiach tell ye how the new lord be treating his tenants?" Seumas probed.

"Only that he be no more terrible than the one before him. But the new lord, he had come less than a fortnight before me cousin paid his visit, so who knows the truth of him?" She lowered her voice to an ominous whisper, "Could be by now he's proven himself to be a far worse monster than the one who come before him."

Chapter 3

Lord Colin Garrick stood before the long, narrow window of his bedchamber, staring out to sea. Yesterday the waters had echoed the stormy grey of the skies, but this morning whitecapped waves of crystal blue danced under the mid-May sunshine. The rhythmic resounding of water meeting land soothed like a whispered lullaby.

He stretched his arms high above his head and indulged his senses a little longer. The lord who had built this stone tower so many centuries ago had chosen his location well. Lord Colin realized the original lord no doubt had built his home upon the cliffs for reasons of defense rather than an affinity for the elemental beauty, but he felt a strange kinship with him. This was his land now. From his chamber atop the tower he could look out in any direction and know all he saw was his—his and no other's.

Six months he had been in Ireland, and they had been the most gratifying months of his life. Not that the Irish welcomed him. To the contrary, when he had first arrived, they had done all they could to drive him from the land. Even now, after he had proven himself to be a fair landlord, many of his tenants remained sullen and wary. No, it was not so much what he had come to in Ireland as what he had left behind in England that made him so content with his new home.

A knock at the door brought his attention round from the window.

"Is his lordship ready to be breaking his fast?" a shy, female voice called from the other side. Her English was halting but improving.

"I'll be down in a moment," he replied.

"Aye, milord. I'll be telling Annie ye said so."

As Colin listened to the rapid retreat of slipper-shod feet upon the stone steps, he smiled. Annie was the only servant he had brought with him from England, and she ruled his household like a tyrant. It was she who was determined all his servants become fluent in English, and she brooked no resistance of her native tongue nor any other dictate of her iron will. Everyone for miles around lived in terror of her temper.

He laughed out loud. He was ofttimes tempted to tell the poor souls who fell victim to her fury she was all blush and bluster, that her heart was as soft as a kitten, but long-held affection for the woman kept him silent. He could see no harm in letting her revel in her moment of omnipotence. The first time one of his servants or tenants found themselves in true need of a champion, they would find her out soon enough.

His eyes darkened and his face lost its merry mien as his mind filled with the memory of the day they had taken Annie away from him. He'd been only seven years of age when they'd thrown her out in the cold, and there was not a thing he could do to help her. For years he had worried over her welfare. As soon as he had turned into a man, he'd set out in search of her. Annie had done well enough for herself without his help, but when he'd asked her to head his household, she had not hesitated to return to him. Annie was his friend. Annie was the one person in this world he truly trusted. The smile returned to his lips.

Knowing full well he too would be subjected to one of his housekeeper's famous tongue lashings if his breakfast was cold when he arrived below stairs, Lord Colin straightened the lace of his sleeves, abandoned his musings, and followed the steps of the serving maid down the spiral staircase to the great hall.

With each step she took Meary felt the odd excitement within her mount. They had been walking for several hours, and she knew they must reach their destination soon.

She had no idea how pleased Lord Colin Garrick would be to see them, but she knew *she* would be pleased when they arrived at his door. All morning she had thought of little else, and her curiosity was driving her to the brink of distraction. Patience had never been a virtue to which she could lay claim, and she was eager to discover just what fate had in store.

The heavy rains had released the rich, sweet scents of the soil, and they mingled with the salt spiced breeze blowing off the sea.

Brendan softly whistled the tune of a popular tragic ballad. The wheels of the pony cart produced a continuous slurp-squish as they rolled over the sodden earth. The raucous cries of kittiwakes and puffins and the deep voice of the sea joined in to create a symphony of sounds.

Meary raised her face heavenward, inviting the sun to beat down upon her pale skin. It warmed her and she sighed contentedly as she walked along side Seumas.

A rumbling of indiscernible words rolled from her mentor's lips, punctuating the sounds of sea, sky, and earth. She smiled sympathetically. Poor man. He had been uncommunicative all morning, but his sporadic bursts of muttered curses made his mood easy enough to read.

Meary understood his motives far better than her own, and she could only pray his prediction that she was leading them "into a kettle full of trouble" proved false for his sake as well as her own.

A few moments later, another string of curses burst forth from Seumas's lips, this one longer and louder than the ones that had preceded it.

"What 'tis it, Seumas?" she asked genially.

"I can be seeing the tower up ahead, standing on the cliffs just where the Deanes said it would be," Seumas informed her.

Meary felt her heartbeat quicken, but she repressed all outward sign of her excitement. "'Twill be good to rest our feet for a day or two," she casually commented.

Seumas responded with a forceful, "Hrmph."

Meary had no intention of arguing with his assessment of the situation. Not only would it do not a whit of good, but his worry might be well-founded. The voice in her head was telling her it was important she go to the Englishman's estate. It was not telling her why.

The closer they came to their destination, the more sounds of human activity Meary discerned. She concentrated on translating the information her ears brought

30

her into a vision of the scene in her head. If her ears were to be believed, Lord Colin made his living from tenants who tended cattle in the main and sheep to a lesser degree. Such was not unusual for this part of Ireland. They passed one plot where the cackle of hens could be heard and another where the squealing of several pigs evinced a moderate level of prosperity.

By focusing her thoughts on her physical surroundings, Meary was able to keep the niggling doubts that might have undermined her confidence at bay. Let Seumas and Brendan do the worrying if any worrying needed to be done. She preferred to interpret the tension in her muscles as anticipation rather than trepidation.

A flurry of activity around her alerted Meary to their arrival in the yard of the manor house. Two women engaging in earnest conversation scurried across the grounds. A male voice shouted orders. Someone was scratching the earth with a hoe. The sharp ring of a stone-mason's hammer striking his chisel grew louder and louder as they approached the house.

Seumas touched her hand to signal the pony cart ahead of them had come to a halt. She stopped, her fingers reflexively polishing the head of her walking cane as she awaited the announcement of their arrival.

"Shall ye be wanting me to do the knocking at the door?" Brendan asked apprehensively when Seumas hesitated to move in that direction.

"Nay, I'll be doing the deed meself," Seumas put his mind at ease. "Ye come here and stand by our Meary."

As soon as she felt Brendan's presence by her side, Meary extended her hand to him and enfolded his hand in hers. His was icy cold. Brendan was habitually timid when they arrived at a new house, and she was not overly concerned by the anxiety manifest in his voice and the temperature of his skin. Still, she felt compelled to reassure him. "'Twill be all right, I promise ye," she whispered.

"Do ye promise ye won't be letting him hurt ye?"

"I promise, but ye worry for naught. There is no more danger in this house than any other."

Brendan started at the sound of Seumas's fist striking the door, his hand tightening around Meary's. "But Mrs. Deane said he be a monster."

"Ye misunderstood the lady's words, Brendan," Meary explained. Before she gave offense, she was quick to add, "'Tis not your fault. Seumas has filled your head with nonsense where the Englishman is concerned. What the lady said was that the man before him was a monster. This lord she knows little of."

"Are ye sure?"

"Very sure." Meary professed absolute confidence, but she was not quite so certain as she proclaimed to be. All this talk of trouble and the threat of harm was a bit unnerving. What if the feeling she had was false or the path fate desired to lead her down was a road to disaster? She shifted her weight from one foot to the other. She was no meek lamb to be led to slaughter. She had no desire to further their acquaintance with this lord if the price was to be too great.

"But why would Seumas be lying to me?" Brendan's plaintive question interrupted her frenetic flow of thoughts, and she pushed down her misgivings with a firm mental hand.

"He didn't lie to ye, Brendan. Ye know he would never do that." Meary paused, choosing her next words carefully so they would bring both solace and understanding to Brendan. "Seumas is sometimes overprotective where I am concerned. We both know that. We cannot condemn him for it because he is so because of his love for me, but we need not be taking everything he says so seriously."

"I wish I was more like ye are, Meary," Brendan stated wistfully, his voice evincing little of the calm her words had been designed to promote. "Ye are always so brave."

The staccato pounding of Meary's heart, for what she judged as no good reason, belied his words. Sighing out a deep breath that did scant to steady her nerves, she said, "I fear 'tis far from true, Brendan, but I thank ye for the compliment nevertheless."

Their conversation ceased at the creaking of the door upon its hinges followed by a proprietary, feminine voice asking in English, "What is it you want?"

"The master of this house if he be Lord Colin Garrick. Is he within?" Seumas responded in kind.

"He is but you'll not be seeing him unless you tell me who you are and what business you have with him."

"I am Seumas O'Hanlon. I be having no *business* with yer lord. We are musicians. He invited us to his home to play for him."

"He told me naught of any such invitation."

"If we are not to be welcomed, we'll be more than happy to be traveling on our way," Seumas informed her, his voice positively singing with satisfaction and relief. "Good day to ye, ma'am."

Her lips compressed with annoyance, Meary stepped forward. Seumas must hold a mean opinion of her indeed if he thought she would allow herself to be so easily outmaneuvered. Privately she might entertain her own doubts about the wisdom of fraternizing with this English lord, but having come so far, she saw no purpose to be served in running away at first opportunity. The door would not be locked. If coming here proved a dreadful mistake, they could leave any time they chose. "Please, tell your lord we are here," she firmly requested, her determination to stay—at least until they had had a chance to speak to Lord Colin—as strong as Seumas's desire to avoid the man.

"And who are you?"

"I am Meary O'Byrne. 'Twas to me Lord Colin extended his invitation, and I must be insisting ye tell him we have arrived."

"Meary, if we are not welcome here . . ."

She turned from the woman blocking their way to face Seumas. "How can we be knowing if we are welcome or not if this woman will not be telling the master of the house we are here?"

"Who is here?"

Immediately, Meary recognized the voice belonged to the man she sought, and she turned back to face the door, squaring her carriage as she listened to the clack of booted feet striding across a stone floor. A moment later, she felt his presence in the doorway. A surge of exhilaration suffused her being, sweeping from the top of her head down to her toes.

"Oh, it is you," he said without a trace of warmth or enthusiasm.

"They say you invited them here," Annie informed him.

"I did. They refused my invitation," he curtly replied.

It was not the reception Meary had hoped for, and she struggled to hide her disappointment. She had no idea what she expected to find here, but his lordship's present indifference when he had seemed so friendly and eager for their company on the road was hard to reconcile. From the sound of things, Seumas would be having his way after all.

"We have reconsidered. . . . But, mayhap ye have also. Would ye be liking us to leave?" Meary asked.

Lord Colin restrained his tongue when it would have seized the occasion to banish them from his property. Much as he despised being trifled with, he also hated to waste an opportunity. Diversions were few and far between on this remote stretch of Irish coast. Too, the old man and the boy looked none too eager to be standing at his door. It was clear to him the only one of their troupe who desired to be here was the girl, and even she appeared less than sure of herself. A grin twisted his lips, and he rubbed his chin. Mayhap he should consider letting them stay. It might serve as just punishment for their earlier rudeness upon the road.

"Shall I send them on their way?" Annie asked after the space between Meary's question and any response had stretched to the point of discomfort.

"No. Let them stay," Lord Colin abruptly commanded. "Treat them as guests. I'll depend on you to see to the details." On that comment, he stepped passed both Meary and his housekeeper and strode across the yard toward the stables.

"Well, I best be getting the maids to make up your rooms," Annie ushered them into the great hall. Her tone had gone from pugnacious to polite. "My name is Annie Baine. You may call me Annie or Miss Baine, whichever suits you; Annie suits me and I'd prefer you use it if you've no objections. I run his lordship's home. Any-

35

thing you need, you come to me. Now, sit yourselves down and I'll have Cathleen bring you some good English tea."

As soon as Annie left, Meary repeated the house-keeper's words in Gaelic to Brendan, and he led her over to a cushioned chair.

Seumas remained morosely mute.

Unwilling to brave whatever comments the older man might have for her, Meary asked Brendan to describe the room to her, which he did, giving the location of each piece of furniture from the stretcher table and benches to the tall chest on heavily turned legs to a small stool. He also provided her the bearings of the stairs, the large open-hearth fireplace, and every doorway leading into the room. Meary committed it all to memory. Most times, if she was attentive, she could sense the presence of objects in her path, but her vanity suffered whenever she fumbled, so she preferred the added security of having Seumas or Brendan map out the manors they visited.

Today, she felt a special desire for grace of movement. As yet the lord of the manor was ignorant of her blind-ness, and keeping him ignorant for as long as possible suited her mood.

Cathleen entered the hall, bearing a tray of tea and scones, saw them served, and left again.

"Well, ye got us in the door. Now what?" Seumas at last deigned to speak.

"We settle ourselves in, play for the lord a night or two, then be on our way." Meary suggested a routine course of events.

Seumas snorted. "As simple as that. Are ye forgetting about yer blasted *feeling?*"

"Nay."

36

"Well," he prodded.

Meary took a sip of tea and sighed loudly. "I'd be more than willing to be telling ye why we are here if I knew the answer," she said.

"He's not wanting us here any more than I am."

"I know. His lack of joy 'twas more than obvious. I wonder why he invited us in."

"Now, how would I be knowing that? I was too busy praying we would yet escape his clutches to be reading the man's mind."

"A pity. 'Twould be nice to know his thoughts. Mayhap they would tell us why we are here."

"A bad bit of potato, that's what I'm hoping 'tis. Ye mistook indigestion for one of yer feelings, and we're here by mistake. His not wanting us here 'tis a sign."

"Seumas." Meary laughed as much from a need to dispel the inexplicable nervous tension afflicting her person as amusement at Seumas's words. A subtle timbre of infirmity of purpose infected her voice. "If ye are so sure 'tis indigestion, why not order me to go? Ye know I love ye too much to defy such an order."

"Aye." Seumas combed his fingers through his unruly hair, his pale eyes taking on a faraway glow. His voice betrayed the depths of his uncertainty. "And what if I'm wrong and 'tis not a bad potato? Would ye have me tempt the Fates?"

"Nay, I would not have ye put yourself in peril of that." She reached out a hand to comfort him. "I guess we will both have to wait and see what comes to pass."

"Ye speak the dreary truth," Seumas agreed.

By the time they finished the tea, another maid came to announce their rooms were ready.

Meary followed behind Seumas and Brendan followed

37

behind her as they made their way up the narrow staircase leading to the bedchambers. Meary kept close to the wall, trailing her fingers along the cold, rough stones to guide her way.

"This is to be yer room, miss," the serving girl said, stepping aside so Meary could enter the chamber. "I hope everything be to yer liking."

"I'm sure I'll be quite comfortable," Meary replied.

"Then, if there's nothing ye'll be needing, I'll be tending to the gentlemen."

"Where will they be staying?" Meary asked.

"They'll be sharing the room next to yers."

"To the left or right?"

"The left."

"Thank ye."

As soon as the maid exited, closing the door behind her, Meary set to exploring the room. It was modest in size. The outer wall followed the curve of the tower and was the longest in the room. The side walls were straight. The curve of the outer wall was repeated on the last wall, making the room shaped like a wedge of pie with the tip cut off. The configuration was typical for an ancient round tower converted to a more modern residence.

She located a single, narrow window. It was bereft of drapery, but a wooden shutter had been affixed to keep out the cold at night. The only pieces of furniture were a canopied bedstead in the middle of the room and a small trestle table near its head.

Meary ran her hand down the bed hangings and determined them to be plain, constructed of heavy linen, and slightly dusty.

The tramp of feet outside her door was followed by a knock and a gruff half-English half-Gaelic, "We've come with yer clothes chest, miss."

Meary crossed the room and opened the door.

"Where would ye be liking us to put it?" the same man asked.

"Against the wall near the door," she instructed.

When she was again left alone, Meary stood at the window and gave her thoughts free rein. The territory they covered was all too familiar. She was not a whit closer to knowing the answer to the question *Why were they here?* and it frustrated her. She really had been counting on some sort of flash of insight upon their arrival. She had also counted on being welcomed. Lord Colin's attitude perplexed her. But no more so than her own. She wasn't feeling like herself at all. Mayhap Seumas was right and she *was* suffering from some bizarre form of digestive upset. It certainly made more sense than any explanation she could conjure.

Meary turned each fact of their present situation over and over in her mind until she grew impatient with herself. With an exertion of stubborn will, she pushed her concerns out of her conscious mind. Lord Colin Garrick was an ordinary Englishman—an insignificant speck of dust on Irish soil. She had better things to do with her time than grow grey hair worrying over trifles.

Lord Colin reined his lathering horse to a halt; then, with a flick of the reins, he set the animal in motion again, this time at a sedate walk. Having ridden off the edge of his irritation, he felt better now.

The Irish loved to annoy the English. He knew that. He shouldn't have let the unexpected arrival of a wisp of an Irish girl get under his skin. Certainly she was beautiful, and no healthy male could be expected to remain unaffected in her presence, but she was nothing to him. He was sure she had her own reasons for changing her mind, and they, too, were none of his concern.

The only thing that concerned him was his own pleasure. If she proved a pleasant diversion, he would let her stay as long as she liked. If not, he would send her and her friends packing. It was a simple solution to a simple situation. It didn't warrant a moment's thought.

He held full control over his guests, and if they proved more trouble than they were worth, he could easily be rid of them.

Despite his conclusion, Lord Colin was in no hurry to return to the tower house. A few surprise visits of his own to his tenants' farms better suited his mood. It helped keep them honest and would help keep him occupied. For while he might be willing to let the lovely Meary O'Byrne share his roof a day or two, he was not about to appear eager for her company.

Meary spent what remained of the afternoon sitting in the great hall, tuning her harp and eavesdropping on the servants' gossip in an effort to learn all she could about her conspicuously absent host.

His household seemed to like him well enough, though they came far from singing him praise. From the information gleaned she was able to conclude his servants thought him distant in manner but generally fair and never overdemanding. Since as far as she could determine his entire household, with the notable exception of Annie Baine, was Irish and not disposed to bestowing credit to an Englishman when none was due,

40

she happily concluded he could not be the monster Mrs. Deane feared him to be.

A footman entered the hall to announce the dinner Meary could smell cooking in the adjacent kitchen. The retreat of his footsteps was shortly followed by the entrance of a pair of booted feet and Lord Colin's voice.

"Ah, I see you are preparing to play for me," he drawled.

She could feel his gaze moving over her. Meary's pulse accelerated under his regard. Folding her hands in her lap, she mentally scolded herself for the reaction and willed herself to offer up an illusion of impeturbability. "Aye. 'Tis why we are here."

"Do you play well?" he queried, crossing the room and coming to stand mere inches from her.

"Better than some; worse than others."

"Where are your companions?"

"I left Seumas in his room to sleep off the ache in his bones. Brendan is out of doors with our pony," she informed him. "I'm sure they'll be joining us at any moment." The last comment she added more for her own benefit than his. He was standing too close to her for her comfort, but she dare not protest or remove herself to a more secure position for fear of announcing her agitation of spirit. If she was the only one in the room who could feel the sparks of energy setting the air on fire, she had no intention of apprising his lordship of the fact.

"I know Mr. O'Hanlon acts as your guardian. What relation is this Brendan to you?" he continued to casually question her.

"A brother of sorts. Seumas took him under wing years before me when he was but a lad of six years."

"What of his parents?"

41

"We know nothing of his true family."

"How is that?"

"Seumas found him wandering in the woods alone and half starved. No one in the county would claim him as kin, so Seumas did. If any of his family still be alive, I'm sure they'll suffer damnation in the next life for their disloyalty in this one," she added vehemently.

"Or so you hope."

"'Twill come to pass," Meary confidently assured him. "The Lord does not look kindly on those who turn innocent children out into the cold."

"And were you turned out too?" he inquired, his voice still manifesting polite indifference."

"Nay. Me parents were devoted to me. They could not help that they died of the fever."

"And the rest of your family?"

"If there is any other left of the once-great O'Byrne *tuath*, no one knows of their existence." Meary shifted on her chair. She was growing tired of being interrogated, and she decided to put a stop to it. "Ye ask a lot of questions. Is there a reason?"

"Curiosity, I suppose. Or perchance it is because I have found it prudent to know all I can about those I invite to stay under my roof. I am told it helps assure a long life."

"Are ye afraid one of us might try to murder ye in your sleep?" she frankly questioned.

"Should I be?" Lord Colin demanded, his heretofore dispassionate voice unexpectedly bristling with suspicion. Meary winced.

"Ye need not sound so angry. 'Twas a jest," she protested.

"A poor one considering the history of our peoples,"

he growled at her.

"There's no murderous wish lurking in me heart, I assure ye."

"But I am English and you are Irish," Lord Colin reminded, leaning so close his nose brushed hers. Meary bolted from her chair and put it and her back between them.

" 'Tis true. But what would be gained by sending ye to your maker. If we killed ye, would not another Englishman come to take your place? 'Twould be a wasted effort," she argued as calmly as she was able.

"I'll sleep well knowing you have such a noble reason for not plotting my demise," he avowed dryly.

"Meary, Lord Colin."

The entrance of Seumas into the room brought a halt to their strange conversation, and none too soon to Meary's way of thinking. If Lord Colin truly feared they wished him harm, why had he invited them to his home in the first place?

She reminded herself his words had been spoken tersely not with a quaver of fear, but it did little to ease her mind. There was something he was not saying. Something that made her believe he was long accustomed to expecting the worst from everyone who crossed his path. Something profoundly lonely in his laconic tone.

Compassion washed over her soul like a wave engulfing the sands. Meary's shoulders sagged under its weight.

Chapter 4

All was not as it seemed. Lord Colin was as sure of it as he was of his own name. Every time he looked at Meary, and he had not taken his eyes off her since entering the hall, he was aware of it—an insistent voice whispering at the edge of his conscious thoughts.

He ran his hand across his jaw. Despite his sarcastic comment, he believed her when she said she did not wish him bodily harm. It was something else. The play of emotions across her face. The way she looked through him not at him. The walking cane.

He focused on the concrete. She still had the uncommon cane with her. Though he had witnessed her take less than half a dozen steps during their three brief encounters, he had seen no indication she was lame. Every evidence of his eyes told him she was physically perfect.

She might carry the walking cane for fashion's sake, but it seemed an odd affectation for a woman, especially of her station. . . . Or mayhap not . . . He knew the Irish regarded their poets and musicians with almost mystical reverence. In recent years, with the immigration of so many Englishmen, the influence of the poet class was waning. It was logical the members of the class would do all they could to hold on to their power over the people. Mayhap she carried the ornately carved walking stick as part of the costume of her trade.

"Meary . . . Lord Colin," Seumas announced his continued-to-be-ignored presence by loudly acknowledging theirs once again.

Reluctantly, Colin turned from Meary to greet his other guest. "Mr. O'Hanlon. I trust you found your accommodations agreeable and have had a restorative repose."

"Aye," he responded unenthusiastically as he ambled across the room to Meary's side.

He whispered something to her in Gaelic. She replied with a stoical "Nay" and turned back to face the room.

It annoyed Colin he could not understand what was being said and he brusquely asked, "Have you come only to play for me, or have you reconsidered teaching me your tongue also?"

Before Seumas could refuse him, Meary queried, "Do ye truly wish to learn our language?"

"Yes."

"Why?"

"My inability to understand the conversations of those around me puts me at a disadvantage," he explained coolly.

Meary cocked her head to one side as she contemplated his answer. Lord Colin once again was divulging his cautious nature. She was still feeling a strong sympathy for him, and the feeling was unwelcome. She tried with fractional success to banish it with an exertion

45

of will and replace it with inquisitiveness.

To her mind Lord Colin had everything men dreamed of: land, wealth, the power of a title. If he had attained all, what made him so distrustful?

Rather than risk another uncomfortable confrontation by addressing the issue in a straightforward manner, she chose instead to explore his attitude by the backdoor approach of twitting him. Besides, humor was ofttimes the best way to fortify oneself against the hazards of life, and at the moment she was feeling in dire need of some sort of buttress.

Pulling her lips into a thoughtful frown, she asked, "Would I not be doing your servants a disservice if I taught ye how to eavesdrop into their conversations?"

"That depends on what they are saying," he replied.

Despite her best efforts to appear worried, her rosy lips quivered into a waggish grin. "And what will ye do if ye find ye don't like what they be saying?"

"Why, I'd have them hung, of course," he stated blandly.

Meary gasped and Seumas sputtered in outrage.

Lord Colin grimaced at their gullibility. This Meary possessed a ripe wit, and it was best she learn now if she persisted in trifling with him, she would get as good as she gave. "'Tis just a jest," he mimicked her earlier words. "It seems you are as wary of me as I am of you. Rest assured, I have never hung a man for an unjust cause nor do I have any plans to take up the habit now. As long as my servants do their work, they can say anything they like about me. I've no need of their love." He adjusted the lace at his sleeves and raised a brow, exhaling an impatient breath before he continued, "Are you not the one who said if I wish to trod on Irish soil, I should learn

46

to speak with an Irish tongue?"

"Aye."

"Is a sincere desire to better communicate with my fellow man too implausible a concept for you to accept?"

"Why should we be believing anything ye say?" Seumas answered his question with a question. "In one breath ye threaten death to our countrymen. In the next ye vow indifference."

"'Tis a poor jest," Meary muttered under her breath, borrowing Lord Colin's words as he had borrowed hers.

Colin nodded. "You are right. Shall we consider the score even?"

"Meary, what in all Ireland is the man prattling about?" Seumas demanded.

Reverting to their native tongue, Meary rapidly recounted their earlier conversation and her opinion of it. When she finished, Seumas addressed Lord Colin.

"We be musicians not murderers," he firmly announced. "If ye expect us to be playing for ye, do not insult us by assigning common English morals to decent Irishmen."

"My mistake," Lord Colin drolly replied. "I was merely curious as to why you changed your mind about coming here."

"Fate," Seumas sputtered the single-syllabled, cryptic reply.

Brendan entered at that moment, addressing a rapid string of Gaelic sentences to Seumas and Meary.

Though Colin was only able to catch the meaning of a few of his words, from his contrite demeanor and posture, Colin guessed he was making some sort of apology.

Colin stood silent and watchful as both Meary and

Seumas spoke to Brendan in soothing tones. As she spoke, Meary gently stroked his cheek, treating him as if he was a boy rather than a full grown man. Colin's gut tightened at the open display of intimate affection.

He opened his mouth to point out their rudeness in repeatedly using a language they knew he could not understand when they were able to speak in his, but he clamped his lips shut. His instincts urged him to keep his opinions to himself, at least for the present.

Instead of a rebuke, he interrupted their private conversation with a punctilious, "Shall we be seated so the servants can begin laying our meal?"

Everyone moved toward the stretcher table. "Meary is to sit at my right," Colin instructed. "Mr. O'Hanlon and Brendan, there and there." He pointed out their places.

"Yer familiarity with the lady 'tis unseemly. Ye should be calling her Lady Meary," Seumas censured, placing a proprietary hand on Meary's waist.

Meary inwardly smiled at Seumas's protest. Strictly speaking, she was never entitled to the title of lady. English politics and greed had seen to that. But it was clear Seumas wanted to impress upon their host her noble lineage. Since she knew Seumas to be a man who put little stock in titles, she could easily guess his purpose.

Lord Colin handsomely offered to replace Seumas's escort with his own with an outstretched arm, but found his gesture ignored. "You are quite correct," he said. "However, we were never formally introduced so I pray you will forgive my lapse in manners."

"'Tis God's decision whether or not to be forgiving ye yer sins not mine," Seumas muttered as he guided Meary past his lordship to her seat.

Meary shook her head at his words. Never had Seumas treated a patron so rudely. It was usually he who chided Brendan or her for making imprudent speeches. But tonight his tongue was as loose as a pup's tale and his comments as vicious as a cur's bite. Her only comfort was Lord Colin thus far had taken his open antipathy in stride.

When they were all seated around the table, the servants entered bearing trays laden with food.

In contrast to last night's supper, the aromas filling the room were rich and varied. Meary detected the presence of roast mutton, cabbage, leeks, and rye bread as she surreptitiously confirmed the location of her knife and spoon.

When the first footman approached her, she nodded affirmatively to his offer of meat.

Silence reigned at the table for a considerable length of time while everyone earnestly applied themselves to the meal. It was Lord Colin who finally breached the conversational void.

"How long have you been playing together?" he addressed the question to Seumas while he continued to covertly observe Meary consume her meal.

"Brendan has been with me fourteen years. Meary has been with us six," Seumas responded.

"I have observed Lady Meary plays the harp. What instrument do you play?"

"I play them all, but these days I'm fondest of the fiddle."

"And Brendan?"

"He plays the hornpipe and *bodhrán*."

"Brendan, you look to be a strapping lad. Does no other trade besides music making interest you?"

"He won't be answering ye. He speaks Gaelic only," Seumas informed him.

"Why is that, when you and Lady Meary are fluent in both tongues?"

The older man's gaze came to rest on Brendan and his eyes filled with affection. "Brendan tries hard but he cannot learn as others do."

Having observed the childlike demeanor of the young man, Colin accepted his guest's statement and didn't pursue the issue when Seumas did not elaborate. "A pity," he civilly opined.

Seumas slapped his knife down on the table with a loud clack. "Ye can be keeping yer pity, thank ye. Brendan has been doing just fine without it."

"Is it English pity you despise or all pity?" Lord Colin queried, keeping his tone conversational despite his guest's contentious mien.

"All pity."

"Why is that?"

"I've never seen it do a soul a whit of good," Seumas explained. "And I've seen it do oceans full of harm. Pity saps a man's strength. Pity makes him think less of himself than he is. Pity, milord, is a double-edged sword that draws the life's blood from both the giver and the receiver."

His lordship fell silent once again. He was not sure he agreed with the man, but he saw no purpose in engaging in a debate. Considering his ravaged looks, O'Hanlon had probably had more experience with pity than most, and his opinion would not be easily swayed. Shrugging his shoulders, Colin transferred his full attention to Meary. It was she he really was interested in anyway.

She was more than lovely. She was . . . he couldn't

find the word for what he was trying to express but the tightness in his loin made him shift on his seat. He felt drawn to her in a way he found difficult to ignore.

The component of lust was easily identified, but he was feeling more than common lust. This feeling was new to him, and he wasn't sure what to make of it . . . or if he liked it.

As he continued to feast his eyes upon her, a thin furrow formed across his forehead. She was not exactly clumsy, but there was something in the way she handled her eating utensils that intrigued him. Her movements were slow and deliberate, and twice she had missed her mark when attempting to spear a bite of lamb. When she reached for her glass of wine and grasped thin air before her hand found the stem of the goblet, he tried to capture her gaze with his. He failed.

As he scrutinized her every movement, many a detail began to fall neatly into place—so neatly he could not comprehend how he had overlooked the obvious for so long. Her profession as a harper. The use of the walking cane. Her unblinking gaze. But just as he was reaching the unwelcome conclusion she was as bereft of sight as Brendan was bereft of rapier wit, Meary overset his discomfiting discovery by asking, "Why are ye staring at me?"

His eyebrows pulled together in a tight line, and he groped for words. "I find your eyes . . . fascinating."

"They are ordinary eyes," she argued.

"Are they?"

Meary lowered her head and shielded her eyes with her thick blonde lashes. Was she found out? She wasn't sure. She wasn't certain she cared all that much. Her mind was presently occupied with a far more disconcerting matter.

Throughout the meal she had felt Lord Colin's gaze upon her. Even as he was conversing with Seumas, he had been watching her. His intense regard conjured all sorts of emotions she didn't want to recognize. To do so would be hazardous to her peace of mind. Meary nibbled on a piece of bread, trying in vain to set her emotions in order and think up a witty yet noncommital reply. At length, for lack of a better response, she stated, "Staring 'tis rude."

"You do it all the time."

"Do I?"

"Yes."

"I beg your pardon."

"Pardon given."

She could still feel him watching her. It was extremely unnerving and she fumbled for her spoon.

Colin clenched his jaw as he observed the mistake. A moment ago he'd been sure she must be blind; then, she had *seen* him staring at her. He mulled over every word and gesture he had observed her make since meeting her, but the evidence was inconclusive. If he embraced one set of facts, he was certain she was blind; another and he was equally certain she was not.

Unable to resolve the issue in his mind, he picked up her goblet and moved the wine out of her reach. When she reached for the goblet, Meary's hand groped the air. She frowned as her fingertips glided over the table and found nothing.

"He moved it," Seumas informed her. "It appears this Englishman likes to be playing tricks."

Meary withdrew her hand from the table and folded both hands on her lap.

"Why didn't you tell me you are blind?" Lord Colin demanded.

"Ye never asked," she replied.

"I knew there was something different about you from the first, but I had no notion . . ." Disappointment mixed with the satisfaction of discovering the truth and a quaver of sudden indecision to color the tone of his words a muddy shade of grey. ". . . until now."

Despite her regret over being found out, Meary's pride made her smile. She had known from the beginning she could not keep her blindness a secret forever, and that she had done so under such close scrutiny for so long pleased her immensely.

"Why didn't you want me to know?" Lord Colin intruded upon her thoughts.

"'Tis a game I sometimes play to test meself," she answered him with half the truth. No good purpose would be served by informing him or Seumas she had felt a special need to hide her vulnerability from him, she told herself. Explanations would be demanded, and she had none to give. She only knew Lord Colin had a strange effect upon her person, and it seemed prudent to hold unto herself every advantage for as long as possible.

"You are very good at keeping your affliction a secret," Colin observed.

"Aye. I cannot let a little thing like being blind interfere with conducting me life," she declared with conviction born from the personal knowledge and experience of having once let her blindness take complete control of her life.

"A saintly attitude."

"Nay, merely sensible."

"Have you always been blind?" he continued to question her.

"Nay. I fell from a horse and hit me head on me fourteenth birthday."

"It must have been very frightening for you." There was charity in his voice, and Meary found it even more vexatious than his earlier suspicion of her and the present disorder of her emotions combined.

She did not need nor want anyone's charity, and she especially did not want it from him. With a rush of awareness, she realized the true reason she had desired to keep her sightlessness a secret from him had far less to do with exposing a vulnerability than it did with protecting herself from Lord Colin's charity. She wanted him to accept her as his equal. It was important. She wasn't sure why it was important, but she knew it was.

Straightening her spine and squaring her shoulders, Meary faced their host without flinching. She had played the passive maiden long enough. It was past time she reacquaint Lord Colin with her true character.

"Aye, 'twas not the best way to celebrate one's birth. But enough of me." She effectively dismissed further discussion of her blindness. "Ye are overly fond of asking me questions. 'Tis a fault, I think. Ye already know far more of me than I know of thee."

"What do you want to know about me?" Lord Colin posed the question as a tentative offer to balance the scales.

Meary contemplated his question and decided as long as he was offering, she may as well ask what she most wanted to know. "Do ye have any secrets?"

"Yes."

"Will ye tell them to me?"

"No."

"But ye know mine," she argued without rancor.

"I discovered it on my own. You did not gift me with the information," he reminded, breaking his pattern of one-syllable replies.

" 'Tis true," she admitted. "For now ye may keep your secrets. . . ." Her smile was both scampish and serene. "I have heard your uncle willed ye these estates. 'Tis true?"

"Yes."

"He must have been very fond of ye," Meary stated with heartfelt conviction.

Colin grinned at her blithe assumption that all men would deem the gift of Irish lands an honor. His acquaintances in England had been sympathetic, not envious, when he had apprised them of his inheritance. They had been positively appalled when he told them of his intention to reside on the land. He contemplated enlightening her with these facts, but decided against it. "My uncle bore me no great affection, but he bore my brother even less," he dispassionately informed her.

"He had no children of his own?"

"None that he knew of."

Pursing her lips, Meary rested her chin on the second knuckle of her forefinger. " 'Tis your uncle the black sheep of your family or are ye trying to politely let me know ye come from a family of cold-hearted philanderers?"

Though she spoke the words in a teasing tone, Colin was a little disturbed by the accuracy of her description of his family's nature. His mood abruptly darkened. Charily, he replied, "The second of your statements is the closest to the truth."

"Ye do not sound overly fond of your kin."

"I am not." The curtness of his statement did not invite further inquiry into his family affairs.

Meary felt the tide of compassion rise once again within her breast. Her family had meant everything to her. It was nearly impossible for her to comprehend a man not esteeming his family.

With this fresh wave of pathos came the surging of another emotion, if one could call it that—an emotion she had been doing her utmost to ignore throughout the meal. Lord Colin's person radiated a force. A force that pulled at her heart, made her want to draw near him, to comfort him, to touch him, to be touched by him. The force did not feel sinister, but the potency of his need was so powerful she felt intimidated. Desirous of expeditiously banishing these sentiments, she hastily changed the subject again. "Are ye fond of Ireland?"

His curt tone turned meditative. "Yes. It suits me well."

"So, ye are planning to stay indefinitely?"

"Indefinitely," he confirmed. He paused. His voice was husky and laden with speculation when he continued. "Does that please you?"

"Aye. 'Twill allow us to further our acquaintance." She spoke the words with an earthy earnest that, much to her discomfort, revealed her profound awareness of the man sitting to her left. Squirming on her seat, she fervently prayed Lord Colin had not noticed even as she sensed his awareness was as acute as her own.

"If we are going to be playing for ye tonight, we best be getting ourselves ready." Seumas abruptly interrupted the conversation. Hopping from his bench, he rattled off a list of orders to Brendan, then took Meary by the hand and led her to the stool near her harp. He placed himself

56

between Lord Colin and Meary.

"We hear ye be the second son of an English marquess," he stated with his next breath. "If I were walking in yer boots, I know I'd be missing me homeland by now. Aye, the longing in me breast would be too fierce to resist. . . ." He continued to vigorously expound on the soul-wrenching suffering borne by a man absent from his native land and to extoll the glories of England despite having never set foot in the country, leaving no opening for any other conversation.

Neither Meary nor Colin were ignorant of his purpose, but they both listened without protest—each for their own reasons grateful for his timely intervention.

Brendan returned shortly with Seumas's fiddle and his own hornpipe and *bodhrán*. Lord Colin settled himself in a carved chair by the hearth, while the three prepared their instruments for the evening's entertainment. He watched them all, but mostly he watched Meary.

She appeared to have dismissed him from her mind, and he wondered if mayhap he had imagined the enticing tone of her last statement. From the moment he'd laid eyes on her the possibility of seduction had not been far from his thoughts . . . but now . . . knowing she was blind . . . a moral man would reconsider. . . .

A moral man: he had always considered himself as such, but as his gaze traveled over the sensuous curves of Meary's lips, throat, breasts, hips, his commitment to morality wavered precariously.

Why shouldn't he seek his pleasure in his comely guest's arms if she was willing? She was a full grown woman. She had announced herself she saw no reason to let her affliction interfere with living life. She knew the consequences of surrender. As he had sailed from

57

England, had he not promised himself he would devote the rest of his days to looking to his own gratification?

Stiffening his carriage, he slammed the gate on such thoughts. There were plenty of available women if he was in the mood for a little wenching. He didn't need to solicit passion from a blind girl to satisfy his lusts. She warranted pity, not lust.

As his gaze slowly moved up from her tiny, slipper-shod feet, over her inviting figure, and back to her heart-shaped face, his loin physically manifested its refusal to heed the dictates of his will.

He must concentrate on cultivating pity. A battle raged within him as his head struggled to gain supremacy over his animal instincts.

It was a pity so beautiful a maiden had been deprived of her sight—but he could easily guess what her reaction would be if he communicated his opinion. She had given him more than one taste of her spirit. In his gut he knew she would voice no more fondness for pity than the old man had. Mayhap, he should adopt her professed non-chalance toward her affliction and proceed as if she was any other woman.

Still, he wondered deep inside, underneath her exterior of cheerful competence, if she was truly as accepting as she proclaimed.

He couldn't reconcile her attitude with his experience of humankind. People, able-bodied people, loved to be pampered and loathed self-responsibility. The trick was to find some fool willing to do the cosseting. Surely, Meary O'Byrne must long to have her needs taken care of by someone else. It made good sense. She must be deceiving him, hiding her true character just as she had hidden the fact of her blindness. She was no different than all the others. He nodded his head knowingly.

Despite his conclusion, Lord Colin could not help but admire her for going to the effort of putting on the act. It showed initiative, and he admired enterprise wherever he found it. He was not sure what she hoped to gain from him, and he was determined she would fail to secure it, but he had to admit that she was very good at pretending independence, very good indeed.

Chapter 5

"Be there anything special ye would like us to be playing for ye?" Seumas's question called Lord Colin out of his thoughts.

"No. I believe any song will do."

"Then, the first tune Brendan and I will be performing for ye 'twill be an old Irish air."

Meary moved her fingers into position on her harp strings.

"Nay, Meary," Seumas admonished. "We'll not be wanting yer harp to accompany us on this song tonight. Ye just sit back and make yerself comfortable till I tell ye I'm ready for ye to be joining us."

Obediently, Meary did as she was told.

Seumas tucked his fiddle under his chin, and Brendan brought the hornpipe to his lips. The first notes of the air filled the hall.

Lord Colin leaned back in his chair and listened, pleasantly surprised by the skill of the pair. Their timing was impeccable. Each note was true and clear. He had not heard musicians of their caliber perform even in the noblest homes in England. He silently congratulated himself on his good fortune.

He glanced at Meary. Her slender hands lay upon her skirt, but her fingers were not idle. They caressed the air, plucking silent notes on invisible harp strings. The movements of her hands were sublimely graceful, yet he sensed an impatience in them as well. An eagerness.

The erotic image of her hands moving with the same grace and eagerness upon his flesh cloaked reality in his mind's eye, setting the blood in his veins on fire.

Colin jerked his attention away from Meary and back to her companions.

O'Hanlon leaned toward Brendan and whispered something as he stroked the final notes of the song with his bow. In the space of a quarter beat, both men launched into a second air the moment the first was over.

After a third song, he announced, "Brendan will now be singing *The Fairy Queen* for ye."

Meary lifted her hands to her harp.

"Nay, Meary," Seumas admonished. "We're not needing yer help yet."

She frowned and dropped her hands on her lap.

Brendan lay down his hornpipe and stood soldier straight as Seumas played a short musical introduction. Then, Brendan opened his mouth wide and began to sing. *"Ciste nó stór go deó ní mholfad, Ach imirt is ól is ceól do ghnáth . . ."*

Again Lord Colin was taken by surprise. The music Brendan made with his mouth was as excellent as what he produced with his hornpipe. He had a tenor voice and his tongue glided over the convoluted phrasing peculiar to Irish melodies with graceful ease. Brendan might be counted lacking in some arenas of life, but as a musician

61

he was twice blessed.

When Brendan finished his song, Lord Colin enthusiastically applauded him. "Lady Meary, pray tell him he is a gifted musician," Colin instructed. "And my home is honored by his performance."

She repeated his compliment in Gaelic. Brendan eyed him warily and said nothing, but the corner of his lips gradually twitched into a tentative smile.

"Now, I will be playing *One Battle More* while Brendan accompanies me on the *bodhrán*," Seumas announced.

The two immediately commenced playing, Seumas making his fiddle sing while Brendan beat out the meter on the *bodhrán*. The tune was as pleasing as all the others, and Lord Colin had no complaints about the quality of the evening's entertainment, but he was beginning to wonder why Meary had yet to be allowed to join in a single song. Could it be her skill did not equal her companions and her function in the troupe was merely to serve as enticement to gain invitations to the homes of noblemen? He disliked the notion of her being used as a lure, but it made more than a little sense considering her continued silence. She certainly had not boasted of her skill when he had asked her about it.

Having no way to test his theory unless and until she played for him, Lord Colin abandoned his speculation concerning her talent if not his speculation concerning the woman herself and concentrated on enjoying the music of the men and the beauty of the woman, to whom his gaze kept drifting despite his best intentions.

Following a gentle but firm "Nay" to Meary, Seumas and Brendan played yet another air, continuing without pause into a medley of currently popular jig and reel tunes.

When they finished playing the set of songs, Meary readied her hands on her harp but before she could pluck a note, Seumas cleared his throat and began to recite the tales of Fionn MacCumail.

Tale followed tale until his booming voice started to fade. Again, he lay his bow to his fiddle and again, he forbade Meary to join in that song and the next.

Meary compressed the back of her lips between her teeth and exhaled loudly. Whatever Seumas was up to, she didn't like it one bit. Never had he left her sitting idle for so long.

She loved to play and he knew it. Music was a part of her. It was her soul. To sit silent was pure torture—especially tonight when she needed its comfort, needed to go to the special place only her music could take her, to restore her equilibrium.

She rolled the fabric of her paduasoy skirt between her impatient fingers as she glared in Seumas's direction through unseeing eyes. If there was some logic behind this punishment, she was as blind to it as she was to the world. He was going to have to explain himself.

Choosing to employ discretion by the use of Gaelic words but without waiting for him to finish his latest piece, she plaintively demanded of her mentor, "Am I to sit on this stool pretending I'm a mushroom all night or are ye going to let me play?"

Without missing a note, Seumas responded as he continued to stroke out the notes of the song, "I think it best ye do not play tonight."

"Why?"

"Ye've bewitched Lord Colin enough for one evening."

Meary's heart skipped a beat, but she was determined not to be distracted from her purpose. "Ye are talking nonsense."

"Am I now?"

"Aye. Utter nonsense. I only want to play as is me right. 'Tis not fair to ask me to sit silent while ye and Brendan have all the joy."

"I'm only trying to protect ye."

She grinned determinedly. "Me harp represents no danger."

"But our host does. Ye felt him watching ye before?" His words were more statement than question. "He's still doing it. Watching ye like a wolf watches a lamb he's about to devour."

The image was not a comforting one, and for a brief moment Meary wavered. If what Seumas said was true . . .

Preferring to believe Seumas was stubbornly clinging to the hope he could distract her from the issue at hand rather than contemplate the possible implications of Lord Colin's supposed lust, she confidently proclaimed, "I think ye exaggerate. Besides, I told ye before I can be taking care of meself where his lordship is concerned. And another thing, what does playing me harp have to do with him?"

"I don't want ye to give him any more reason to be wanting ye."

"Bah! I can see ye have abandon all sense of logic. Shame be upon ye for thinking like a fool. I am asking to play me harp not strip down to me garters and strut about the room."

"Seduction comes in many forms."

"Ye now are accusing me of desiring to seduce the

64

man?" Meary asked in genuine outrage and disbelief. She might not be able to deny with complete honesty that there was anything out of the usual about her reaction to Lord Colin, but she most certainly could honestly avow never had there been a moment's contemplation on her part of seducing the man. "If ye say aye, 'twill be the vilest thing ever said to me."

"Willfully seduce him? Nay. I know ye better than that," Seumas assured her. "But tonight ye have a look about ye, Meary. I've never seen it before and it worries me."

Folding her arms across her chest and raising her chin to a pugnacious angle, she argued, "I look as I always do."

"Nay. Ye do not."

"Then what about me is different?"

"I cannot be saying exactly . . . but . . ."

Her lips curled into a mulish smile. "If ye cannot be saying, I am going to be playing the next song with ye."

Seumas deftly guided his bow through several difficult measures of lightning-fast notes before dolefully replying, "Aye, I can see ye are."

"I am glad ye at last have come to your senses."

"I am always in full possession of me wits," Seumas tersely informed her. "And I'm not agreeing with ye. I'm merely accepting what I cannot change. I see ye are stubbornly determined to put yerself at further risk, and I know well the boundlessness of yer obstinacy. Play for the man if ye must, but do so with the full knowledge that ye are begging for what misfortune follows."

As Lord Colin listened to the covert conversation,

struggling with scant success to catch the meaning of the volley of whispered words, his determination to have Meary begin his language lessons at once became stone hard. He repeatedly cursed himself for allowing Annie to impose English upon his household servants. He had been so busy establishing his authority over the land, he blithely had allowed her to do as she pleased. It made his life convenient. It allowed him to concentrate his energies elsewhere. He had no doubt, in time, English would become the predominate language of this country, but it had yet to become so, and here he sat like an oaf unable to comprehend what was being said.

Before meeting Meary his ignorance of the Irish tongue had been a slight inconvenience. Now, it felt like a prodigious deficiency.

Before meeting Meary . . . He repeated the phrase in his mind as he gazed at her and grimaced. The woman was insignificant. She was a fleeting diversion. His invitation a whim. He did not like that his desire to understand her was somehow greater than his desire to understand others.

He rubbed his jaw. Whatever they were saying, he was fairly certain it concerned him. O'Hanlon kept glancing in his direction and scowling. *Her* face displayed a cornucopia of emotions. She pouted, then grinned, then appeared lost in thought—smiles chasing frowns and frowns chasing smiles. He wondered if she knew how plainly her face communicated her feelings to the world. He wondered how one person could feel so many different emotions in the space of one conversation. He wondered if ever there had been a face more beautiful than hers.

He wanted to hold that face between his hands, kiss

those rosy lips, rub his cheek against the blushing velvet of her cheeks. His gaze lowered. He wanted . . . Lord, how he wanted . . . He abruptly halted the direction of his thoughts.

No wonder the old man disliked and distrusted him. He had good reason to distrust him. He was itching with his need to have Meary O'Byrne.

Lord Colin tore his gaze away from the object of his leviathan lust just as the conversation and the song ended.

He focused his attention on O'Hanlon. Hunching his shoulders and sighing loudly several times, his face evincing both affliction and affection, O'Hanlon's attention was on Meary. Colin's gaze drifted back in that direction.

Her fingers poised on the strings of her harp, and she wore a triumphant expression.

So, at last, she was going to play, Lord Colin noted with no little interest. Taking into consideration Seumas's previous reluctance to let her play and his present pained expression, Colin concluded his earlier conjecture to be true. Fair Meary played the part of ornament not musician in this little troupe. But plainly she was not fully cognizant of her assigned role and fancied herself to have more skill than she possessed.

That her guardian had given in to her persistently expressed wish to play surprised him not at all. It was readily apparent to anyone who cared to be observant that she had both O'Hanlon and Brendan in the palm of her comely hand. It was a fact worth remembering—a fact he intended to take full advantage of should he decide to pursue her.

Crossing one booted ankle over the other, Colin braced

himself for what he predicted would be an amateurish performance.

A part of him welcomed the coming assault upon his ears. He did not like the strong effect Meary O'Byrne had upon him. It unsettled him. It made him feel uncomfortable, less under his own control than he liked to feel. A bad performance would surely help. He wanted her to play dreadfully. So dreadfully he would be able to use the memory of her discordant performance as antidote to the powerful allure he felt whenever he was in her presence.

With a final sigh, Seumas raised his fiddle to his chin and bowed the opening note. Meary's fingers began to move upon the strings of her harp.

She plucked and stroked, calling forth sounds so sublime they were celestial. Every note was perfect. Every movement a study in grace. Her slender fingers danced upon the harp strings. A half smile adorned her lips. Her chest rose and fell to a rhythm of deep contentment. It was as though the harp had become a natural extension of her person, completing her. Why O'Hanlon had not wanted to let this paragon play was beyond comprehension. Her skill not only equalled her companions but exceeded it. She evoked more than skillful music from her instrument; she evoked its spirit, filling the hall with rapture.

When, after the space of two musical pieces, she began to sing, Lord Colin found himself completely undone.

If her harp music was celestial, her voice surpassed even the angels'. Its beauty caused a physical reaction in every fiber of his being, a reverberation in the very marrow of his bones. It was a strange sensation, intense excitement and utter relaxation felt as one. Profoundly moving. Indescribably soothing.

If there were still others in the room, Lord Colin ceased to be conscious of their existence. He only had eyes and ears for Meary. Her lips fascinated him as they formed each word. Her eyes changed hue with the mood of each song. He was of a sudden acutely aware of the frangipani fragrance she wore. Her presence so filled his senses, he could almost taste it in the air.

Before, he had merely feared himself beguiled. Now, he knew himself to be so.

As soon as she began to play, the much-sought serenity stole over Meary. Seumas's accusations and warnings faded from mind. Her own worries and doubts ceased to plague her. She was where she needed to be. Inside her music. Safe from all worldly cares.

She played and sang one song then another and another. Her fingers and voice were in splendid form tonight. Even to her own ears the always fine music she made sounded sweeter than usual. She credited it to the suffering she had borne by remaining silent for so long. Depriving of quantity, the saints of music had gifted her with an extra measure of quality. She thanked them with another sweetly sung song.

Seumas and Brendan had long since fallen silent, but Meary continued to play and sing. Some songs she sang in Gaelic. Others she translated into English. She sang of the ancient ones, heroic quests, bungling squires . . . and love gone awry. Sad though they were, she esteemed the love songs best. They touched her heart and made her feel the deep sense of yearning of the tragically parted lovers. She liked to imagine those separated in this world united in the next, holding hands and watching over all the earth's troubled lovers with knowing eyes. Romantic, yes. Foolish, very much so. But she found the notion appealing, and she held on to it because it gave her pleasure to set the world in order if only in her own mind.

While she played and sang, Meary was completely absorbed in her music. She did not think of Lord Colin or Seumas or Brendan or what the next minute might hold in store for her. She existed to make music. Nothing else mattered.

It was a heady feeling. A feeling of utter peace and joy, more powerful than the most potent wine.

Meary played on until her voice and fingers grew too weary to continue. As she plucked the last note of the song, slowly, she became aware of her surroundings. The room was utterly silent except for the rhythmic breathing of its occupants. She could feel Lord Colin's gaze fixed upon her. The keenness of his gaze made her breath catch in her throat.

Seumas's disregarded warnings echoed in her head, and she knew in her heart he had been right. Playing for Lord Colin *had* been a dangerous thing to do.

Dangerous, not because she feared Lord Colin would try to force himself upon her. She could handle unwanted lust with aplomb. She had dealt effectively with more than one overly amorous patron. It was dangerous because she feared her own proclivities, not his.

The pull she had felt earlier had intensified tenfold. He needed something from her. He needed it desperately. She needed to fulfill that need. Only she wasn't sure what it was she was suppose to give him or if she was willing to give it.

The intensity of the emotion and her frustration at her

70

inability to discern how she should react made her shiver. She wrapped her arms around herself and lowered her head.

"Lady Meary?" Lord Colin's expression of concern broke the spell of silence. "Are you chilled?"

"Nay. But I am feeling a bit spent. I'd like to be retiring to me room now if ye have no objections."

"How could I object after you have played so well for me? I'll call Annie and have her lead you to your room."

Rising to her feet, she shook her head. "There is no need to trouble her. I can find me own way."

"Are you sure?"

"Aye . . . Good night."

Chapter 6

The gilded rays of the morning sun still kissed the horizon as Lord Colin reined in his mount and sat silent, staring off into the distance. Behind him was a row of thatched roof cottages, ahead the heath stretched as far as the eye could see.

He hadn't slept well last night. Thoughts of *her* had kept him awake. Thoughts of her still plagued him. That she had invaded his mind so thoroughly in so short a space of acquaintance set poorly with him.

He had not come to Ireland seeking to burden himself with human attachments. He had come to Ireland to escape all ties that bind . . . and twist . . . and strangle. He was determined to remain responsible for no one but himself.

Lord Colin straightened on his saddle and scolded himself for a fool. The direction of his thoughts was absurd. He was not contemplating forming any sort of permanent attachment with his comely house guest.

Lady Meary O'Byrne—he purposely used the formal

address to distance himself from her—was a saucy-tongued, talented, sexually intriguing piece of Irish fluff, nothing more. He desired nothing more from her than entertainment. There was nothing to think about. The only issue he must decide was whether or not he intended to seduce her before she left his household. Lord Colin laid out the facts as he saw them with ruthless logic.

Since seduction held promise of better reward than self-restraint, some time during the long sleepless night he had begun to lean heavily towards the former. True her blindness complicated matters, but as long as he was honest about his intentions, he saw little sin in pursuing his desire. He fully intended to reward her for her services. And if he found his conscience bothering him more than he anticipated, he could give her an extra trinket or mayhap a jewel or two when he sent her on her way. She would not leave his household feeling abused.

This line of reckoning provided motive enough for Lord Colin to grant himself permission to give into temptation, but another was what settled him on his course.

The best way he knew how to get a woman out from under his skin was to have her. He needed to take Meary to bed if for no other purpose than to rid himself of his growing obsession for her.

In his experience, familiarity truly did breed contempt—on both sides of the mattress.

But before the inevitable contempt set in, there was much pleasure to be had. With this Meary, his instincts told him, it would be doubly so.

There was no reason to feel uneasy. There was no

reason to lose sleep. There was every reason to look forward to the carnal pleasures that awaited him.

Despite a sound sleep, Meary awoke feeling little better than she had when she had retired. She was still just as confused and had little hope of finding relief any time soon.

The last person she wanted to think about was Lord Colin, but thoughts of him invaded every corner of her mind.

What was it about the man that piqued her interest so? She most certainly could not claim she had been waylaid by his effusive charm. At times, his behavior bordered on caustic.

But his voice, whether his words were courteous or churlish, enchanted her ears. His scent roused like exotic perfume. And the proximity of his person sent bolts of lightning through her nerves. The mere memory of her encounters with his lordship caused waves of warmth to radiate from the pit of her belly to every limb and her heart to beat a little faster.

Were these the stirrings of lust she felt in her breast? Meary fervently prayed it was not so. It couldn't be. Not for an Englishman. Not for a man she barely knew. It had to be something else. But what?

Sighing heavily, she rose from her bed and padded across the stone floor on bare feet to her trunk. The cold of the floor provided an astringent contrast to the warmth of her thoughts, and she welcomed its bracing effect.

Rummaging through her trunk, she gathered up the necessary toilette articles and underpinnings and selected a gown with a deep blue damask overskirt, pale pink silk petticoat, embroidered stomacher, and lace-festooned modesty piece.

The gown was a favorite of hers. A gift from Lady O'Doherty to thank her for her singing at her daughter's wedding feast. Though she could not see its beauty, she could feel it in the finespun weave of the fabrics and the combination of textures. She always wore it when her confidence needed a little boost.

Deciding the vanity of wearing her hair flowing loose about her shoulders in defiance of propriety and fashion as was her usual habit should be resisted, Meary returned to her trunk and selected a riband to match the blue of the gown, making the match by rubbing her fingertips across and counting the number of tiny French knots Seumas had helped her embroider on the ends of the strips of satin.

After brushing her hair until the flaxen tresses began to crackle and rise into the air in protest of her prolonged grooming, Meary neatly plaited her hair into a single braid and tied the end with the riband. The braid was no more fashionable than her usual style, but it was more reserved.

As Meary made her way down the spiral staircase, she struggled mightily to conjure a soothing dose of good humored acceptance of her present predicament. Unfortunately, she found the thought of having to face Lord Colin before she had fortified herself with a hearty breakfast too daunting to overcome. In truth, the thought of having to deal with him at all left her more inclined to dash back up the stairs and bolt her door than face the new day.

The notion of informing Seumas she was ready to leave

this house crossed Meary's mind. She wrestled with temptation. She knew Seumas would be overjoyed to hear such words from her lips, but running away might be as detrimental to her peace of mind as staying. More so. She would always wonder what had brought her here. She would always wonder what she had left undone. Nay, she could not take the coward's way out. Meary squared her shoulders.

As she continued to make her way down the stairs, her shoulders rapidly lost their starch. Seumas called her ability to sense things yet unknown a gift, but today she was more inclined to call it by the name of curse. She knew enough to feel she must stay, but not enough to feel confident or comfortable to be doing so. It was vexing in the extreme.

She had absolutely no power over this gift/curse of hers. It came and went at will with no regard whatsoever for her wishes. She comforted herself by reminding herself her precognition had never led her into trouble before, then dispelled the comfort of the thought by bluntly reminding herself there was a first time for everything.

Upon reaching the great hall, Meary paused to listen. She could hear activity in the adjoining kitchen, but the great hall sounded vacant. She listened a moment longer, then rounded the room touching each corner and piece of furniture to be sure they were empty. They were, and her feet danced a little jig to celebrate her good fortune.

"You're in fine spirits this morning," Annie commented as she entered the room. "You must've slept well."

A slight blush stained Meary's cheeks upon being caught prancing about the room like a jittery goose, but

Annie's voice sounded unexpectedly friendly, so she did not feel as embarrassed as she might have. Neatening her posture, she smoothed the fabric of her skirt. "Me room 'tis very comfortable," she responded politely.

"I stood in the kitchen and listened to you singing and playing last night," Annie changed the subject. "I've never heard lovelier."

"Thank ye."

"I know my Colin was impressed with you as well."

Meary stood blank faced and silent, unsure how she should respond.

"Well, I best be getting you something to break your fast," Annie continued.

"Will the master of the house be joining me?" The question escaped Meary's lips before she had time to consider it. She feared it made her sound eager for his company when the opposite was true.

"No. I'm sorry; he ate some time ago and is out tending his estate. But before he left, he ordered me to see your every whim fulfilled."

"Surely, ye exaggerate," Meary protested.

"No," Annie replied without hesitation, but Meary detected an underlying note of merriment in her voice and was inclined to disbelieve the housekeeper.

Just as Meary was being served her breakfast, Seumas and Brendan came down the stairs and joined her. Meary braced herself for a scolding from Seumas, but it did not come. He kept his conversation strictly neutral. If not for her awareness that her guardian was constantly studying her, Meary would have judged the day like any other in any other household.

She feared she would have to bear Seumas's scrutiny all day, but upon learning that Lord Colin was occupied with duties away from the house, he announced his intention to retire to his room to work on a poem he was composing for Squire Randolph.

Brendan lingered longer by her side, but yesterday he had discovered milord's stable housed a considerable collection of fine horse flesh, and at length his desire to keep them company became too great to resist.

Left on her own, Meary decided a stroll in the fresh air suited her mood. Walking ofttimes helped her think, and she was confidently hopeful given enough time alone and without interruption she could think her way through her present confusion and arrive at a comfortable state of mind.

Retiring to her room to fetch a shawl, she returned below stairs and stepped out the door.

There was a steady breeze blowing off the ocean, but the sun was warm and no scent of coming rain rode upon the air. A sea eagle cried overhead. The measured ring of stonemasons' hammers vibrated through the air.

Pausing to take her bearings so she would have no trouble finding her way back to the tower house, Meary set off in the direction of the sea.

As she walked, Lord Colin filled her thoughts. She wanted to know him better, and yet . . . Was he a threat to her? A threat to her peace of mind most definitely. If she came to know him better, would she understand why she had come here? If she understood, would she be more or less comfortable with her situation?

Her physical attraction to him was undeniable, but she refused to believe that had anything to do with why she had wanted to come here. Her physical response to him was something to be ignored, overcome. It was merely an obstacle thrown in her path to distract her from her true

purpose which was to . . . Was what? To give him . . .
What was she suppose to give him?

Frustrated by the abundance of questions and dearth
of answers filling her mind, Meary tried to cultivate a
healthy dislike for her host. He was English after all. The
trouble was she had never been able to apply her general
prejudice against the English on a personal basis. Every
Englishman and woman she met she found herself
judging on their own merits.

So, she was back where she had started concerning
Lord Colin. She knew not enough about him to make an
intelligent assessment of his character. She had only the
feelings he evoked within her to judge him by, and they
were so plethoric and chaotic she rapidly was becoming
bereft of all hope of settling on one opinion over another.
Why must she be subjected to this confusion? What
possible purpose could it serve?

The wind was becoming stronger as Meary approached
the sea. She could hear the waves crashing against rock.
The sound came from below, far below, signaling to her
there were cliffs nearby. She stopped, listened intently,
then proceeded with an extra measure of caution. When
she had gone as far as she deemed safe, she stood facing
the ocean, enjoying the feel of the wind as it flapped the
ends of her shawl and teased the wisps of hair framing her
face. Drawing in deep breaths of air, Meary tasted salt
upon her tongue.

She did not know how long she stood there. Having no
pressing business elsewhere, she had no care for time.
The sea made a music all its own, and she loved the
melody. It was vibrant, forceful, never changing. The sea
would still be there long after she with her petty problems
vanished from the earth. Listening to the sea always

helped her put her concerns in perspective.

The pounding of horse hooves—the rhythm of the particular horse disquietingly familiar—caused Meary to turn from the sea and face the approaching rider. He reined to a halt inches from her and leapt to the ground. As he roughly grabbed both her hands, her walking cane fell to the earth with a dull thud.

"What in the name of heaven are you doing here!" Lord Colin's voice roared above the waves.

"Enjoying the sea," she responded calmly, though heat surged through her hands and her heart beat more rapidly than it should.

"Do you realize how close you are to falling to your death?" he demanded.

"Ten, mayhap twelve footsteps," Meary accurately informed him of the distance between herself and the cliff's edge.

"Are you insane? Why are you out here with no one to guide you?"

His unjust questioning of her competency hit a tender nerve, causing annoyance to quell the agitation that had assaulted her when he had come thundering onto the scene. "I am in full possession of me mental faculties, I assure ye. As to your second question, I desired to be alone."

"It is foolhardy to venture out on your own!"

"Pray lower your voice. I am blind not deaf."

"Then pray *you* explain yourself."

Meary pursed her lips. "I already have. I like the sea. I like me own company. I am perfectly capable of taking meself on a short stroll. I've done it hundreds of times and will do it hundreds more."

"But the cliffs?"

"I know where they be."

"And if you mistake your guess?"

"I do not guess. I know." Vainly, Meary tried to extract her hands from his. Short of kicking the man, she doubted she could get him to loose his grip on her. Not wishing to provoke him unnecessarily, she attempted to reason with him. "Ye measure the distance with your eyes. I measure the distance with me ears and skin. We use different senses, but the accuracy of the results 'tis the same."

He lowered the volume of his voice, but his tone remained strident. "I still don't like it."

"Why?"

"You are too beautiful and talented to brashly court tragedy."

The gruffly spoken compliment fell sweetly upon Meary's ears, but her pride rebelled at his continued lack of faith in her ability to make her own way in the world. "Praise God I am not ugly and lacking a pleasing skill, else I fear ye might be helping me over the cliffs' edge."

"You turn my words," Lord Colin protested.

"Ye do not listen," she countered with her own complaint. "If ye did, ye would not question me judgment. I assure ye, if I require assistance, I am fully capable of asking for it."

Lord Colin fell silent while he considered her words. Was there truth in them? He didn't know. Whether or not she was capable of tromping about the countryside was a matter of pure conjecture. He preferred concrete facts . . . and they were plain. He had found a beautiful, blind woman standing precariously close to certain death. As far as he could discern, she cared not a whit for her own safety.

81

The thought of her body being broken by the jagged rocks below left him feeling sick. A man would have to be daft not to use his authority to put a stop to such reckless behavior. "While you are here, you will not venture near these cliffs without escort," he decreed.

"Shall ye lock me in me room? 'Tis the only way ye will keep me from going where I please with whom I please," she warned.

"Why are you so stubborn?" he answered her query with a query.

"Because I need to be."

Lord Colin again fell to silent contemplation. Her statement was made with such conviction it was impossible not to believe she believed it. He didn't understand her. His question had been meant as a barb. He had not expected her to answer it. She did not seek to refute his slight to her character. She claimed it with no more rancor than if he had noted her gown was blue. What manner of woman was she? How had she become what she was? His voice suddenly gentle, he requested, "Tell me more about yourself."

The abrupt change in his tone baffled Meary, but the timbre of his voice inexplicably soothed, robbing her of any desire to thwart him. "What more about me do ye want to know?"

"How old are you?"

"Twenty years."

"Your guardian bids me to call you Lady. What was your station before you took up the life of a harper?"

"I come from a long and noble line of Irish gentry. Once we were numbered among the ranks of the great kings, but that was a long time ago. Though Seumas would have ye believe otherwise, in truth, the title of

82

Lady was never rightfully mine. 'Twas lost to the women of me family long before I was born."

"Did your family own much land?"

"Our fortunes shifted with the tides of politics. When Queen Mary was on the throne, we were rich in land. Cromwell made us poor. We recovered the land stolen from us when King James came to the throne, then lost most of what we had regained when the Protestant Parliament imposed the Penal laws," Meary chronicled the history of her family with little show of emotion.

"So you are Catholic."

"By birth, aye. But me heart 'tis far more fond of God than any system of Church designed by man. One 'tis no better nor worse than another."

"There are those who would despise and revile you for holding such an opinion."

"'Tis why I keep it to meself."

"But you told me," Lord Colin observed.

"Ye will not despise or revile me."

"How do you know?"

"I just do."

As they conversed, there was a caressing quality to each softly spoken word—a provocative, honeyed quality that had nothing to do with politics or religion and everything to do with the fact that they were a man and a woman.

"What else do you know?" Lord Colin murmured.

Powerless to resist the appeal of his velvet-toned words and too lost in the moment to care where her own words might lead her, Meary quietly replied, "I know I have come here for a reason."

"And what is this reason?" Lord Colin coaxed.

"Would that I knew."

"You sound frightened."

"I am, a little."

Stroking the back of her hands with his thumbs, he queried, "Do you fear I wish to do you harm?"

"Nay."

"I am glad it is not me you fear."

Ah, but 'tis ye I fear, Meary countered in her head. I only said I do not believe ye *wish* harm upon me, not that ye would not do it. She stifled a sigh. There must be something she could do to restore the equilibrium she invariably lost merely by being subjected to his presence. Mayhap if she bowed to intuition and became better acquainted with him . . .

"May I touch your face so I might know it as ye know mine?" The request was made before Meary realized she had spoken it out loud. Prudence urged her to call it back, but she found she had neither the wish nor will to do so.

Lord Colin released his hold on her hands. "You have my permission."

Raising one hand, Meary lay her fingertips on his chin and carefully traced his jaw to the lobe of his right ear.

The moment she touched him, a mantle of contentment settled over her. It was right that she do this, right that she learn to know his face intimately. The sensation was not unlike that which she called forth when she played her music, only there was an added dimension—a stimulating quality to the serenity touching him evoked.

Her second hand joined the first, and it followed the same path on the opposite side of his face. His skin felt warm and smooth and clean beneath her fingertips with just the barest rasp of whisker roots. Her forefingers traced the sea shell whorls of each ear before traveling across his cheeks. The flesh of his cheeks was softer than that of his jaw. The bones were high and slightly angular. On his left cheek her fingers detected the seam of a scar running from an inch below the corner of his eye and extending a length equal to the distance from the tip of her ring finger to the first knuckle.

Moving her fingers upward, Meary traced the hollow of his eyes. His lashes tickled when he blinked as she brushed across them on her way to his brows. Moderately dense and growing in a straight line on the hard ridge of the bone that defined his eyes, the hairs of his eyebrows were coarser than the feathery fringe of his lashes. The contrast of textures delighted her senses.

She measured his skull with splayed fingers as she moved her hands upward to his hairline. Just as Seumas had said, he wore his hair tied back like a tradesman. It grew thickly upon his head. The strands were heavy and possessed a natural wave. She combed her fingers through his hair, letting it graze the sensitive skin between her fingers.

Though she was wont to linger, she did so only slightly longer than was necessary to fill her senses with every detail of his generous head of hair.

Trailing her fingers earthward, she turned her attention to his nose. It was lean and arrow-straight with only a subtle flaring at the nostrils—very English.

Her fingers lowered to his lips, following their outline. His was a broad mouth, and she could feel the hint of a smile. His lips were neither thin nor full, firm nor soft. What impressed her most was their temperature. They were exceedingly warm. Fascinated, she traced their outline again and again.

Lord Colin stood perfectly still as Meary's fingertips roamed over his face. He gazed at her upturned face and read intense concentration *and* pleasure there. Her pleasure pleasured him and his lips echoed the delicate, heavenward curl of her lips.

Her fingers were soft and gentle as they explored his face. She touched him as one might touch the petals of a flower. The reverence of her touch was in sharp contrast to the irreverence of his Dionysian reaction to her caressing hands. As she continued to touch him, the coil of tension in his loins twisted tighter and tighter.

He wondered if she knew how erotic her exploring fingers felt against his face, then decided she did not. Her half-smile was too innocent. Her demeanor too tranquil. She was studying him with her fingers as he had oft studied her with his eyes. Gathering impressions of him . . .

He longed to caress her face as she caressed his, to trail his finger down the bridge of her nose, feel the silk of her skin, brush his thumbs across her rosy lips. But he had not the excuse of blindness as she did. For a fleeting moment he half wished God would strike him blind so he would have the excuse; then he realized that would deprive him of the sight of her. He could not bear that. Never could he bear to deprive his eyes of such delight.

He drew in a deep breath. Standing here being touched and not touching was pushing his self-control to its limits. He didn't know how much longer he could resist the impulses surging through him. He clenched his hands into fists at his side to prevent himself from pulling her against him and startling her with the boldness of his desire.

"Ye are angry with me?" Meary lifted her hands from his face and dropped them to her sides.

"Not at all," he assured her, the confusion in his voice

mirroring her own. "Why do you ask?"

"Ye are clenching your fists." She stated what was to her the obvious.

Lord Colin frowned. "How do you know that?" he demanded, a little intimidated by her ability to accurately "see" things she couldn't see.

"I can feel it in the muscles of your face. A body 'tis much like an intricately woven cloth. Pull one thread and the whole reacts," she explained.

Her answer satisfied, even though it was difficult for him to conceive being possessed of such a discriminating sense of touch. He relaxed his fists. "My apologies."

It was Meary's turn to look perplexed. "Have ye done something for which ye should be feeling shame?"

Lord Colin decided to take advantage of the opening her question provided . . . for while his fingers might lay slack at his sides, another portion of his anatomy remained as taut as ever. "Not yet, but I am contemplating such action."

"And it makes ye tense?"

"Very tense."

Meary mulled his words over in her mind. The lulling sense of contentment touching him had spread through her veins was still enough upon her she only had concern for his comfort. "Mayhap ye should not do this thing if it causes ye discomfort merely to think of it," she opined.

"Mayhap it is the thinking that does me harm . . . and the doing would bring relief."

" 'Tis possible."

"Then, I shall test the theory for I am sorely in need of relief." Reaching for Meary's hand, Lord Colin brought it to his lips, drawing her against him as he favored her palm with a lingering kiss. His lips traveled to her

87

face, brushing across her blushing cheek on their way to her lips. He kissed her once—a feather-light caress. When she did not pull away, he cupped her face between his hands and kissed her again, this time with more passion. A third kiss followed, more demanding than the second, then a fourth. His lips hungrily devoured hers again and again, each time growing bolder and more impassioned.

He felt Meary's cheeks warm beneath his fingers and gloried in the heat he created. So consumed was he by the profoundly pleasurable sensations produced by the mating of their lips, it took several moments for his brain to register that her hands, which earlier had lain passively upon his shoulders, now were exerting an insistent pressure against his chest. Reluctantly, he released her.

Meary turned her back to him, struggling to catch her breath without calling attention to the fact he had taken it away. The press of his lips against hers had felt divine. She didn't want it to be so. He was an Englishman, a stranger. She should have pushed him away sooner. She should not have let him kiss her at all. But she had wanted to feel his lips against hers. She had wanted every titillating moment of every kiss. Only the fear that she would not have the will to stay him should he attempt to carry his caresses beyond a few stolen kisses had compelled her to shove him away. Groaning out the agony of her overwrought soul, Meary hugged her arms about her waist.

"You are vexed with me," Lord Colin stated matter-of-factly.

She shook her head negatively.

His voice took on a dubious, hopeful timbre. "Are you pleased?"

Again, she shook her head negatively.

Lord Colin stared at her back, his bottom lip protruding slightly. What was he suppose to make of such answers?

For his part, kissing her had been everything he had imagined and more. She was soft and yielding, and unless he was deluding himself, every bit as hungry for his touch as he was for hers. But there was also an innocent, inexperienced quality to the way she had responded to his kisses. And she *had* pushed him away. As he continued to scrutinize her, he noted the quivering of her shoulders. "You're shaking."

She shook her head affirmatively.

"Are you going to talk to me?"

A long silence stretched between his question and Meary's reply. "I would like ye to go away," she brusquely informed him.

"You *are* vexed with me," he stated, disappointment tingeing his voice. "I admit I should not have been so bold, but I am a weak man and the temptation was too great."

"I told ye I am not vexed with ye!" Under her breath she muttered, "I am vexed with meself." Lord Colin heard her plaintive confession.

"You have done nothing wrong," he cajoled, reaching out to touch her. Meary spun around to face him and stepped out of reach.

"I should not have let ye kiss me!"

"Why?"

"'Twas unwise."

"I thought the experience pleasurable. So pleasurable I would like to repeat it long and often while you are here," he voiced his own interpretation of their kisses.

"Why?"

"'Tis unwise," he drawled. From his lips the statement sounded like a compelling invitation to passion rather than an indictment of their behavior.

"Do not mock me."

Lord Colin chuckled at her flustered expression. He knew he shouldn't, but he found it impossible to repress his good humor. A more dismal countenance he had yet to see, but it was dismay brought on by an excess of desire not a lack of it. And he was the object of that desire. Rather than give into the urge to stoke the fires causing her distress, he decided he might be better served if he pretended at least a little sympathy. "Have you never been kissed before?" he delicately queried.

"Aye. Other of me patrons have tried to take liberties with me."

"And what did you do?"

"I beat them off with me cane." Meary seized upon the ire memory of the incidents evoked and used it as armor against the wanton desire filling her breast.

"Why did you not beat me off?"

"I dropped me cane," she grumbled.

"You still have fists."

Why wouldn't he let her be? She was not in the mood for conversation! She needed to be alone so she could think! It was why she had come out here in the first place. Kicking a clump of peat in the general direction of his voice, she shouted, "'Tis impolite to deny a lady's request, and I have asked ye to leave!"

Prudence sometimes demanded a man retreat even

when he held the clear advantage. Lord Colin judged this one of those times. "Let me walk you away from the cliffs, and I will honor your request," he calmly responded to her shouted request.

"Nay!"

"I will not leave you here alone."

"I got here by meself, and I can be returning the same way."

"I will not leave you here alone," Lord Colin repeated.

Meary mentally sputtered string after string of colorful curses until she had dissipated enough of her exasperation to renew some acquaintance with rational thought. When she did, she realized it was futile to argue with the man. "'Tis unnecessary to lead me about like a child, but if 'tis the only way I can be rid of ye, I suppose I will have to humor ye."

"Thank you."

Bending low, Lord Colin scooped up her walking cane from the ground and placed it in her hand. He then placed a gentle hand on the small of her back, pointed her in the right direction, and began to walk.

The feel of his hand on her back was like fire, and Meary longed to escape it. She accelerated her gait, but he kept pace. When subtlety failed her, she grasped his hand by the wrist and firmly planted it on his thigh.

They had gone about a hundred yards, and Meary was in the midst of thanking the saints for at least saving her the misery of making conversation, when Lord Colin interrupted her thanksgiving.

"Meary."

"What?" she snapped.

Colin hesitated. He wanted to tell her the truth, but the truth might very well thwart . . . Still, he had made a vow to himself he would deal candidly with her and waiting till the deed was done would not qualify. Taking a deep breath, he firmly stated, "In all fairness I must tell you my intentions toward you are less than noble."

"What *are* your intentions?" Meary asked, even though she did not want to hear the answer.

"To seduce you if I can."

Though she was not surprised by his answer, Meary was surprised he had stated it so bluntly. She had to credit the man. No one could claim he lacked the virtue of honesty. How in the world did he expect her to respond to a statement like that? She nervously polished the head of her cane while she advised herself: when in doubt embrace bravado. "How very courteous of ye to be warning me," she lauded. "And what if I will not be seduced? Need I fear ravishment at your hands?"

"I do not force myself upon unwilling women."

Meary stretched her lips into what she hoped was a gracious smile. "I'm glad to hear it. For I shall inform ye now that I am most unwilling, and we need never be speaking of this again."

"You did not act unwilling when I kissed you on the cliffs," he countered.

"A temporary lapse in me usual good sense. 'Twill not happen again."

"I am disappointed."

"Would ye like us to be leaving your house?" she asked. Meary told herself she would be all too happy to honor such an eviction, but to her misery she could not quite make herself believe it.

Lord Colin considered her question. Mayhap he should tell her to leave. Already, he felt more for her than he wished to feel. Taking her to bed would only complicate his life. There were other less bothersome women to be had. All the reasons he gave himself were good, but they could not compete with the simple fact he did not want her to go. When he spoke, he spoke forcefully. "No. I would like you to stay a while longer."

Meary's brows drew together and her lips went slack. "But why? I have told ye I will not be falling for your charms again."

"If all you choose to do is sing and play for me, I shall consider myself well rewarded. As to other matters . . ." his words hung warm and heavy on the air, "I am prepared to let *you* make the choice as to what other pleasures we shall share."

Chapter 7

Seumas O'Hanlon struck his forehead with the heel of his hand then drew his hand down the length of his face. His eyes narrowed as he stared at Lord Colin and Meary strolling side by side toward the house.

Lord Colin was suppose to be off seeing to his tenants. Why was he with Meary? Where had they gone together? What had they said and done?

A feeling of sick dread suffused his gnarled bones. He never would have withdrawn to his room if he had known his lordship was lurking about.

There was something between the two of them. It crackled in the air whenever they were in each other's presence. That something frightened him, for *he* recognized the lightning charge of desire when in its presence even if Meary did not.

Seumas combed his fingers through his hair as his gaze remained fixed on the approaching couple. Meary. She was the true source of his fear. For all his caterwauling about the lusty gleam in Lord Colin's eyes, it was Meary's reaction to his lordship and not his lordship's reaction to

94

Meary that caused his heart to constrict.

Other men's eyes had held that same lusty look, and he had not lost sleep over them. In his bones he had known Meary would waste no time putting them in their place with a few well-chosen words. And, she was not above using the wolf-head cane he had carved for her to bring home her point when added emphasis was needed. Seumas grinned. He had taught her well.

But with Lord Colin the situation was different. As his thoughts came back to their host, his grin of pride faded into a grimace of pain.

The day they had met his lordship on the road, he had had his suspicions, but last night suspicion had turned to dead certainty. Meary glowed like a candle.

He continued to watch Meary's approach. He observed nothing the least bit untoward in her behavior or in his lordship's, yet he found it gave him no ease. Seumas lowered his gaze then quickly raised it again as if trying to catch some unseen detail unawares. His scowl deepened. There it was. Now that they were closer, he could see it— in her heightened color and the animated way she gestured as she spoke. Seumas heaved a ragged sigh.

He did not wish to deny Meary the passions of youth. Never before had she shown interest in a man as a man, and ofttimes he had worried about her lack of interest. He *wanted* her to experience life at its fullest. But when and if Meary became enamored, he had always assumed it would be with a genial and honorable Irishman—someone worthy of her affections.

Lord Colin was no Irishman, and worse, what Seumas believed he would be willing to offer Meary was a poor substitute for the devotion he wished for her. He was an excellent judge of character, and the man had walls around his heart. Thick, impenetrable walls. There was an empty, icy glint in his eyes. The set of his jaw announced he was an angry man. His words revealed cynicism and studied indifference for his fellow man. What Lord Colin would offer Meary, if he offered her anything at all, would be heartache.

Meary might wisely rebuff him. She had a good head on her shoulders. She understood causes and consequences. Unfortunately, he found little peace in this knowledge for during his fifty-five years upon this earth he had witnessed many a good head turned to oat gruel by lust. Those involved would name the overwhelming passion they felt for the other love, but he refused to glorify lust by calling it by other than its correct name.

Lust could lead to love, but they were not one and the same.

Lust could also lead to untold suffering.

He could not see this ill-timed visitation of lust leading to anything but suffering for his sweet Meary. He wanted to save her that suffering, but he did not know how.

He had seen what happened when he voiced his concerns. She called him foolish and refused to acknowledge she was the least bit attracted to his lordship.

And if he outright forbid her Lord Colin's acquaintance, he feared she would only want it more. Forbidden fruit always seemed more delectable to the young. It was in their nature, this morbid curiosity that compelled them to defy the sage counsel of their elders and experience the pain of life firsthand.

Seumas combed his fingers through his hair again. How comforting it would be if he wholeheartedly could believe Meary immune to the folly of youth.

He could not deny she was wise in ways other young

women were not. She possessed more than intellectual acumen. She understood people well. When had he ever known her to behave recklessly when dealing with her fellow man? Never, unless one counted the handful of times she had plainly spoken her mind when silence would have served her better. And he should not discount the voices she heard in her head. Though he was angry with them for bringing her here, he had not lost his respect for them.

Mayhap he was letting his own discomfort and inexperience in dealing with matters of female passions color his judgment unduly black.

Up to this point in time playing parent to Meary had been joyously uncomplicated. He loved her and that had been enough. Was it still? He feared it might not be. If it was not . . .

Meary deserved his faith, but she also deserved his guidance. Striking the proper balance between the two was a daunting task. If he failed, the consequences for Meary would be dire. *He could not fail.*

Seumas O'Hanlon cursed his own insufficiencies, cursed Lord Colin for forcing him to face them, and fervently prayed Meary would be blessed with the necessary clearheadedness to survive this situation unscathed.

Upon arriving at the tower house, Lord Colin gave Meary over to Seumas's care, sternly admonishing him to keep a better eye on her.

"What 'twas that about?" Seumas queried the moment Lord Colin was out of hearing.

"He fears I will be coming to harm if I am allowed to

wander about on me own."

"I share his fear."

"I cannot believe me ears. Ye have never discouraged me from taking meself about before. I know how to . . ."

"I'd like ye to be thinking over the wisdom of walking alone with his lordship," he interrupted her protests.

"Oh." While Meary was relieved that Seumas had not suddenly concluded she was an invalid, she was not particularly happy to have her painfully recent lapse in good judgment recalled to the forefront of her mind. Her lips tightened as she felt the roseate warmth staining her cheeks spread across her face and down her neck.

"I can see by yer face I am right to be feeling fear for ye. I beg of ye, Meary. Not for me sake, but for yer own, be wise."

"I intend to be," she stated resolutely, having full faith in her own words. After all, she counseled herself, regardless of the lingering longing she presently felt or any longing she might have the bad luck to feel in the future for Lord Colin's person, there was certainly no law she must act upon it. Lord Colin had said the choice was hers, and her choice had been made. A twinge of regret clutched her heart, but she refused to attach any significance to it.

"Then ye'll not be minding if I keep ye company," Seumas said.

"Not at all," Meary responded enthusiastically, having no desire whatsoever to be alone lest her thoughts turn traitor. Keeping her mind thoroughly occupied with some challenging task was her best defense against errant thoughts, so she suggested, "Mayhap we could review me lessons. It has been so long since I've practiced me Latin, I fear me mind grows rusty."

Seumas agreed to her suggestion.

After spending considerable time drilling her on the conjugation of irregular Latin verbs, he had Meary recite several epic poems of Irish history. Each time she misspoke a word or lost the meter of the verse through hesitation, he required her to begin anew. These and other exercises of the mind brought Meary the sanctuary she sought.

Evening came upon them unnoticed.

"Ah, I see you are already here. Good," Lord Colin commented as he strode into the room. "Annie has just informed me our supper is ready."

A second pair of feet had entered with Lord Colin. Even before he began to chatter excitedly about the quality of his lordship's stables, Meary recognized Brendan's presence.

They retired to the trestle table to take up the places they had occupied the previous evening.

The atmosphere at the dinner table was even more strained than it had been the night before.

Meary may have succeeded in keeping her wayward thoughts and emotions in check in Lord Colin's absence, but she found it impossible to direct her thoughts elsewhere when he was sitting but a few inches away from her doing his best to engage her in cordial conversation. However, she could present a stoic mien.

"Did you have a pleasant afternoon?" he queried.

"Aye."

"How did you occupy yourself?"

Having already revealed her Catholic heritage, and since it was presently illegal for an Irish Catholic to receive education, Meary offered up an abridged version of the truth. "Mostly, I practiced me poetry."

"A poetess as well as a singer and harper? Is there no limit to your talents?"

"The limits are many. I recite poems, I do not compose them. Or, at least, the ones I've composed are not worthy of recitation."

"Mayhap you should let another be the judge."

"There is no one upon this earth I despise so much I would subject them to me awkward verse."

"Is this false modesty I hear? I would think you above such ruses."

"I assure ye 'tis the truth and not false modesty that guides me tongue. If ye will not be believing me, ask Seumas."

"Mr. O'Hanlon?"

"She be telling ye the truth. She has mastered the meter well enough, but her sense of rhyme 'tis still wanting," Seumas said.

Lord Colin brushed his fingertips across her knuckles causing Meary to withdraw her hand to under the table.

"Nevertheless, I would like to hear one of your poems. Will you say one tonight?"

"Nay. I prize me dignity too much. Ye might be able to endure the assault upon your ears, but I would not survive the humiliation."

"I bow to your wishes, but not without disappointment." His voice retained the subtle, velvety tone it had had since he had entered the hall. "If you will not recite for me, you must promise not to sit idle half the evening but to play and sing from the start."

"That I will do with pleasure." Meary announced, seizing the invitation to escape into her music. "'Tis me weaknesses I seek to hide. Give me a wee hint of an invitation, and I'll be first in line to flaunt me talents."

"Don't we all," Lord Colin opined. "However, it is refreshing to hear someone admit such is the case." He paused to chew a bite of roast pigeon. "I have witnessed for myself the excellence of your music. What other talents do you have?"

"I can make the lightest scones ye will ever eat. I possess a good memory for facts and figures and the like. I'm a passable dancer. I can take meself anywhere I desire to be going in this world without the least bit of trouble." She added the last in hopes of provoking him into a less amiable mood for, despite her best efforts, her resistance to his charm was flagging at an alarming rate. She feared if he chiseled many more chinks in her wall of resistance it would crumble to dust at her feet.

"Impressive."

How dare he respond with a compliment, Meary objected. He wasn't playing fair. Mayhap if she turned the discussion to him she would be better served. "And what are your talents?" she queried.

"Money. Money is my talent. I can turn a handsome profit in most any venture."

"So, ye are exceedingly rich."

A long moment passed before he answered. "Rich enough. Does that please you?"

She thought she detected a note of suspicion in his voice, but she was feeling too off-balance to be certain. "I care not one way or the other how well-lined your pockets be. 'Tis none of me concern. What other talents do ye have?"

"I have no other talent."

"None?"

"None."

"Surely ye underestimate yourself."

101

"I tell the unvarnished truth."

"Then, ye have sorely neglected yer soul," Seumas tersely informed him.

"How so?" Colin asked.

"Gold be only as good as the man who holds it, and a good man does not found his life on greed."

"I have never considered myself a greedy man," Lord Colin said without animosity.

"Then why have ye neglected all else for the pursuit of wealth?"

Again, there was a noticeable lapse of time between the question asked and Lord Colin's reply. "I have had financial obligations to satisfy."

"So, ye be a gambling man." Seumas spoke the words like a magistrate handing down a guilty verdict to a low-life villain.

Lord Colin opened his mouth to deny the accusation, then clamped it shut. The truth was more discomfiting to him than the misconception, and he had no desire to explain the circumstances he had left behind in England. He didn't want to reveal the monumental waste he had made of his life.

"If you have finished your meal, let us retire from the table. Lady Meary has promised to entertain me," Colin announced as he rose from the table. "Lady Meary." He guided her hand to his arm. "I would be honored to escort you to your stool."

The courtesy he offered was common. To refuse it because she was afraid to touch him was to admit she felt something out of the ordinary for him. Meary left her hand on his arm.

Her fingers felt on fire. The heat radiating up her arm conjured memories of the prurient sensations she had felt upon the cliffs. Why was this man doing this to her? How did he do it? And why was he calling her "Lady" when he knew she had no rightful claim to the title? He had not done so when they were alone. He made the mere speaking of her name sound like a psalm.

Never had Meary been so eager to begin playing her harp. She needed to retreat from the tension of the room, and she needed to retreat *now*. She was frightened to find herself so weak when she had vowed to be strong. It made no sense. Where was the logical mind in which she took such pride? She could not accept its cruel desertion. She could not accept she was no longer the mistress of her own will. The moment she settled herself on the stool her fingers began to stroke and pluck the strings of her instrument.

Slowly, her earthly cares began to fade, and soon there was nothing but music filling her soul.

As the notes washed over him, Lord Colin settled comfortably into his chair, arranging his long arms and legs negligently. He closed his eyes, savoring the sounds that filled his ears, then opened them again and savored the sight of the beautiful woman who filled his hall with such divine music.

He had spent the afternoon trying to conjure a little genuine remorse for giving into his impulsive urge to kiss her, without a whit of success. He knew he'd gladly do it again given half an opportunity.

And he intended to make sure he did have the opportunity. For while he may have told Meary the choice was hers, he did not propose to leave the matter of her surrender to luck. He would make certain her "choice" was his choice.

There was no point in pretending compunction. His lust had conquered wholly what sense of decency he owned where Meary was concerned. The kiss had sealed her fate.

It was not his fault she was beautiful. It was not his fault she was blind. When he had first asked her to come play for him, he had warned her he was a mortal man. He had warned her he was capable of sin. Colin crossed his legs at the ankle. Lord, how he needed to sin with this woman.

If he was feeling any regret at all about his behavior today, it was regret that his boldness had put her on her guard, thus making the task of seducing her more prolonged and difficult.

Difficult he had no doubt he could handle with aplomb. He enjoyed a challenge. A hard-won battle made victory that much sweeter. It was the *prolonged* that set his teeth on edge. He had never felt such a potent stirring in his loins for a woman, and he was eager to work it out of his system. He had more important things to concentrate on than indulging basic animal needs, and these last two days he had been able to think of little else.

Once the deed was done—more than once if necessary—his mind would be entirely his own again. He could go back to concentrating on what he knew best: turning a profit. He looked forward to the day.

But he was getting ahead of himself, Lord Colin cautioned. First came seduction, then came release and relief. He must achieve the first goal before he could hope to attain the second.

The concert continued, each musician taking a turn at singly displaying his skills, but more often all three played and sang together. Their instruments and voices blended in faultless harmony as they made their music for him.

Lord Colin judged it a fine way for a man to end his day, despite his desire to have Meary play a very private sort of concert with him. She would entertain him soon enough.

His flesh would be her instrument, each nerve as sensitive to her touch as her harp strings. The thud of his heart would be as the drum of the *bodhrán*. And the songs he would coax her to sing would be poems of earthy pleasure. . . .

He sighed heavily and shifted on his chair, reining his thoughts back to the scene at hand. Patience, he lectured himself. Patience. Such imaginings could lead a man to imprudent behavior, behavior that would ultimately interfere with the attainment of his goals. He must find some way to distract himself, or he risked being undone before he began.

Forcing his attention away from Meary and onto Brendan and O'Hanlon, Lord Colin clenched his jaw in determination. He would be the master of his own thoughts. They were his to command. He commanded them. . . . His shoulders stiffened and one corner of his lips curled into a rueful grin as his gaze gravitated back to Meary. He commanded them . . . to think of a speedy way to bring Meary O'Byrne, willing and eager, to his bed.

The next morning Meary was halfway dressed when a knock came at her door.

She sighed. The night had not been a restful one. It had

105

been one plagued with confusion, self-doubt, and unwelcome yearnings. Playing her harp had given her respite from her cares, but the interlude had been all too brief, and the moment her fingers had stilled, all the unwieldy feelings she had hoped to banish rushed back upon her. She did not feel ready to face a world of inquisitive eyes, eyes she feared might perceive her inner turmoil despite her stalwart determination to conceal it. The knock came again.

"Good morning, miss," a feminine voice greeted. "Me name be Doreen. The master sent me up to take care of ye. I'm to be yer personal maid."

"Thank ye, but I can see to me own needs," Meary called through the door.

"The master said I was to persist no matter what ye said."

"Did he now."

"Aye. He was most adamant about his wishes."

"And I am most adamant about me refusal."

"Please. I'd deem it a personal favor if ye'd be letting me do as he says. There's no thwarting of the master's wishes in this house. I'll be sent packing for sure."

Meary ground her teeth and made a face at the door. She detested being maneuvered every bit as much as she detested being mollycoddled, and Lord Colin's "offer" of a personal maid did both. He should have asked before he commanded Doreen to her threshold. She did not need nor want a maid . . . but she could not in good conscience allow the girl to lose her position on her account. Meary reminded herself, if she was sighted, she would not refuse the offer of a maid. She would accept it as her due. Then, again, if she was sighted, pampering would not threaten her survival. She could not afford to grow lazy. It had taken a long time to relearn to do everyday things for herself, and she was loath to fall out of practice.

"Please, miss."

Meary weighed the pros and cons of giving into the maid's pleas. She didn't like it, but she supposed for the maid's sake, just this once, she could bend her rule of strict independence. But she intended to have a word with Lord Colin at first opportunity.

"Ye may come in," Meary informed her.

"Oh thank ye, miss. I'll be forever grateful." Doreen announced as she stepped through the doorway. She immediately set to cinching the laces of Meary's corset where Meary had left off.

Meary surrendered herself to Doreen's hands, letting her mind wander where it willed. Predictably, her thoughts settled on Lord Colin. "Is your master really such an ogre he would dismiss ye if I refused ye entry?"

"Not him," Doreen protested. "'Tis her. Annie Baine be a tyrant worse than any that's sat upon England's throne."

It was not the answer Meary had hoped for. She had hoped Doreen would reveal Lord Colin a man to be despised as one despised the devil. She wanted a reason to despise him, for she knew her heart would never allow her to feel the things she was feeling toward an evil man. Unfortunately, it was not to be. Shrugging her shoulders into the sleeves of the bodice Doreen slipped onto her arms, Meary offered a bit of friendly advice, "If she is such a tyrant, I would not go about so freely expressing me opinions. Tyrants have been known to post spies to eavesdrop and report on what is said behind closed doors."

"Oh, she knows we all think her a tyrant," Doreen

107

reassured her. "And proud of it she is. I once lost me temper and called her so to her face, and she stood there with her chest puffed out grinning from ear to ear as she shouted more orders at me."

Remembering the greeting they had received upon their arrival, Meary did not doubt the maid's accounting of the head housekeeper. Now that they were considered guests, Annie's manners toward them had improved, but Meary still felt the strong sense the housekeeper was not a woman one would want to cross.

Doreen finished helping her dress, found her brush, and sat Meary down on the edge of the bed.

As the maid drew the brush through her hair, Meary smiled. She had forgotten how good it felt to have someone else tend one's hair. Her own maids and mother used to take turns brushing her hair. She had been an only child and the entire household doted on her. She had wanted for naught and was given far more freedom than other girls of her age and station. But that was a long time ago, before she recklessly had tried to jump a hedge far too high for her horse. Before her parents' death.

"How would ye be liking me to dress yer hair today?" Doreen's question brought Meary's thoughts back to the present and perforce to Lord Colin.

"Something austere, if ye please."

"Aye, miss."

As Doreen twisted and coiled Meary's hair into a high bun at the back of her head, she continued to converse with her. "After ye break yer fast, his lordship would be liking to see ye."

Meary instantly tensed. "Did he say why?"

Surveying her work, Doreen frowned and teased two tendrils of hair loose from the bun, arranging one over each of Meary's shoulders. "Nay. Just that ye were to wait for him to come to ye in the great hall."

Meary nodded for lack of a more dignified response. She could not refuse to honor the request, but she was not particularly eager to do so. She had thought to spend the day avoiding Lord Colin. Not because she disliked his company but because in light of her present peculiar thoughts and behavior, it seemed the prudent thing to do.

And, as if reality had not given her enough with which to contend, she had dreamed about him last night. She dreamed he had kissed her again. Only these kisses were far more daring than the real ones they had shared on the cliffs yesterday. *Far more daring.* Meary felt her cheeks warm at the memory and silently prayed Doreen would not comment on her heightened color.

Her prayer was answered. "If yer ready, I'll be taking ye down to the great hall now," Doreen said.

Rising to her feet, Meary took several steps toward the door. She heard Doreen scurry to place herself in front of her. "I can be finding me own way, and I'll not be compromising with ye on the matter, so there's no use pleading with me," Meary stated, feeling a sudden need to reassert her own will. "Thank ye for your help. I'll be sure to tell Annie how well ye have done."

On that comment, Meary swept passed the maid, placed her hand on the wall, and regally descended the stairs.

Doreen silently trailed behind. When they reached the base of the stairs, she excused herself. Another maid entered momentarily, carrying a tray of oat porridge, muffins, sweet butter, honey, and tea. Doreen reentered as the kitchen maid left. She said not a word, but Meary could hear her puttering about the hall.

Meary had barely swallowed her last bite of breakfast when she heard Lord Colin's boots striding across the stone floor toward her and Doreen's slippered feet scurrying in retreat.

Dabbing her lips and fingers with her napkin, Meary clenched her hands in her lap. "Good morning to ye, Lord Colin. I've been told ye wanted to see me?"

"Yes."

She could feel his gaze upon her as she waited—her fingers nervously drumming upon her knuckles—for him to say more. When he did not, she felt compelled to prod him. "What is it ye wish of me?"

Several delightful possibilities sprung into his mind, but Lord Colin resisted their siren song and remained committed to the more subtle path of seduction he had earlier settled upon. "I would like to begin my language lessons this morning."

"Oh." Meary was unsure whether she felt more relief because his request was so innocent or distress that honoring his request required her to keep his company.

"You do not sound enthused," he observed. "Do you intend to deny me?"

"Nay. I will teach ye," Meary assured him, cursing herself beneath her breath for failing to come up with some reasonable excuse why she could not.

"I am not a stupid man. The task will not be as onerous as your frown says you predict."

She hadn't realized she was frowning, and Meary quickly turned up the corners of her lips. What was she worrying about? she chided herself. Here in the great hall, there could be no repetition of yesterday's misbehavior. Why, at any moment Seumas or Brendan or any one of a dozen servants would enter the hall, and they no

110

longer would be alone. Even if no one came to interrupt their solitude, she had the wide barrier of the stretcher table between her and temptation, and she intended to keep it that way. "Please be taking the seat across from me, and I will begin your lesson," she instructed in an authoritative voice.

Lord Colin took up the seat next to hers.

Meary stiffened, her tone becoming even more imperious. "If ye expect me to teach ye, the first thing ye must learn is that I expect me instructions to be followed. If ye are unwilling to do so, I'll not be wasting me time on ye. Take the seat across from me."

Chuckling at her agitation, Lord Colin complied. Meary ignored his bad manners.

Even though she had secured a more comfortable physical distance for herself, Meary still felt vulnerable. In the fervent hope she could secure for herself emotional safety as well, she decided to court controversy by broaching the issue of Doreen. "There is another matter we must be settling before we begin."

"What is that?"

"Doreen."

"She has done something to displease you?" he asked, his tone evincing concern.

"Nay. She is as sweet and efficient as can be, and I don't want her to be suffering for me words," Meary enjoined. Wishing to appear as commanding as possible, she squared her body for a frontal attack. "I don't require the services of a maid."

"What one requires and what one desires are ofttimes at odds. Think of her as a gift," he magnanimously proffered.

"But I don't want to be accepting this gift."

111

"Why not?"

Why must he sound so damnably pleasant? Meary wrinkled her brow. She had expected him to meet her statement with insensitivity and arrogance, not sympathy and civility. Her resolve to put him pithily in his place began to waver. "Pampering puts me ill at ease and . . ."

"And?"

She took a deep breath. "It has occurred to me, ye might have sent her to spy on me because I refused to submit to your order not to be wandering about without escort."

"You insult me with your false accusation," Lord Colin lied, as he simultaneously cursed and congratulated her for her perceptiveness. He continued in an injured tone, "My sole motivation is your comfort and convenience. I thought you would be pleased."

A wave of contrition washed over Meary. It had never been her intent to abuse his feelings. She should not have been so frank. Reaching across the table, she gently stroked his hand. The instant she touched him, her mind registered the folly of the gesture of comfort, but her concern for him overcame her dread of the sultry sensations assailing her person. "I am sorry if I have given offense."

"Then you will keep her?" he asked, tendering the question as a plea.

To do otherwise seemed mean-spirited, and Meary felt she had no choice but to acquiesce. "I suppose."

"Thank you."

Meary's stomach constricted and she retracted her hand. Was that a subtle note of triumph she heard in his tone, or was her imagination playing tricks on her? Was

112

the niggling feeling she had somehow been hoodwinked into saying and doing exactly as he designed to be heeded or ignored? With any other man or woman she would have no trouble discerning the truth of the matter, but with Lord Colin . . .

Abandoning the debate until her nerves were less jangled presented itself as her only rational course. "Shall we be commencing with your lesson?" she proposed, feigning a level head. Before he could say otherwise, she demanded, "Tell me what ye already know."

Lord Colin obediently listed the words and phrases he had gleaned on his own. As Meary listened, she became increasingly distressed. It was not what he said, but the tone he used to say it. Every word out of his mouth sounded like a caress—every pause like a wistful sigh. Before this day she would have laughed herself breathless had someone tried to convince her a phrase like "the cattle are in yonder pasture" could be used to heat the blood. She wasn't laughing. But she did feel a bit breathless.

She was beginning to feel bereft of her sanity. There was absolutely no reason she should be letting him affect her this way.

When Lord Colin had exhausted his store of Gaelic words, Meary took her wayward emotions firmly in hand and brusquely stated, "Well, 'tis a start anyway."

Meary spent the next two hours teaching her pupil the basic rules of Gaelic grammar and a series of common phrases she deemed he would be most likely to encounter in his day-to-day dealings with his people.

Though his lordship learned quickly, Meary was not at all pleased with her pupil and even less so with herself.

113

Despite the barrier of the table, Lord Colin had somehow managed to keep her nerves so on edge it was nearly impossible to keep her wits about her. And the nervousness he evoked was not the kind one might expect to feel if one was called upon to perform before a great lord or found oneself lost in the woods. It was an entrancing kind of nervousness, a delicious anticipation that suffused every fiber of her being.

How he did it, she did not know. If she knew she could guard against it. He had not spoken one provocative word, made one untoward advance upon her person. Often he had lain his hand so close to hers she could feel the heat of him, but he had never tried to touch her. He was full of compliments, but none had overstepped the bounds of propriety. In short, his behavior was that of a perfect gentleman.

There was nothing she could fault him with. Nothing. Except, mayhap, his penchant for staring at her and sighing. She could rebuke him for that, but she dare not. What if the stare she felt was merely the innocent gaze of a pupil concentrating on his teacher, and his sighs the sighs of a weary scholar? She did not want to call attention to her own amorous reactions by falsely accusing him of harboring like feelings.

Nay! What she was feeling were not romantic stirrings, Meary adamantly denied her own assessment of her emotions, pretending not to hear the voice of her conscience screaming "liar" over and over in her head. She had told Lord Colin she would not fall victim to his charms, and that was the end of it. She wasn't about to let herself be beguiled by any man, especially not Lord Colin. He was an Englishman. A usurper. She didn't trust him. She was Irish, blind, and too sensible to fall prey to imprudent passions.

And another thing, Meary continued to mentally bemoan. Where were Seumas and Brendan? She had been sitting here for over two hours fervently praying one or the other would enter the hall and save her from this discomfiting situation, and she had yet to hear a whisper of a footstep. Surely, they could not still be abed.

"I believe my mind has absorbed all it can for today," Lord Colin announced, calling Meary out of her turbulent thoughts. "Good day to you." Rising to his feet, he strode toward the door.

If Meary gave reply, he did not hear it.

Lord Colin stepped through the door and tipped a salute to the sun.

Although his statement concerning the capacity of his mind was true, the real reason he had called a halt to the lesson had to do with Meary. He'd toyed with her and tempted himself as much as he dared.

Everything had gone exactly as he planned. He had given his servants strict orders to stay out of the great hall until he informed them otherwise. Those assigned to keep Seumas and Brendan occupied elsewhere had performed their tasks admirably. And Meary . . . she had blushed and fidgeted and blushed some more. Her words were those of a stoic teacher. Her actions were those of a woman very much aware of her pupil as a man. She was fighting her feelings, but his instincts told him she wanted him every bit as much as he wanted her. That was good—very, very good. He would hone that want as one honed a sword. When it was razor sharp, he would wield it to his advantage.

But now it was time to withdraw. Press too hard and he risked frightening her off. Besides, if he had stayed with

115

her much longer, he would not have been able to resist the urge to pull her into his arms.

Seduction was much like a business negotiation. A man who stated his intention, enticed the other party to desperately want something he could give, and exercised a little patience was sure to triumph.

He sensed Meary was new to this game, and it caused him a twinge of conscience, but he summarily squelched it. Sentimentality was for fools, and he was through being a fool.

Lord Colin occupied himself elsewhere for the remainder of the day. There was always plenty to do to keep the estate prosperous, and he made good use of his time.

As he had the two previous nights, he did not make an appearance until it was time for the evening meal.

He kept his conversation friendly and light, addressing O'Hanlon as often as he did Meary. He again requested Meary play for him. She willingly agreed to his request.

Lord Colin closed his eyes and prayed her music would soothe the tension from his muscles. He was sorely in need of soothing. Much to his dismay, he was finding it almost impossible to be near her and refrain from touching her, but he knew he must. At least a little while longer. When he made his next advance, he wanted the assurance of success.

After Meary played the first tune, O'Hanlon and Brendan joined her in performing several others. Lord Colin did his best to focus his attention on them, but his mind kept drifting back to Meary, and eventually he gave up the struggle.

Watching her fingers move lovingly over the strings of her harp, he felt a sharp stab of jealousy. Would that it was his flesh upon which her fingers played so tenderly. It seemed to him unfair the harp strings were freely given what he must scheme and labor to attain. They could not appreciate the gift she gave them.

At length the concert came to an end, and all rose to retire to their separate rooms. Lord Colin deftly placed himself at Meary's side, determined to grant himself the pleasure of her touch at least for the brief space of time it took to escort her up the stairs.

She did not pull away when he lay her hand upon his arm, but her carriage stiffened and her color subtly heightened.

Later, as he blew out his candle and slipped under his covers, Lord Colin wondered how much longer he would have to wait before his mattress knew a body other than his own.

He would not let it be long, he promised himself. Whatever he had to do, he would not let it be long.

Chapter 8

They had been at Lord Colin's estate two weeks, and every morning Meary found it more difficult to face the day. She could not blame her apprehension upon the events of each day. She rose, broke her fast, tutored Lord Colin, then had hours to do as she pleased. Every evening Seumas, Brendan, and she made beautiful music to entertain their host. Nay, it was not the events of the day, it was the storm of emotions churning in her breast that caused her disquiet.

Lord Colin was driving her to distraction. Worse, he was accomplishing the feat without doing a thing. Since the day she had rebuffed his kisses, his behavior had been above reproach. He was an excellent student, an appreciative audience, a generous host. *He* was comporting himself as a gentleman. It was her own behavior she found offensive.

Every time the man entered into a room her heart began to pound like feet gone drunk with joy at a jig. Every time his hand innocently brushed hers, an event which to her seemed to occur with daunting regularity of late, the blood in her veins turned hot and thick. Her cheeks bloomed with color at the slightest provocation. The sound of her name upon his lips sent delicious shivers up her spine.

If not for the fact these symptoms occurred only in Lord Colin's presence, or when she thought of him, she would believe herself afflicted by some dreaded disease. It would be almost a relief if it were so, for the truth of the matter was so much harder to accept.

She was hungry for the man pure and simple. Hungry like the peasant girls she heard giggling in the fields as they frolicked with their beaus. She wanted to caress him, to be caressed by him, to cuddle into the crook of his arm, to lay her head against his chest, to share another kiss. It gave one cause to question one's sanity.

Nothing good could come of her longings. If she indulged them, where would they lead? *To a few brief moments of pleasure and the deprivation of her dignity.* Was she willing to sacrifice her dignity for a few stolen kisses? *Nay.* Did she have any intention of exposing her aberrant turn of heart to Lord Colin? *Absolutely not.*

Since she was determined to be wise, why did she continue to suffer this agitation of spirit?

She had never held to the notion that suffering was good for the soul. Suffering was suffering. It was to be avoided whenever possible. So why didn't she pack her trunk and be on her way? It was a question Meary could not answer.

In truth, several times she *had* packed her trunk and started down the stairs to find Seumas to tell him she wanted to leave this place immediately. But always something stopped her. That something was the still incessant voice in her head telling her she *needed* to stay.

She had argued and cajoled, demanded and pleaded, to be left in peace, to be allowed to remove herself from the presence of temptation, but to no avail. Nightly she fell to her knees and prayed that if she could not be relieved of whatever burden fate demanded she carry, she could at least be told what it was. No reasonable answer was forthcoming. Only a trenchant urge to give herself body and soul to Lord Colin.

She could not accept the idea that she was destined to be an Englishman's whore. Intelligent, forceful, and enticing as he was, she did not believe Lord Colin capable of coaxing the angels into helping him procure a woman to entertain him in his bed. Angels trafficked in more noble trades. Too, the man clearly had lost all interest in seducing her. The thought caused a pang of disappointment, and the fact she would feel such a pang humiliated her to the depths of her beleaguered soul.

She morosely considered the possibility the impulse was the product of her own failings. All her life she had been immune to the weaknesses of the flesh. Had she unknowingly become boastful and unfeeling? Mayhap Lord Colin was some sort of test . . . or punishment for the sin of arrogance. Meary whimpered her dismay.

She didn't know what to do. She couldn't go to Seumas for guidance as she had always done in the past when faced with other difficulties. Embarrassment prevented her from seeking his comfort. He had made it abundantly clear he recognized her feelings for Lord Colin were not what they should be, though she hoped he wasn't cognizant of the magnitude of her hunger. Meary sensed the awakening of her womanly appetites made Seumas as uncomfortable as they made her. She could not bring herself to increase his distress by demanding he give her counsel. It was preferable to profess the feelings did not exist.

Brendan could be of no help.

The only comfort she found was in her music, and though she had taken to playing for her own consolation for hours at a time, it was impossible to spend every waking moment making music.

Never had she felt so completely adrift. Loosing her sight had been terrifying, but the darkness she now found herself plunged into was even more frightening. This was moral darkness, and every hour she felt herself sinking deeper into the abyss.

Today was like every other day. She had finished Lord Colin's language lesson. As usual, he had been a keen student, a fact that pained Meary every bit as much as it pleased her. She had always been attracted to men of intelligence—though not in the ruttish way she was attracted to Lord Colin—and his cleverness was just one more strand in the silken cord that drew her to him. Now, Meary sat alone in the great hall trying to decide what to do with her day.

"I see you've finished your tutoring," Annie commented as she entered the hall. "I can't understand why the master thinks he needs to learn to speak in a foreign tongue, but it's good of you to indulge him," she continued. Her voice warbled with friendliness.

Meary thought it amusing the housekeeper seemed to have taken such a liking to her company. Annie often took a break from her duties to sit and chat with her. They talked of many things, but nothing Meary judged to be of consequence. Considering Annie's reputation among the servants and her eagerness to have them banished upon their arrival, such affability was unexpected.

There was a lot about Annie that was unexpected. While requiring the servants of the household to treat the master of the house with exaggerated respect, *she* addressed him in a manner far more familiar than deferential. She had a voice that carried for miles, or so it seemed when she was scolding one of her charges; yet Seumas had described her as a frail-looking woman. There was little doubt she believed everything English superior to anything Irish, but Meary could not recall one instance where Annie had let her prejudice interfere with fair-mindedness when it came to disciplining the staff.

Deciding some sort of response to the housekeeper's comment was required, Meary, at length, replied, "He is a very good student."

Annie settled herself on the bench opposite Meary. "Always was smart as a whip. Even when he was but a babe."

"You knew him then?" Meary asked, curiosity overcoming her reluctance to discuss the source of her frustration with herself.

"I've known him since the day he was born," Annie stated proudly. "I was his nurse till his mother, the beastly woman, shoved me out the door. I can tell you, I wept a bucket of tears when they deprived me of the boy." She cleared her throat. "Not for myself of course, but for his sake, poor little angel."

"Poor? How so?" Meary was so intrigued to hear Lord Colin described in such terms she forgot to sound detached.

"They never treated him right, him being a second son. He was a thousand times sweeter than that brother Edwin, but they just ignored him. Treated him worse than the meanest servant and him always trying so hard to please."

Though Meary assumed Annie's account was wildly exaggerated—she had never met a servant who after being summarily dismissed had good to say of a former master—it did give her pause. The loneliness she sensed whenever she was in Lord Colin's presence, was this the cause? Did her heart see behind the facade of a formidable man the forlorn child?

As she tried to assimilate Annie's view with her own experience of Lord Colin, Meary diplomatically commented, "It sounds like he was very fortunate to be having ye to champion him."

"Oh, I couldn't save him much misery, but I gave him my love. It was little enough, but he never forgot it. Most gentry has trouble remembering your name, but not my Colin. When he grew up and needed someone to run his household, he came looking for me."

Meary smiled. "I like stories with happy endings."

"So do I, but so far this story don't have one. They did something to my Colin in all those years I was away. They killed his sweetness. But that wasn't enough for them. Oh, no. They had to keep plaguing him till they sucked his heart dry. Chased him out of England, they did." Annie paused to catch her breath and bridle her ire. "Now . . . well . . . what my Colin needs is someone to love him."

Meary was at a loss as how to respond to Annie's tirade. Her information fascinated and frightened her, but she could hardly remark on such feelings. Mayhap the wisest thing to do was try to soothe Annie's ruffled emotions. "Then 'tis lucky he has ye to be giving him the love he needs. I doubt there 'tis a lord on earth who has a more devoted servant than thee."

Annie snorted. "I'm an old woman. What my Colin needs is the love of a pretty young one. He needs someone to make him feel like he's the finest man on earth. It's past time he settled down and started a family of his own. It'd do him a world of good."

Meary stifled a grin as she imagined Lord Colin's reaction if he was ever made privy to the fact his house-keeper entertained herself by charting his life's course and making sweeping proclamations concerning the providential nature of her decisions. Doing her best to sound appropriately sober, she said, "Since ye are convinced he needs this woman, I hope he finds her someday."

"I think he already has," Annie confided.

The twinge that tweaked Meary's heart was as unexpected as it was undesired, and she physically recoiled from it. What did she care for Lord Colin's love affairs, she sternly demanded of herself—but the question that escaped her lips was a tentatively spoken, "A neighbor?"

"Not exactly." Annie bustled to her feet. "I best be getting back to my duties." She paused halfway across the room. "Just remember, you'll never meet a finer man."

"Now that was a strange conversation," Meary said out loud when she again found herself alone. She had the distinct impression Annie hadn't sat down at the table for the purpose of a little friendly gossip. Very distinct. If she didn't know better, she would swear Annie had just informed her she should pursue Lord Colin.

Meary laughed at the ridiculousness of the thought. Not only was she blind, she was Irish. Even if Annie was willing to overlook the former, a very doubtful circumstance, Meary could not believe Annie would ignore the fact that she came from "inferior" Irish ancestry. Not where a bride for her beloved master was concerned. She must have imagined the odd inflections in the housekeeper's tone. Mayhap because a traitorous part of her wished it could be so. But Lord Colin had made it perfectly clear his interest in her, when he had been interested in her, was strictly as a paramour, not a wife.

Meary straightened her spine and pressed her fingers into the tabletop so firmly she could feel the grain of the wood. She had to stop allowing her mind to wander down outrageous paths. If Annie had had something important to say to her, she would have come right out and said it. Annie was nothing if she was not forthright.

Having once again embraced logic, Meary was distressed to find the twinge she had felt when Annie had revealed the existence of the woman she had in mind for Lord Colin's bride settled in her stomach as a pervasive ache.

The man means naught to ye. Naught, do ye hear! If ye don't stop acting the mooncalf this instant, I shall disown ye, she upbraided herself.

A brisk walk was what she needed, she decided. She had been sitting idle too much of late. Moss was growing in her mind.

Rising to her feet, Meary resolved she would seek out Brendan and request he accompany her on a stroll. The last thing she wanted was to be alone with her thoughts. Also, his company would guarantee her some protection

125

from herself should Lord Colin spy her on the heath and take it in his head to join her.

It was no mystery where she would find Brendan. Since discovering Lord Colin's stable, he had spent every spare minute out in the barn talking to his lordship's horses. With the exception of Seumas and herself, Brendan always preferred the company of four-footed creatures to two-footed ones, and horses he loved best of all. It was easy to understand his affection. She had once shared it.

Since her accident she was reluctant to sit in a saddle, but as long as she could keep both feet firmly planted on the ground, she had no fear of the animals.

Walking cane in hand, Meary headed for the stables.

"Brendan, how are the horses this morning?" she greeted when she had located him by following the sound of his cooing voice to the stall where he stood.

"They be in fine form, except for Pansy here. She's feeling a bit melancholy this morning."

"Do ye know why?"

"Says she needs a frolic in the sunshine. Wants to be ridden, she does, but the grooms be too busy and Lord Colin prefers his thoroughbred to her."

"Mayhap ye could ask his lordship if ye could ride her," Meary suggested as she stroked the mare's velvety nose.

"Nay. I could never ask so large a favor."

"But 'tis ye who would be doing his lordship the favor. I'm sure he does not mean to neglect the mare."

"I cannot ask," Brendan insisted.

Meary was well used to Brendan's timidity, and she did not abuse him for it, but she and Seumas shared the opinion that for Brendan's sake whenever possible they should encourage him to overcome it. "If ye are afraid he won't understand ye, ye need not be. His Gaelic is much improved."

"'Tis not that," Brendan stammered. "'Tis his eyes."

"His eyes?" Meary blinked her own.

"Aye. If I talk to him, he'll look at me—hard. Like I've done something wicked and he knows it."

"Lord Colin does not think ye wicked," she assured him.

"Oh, 'tis not just me. He looks at everyone that way. Everyone except ye."

First Annie, now Brendan. Did they all conspire to keep her mind in constant turmoil by telling her these things? She did not wish to hear of Lord Colin's withered heart or piercing eyes. She wished to become less not more intrigued with the man. Rather than further distress Brendan and herself by pursuing the issue, Meary asked, "Would ye like me to do the asking for ye?"

"Would ye?"

"Aye. I'll ask him the very next time we meet," she promised. "But right now 'tis me who is needing a favor from ye." Taking Brendan by the hand, she held fast. The warm, familiar feel of his fingers wrapped around hers provided a steadying effect. "I'm weary of me own company. Can ye leave the horses long enough to accompany me on a stroll?"

"Aye. 'Tis me finest pleasure to do anything ye ask," Brendan responded with enthusiasm.

Meary smiled. "Ye should not flatter me so, I'll grow haughty."

"But 'tis true. Ye know how much I love ye."

"Aye, I do. No maiden could ask for a better friend."

After taking a moment to bid farewell to the horses,

127

Brendan gifted Meary with his full attention, and they stepped out into the sunlight.

"Which direction would ye like to be going?"

"Any will do."

As they walked, she and Brendan talked of horses and music, subjects of which Meary thoroughly approved. The weather was warm and fair, adding to her pleasure. Brendan provided detailed descriptions of the scenery and tenants' activities whenever a sound piqued Meary's interest. Neither made mention of their host.

By the time Brendan returned Meary to the door of the tower house, she was feeling more herself again.

Meary maintained her much improved mood until late that afternoon when her stomach began to gently rumble, warning her the supper hour was nearly upon them. Supper meant the return of Lord Colin, and she knew banishing the man from her mind when he sat at her elbow would prove a formidable task. She tried with scant success to believe tonight would be different and she would no longer be acutely aware of his every word, gesture, and breath. Failing in her first effort, she consoled herself with the knowledge that once she had endured the meal, she could sit down to her harp and gain blessed solace through her music.

"Good evening, Lady Meary, Mr. O'Hanlon, Brendan," Lord Colin greeted when he entered the great hall.

At the sound of his voice, every muscle tensed. Meary stridently scolded herself for reacting thusly as she politely returned his greeting. "Good evening, Lord Colin."

"Annie tells me supper is ready to be served. Shall we

be seated?"

A perfectly innocuous, innocent remark. Highly appropriate for the occasion. So why was her blood trying to rush through her veins like a river at flood? She would not allow it. She would maintain her composure. It mattered little to Meary that outwardly she presented a calm mien. She did not want to act a ninny inwardly, either.

Despite every effort to will upon herself the proper state of mind, no mantle of calm descended upon Meary. The unwelcome sensations plaguing her raged unabated. It was all she could do not to flinch when Lord Colin lay her hand on his arm and guided her to her place at the table. This small triumph over her person consoled her not at all, for as she touched him, she had the sudden and distinct impression Lord Colin was as aware as she of the emotions roiling in her breast. The suspicion heightened her color and her disgust with herself.

When they were all seated round the table, the servants came and went. As usual the meal was generous and every offering tasted delicious.

Lord Colin divided his conversation equally between Seumas and her—and now that he was becoming more fluent in Gaelic, he even was able to draw a few words out of Brendan.

Meary held up her end of the conversation admirably considering her agitation, but she was grateful whenever Seumas or Brendan relieved her of the onerous responsibility. She measured out the minutes left to weather until she could rise from the table and retreat to her harp.

The meal was coming to a close, when the conversation turned to horses. Despite her reluctance to voluntarily call Lord Colin's attention to herself, Meary felt obliged to seize the opportunity to fulfill her promise to Brendan.

"Ye have a mare in your stables by the name of Pansy that is in want of attention." She opened the subject with a direct statement.

"What is wrong with her?" Lord Colin inquired.

"She is melancholy."

"Melancholy?"

Meary heard the incredulity in his voice, but she valiantly pressed on. "Aye. But do not be alarmed. All she needs is a little riding, and she'll be in fine spirits again."

"I'll inform my grooms."

She drew a deep breath. " 'Tis a wise decision, but they already have enough tasks to fill their days. . . . Might I be offering a better solution?"

"You may."

"Ask Brendan to give her her exercise. He would not mind the imposition."

The awkwardness of her machinations to secure a horse for her friend delighted Lord Colin. He detested wily women. Struggling to keep his voice devoid of the amusement quivering in his chest, he asked, "Are you sure?"

"Quite sure."

A slow grin spread across Colin's face. It was the first time she had ever asked anything of him. He had begun to fear she never would. He had been waiting, less than patiently, for just such an opportunity.

The assertion was only partially true. For while it was true he had been biding his time waiting for Meary to gift him with a bargaining tool, it was also true he had willfully delayed a wholehearted effort to seduce her for a less pragmatic reason. The power she had over him made him uneasy. He had needed to prove to himself that he could resist her, that *he* was in control.

He had reined in his lust during their daily language lesson. He had stayed away from her during the better part of the day and tended his duties. He had constrained himself from crawling into her bed at night while she slept.

Lord Colin leaned back in his chair. He judged two weeks of restraint a more than sufficient test of his mettle. Especially when every day of that two weeks had felt like an eternity.

He was ready—confident in his own mastery of the situation—confident that his "innocent" fondling and gentlemanly manners had paved the path to his bed. Now, he must coax her to travel down the path he had laid.

A private outing would be his next move. He needed to lure her away from her friends and his staff to some secluded place where he could more boldly press his suit. He shifted his weight in response to the very physical reaction his prurient plotting evoked.

First he must get her to agree to come, Lord Colin reminded himself, and that was where her request would serve him well. He would trade his permission for her promise to accompany him. But he couldn't do it under the watchful eyes of the old man else he risked finding himself saddled with unwanted company. He would have to graciously give permission now and make the requirements of that permission known to her at some later more privy moment.

His gaze circled round the table. They were all waiting expectantly for his reply.

Turning to Brendan, he asked in halting Gaelic, "Would you do me the service of taking my mare Pansy out for a ride tomorrow?"

"Aye," Brendan responded exuberantly.

"Good. I'll inform the head groom to let you take her out whenever you have the inclination and time."

Though he knew he had botched several words in the course of the conversation, it was evident he had performed well enough to be understood. The warm smile gracing Meary's face was exactly the reward Lord Colin had been hoping his generosity would elicit. His eyes darkened. He would have to think of more favors he could do for her to secure a firm position in her good graces.

Reverting back to his native tongue, he addressed Meary, "Would you like the use of a mount as well? I would be happy to put a groom and any horse you choose at your disposal."

The tone of his voice was too genial. Meary's hand tightened around the stem of her goblet. For Brendan's sake she was glad Lord Colin was in a generous and friendly mood tonight, but for her own sake she preferred, now that she had fulfilled her promise, he revert to a less pleasing mood. Carrying the wine to her lips, Meary took a fortifying sip before politely replying. "Thank ye. I'll remember that should I ever have the urge to go riding."

"Mr. O'Hanlon, my stable is at your disposal also."

"I don't ride," Seumas curtly informed him.

"Why is that?"

"Irishmen aren't allowed to own good horses, or have ye so soon forgotten how ye English have robbed us of our rightful property with yer laws?"

132

"How could I forget with you here to constantly remind me?" Lord Colin maintained his cheerful mien and civil tone, having long grown accustomed to the old man's goading. Still, he did not like to be falsely convicted. "Despite what you would like to think, I am not personally responsible for the enactment of the Penury laws. In truth, I do not approve of them."

"Why?" Seumas demanded.

"They breed resentment."

"What do ye care of Irish sentiment?"

"My tenants are Irish. A man works harder when he is content. Resentment interferes with my ability to turn a profit."

"I can be thinking of a hundred more noble reasons for a man to oppose the Penury laws, but I doubt I'd be believing ye if any one of them had sprung from your lips. Ye may be greedy but at times I think ye may be an honest man, as well."

"I am."

Seumas impaled him with his gaze. "It may keep ye out of hell, but 'tis not enough to make me fond of ye."

"I'm desolate."

Seumas grunted in response.

Colin noted with satisfaction how his politeness provoked the older man. Never had he met a fellow so intent on wholeheartedly hating him, and whenever he could deprive him of his ambition by exhibiting the tiniest of virtues, he did so. Poor O'Hanlon was a prisoner of his own sterling sense of fair-mindedness. For no matter how much he might wish to judge his host a complete wretch, when the evidence said otherwise, he could not. Colin admired the man's principles and sympathized with his dilemma but not so much he was

133

above using them to his own purpose.

He wondered what Meary thought of his view of the Penury laws. He hoped she did not judge him as harshly as her mentor. He wanted her to hold him in better favor, to at least like him enough that she . . .

"I expect ye'll be wanting us to be playing for ye again this evening," Seumas broke into his thoughts.

"Yes. But tonight I have invited the servants to the hall, so you will have an audience of more than one." An inspired thought popped into his head, causing Colin to add, "Some of them may want to dance. I would be grateful if you would take their desires into consideration when selecting the tunes you play."

"That we will."

Colin was pleased to see his invitation to his servants had won him another penny of O'Hanlon's grudging approval. The idea to invite the servants to the hall had really been Annie's—she had informed him they were deserving of a reward—but he saw no profit in apprising O'Hanlon of the fact.

As his guests moved from the table to their instruments, the servants began filing into the hall. Colin smiled. While Annie may have originated the notion of inviting the servants into the hall for a concert, the idea of turning the concert into a dance had been all his. Had Meary not said she was a passable dancer? What better way to begin zealously pressing his suit than to ask her to dance? It would give him a legitimate excuse to hold her as he had been longing to do these many days. It was not all he longed to do with her this night, but it would have to suffice.

As Colin directed two brawny farmers to move the table and benches against a wall and announced the night would be filled with dancing, he crystallized his plans. A little dancing, a little conversation, a little wine—mayhap more than a little wine; then, he would ask her to join him for a midday repast on the heath. If she balked, he would remind her of his generosity to Brendan and gently yet firmly insist she return favor for favor.

When all was to his liking, Colin settled himself in his favorite chair and signaled for the entertainment to begin.

The music as always was excellent. Biding his time, he watched with interest as footmen approached housemaids and grooms bowed before scullery maids and the girls who worked his dairy, making mental note to ask Annie which of those couples she thought most likely to approach him for permission to wed.

His servants proved to be enthusiastic dancers. The sound of tapping feet and laughter filled the great hall.

Lord Colin let a jig and three reels pass before he rose to his feet and slowly approached his quarry.

"Lady Meary, may I beg the pleasure of the next dance?"

Startled, Meary dropped her hands to her lap and crimped the fabric of her skirt. Though she succeeded in producing a watery smile, her brows inched together, further betraying her distress. It was rude to refuse, folly to accept. Her smile slowly sagged as she chewed the back of her lips in indecision.

She adored dancing, but she could not ignore the warning bells pealing in her head. They rang loud and clear. They told her to cling to her harp, to retreat into the celestial world of her music where she did not have to face the untenable messy human emotions of the temporal world.

Meary opened her mouth to refuse the invitation, but before the first syllable escaped her lips, a surge of desire cannily disguised as pride stopped her from choosing the guarded course.

She would not let herself be cowed by this Englishman! If he were any other man she would accept his invitation to dance without hesitation. If his touch evoked an accelerated heartbeat and a warming of her blood, so be it. She was stronger than a lot of silly sensations. Plague take her cowardice! They were in a room full of people. Nothing untoward could happen even if she had wanted it to. She was tired of being overvigilant where Lord Colin was concerned. She wanted to dance and dance she would!

Thus shored by her mental diatribe, Meary rose to her feet, her head held high. "I would love to be sharing a dance with ye, Lord Colin."

"Thank you," Lord Colin stated with heartfelt sincerity, though his words were meant for the powers that be as much as they were for Meary. Whatever battle had been raging behind her comely face, and it was lamentably apparent she had not come to her decision to accept his invitation easily, he had emerged the victor—at least for the moment. He placed her hand on his arm and covered it with his own. What victories the future would hold were now in his hands.

A confident, lecherous grin spread across Lord Colin's face as he led his pretty partner out onto the dance floor.

Chapter 9

Colin and Meary took up their place among the other dancers and waited for the music to begin. When it did not, Colin glanced in the direction of Seumas and Brendan. They were both staring at him. Brendan wore a worried expression. Seumas looked flush-faced and ready to do battle.

"A reel if you please," Lord Colin commanded. At his word the dancers formed two concentric circles, the men on the inside their ladies on the outside.

O'Hanlon muttered something under his breath—most likely he is calling a curse upon my head, Colin guessed—but the old gentleman did not lunge for his throat. Instead O'Hanlon's gaze shifted to Meary. His lips quivered into an anguished smile, and his shoulders sagged.

Colin turned away. He did not seek to give the man pain, just pursue his own desires, and he refused to be made to feel guilty for doing so. He wanted Meary and he would have her.

After a protracted pause, O'Hanlon put his fiddle to his

chin and laid his bow to the strings. Colin took Meary by the hand and led her three steps to the right; then, they reversed direction and stepped a like distance to the left.

As he continued to lead Meary through the steps of the reel, Colin was less amazed than admiring at how smoothly she performed the intricacies of the dance. Only when he led her through a series of rapid turns did she appear the least bit disoriented, and many of the sighted ladies in the hall emerged from the twirls equally bewildered. A guiding hand on the small of her back or a gentle tug on her hand quickly set her back in the right direction.

It was a perpetual wonder to him how she got on in the world so well. The woman was as graceful as a doe and as independent as a hawk. Her musical skills were nonpareil. She was capable of conversing intelligently on a wide variety of topics. She was an splendid teacher. As far as he could discern, she excelled at everything she did—with the notable exception of hiding her feelings. He was glad she was an abysmal failure at that. He doubted he would be quite so eager to have her if he was uncertain of her desire for him.

Now there was a blatant lie if ever he had heard one, he rejected his own statement. If Meary O'Byrne was as cold as a stone toward him, he would still want her. She was too intriguing to resist. Lord Colin pulled her a little closer than was conventional and immediately felt her stiffen. Relaxing his hold, he allowed for a more proper distance between them.

Damn. He would have to watch himself. She was still too much on her guard whenever he was near. Such conditions were not conducive to seduction. Kissing her on the cliffs had already cost him too much time. He could not afford to act brashly again. If he persisted in doing so, she would persist in being too wary of him, and he would be forced to abandon the game or find reason to detain her at his estate for a score of weeks or more. To his surprise, Lord Colin did not find the notion of sharing his home with Meary for an indefinite period of time as repugnant as he should have.

He shook his head to clear it and sternly reminded himself he was not looking for anything more than a fleeting liaison. He lived alone by choice. He liked his life just as it was. He was not about to throw away all he had gained for Meary O'Byrne or any woman.

The reel ended and Meary was pleased she had managed to execute it without indulging in any major faux pas.

The possibility of stepping on her partner's feet had not been among her worries. She had been afraid she would do or say something that would reveal to him how profoundly his touch affected her. That was an embarrassment she did not think she could abide.

He had not said a word throughout the dance, and for that she was grateful. If she was not required to carry on a conversation, the likelihood of verbal blunder was greatly diminished.

Only when he had pulled her against him had she been undone by her emotions. She should not have become so tense over an innocent misstep in the dance. Fortunately the moment had been fleeting, saving her from unbearable disgrace. There was even a possibility he had not noticed. Nevertheless, she would be glad to return to her harp.

Meary allowed Lord Colin to lead her by the hand across the room without protest.

"You look a little flushed. A glass of wine should help ease your thirst," he declared as he pressed a goblet into her hands.

Meary retreated behind the rim of the goblet and earnestly sipped at the wine, not to slack her thirst but to provide herself with an excuse not to respond. She had thought he was leading her back to her stool by her harp. If she had known otherwise, she would not have come so willingly.

"You dance quite well," he complimented.

She nodded.

"One would think such finesse impossible for one consigned to a dark world, but once again you have proven my assumptions false. I cannot fathom how you do it, but I salute your grace and ingenuity."

Deeming she should say something, Meary lowered the goblet to the table and said, "Thank ye."

Full hands were less likely than empty ones to fidget. She retrieved the goblet and found it had been refilled. Rather than feel annoyed, Meary felt grateful to whoever the considerate servant was who had provided her with more of the bracing liquid.

"Will you tell me how you do it?"

Bringing the wine to her lips, she took another sip, welcoming the slightly acid taste on her tongue and the soothing warmth as it travelled down her throat. "How I do what?"

"Manage to keep your feet going in the right direction when you cannot see what the other dancers are doing."

"I listen to the music and follow me partner's lead," she explained.

"But don't you get confused?"

"Not if me partner is a good dancer."

"I shall take that as a compliment."

She had certainly not meant to compliment him, but Meary had no way of calling her words back. In truth, he was a fine dancer and to tell him otherwise was to be a liar. She was already guilty of the sin of lust—though she hoped she was being given some credit for resisting a surrender to temptation. She was not going to add the sin of dishonesty to her burden of guilt. "Ye may consider it so," she said.

"The music is starting again. Since you have ruled me worthy, may I be so bold as to beg the favor of another dance?" He reached for Meary's goblet, but she held fast. "Please?"

Sighing in resignation, Meary nodded her consent. She judged it hideously unfair of him to sound so sincere. He made it impossible to refuse him without sounding petulant; unless, of course, she was willing to tell him the true reason behind her reluctance to dance with him again, and she was not. Before allowing him to lead her back to the other dancers, Meary drained her goblet.

Seumas and Brendan were playing another reel. Lord Colin deftly slipped them into the circle of dancing servants and picked up the steps of the dance.

Meary tried to concentrate on the music rather than her partner. If playing music brought her serenity, she reasoned listening intently to someone else play should evoke at least a modicum of peace. Lord Colin's gentle, guiding hands were too agreeable to her senses, a condition highly disagreeable to her mind. She was not very successful in achieving her aim, but by the end of the dance, the wine was starting to relax her enough she was not feeling quite so harassed.

Without asking her permission, Lord Colin led Meary

into a third reel. All around her she heard the stamping of feet, the rustle of fabric, breathless laughter. There was the occasional grunt or squeal followed by more laughter or an amicable scolding admonishing the offender to kindly keep off the abused one's feet. Whispered flirtations mingled with whoops of glee. Milk maids giggled and old men guffawed. Joyous sounds. Sounds to lighten the heart.

When the dance ended, Lord Colin led Meary back to the table from whence liquid refreshment flowed freely.

"A glass of wine for the lady," he commanded. Almost before he finished issuing the command, Meary found a goblet of wine being pressed into her hand.

She thought to refuse it, then thought again. A little more wine wouldn't hurt. She was still feeling far too tense than was natural and the wine's warm, calming effect would do her good. She would be careful not to overindulge, but one more restorative glass was well within the bounds.

"Drink up," Lord Colin urged. "The next dance will be starting soon, and I don't want us to enter the circle late."

Meary was both flattered by his attention and put off by his blithe assumption they would be sharing yet another dance. "I don't believe 'tis seemly for us to be sharing so many dances in a row," she stated.

"But who else shall I dance with? I cannot ask one of my serving maids to dance. They all seem rather intimidated by me. It would be impolite to put them in an awkward position."

"Ask Annie to dance."

"Annie?"

"Aye. Ye need not worry she will be feeling fearful of

ye, and I'm sure she would be pleased." Meary smiled, delighted with herself for coming up with such an admirable solution to his problem . . . and hers.

Lord Colin chuckled and graciously acquiesced. "I will do as you ask. May I leave you here, or would you like me to lead you back to your stool?"

"I'm just fine here. Ye run along before ye miss the beginning of the next dance."

When she had rid herself of her dance partner, Meary let out a long sigh of relief. The music began and she made her way to the nearest wall, leaning against it as she sipped her wine. The stones were hard and cold against her back, but she welcomed the solid feel of it.

Lord Colin seemed excessively devoted to her company tonight. She had thought to share one dance with him and be done with it. When she had agreed to his invitation, it had not occurred to her she was the only woman present who came close to qualifying as a peer. She was not so foolish as to assign false meaning to his devotion, but she found it as enchanting as it was troublesome. It was further proof of her weakness, but no new harm had been done.

She was safe. She had successfully delivered him into Annie's capable hands. She would finish her wine, then return to her harp. Tonight would be another evening survived while she played a discomfiting waiting game with the voices in her head.

Meary finished her wine just as Brendan clapped the final beat of the song on his *bodhrán*. She had lingered longer than she intended, but she was feeling cozy and was not particularly concerned.

Setting the empty goblet on the table, she started towards her harp. She had not gone three steps when she found her path blocked. Reaching out, she lay her hand on a lawn shirt. It was warm and slightly damp from the exertion of its wearer.

"Lord Colin." She frowned, quickly withdrawing her hand.

"Lady Meary. I have been returned to your side. Annie bids me dance with someone more my own age."

"I thought to play me harp."

"And leave me standing idle?"

"Surely there is one maid among your servants who is brave enough to dance with ye."

"Direct me to this lady and I will leave you in peace; otherwise, I fear I must impose upon your good nature and earnestly beg you to partner me."

A pretty speech but Meary was unwilling to surrender to his blandishments. "I do not know your serving maids well enough to say which one ye should be asking to dance. Since Annie made the suggestion, mayhap she will direct ye."

"I have already discussed the matter with Annie. She agrees with me. A good master must take the tender sensibilities of his staff into account in his dealings with them. There is no one else I can ask but you."

Meary was not at all pleased with Annie. What about *her* sensibilities? Should they not be taken into account also? Reminding herself she had been going to great lengths to hide her feelings concerning her host, giving Annie no cause to know them, Meary abandoned her private parley and changed tactics.

"Your fondness for dancing is unexpected."

"Why is that?"

"I just would not have judged ye to be the kind of man who would be enamoured of such sociable sport."

144

"Mayhap you have misjudged me."

The hairs on the back of Meary's neck rose to attention, and she had an elusive impression his words were referring to something other than dancing, but her mind was feeling pleasantly fuzzy and to pursue the thought seemed too much effort.

"A jig is starting," he stated, his voice imbued with the pleading tone of a child standing before a freshly baked plate of honey cakes.

"I suppose since ye are me host, I cannot deny ye," Meary said, sounding far less reluctant than she meant to sound.

"To deny me would be rude," he agreed.

Again Meary's hairs prickled to attention. This time she brought her hand to the back on her neck and firmly rubbed them back in place.

"Shall we?" Without waiting for an answer, Lord Colin led her back to the dance floor.

A jig required far less physical contact than the reels, and for that Meary was grateful. It made the chore of keeping her lust subjugated ever so much easier. She stood, arms akimbo, swinging her knees to set her skirt swishing in time with the lively music, as she followed the rap of Lord Colin's feet as he danced the cross-step around her.

The next dance was a hornpipe and the following another reel.

Throughout them all Lord Colin entertained her with snippets of conversation, describing this couple or that and interjecting a goodly number of gallant compliments to her dancing skills and her beauty into his discourse. Meary laughed at his descriptions and blushed at his compliments, making her own amiable contributions to

145

the conversation. Apparently, he was having as agreeable a time as she, as on several occasions she was certain she detected a chuckle rumbling up from his throat.

At the end of the reel, Meary was startled to find Brendan at her elbow. Grabbing her hand, he informed her that Seumas had ordered him to dance with her before her head was robbed of sense by feckless notions. Meary cringed, for though he perforce spoke to her in Gaelic, she feared Lord Colin might now be knowledge-able enough to understand all he said. Besides, Brendan did not dance. Even if Lord Colin did not perceive the meaning of his words, she feared Brendan's purpose would be all too readily understood.

Meary had no time to offer Lord Colin a credible pretext, even if she had been able to think of one, because Brendan was already dragging her across the room.

Sharing the dance, another reel, was a painful experience for both her and Brendan. Brendan did his best, but he had no notion how to lead, and they were forever bumping into each other and the other dancers. Her personal awkwardness was an embarrassment to Meary, but she knew Brendan was suffering far more than she. He was sweating profusely. His palms were hot and clammy. His voice became more and more tremulous with each abjectly muttered apology.

Brendan resolutely remained by her side through a second and then a third dance. As he stumbled and apologized his way through the tangle of steps, Meary felt herself becoming more and more angry with Seumas. She knew he had little faith in her ability to handle herself with Lord Colin. These past weeks a thousand times he had told her so, sometimes bluntly with words but more often through subtle inflections in his voice and his uncharacteristic bad manners. She could accept his lack of faith. Her own faith in her wits was precarious at best. But to put poor Brendan through this agony, no matter how honorable Seumas's motives, was cruel.

Her behavior and the results thereof, were her responsibility and no one else's. Brendan should not be asked to pay the price for her shortcomings. Besides, she did not judge herself guilty of any grave trespass. It might not be strictly orthodox to dance so many dances with one man, but in present-day Ireland strict social conventions were routinely ignored when they interfered with practicality. She *was* the only willing woman available for his lordship to dance with. He was behaving as a gentleman, and she was behaving as a lady. She might hold unladylike secrets in her heart, but that was exactly were they were going to stay, and they were nobody's business but her own.

By the time Seumas played the last note of the set on his fiddle, Meary had worked herself up into a fury of righteous determination. She folded Brendan's sweaty palm between her hands and gently tugged to pull his ear near her lips.

"Brendan, would ye like to be sharing another dance with me?"

"Nay," he responded, suffusing the word with a full measure of the agony his ineptitude for dancing and his deep-rooted aversion to social intercourse was causing him.

"I thought not. Get yourself a tankard of ale. When ye are finished drinking it, ye can go back to your instruments," she instructed.

"But Seumas . . ."

"I'll be taking care of Seumas. Ye just do as I ask."

147

When she was sure Brendan was headed in the opposite direction, Meary carefully wove her way through the crowd to Seumas's side. "I'll be having a word with ye, Seumas O'Hanlon," she announced in a low but dogged voice.

"What about?" He feigned ignorance.

"Don't be playing games with me. Ye know very well what this 'tis about," Meary rebuked. "I'll not allow ye to torment Brendan for me sake or anyone else's. I know ye do not like Lord Colin. That is your right. I happen to find the man a fine dance partner. I am having a little fun. No harm is being done."

"It looks to me as though ye be having more than a little fun with the man."

"Then your eyes deceive ye. He is our host. We owe him a little regard. 'Tis the only reason I dance with him."

"I do not believe ye, Meary."

"Then don't. But when Brendan comes back to your side, ye welcome him and do not be sending him out on the dance floor again. Even if ye think ye see me jumping into hell with both feet, I want ye to put Brendan's comfort above me own." On that comment, Meary quit his side.

Never in her life had she spoken so harshly to Seumas, and as she made her way back across the room, a knot began to form in Meary's stomach. She hadn't been completely honest with him about her feelings for Lord Colin. But how could she be? And she didn't intend to do anything about those feelings. She was fighting them with every ounce of her strength. Besides, *she* was not the issue here. It was Brendan. Sometimes, did not noble ends justify less than noble means?

It was not as if she and Seumas never argued. Arguing was a game with them, she consoled herself. But she knew their disagreement over Lord Colin was no game.

Meary was feeling so unsettled she decided to risk one more goblet of wine. She promised herself it would be her last. She was already feeling a tiny bit light-headed and did not want to compound her problems, but her thirst for some kind of buttress to help her get through the rest of the evening was too strong to ignore.

"Is there anything I can do?" As he leaned close and spoke directly in her ear, Meary was startled by the sound of Lord Colin's voice.

"Nay. Nothing. Why do ye ask such a question?" she replied.

"You look dismayed."

"I'm sorry. I did not mean to be looking sour-faced." Meary took a sip of wine and wrested her scowl into a smile.

"You need not feel you must hide your feelings from me. It does a gentleman's heart good to relieve a lady's distress," he drawled.

"Me vexation has naught to do with ye." Shifting her weight from one foot to the other, she retreated behind the rim of the goblet while she contemplated how much she should say. "Seumas and I are suffering from a difference of opinion concerning Brendan. I'm afraid I lost me temper and am now suffering pangs of remorse." It was a varnished truth, but all Meary was willing to reveal.

"You could apologize," Lord Colin amicably suggested.

"Aye. But then he would think me wavering in me resolve."

"Mayhap I could intervene on your behalf."

"Nay!"

"You fear I would make a clumsy diplomat?" he asked, mindfully maintaining his soothing tone.

"Nay." This time she was careful to speak the word more calmly. "'Tis just the problem lies between Seumas and me. 'Tis us who has to be solving it."

"If you will not let me help you directly, mayhap I can do so indirectly." Catching hold of her hand, Lord Colin lay it on his arm and stroked her skin from wrist to fingertips. "I am told dancing helps takes a body's mind off their troubles. Shall we test the truth of the matter?"

Eager to put an end to the conversation, Meary enthusiastically responded, "Aye."

As Lord Colin led Meary back onto the dance floor, he was careful to keep his triumph well-disguised. Old Seumas was giving him the evil eye, and he feared if he appeared too pleased with himself, his winsome dance partner would once again be snatched from his grasp.

Meary was free to believe she had deluded him with her measured truths, but he was not a simpleton. His eyes told him a different story. He'd wager the profits from this season's corn crop, her disagreement with O'Hanlon had far more to do with him than she was willing to admit.

The music began again, and he deftly led Meary through the first steps. Dancing with her was a divine sort of torture. It allowed him to touch her, but the touches were too unenduring to give real satisfaction. Still, he was more than satisfied with the progression of the evening.

She had yet to say so, but she was enjoying his attentions. He could see it in the fleeting half-smiles that graced her lips, the blush upon her cheeks, the sway of her hips. A few more dances, mayhap another goblet of wine, and he would propose tomorrow's outing.

They danced three more dances—two hornpipes and a jig. Plainly, Meary was taking his advice and throwing herself full tilt into dancing away her troubles. He could feel her muscles becoming more and more relaxed with each successive dance. She was more animated. She conversed more. She laughed more.

Unfortunately, he was not the only one to notice Meary's improved mood. Seumas had abandon his fiddle, leaving Brendan to play a set of hornpipes, while he made the rounds of the male servants. His mission soon became apparent. After finishing their conversation with Seumas, several of the men started to approach Meary.

Their intention to relieve him of his dance partner was clear. Lord Colin held them off with an icy stare guaranteed to turn the stoutest man's heart winter cold. None was brave enough to venture more than few steps in her direction.

Inevitably, O'Hanlon was forced to admit defeat. He returned to his fiddle and the dancing went on.

Whether her senses were intoxicated by an excess of wine, merrymaking, Lord Colin's pleasurable proximity, or a combination of all three, Meary not only could not say but did not care.

She was having a lovely time. That was all that mattered. If there was sin in that, then tonight she would be a willing sinner. For the first time in what seemed an aeon she felt comfortable in her own skin.

She credited Lord Colin for making the evening so cheery. He was treating her well. Not like a blind woman; not like a guest or a teacher; but as a friend. He was ordinarily so pensive and formal. She liked this affable side of him.

151

One dance ended and another began. Meary threw back her head and giggled with glee as Lord Colin guided her through a series of dizzying spins.

"I am glad you are having a good time," he commented.

"I'm having a *wonderful* time."

"Then I am doubly glad. I too am enjoying myself."

Meary smiled broadly.

"Since we seem to get along so well, I hope you will agree to share a midday meal with me on the heath tomorrow. The sun set red this eventide, so it promises to be a fair day."

"It sounds like a charming idea."

"Then you will come?"

"Aye. 'Twill be a pleasure."

That's what I'm hoping, Lord Colin said to himself as he mentally licked his lips in anticipation. Getting Meary to agree to his plans had been shamefully easy. He hadn't even needed to mention Brendan and the mare. He was glad he hadn't had to stoop to such underhanded methods, but still he felt a bit squeamish about his ambition to lead such a tender woman astray. His compunction perturbed him, and he ruthlessly spurned it.

Having accomplished what he set out to do, Lord Colin was free to give himself up to the delights of the dance, and he could not recall a dance ever being so agreeable. In fact, now that he thought about it, before this night he had always danced out of social necessity rather than for pleasure.

His servants seemed to be enjoying themselves as much as he, and he was glad for it. It had taken little effort or expense to provide this evening for them. In the

152

future, he would have to give more mind to providing his people with regular opportunities for revelry.

The music and dancing continued until every candle wick, despite judicious trimming, had sputter out in a pool of tallow. As the weary dancers made their way to bed—some to their own beds but more than few to shared mattresses—Lord Colin's face was not the only one to bear a satisfied grin.

"The master says ye are to be joining him for an outing this noontide," Doreen announced as she bustled into Meary's room. "I suspect ye'll be wanting to wear something extra pretty."

"An outing with his lordship?" Meary moaned as she pushed back her blankets and clambered to a sitting position. She already had been awake when Doreen had enter, had been awake for quite some time. Disconcerting memories had been flitting in and out of her head. . . . Lord Colin's strong arms encircling her waist as he twirled her around the great hall; whispered compliments followed by hot blushes; the warmth and pleasure of his hands enfolding hers; her lips offering up flirtatious comments; the bold sway of her skirts; leaning provocatively against the long, lean frame of her dance partner . . . Having been lying here reliving the events of last night in her head and trying to sort out her feelings concerning them, the reminder she was now to be required to spend time away from the house alone with Lord Colin was as unwelcome as a bucket of icy water poured on her head.

"Aye," Doreen confirmed. "He says to tell ye not to be worrying about his lessons this morning. He had other duties to be tending, and after last night's late hours, he doesn't begrudge ye staying abed."

"What time is it?"

"Well nigh half past eleven."

"It can't be," Meary protested as she scrambled out of bed.

"Aye, it can. But I already told ye ye're not to fret. The master be in a fine mood this morning. The finest I've ever seen him. I don't think a body could cross him even if she was of a mind to. Now, which will it be? The yellow paduasoy gown to show off yer figure or the blue damask to be bringing out the color of yer eyes?"

"I'm not sure I want to be going on this outing," Meary murmured.

"Why not?"

"I . . . ah . . . I . . ." Meary's lips went slack. She had no notion how to put her feelings into words. The idea of sharing a private meal with Lord Colin simultaneously filled her with delight and dread, overlaid with a delicious sense of anticipation. They made no sense these feelings that heaved within her. Then, nothing about herself made sense as it used to. It was as if her mind was trapped in some queer dream. The only verity she was sure of was that she felt as tremulous as an aspen. But she was not about to admit her trepidation to Doreen or anyone else. Her pride was the only familiar attribute left from her former self, and she embraced it like a lost child.

"Well?" Doreen prodded.

"I'll wear the blue gown," Meary abruptly stated. "And dress me hair with ribands, if ye please. If I'm to be going on an outing, I ought to be looking festive."

"Aye, indeed, miss."

Having once decided to face her host, Meary was

154

stubbornly determined to do so with dignity and grace. Lord Colin would see she was up to this outing. He would see she had fully recovered from the dance and would not be besotted by his warm touch and his velvety voice again.

Not that she was sure he knew how affected she was by his person. He might have attributed her friendly manner to an excess of wine. But just in case he *had* noticed, she would show him another, more resolute side of herself today.

By the time Doreen had readied Meary to present herself downstairs, Meary had managed not only to cozen herself into believing she was up to handling being alone with Lord Colin, but that the planned venture would be an enjoyable excursion. Instead of being put off by his attentions, she should be flattered, she told herself. He was an intelligent, handsome, powerful, and wealthy man. How many other chances would she get to keep company with such as he? Had he not proved himself a gentleman these past two weeks? And she was no giddy girl. She was in no danger of losing her heart or her head. She was Meary O'Byrne, daughter of the noble Conall and Mairead O'Byrne, protégé of the great Seumas O'Hanlon.

If Meary had been thinking clearly, she would have remembered she had had a similar conversation with herself the evening before and circumstances had not proceeded at all as she had planned. But Meary was not thinking at all clearly. Consciously, she did not recognize the trick she played on herself by desperately denying the reality of her situation in the vain hope by doing so she would alter it. She was only cognizant that she felt better. Picking up her walking cane, she stiffened her spine and stepped out of her room.

"Lord Colin, I understand we are to be sharing a meal upon the heath," Meary greeted as she descended the last step of the staircase and sensed his lordship's presence standing a few feet to the right of the base. She forced a friendly smile upon her lips.

"I was not sure you would come," he said, stepping forward. "I am glad you have."

"Why would I not?" Meary demanded.

So, she was playing the stoic maid again, Lord Colin noted with approval. It boded well for his plans for the day. She was always the most vulnerable to his stratagems when she behaved as though she cared the least. "No reason in the world," he assured her. "No reason at all. Shall we be off?"

Laying Meary's hand on his forearm, he led her through the door to the kitchen where they paused to pick up the basket he had ordered prepared; then, he led her out the side door.

As they walked away from the house, Meary pretended not to perceive the warm energy seeping up her fingertips, through her arm and into her breast.

"It feels like a fine day," she said.

"Not a cloud in the sky," Lord Colin confirmed.

"Whatever 'tis in the basket, it smells delicious."

"Yes, it does."

"Have ye seen Seumas and Brendan this morning?"

"The last I saw Seumas, he was with Annie. Brendan I haven't seen since we met early this morning in the stables, but I'd wager a bet wherever Pansy is is where we shall find him."

" 'Tis kind of ye to give him free rein with the mare."

156

"It suits my purpose," Lord Colin responded nonchalantly.

The hairs on Meary's neck and forearms prickled, but she refused to be abashed. Lord Colin had proven himself a gentleman; he was speaking of providing needed exercise for his mare; suspecting him of base intentions just because her imagination was wont to wander down prurient paths was unfair. Had not Annie told her he was enamored of some other woman? If she truly believed him guilty of nefarious motives, she should not have agreed to come.

Falling silent, Meary forced herself to allow Lord Colin to lead her where he willed.

Though Meary was successful in convincing herself Lord Colin's thoughts were pure, she could not say the same for herself. It was disheartening to discover that despite her grim determination to honor her ancestors' name, despite Lord Colin's clear lack of interest in her as a woman, despite every logical argument and noble intention, the lustful urges she sought to banish persisted in mocking her with their intensity.

Lord Colin's scent—a delicious mingling of man, soap, and leather—surfeited her senses. The feel of his muscles through the fabric of his coat sleeve made her ache to knead them. The tread of his forceful, masculine stride conjured primitive thoughts. And his voice—deep, vibrant, and caressing—all by itself was enough to annul her vow of prudence.

What on earth had possessed her to believe she could blithely walk along with Lord Colin let alone calmly share a private meal with him? Aye, she could staidly engage in cordial conversation and pretend dispassion, but she could not make herself feel it. Not in her breast. Not in her loins. They had already gone too far from the house. She was feeling too frantic. She couldn't trust herself to maintain her dignity.

And how would Lord Colin react if, after vowing she was uninterested in a carnal liaison, she threw herself into his arms like a vixen in heat? Would he be amused, repulsed, bored? She didn't know him well enough to make a rational judgment, even if she still possessed the ability to make rational judgments, which recent evidence proved beyond all doubt she did not. In any case, none of the cataloged responses was pleasant to contemplate.

Finding the lack of conversation was allowing her mind to travel paths she was determined it not take, silence became even more intimidating than the effort it took to maintain a calm facade while conversing. Meary sucked in a deep breath, screwed up her courage, and asked, "Where is it we are going?"

"There is a small stand of hawthorn not too much further."

"We call them fairy thorn, ye know." She seized the opportunity to steer the conversation in an innocuous direction.

"Why is that?"

"When the wind blows, the petals of the flowers seem as a thousand fairy wings fluttering on the breeze."

"You Irish are a whimsical people."

"'Tis one of our finest virtues," Meary proclaimed.

"Do not take it amiss that I ask, but to your way of thinking do the Irish have any faults?"

Her expression became thoughtful. "Mayhap one or

two, but at the moment I cannot recall what they might be."

Lord Colin chuckled. "Has not anyone ever read to you the scripture: *pride goeth before destruction?*"

"Aye, but I have always been believing that the Lord was referring to false pride and not the valid assessment of one's own worth."

"An interesting interpretation."

"I take it ye don't agree."

"I did not say that. I will have to give the matter further contemplation before I decide one way or the other. Are your feet sore?" He suddenly changed the subject.

"What?"

"I asked if your feet are sore from all the dancing we did last night. If they are, I would be happy to carry you the rest of the way. I doubt you weigh much more than one of your Irish fairies."

"Ye will not be carrying me anywhere!" Meary decreed, a bit more stridently than she intended.

"There is no need to get peevish," Lord Colin comforted in honeyed tones. "I merely asked because it just came to my mind your question about the distance left to travel might have been prompted by tender feet, and you were merely too polite to complain."

He sounded as innocent as a lamb, and it distressed Meary, she again was guilty of letting her own hunger for *his* touch color her judgment of his motives. His chivalrous offer did not warrant condemnation. She was the one who could not be trusted.

Though she was determined to be charitable, she felt compelled to make her position firmly understood. "I

159

have walked the length and breadth of Ireland. I don't think one night of dancing 'tis going to make me lame."

"You promise you will tell me if you find you are wrong?"

"Aye," Meary promised, praying he would abandon the topic.

The faint scent of hawthorn blossoms wafted into Meary's nostrils, and the muscles of her face tightened her lips into a thin line. "We are almost there." She snatched her hand from his arm. "Was your concern for the comfort of me feet naught but a ruse to get your hands upon me person?"

"I believe it was," Lord Colin stated without remorse.

Chapter 10

Meary felt the blood drain from her face then rise again as a hot blush. It was one thing to put herself in harm's way when she thought she had only her own desires to contend with, quite another if she must fight off Lord Colin's advances as well. Her mind reeled in protest. It made no sense. Had he not behaved as a perfect gentleman these many days? He spent more time away from her than in her company. He had not exhibited the slightest appetite for anything more than platonic friendship between them. Was that not proof enough he had accepted her dictate she would not be seduced? Proof enough he had lost what little interest he had in debauching her? Mayhap she had not heard him accurately.

"I beg pardon, I fear I did not hear ye correctly," she whimpered.

"Mayhap not. Will you help me spread the blanket?" Lord Colin dismissed the matter.

Meary stopped. She had been traveling at a brisk pace in an effort to escape the hand he had placed on the small of her back when she had yanked her hand from his arm. Too late she realized, in her agitation, she had continued in the direction he desired. The sweet scent of hawthorn blossoms now saturated the air.

"I'm not sure I should," she replied warily.

"Not to worry. I can do it by myself if you would rather."

A puff of air rustled Meary's skirt as he shook out the blanket and spread it on the heath. She stood, soldier straight, listening to him lay out the contents of the basket.

"There. All is ready. You may have a seat now."

His tone was conversationl and unthreatening. Meary contemplated demanding he explain his earlier statement or take her back to the tower, but in the end the fear her own sins were causing her to be irrationally chary kept her mute.

She settled herself on the far corner of the blanket, taking care to lay her walking stick within easy reach— just in case she found herself in need of a good, stout club.

"It looks like Annie packed us quite a feast. We have ham, smoked herring, pickles, biscuits, roasted walnuts, and fried cakes," Lord Colin listed the food spread before him as he removed his coat and sword belt and lay them at the edge of the blanket. He had purposefully chosen every item himself, selecting a dry and salty diet to insure Meary would acquire a healthy thirst. Last night the wine had had an agreeable result. He hoped to enlist its salubrious effects again today. He did not wish Meary drunk, but he did wish her to be sufficiently languorous she would be robbed of the will to resist him.

With that goal in mind, he filled her goblet with wine,

stretching across the blanket to deliver it into her hands. "Do you think you might sit a bit closer?" he cordially queried. "It is inconvenient for us to sit so far apart."

"I am quite happy just where I am, thank ye."

"Then I will move," he announced without umbrage.

Meary tensed as she listened to him shifting his position. She relaxed a little when he planted himself a completely respectable distance away.

"There. This is much better," he said. A minute later he handed her a plate piled high with food.

"Thank ye."

"You are very welcome."

Meary nibbled at a biscuit as she tried to think of a suitable topic for the making of polite conversation. She was becoming more and more convinced her imagination had caused her to mishear Lord Colin's earlier statement, and she wished to nullify her overreaction by behaving as though she had never believed anything amiss. Unfortunately, her mind was a total blank.

"I think my servants enjoyed last night's dance." Lord Colin saved her by proposing his own topic.

"Aye. I'm certain they did. There was much laughter, and I overheard many a complimentary comment," she eagerly responded.

"Did you know your Mr. O'Hanlon danced a hornpipe with my Annie?"

"Nay." Meary voiced her amazement. "They seem an odd pair."

"My thoughts exactly."

"Who asked whom to dance?"

"He asked her."

"I don't know which astonishes me more: his asking or her accepting. Annie is so very English, and Seumas . . ."

163

"Is an Irishman through to the marrow of his bones," Lord Colin finished the sentence for her. "Nevertheless, both appeared to enjoy themselves despite their prejudices. Of course, your friend was well into his cups when he asked her to dance."

"That might be explaining his behavior, but how do ye explain hers?"

"I cannot. Then, Annie has been acting a bit out of character lately. She has taken to singing as she goes about her duties, something I have never known her to do before, and she has mentioned more than once what a pleasure it is to have company in the house."

The obvious explanation for Annie's changed nature sprung into Meary's mind, but the notion of Annie being enamored of Seumas was so ludicrous Meary could not conceive it being true. Certainly Seumas would make a fine mate for any woman, but Annie? Now that she stopped to think about it, more times than not when she ask of Seumas's whereabouts, the answer was "with Annie". Had she been so absorbed with her own wayward emotions she had missed noticing the sweet flowering of romantic feelings between her mentor and Lord Colin's housekeeper? Meary shook her head. Her world might seem a topsy-turvy place of late, but she was not prepared to believe it completely gone mad.

"Well, what do you think?" Lord Colin prodded.

"I think the only way we will be knowing what 'tis in their minds and hearts is to be asking them, and for meself I possess not the courage."

"Nor do I," he proclaimed.

As they consumed their meal, they continued to discuss the dance, both carefully avoiding any mention of their own participation in the evening's revelry. When

164

that subject was exhausted, they discussed other matters of an equally innocuous nature.

"The work on the new wing to the tower house is proceeding well. The masons tell me the walls will be ready for the roof in little more than a fortnight."

Meary swallowed the bite of ham she was chewing and took a sip of wine. "I have heard the stonemasons' hammers and wondered what they built."

"Mostly the new wing will house my servants," Lord Colin explained. "The tower was built at a time when servants were expected to share the floor of the great hall, and the new accommodations are sorely needed. At present, many of my house servants must walk home to the cottages of their families at the end of their day. Others make do with the stable or kitchen floor. It is most inconvenient for all concerned."

"I can see how it would be. 'Tis kind of ye to look after their comfort."

"It is my duty as their master."

Both the food and the conversation were satisfying, and Meary could not complain she was being ill-treated. Only two circumstances marred what would otherwise be a perfect afternoon. She was far too aware of the man sitting next to her and the excessive saltiness of the meal made her tongue sting, compelling her to consume far more of the excellent wine Annie had provided them than she liked, so that she would not become completely cotton-mouthed.

By the time they finished the meal, the combination of the warm wine within her and the warm sun overhead left her feeling agreeably lazy. She stretched her arms above her head and yawned.

"Would you like me to stand guard while you recline

and take a nap?" Lord Colin offered.

"Nay. I have barely been out of bed two hours." She yawned again. "Despite appearances, I am not in need of more sleep."

"I imagine you look like an angel when you sleep."

"Who's to say?" she shrugged off the compliment. "I have never seen meself asleep, and Seumas and Brendan are not inclined to make such judgments." Another yawn overtook her and she pressed her hand to her mouth. "Mayhap we should be getting back to the house," she suggested.

"If you do not mind, I would like to sit here a little while longer. My duties are many, and I rarely have time to just sit and enjoy the wide world around me. You can understand; I would like to prolong the moment."

"Aye, I understand. I sometimes worry ye work yourself too hard. Gone all day doing this and that." She gifted him with a half sigh full of warm rapport. "We can be staying as long as ye like."

The knowledge that she sometimes worried about him pleased Lord Colin on some elemental level. He had never known anyone to worry over him except Annie. "Thank you." He reached out his hand and stroked her cheek with his knuckles.

Meary trembled, but she did not move herself out of his reach. Lord Colin smiled.

They sat, side by side, in compatible silence for the space of several minutes.

"Meary."

"Hmm."

"I believe you to be the most beautiful woman I have ever lain my eyes upon. No one comes near your loveliness."

" 'Tis a false belief, I'm sure. Or mayhap ye have lived a sheltered life or have recently imbibed too much wine." She placidly refuted his flattery. As an afterthought, she added, "But I do thank ye for the delusion."

"I like modesty in a woman."

She shrugged.

"I like many things about you. Your music, your wit, and your grace . . ."

Definitely too much wine, Meary settled on the reason for his loose tongue. It was little wonder he had overindulged. The man had eaten the same food as she, and it was to be expected he would develop a similar compelling need to slack his thirst.

". . . your lips." He leaned close and kissed her tenderly. Rivers of fire coursed through Meary's veins, leaving her disoriented and limp.

"Please do not be doing that," she begged.

He kissed her again. "Don't you like it?"

"Of course I like it. 'Tis why I must be insisting ye stop." It wasn't at all what she had meant to say, but she didn't know how to call the words back.

"But I don't want to stop," he breathed against her ear.

Meary could not fathom when he had moved so startlingly near, but she felt herself being pulled onto his lap as he continued to tease her lips with tender kisses. Warm, needy, persuasive kisses. He cradled her in his arms, holding her so near she could feel his heart beating against hers.

One of his hands buried itself in the hair at the base of her skull, the heel of his hand massaging the muscles of her neck. His other hand roamed up and down her spine, coaxing her to relax against him with long, soothing strokes. All the while his hands worked their mellowing magic, his lips worshipfully caressed hers. He plucked kisses from her lips as one plucks petals from a dewy flower quivering in the morning breeze, suckled the sweetness of her lips as a bee sucks nectar. His lips did not demand she return his kisses; they prayed her to do so.

Meary felt herself melting against the strong arms embracing her, leaning closer into the broad chest that housed his urgently beating heart. Every sense seemed multiplied tenfold. Her ears were filled with the sound of the sea, the singing of birds, the rustling of the grasses, and *his* breathing. The musky scent of man surrounded her, crowding out both the delicate fragrance of hawthorn blossoms and the earthy aroma of peat. She was aware of the fine weave of his lawn shirt, every button and piece of braid, the silk of his hair, the smoothness of his freshly shaven cheek. And the taste of him. He was slightly salty. She could detect the subtle bouquet of the wine they had drunk. But he possessed a flavor all his own, some indescribable, heady taste that intoxicated her senses in a manner far more besotting than the most potent spirits gulped by the tankardful.

She found herself returning his gentle kisses, tentatively at first, then more boldly. Her hands kneaded his shoulders and fondled his neck.

Meary was only vaguely aware when her hair came cascading down around her shoulders. She was too preoccupied discovering the many pleasures of the kiss. She was pliant in Lord Colin's arms, allowing him to guide her lips to his again and again. He kissed her quickly, showering her lips with butterfly pecks. Then, he kissed her slowly, drawing out the kiss until the heat created caused them both to gasp for breath. He not only kissed her lips, but her cheeks and hair and eyes and chin. Though she had ofttimes heard herself called such, he made her *feel* beautiful.

When Lord Colin smoothly lowered her to the blanket, Meary murmured only a token protest. Her lips were too busy to say more. The weight of his body leaning against hers felt solid, not menacing. His arms felt sheltering, not constricting. He did not embolden his caresses. He merely continued to gift her with entrancing kisses. It was heavenly lying here kissing him and being kissed by him. She wanted the moment to last forever.

Meary remained lost to the earthbound world, forgetting all her promises to be wise, until she felt Lord Colin's fingers at her neckline, followed by a cool gust of air wafting across her bare skin as her bodice fell open. Frantically she tried to cover herself, shaking her head from side to side.

"Nay! I am sorry. I should not have let ye . . . I should not . . ."

"Shh. Do not be sorry. Be glad. Be glad we can give each other so much pleasure. Do not try to rise. Lie back and relax. This is good. This is very very good," he whispered as he gently pressed her down on the blanket.

His softly spoken words were like an irresistible incantation. Meary's limbs lost their will to obey her command. Her lips, rather than protesting, sought out his. Only her mind continued to demur, repeating the single word *nay* over and over in her head. Even her mental denials began to drift in and out of existence as Lord Colin relentlessly plied her with fiery, thought-numbing kisses.

His fingers played at her collarbone until he felt the tension in her limbs ease; then, almost imperceptibly, they began to inch downward.

While his fingers crept every so slowly toward their pillowy prize, his lips escalated their seductive onslaught. After kissing her lips until they blushed rose red, he parted them and slid his tongue into the warmth of her mouth. He paused, waiting to see if it would be rejected. When it was not, he began to lightly stroke the moist, sensitive, flesh inside her mouth, drawing moans of pleasure from her throat. Sucking gently, he invited her tongue to enter his mouth.

Meary was vaguely aware of the thought that there was much about kissing that had never been made known to her. Whether the omissions had been willful or merely an oversight was of little concern to her. Her interest was in expanding the boundaries of her present knowledge. When Lord Colin invited her tongue to join his, she did not hesitate to accept the invitation.

The inside of his mouth felt wet and hot. His teeth grazed her tongue as she moved it in and out in echo of the erotic caresses he had given her.

So enraptured was she with exploring this newly discovered and highly stimulating aspect of the kiss, Meary was caught unaware when his hand grasped her breast. He brushed the pad of his thumb back and forth across her nipple, sending rivers of hot pleasure radiating from her breast to her loins with every pass.

The voice of logic cried for her to stop him. An even louder voice beseeched him to continue. Hands she told to beat against his chest pulled her tighter into his embrace. She felt her mind separating from her body.

Meary valiantly fought to muster the tattered remnants of her will in a final attempt to cling to reason, determined her mind would regain dominion over her body. But when the final wrenching of mind and body came, it was a relief.

Blessed freedom washed over her. She was free to indulge her finely attuned senses. Free to explore and express the earthy side of her nature without reserve. Free to follow the path of yearning to whatever fulfillment lay at its end.

Reaching up, her fingers found the buttons of his waistcoat. She made quick work of these, then turned her attention to undoing the fastenings of his shirt. Tugging at the lace of his cravat, she loosened his neck cloth. Colin aided her efforts to disrobe him by yanking off the cravat and tossing it aside. Eagerly, Meary slipped her hands inside his shirt, stroking the thick matt of hair covering his chest and kneading the muscles beneath.

Colin murmured his approval, bestowing a profusion of grateful kisses upon her passion-ripe lips as he shrugged out of his waistcoat and shirt.

Straddling her hips with his knees, he rose enough to give himself access to the buttons and lacings barring him from her pale flesh, though he was careful not to let more than a moment elapse between his supplicating kisses lest her common sense make an untimely reappearance.

After laying open her overdress and discarding her pink silk petticoat and quilted underpetticoats, he tended to the lacings of her corset, noting with mild amusement the undergarment was of French, not English, design.

When he had Meary stripped to her chemise and stockings, he lay back down beside her, pulling her so she lay atop him.

His hands roamed up and down her frame following the lithe curves of her figure. He teased the tip of her breasts with his mouth, reveling in her mews of pleasure.

Meary's hands and lips were not idle as Lord Colin tempted her flesh to a rosy glow. She could not get enough of the feel of him. His skin was some places velvet smooth, other places rough as a quarry stone. The texture of the hair covering his body ranged from curly to straight, coarse to fine. The hardness of his bone and muscle contrasted delightfully with the softness of his lips and brows. She found his body fascinating in the variety it offered her exploring fingertips.

Their lips continued to meet as their hands freely roamed. There was no longer a tentative quality to their kisses. They were ravenous, almost violent in their intensity. Her flaxen hair cascaded in a golden waterfall round their heads as they passionately devoured each other.

The heat of his skin seeped through the thin fabric of her chemise, searing her flesh. The leather of his breeches was soft against her legs, but she desired no barriers between them. Meary felt delirious with a feverish need to feel all of him.

When Lord Colin eased her from his chest, she tried to cling to him, but he gently peeled her hands from him. In one swift movement he yanked her chemise over her head, growling in appreciation as he did so; then, he began removing her stockings and garters, kissing his way down the length of each leg until his lips caressed the arches of each foot.

Ever so slowly and with great care to leave no inch of flesh ignored, he kissed and caressed his way back up to her face. There he lingered for a long while, his lips adoring her eyes and ears and petal soft lips.

Burrowing his hands in her hair, he drew his fingers through the silken strands again and again.

172

Lifting a golden lock, he brushed it across his lips, breathing in the subtle jasmine scent of her frangipani perfume.

He neglected her, ever so briefly, to wriggle out of his breeches and boots. When he again lay down beside her and gathered her in his arms, there was nothing to shield Meary from the knowledge of his hard arousal.

Rather than intimidate her, the evidence of his need for her impassioned her. She wanted to give herself to him, wanted to have him give himself to her. The pounding of the sea and the beating of his heart became one sound. The summer breeze and his warm breath mingled into a single sensation. The musky scents of rich earth and passion-enflamed man were indistinguishable. Meary pulled Colin closer, molding her lips to his, tasting the salty sweetness of him as she wordlessly invited him to make them one.

Colin needed no other overture. He was close to bursting from the pressure of desire too long held in check. He had been waiting for this moment for an eternity, and now the waiting was over.

Easing Meary's thighs apart, he buried himself between the moist folds of her feminine flesh with a single, forceful thrust. She arched against him as he entered her body, crying out in pain and pleasure.

He wasted no time soothing her sensitive flesh with long, slow, powerful strokes of his male shaft, quickly erasing the memory of the pain of her deflowering with titillating sensations.

Though Meary clung to him, at first she lay passive in his arms, but as he continued to move within her, her hips instinctively began to rise to meet each thrust.

Colin felt himself losing control, and his thrusting

became more and more vigorous. Meary matched his urgent rhythm, driven by her own need for release from pent up passions.

They were like wild creatures of the forest, so frantic was their need to reach fulfillment. Colin held Meary so tightly she could no longer discern the galloping beat of her heart from his or where her flesh left off and his began. She shackled Colin to her with her legs as they strained together. Between fierce kisses, their gasps and groans joined the cries of the birds overhead.

Relief came crashing upon them in wave after wave of pulsating pleasure, leaving the lovers exhausted and too breathless to speak.

Shifting his weight to his hip, Colin cradled Meary's limp, sweat-soaked body in his arms. Meary buried her face in the crook of his neck.

Chapter 11

Lord Colin lay on his back, his bare skin bathed in the warm rays of the afternoon sun. He tightened his arms around Meary, nestling her full breasts against his chest. Never had he felt so content. Never. Making love to Meary had been everything he had fantasized it would be and more.

There was something refreshing about the way she gave herself to him. He surmised her lack of experience had much to do with it, but there was another subtle attribute to her lovemaking to which he could not put a name. He heaved a quiescent sigh. Whatever it was, he liked it.

His original assumption he would soon grow tired of Meary O'Byrne mocked him for a fool. He should have known a woman as clever as she in all other areas of her life would prove equally as adroit in the game of lovemaking. That he would grow tired of her some day, he had no doubt, but he now predicted that day to be a good way off into the future.

But what if she grew tired of him first? He did not like

the thought marring his present contentment. He would have to lavish her with attention, cosset her, entice her with gifts—in short treat her so well she would never even think to reject his company. He would make his companionship too profitable to resist.

"Meary."

"What?" she replied in a muffled voice, refusing to lift her face from his neck.

"I think we should dress and return to the house."

A squeaky moan escaped her lips.

Colin winced at the pitiful utterance, wishing with all his heart he knew the right thing to say to make her feel at ease about what had just transpired between them. He wanted her to be as enchanted with their lovemaking as he. "There is no need to feel regret about what has happened here. It is natural that man and woman come together in this way."

"I should have been stronger, wiser."

"You could not resist the attraction between us any more than could I."

The truth of his words was of little comfort to Meary. She had *not* possessed the strength or will to resist him. And now, she knew her will would be even weaker. Having tasted the sensual delights of Lord Colin's lovemaking, she knew her craving for his touch would be even more truculent. What she didn't know was what she was going to do about it.

Pride goeth before destruction. His words had been spoken in another context, but why had she not recognized them as an omen? She had no one but herself to blame.

. . . and a haughty spirit before the fall, Meary finished the line of scripture. She should have heeded Seumas's

warnings, not shunned them. She should have left Lord Colin's estate at the first sign of carnal stirrings. But instead, she had blithely walked into perdition, beguiled by an inflated opinion of her own ability to resist temptation.

Meary was not dense to the knowledge she had been invited onto the heath for the express purpose of depriving her of her virtue. Hindsight provided clearer vision than that of the moment, and words and behaviors she had once perversely convinced herself were innocent, she now saw in a more honest light. Lord Colin had stated his intention to seduce her, and he had done just that. The fact he had lulled her into complacency by playing the gentleman was not particularly admirable, and a part of her was furious with him, but she could not in good conscience say he had forced himself upon her. She had been a willing, nay, *eager* participant in her own downfall.

Why her good sense had deserted her was a question Meary could not answer. She was more than a little appalled with herself that she had succumb to a virtual stranger. Two weeks was not enough time to know a man. Her attraction to Lord Colin was more than physical; he engaged her heart in some uncommon way; still, in her mind, this did not justify amending her belief of right and wrong. Or did it? Nay, it could not. Despite her claim, her contrition warred for supremacy with a nagging sentience that giving herself to Lord Colin had *not* been wrong—that she was meant to be with him in this way.

"Meary."

"What?" This time her reply was tinged with annoyance. She did not want to face the world. She preferred to hide in the hollow of his neck forever. The illogic of her strategy to deal with her situation did not matter to her.

"If we lie here all afternoon, we risk sunburning parts of our anatomy that could prove quite vexatious." When that didn't budge her, he added, "If we are gone too long, someone at the house may come in search of us."

Meary bolted upright, in her haste spearing him just below the breastbone with an elbow. Lord Colin let out a *whoof*, but Meary paid no attention. "Where are me clothes?" she desperately demanded.

"Calm yourself," he admonished as he handed her her chemise. "There is not a soul on the horizon."

Meary snatch her chemise over her head, jabbing her arms through the sleeves. When Lord Colin did not immediately thrust the next item of clothing into her hands, she began crawling about on her hands and knees, sweeping the blanket for the articles she sought. Once retrieved, she pulled on the remainder of her clothing and worked her way through the intricate fastenings with amazing speed.

She breathed a sigh of relief; then, her hands flew to her head. "Me hair," she wailed. "I'll never be getting it back in the style Doreen fashioned."

"Let me get dressed and I will try to help you," Lord Colin soothed.

"Ye mean to say ye are still sitting there as naked as the day ye were born! What is the matter with ye! Are ye mad?"

"No." He rose to his feet and began to dress in a leisurely fashion. He could understand why Meary might not be as good humored as he. She was after all, young, relatively unworldly, and Irish in temperament. Still, the extent of her distress chafed him. Nevertheless, he was

178

determined not to let her unwarranted agitation ruin his fine mood or goad him into speaking harshly. As he tucked his shirt into his breeches, he began to hum a jaunty tune.

Meary wanted to kick him for being so nonchalant. He seemed not to realize her whole notion of herself had been crushed to rumble, and she needed time to come to terms with her new, less admirable self before she was forced to face the opinions of others.

She was not so self-involved she believed all of the human race cared one way or the other if she had fallen from grace. But Seumas would care. Brendan would care. Any castigating she received would be well deserved; however, she wished to spare them the painful knowledge of her folly for as long as possible.

"There. I am modest as a monk," Lord Colin announced after an eternity. "If you will turn around, I will see what I can do to repair the damage I did to your coiffure."

Meary presented her back to him and braced herself to receive his touch. Having no other implement, he was forced to use his fingers to comb the tangles from her flaxen mane.

Every time he brushed the hairs near her scalp, waves of tingling pleasure surged down her spine. Meary did her very best not to be effected, but to no avail. Lacing her fingers together, she held onto reason with all her might.

When he had freed her hair of all snags, he said, "You will have to tell me what to do next."

"Have ye never braided a woman's hair?"

"I'm afraid not."

"Ye do remember how the braids were arranged upon me head?" she half-stated half-questioned, her tone

179

evincing a goodly amount of fatalism.

"I believe I remember well enough to fool the casual observer," he replied.

Seumas O'Hanlon was anything but a casual observer, Meary bemoaned; then, she remembered he had not seen her when she went out this morning and her spirits brightened a little.

"All right. I want ye to be dividing me hair into three equal sections, two on the sides of me head and one in the back. Each must be made into a separate braid. I can manage the two on the sides well enough, but ye will have to watch carefully so ye can do the one in the back," Meary began. Though the occasion behind the necessity of the task was mortifying, she was grateful to have a solid occupation for her mind and hands for it provided much needed, if only temporary, relief from the chaotic, raucous riot of emotions raging in her head.

Taking the first section of hair in her hands, Meary split it into three smaller strands and deftly twisted it strand over strand for the space of several inches. "Do ye see how 'tis done? Ye lay the outside hair over the middle strand alternating sides every time."

"It looks simple enough."

"Good." Meary continued with the braid until she reached the end of her hair. She then fastened the end with one riband and turned her attention to the other side.

Behind her, she could feel Lord Colin twisting and tugging at her hair. A section went slack. He cursed under his breath, picked up the strand, worked industriously a little while longer, dropped the whole, and cursed again. "It is not easy as it looks," he complained.

180

"If ye can get the first few inches tight, I can probably be managing the rest meself," Meary encouraged.

"Are you sure you cannot manage the whole?"

She shook her head. "The ends will become hopelessly tangled."

Lord Colin lifted her hair and began again. He made another mistake, gritted his teeth, and began once again. He was determined if even the lowliest maidservant could manage the task, then so could he. Of a sudden, he began to chuckle at his own predicament. How could these silken strands of pale gold, which had but a short while ago given him such pleasure, now be the cause of so much frustration?

"What is it ye find so amusing?" Meary demanded.

"Nothing really," Lord Colin admitted. "It is really quite sad that a man of my accomplishments should be laid low by a simple braid."

"But ye have to do it," she insisted. "I cannot be going back to the house with me hair half undone or in a style that 'tis different than when I left. Everyone will know we . . ."

"They will know soon enough anyway," Colin calmly informed her.

"Ye plan to announce me disgrace to the world!"

"I would never do anything so unchivalrous. I only meant to imply that it is only reasonable to assume the members of my household will notice the public exchange of small affections between us."

"I beg ye to have mercy on me and do not be exchanging anymore 'affections' with me publicly or privately."

"There. I've got it!" Lord Colin declared. Refusing to

relinquish the braid, he finished plaiting the hair to the end. Then he asked, "What do I do next?"

Meary was acutely aware of how neatly he had evaded her plea for the consideration of her feelings, but she was at a loss what to do about it. Since repairing her hair presented the more immediate and manageable problem, she did her best to concentrate on it. "Loop the braid end over end like ye be coiling a rope; then, tie the whole with the riband to the crown of me head." She paused, trying to recall exactly how her hair had felt earlier in the day. "The loops should be long enough to brush me shoulders and pulled apart once they are tied."

Lord Colin did as he was instructed, calling upon his own memory to arrange each braid and riband as he had seen it this morning. After considerable fussing, he stepped back and pronounced himself satisfied. "If you will give me a moment to gather up the remains of our meal, I will be ready to escort you back to the house."

Meary's first thought was to escape his companionship without further delay; then she was struck by the realization she had no idea which direction led back to the house. She had been so preoccupied with her emotions on their walk away from the tower house, she had neglected to pay strict attention. She pursed her lips and stood perfectly still, taking her bearings by the location of the sun, the direction of the breeze, the sound of the sea. The information gathered was helpful but not nearly enough to guarantee her any degree of accuracy.

She was not happy to be dependent on Lord Colin's guidance, but there was naught she could do to change the situation. Her pride had already led her down one road to disaster today. She would not allow it to lead her down another.

Though she could not gain complete independence, Meary *was* determined to maintain as much self-sufficiency as her situation allowed. "Would ye do me the kindness of handing me me walking stick?" she firmly requested.

Lord Colin obliged. He returned to his previous task, and a moment later presented himself at her side. When he tried to lay her hand upon his arm, Meary pulled it back and adamantly shook her head.

"I don't want to be touching ye," she informed him.

"I see." He was rankled by her reaction, but he kept his voice devoid of emotion. "Do you intend to pretend this afternoon never happened?"

More than anything in the world, Meary wished she could do just that, but she was through lying to herself. Her refusal to face reality was what had brought her to this sorry pass. She had given herself to Lord Colin, and there was no taking the moment back. Facing reality also required her to accept that while they had been making love, she had been blissfully content to behave wantonly. The regret had come only afterward and had far less to do with wanting to erase the experience than it had to do with a sense she had betrayed her friends and herself. "I cannot pretend this afternoon did not happen. It did. But right now I am feeling exceedingly distraught and confused." She paused to take a deep breath. "Ye said ye would seduce me, and ye did. I cannot claim to admire ye for it. 'Twas an ignoble thing to be doing. But I will not feign blamelessness and argue I did not give meself to ye willingly. Nor will I prevaricate and say that I did not find lying in your arms pleasurable. I am terrified by how

183

pleasurable what we did together was." Meary bowed her head and lowered her voice to barely above a whisper. "I grant ye the victory. Now, I am asking ye to grant me a space of time to compose me thoughts so I can get on with me life with what dignity ye left me."

Colin was gratified to hear he had pleased her as well as she had pleased him, but he could see how much her admission was costing her. All trace of his previous ire at her unhappy mood vanished, and he reached out to comfort her. As he did, she backed away from him. He dropped his arms to his side. "It was never my intent to deprive you of your dignity, and I do not think less of you because of what has occurred here," he assured her. "I promise I will treat you well. Ask, and if it is within my power to give it to you, anything you want is yours."

What she wanted, Meary knew could not be asked for. He must give it to her freely without prompting. And, if she was completely honest with herself, she was not even certain she would welcome a declaration of his love. If he said he loved her, if he wanted her for a wife, she knew it would be easier to accept the lusty events of the afternoon. Love lent morality to unbridled passion. But . . .

First she needed to discover if her own heart harbored that gentle emotion for him. She needed time to come to grips with the powerful feeling in her breast, time to discern if it was enduring love or merely a passion of the moment. She had never been in love and knew not what it felt like. Even now, amidst all her pain and confusion, she felt a kinship with him, a desire to put his comfort above her own, but she also felt a precipitous distance between them and a strong wish to protect herself and so many other conflicting emotions it was

184

impossible to know what she felt. "Ye need not be making me promises," she said. "All I want of ye is the gift of a little time."

His tone dubious, Colin inquired, "How much time?"

"I know not."

"Now that we have become lovers, I do not want to waste any more time. I want us to make love again and again, today, tomorrow, as long and as often as we like."

"I do not consider the restoration of me sanity a waste of time," she argued.

"If that sanity causes you to push me away, I cannot support it. I am most eager to have you share my bed."

He sounded so matter-of-fact Meary knew not how to answer him. He clearly intended she take up residence in his bedchamber, which gave answer to her earlier supplication he have mercy. He was not a merciful man. She needed to say something, anything to gain reprieve. "I do not understand ye any more than I understand meself. Why do ye profess to want me so keenly? There are other women to be had."

"But none so beautiful as you."

"Beauty 'tis a gift from God. It has naught to do with the person inside the skin. Close your eyes and would not a plain lover do as well as a comely one?"

The logic behind her opinion was irrefutable, so he offered a different reason, "I find you intriguing."

"I am an ordinary woman."

"You are far from ordinary."

"I cannot think how," she pleaded.

"Then you are right when you say you are exceedingly confused. I will grant you the time you request, but you may only have a little time. If you take too long to come to terms with being my lover, I will come for you and carry you up to my bed."

"What is your measure of 'a little time'?" Meary asked, disheartened by the resolute tone of his voice.

"Twenty-four hours. No more, no less."

She quailed. "Ye are not a generous man."

"I think you will find I am very generous . . . with those who are generous to me."

Chapter 12

The walk back to the tower house seemed miles long, and more than once Meary was tempted to accuse Lord Colin of leading her astray. However, since such an accusation would invite an exchange of words between them, she did not give in to it.

Lord Colin was not altogether mute, but he did restrain his conversation to the occasional comment, which thus far she had been able to ignore. He was also keeping his hands to himself, allowing her to walk unfettered beside him. She was not about to say or do anything that might encourage him to abandon his present behavior.

Twenty-four hours. She could hear the minutes ticking away in her head. Twenty-four hours to embrace the life of a paramour was not long enough. A lifetime would not be long enough. But how could she blame him for thinking himself generous when she had so readily surrendered her virginity? He had nothing to judge her by but her actions, and they did not speak well for her.

Though her heart constricted at the thought of never again hearing his voice or knowing his touch, she knew what she must do. She must leave his estate immediately. Running away might be cowardly, but if she did not, she knew of a certainty, she would succumb to temptation again and again . . . and again. Whether she loved Lord Colin or not, she did not want to be any man's whore.

The clamorous activities of the courtyard were the sweetest sounds Meary had ever heard.

"I'll leave you now," Colin said.

"Thank ye."

She quickened her stride. Without slackening her pace, she pushed open the heavy wooden door of the tower, crossed the hall, and started up the stairs leading to the sanctuary of her room.

"Meary."

She spun on her heels at the sound of Seumas's voice, coming precariously close to losing her balance. One hand clutched the wall, the other gripped her cane.

"I didn't mean to be startling ye," he apologized. "I only wanted to be speaking with ye a moment." His last statement had the tenor of a command.

Meary's hand gripped the head of her walking cane a little tighter. He couldn't know what had transpired between Lord Colin and her on the heath, could he? Nay. Lord Colin would have warned her if Seumas had stumbled upon them. Even if he would not have, had Seumas wandered onto the lusty scene, surely he would have tried to put a stop to it.

Somewhat calmed by her reasoning, Meary began to breathe again. Still, she was not eager to descend to the floor of the great hall. Whatever Seumas wanted to be speaking to her about, she was in no mood to be listening. All she wanted to do was hide in her room . . . and pack her trunk.

With great effort, she forced her feet to carry her back down the stairs.

"What is it ye need to be saying?" she asked when she stood before him.

There was a long pause. She could feel his eyes studying her intently. She could hear the inhaling and exhaling of his every breath.

"I want to be talking to ye about last night," he began. "Ye were still asleep when I checked in on ye this morning and . . ."

"What about last night?" Meary prompted when his sentence trailed off into pregnant silence. She certainly wasn't eager to be scolded about her behavior last night, but it was vastly preferable to discussing what had occurred this afternoon.

"Are ye feeling all right? Ye look a bit flushed," he observed, temporarily abandoning his initial purpose.

His words caused her color to deepen, and Meary turned away slightly, her fingers worrying the head of her cane. "I fear I took too much sun." She offered an excuse that was not an outright lie, but the deceit was enough to make her squirm.

"'Tis not the sun turning ye a rosy red. Methinks ye are feeling shame for the way ye flirted with Lord Colin last night."

"I did not flirt with him," Meary argued unconvincingly.

"Aye, ye did."

"Nay. I may have been overly indulgent, but I did not flirt," she repeated the hollow assertion. She knew it was not true, but to her considerable shame her tongue would not obey her conscience's dictate to be unflinchingly honest.

189

Seumas did not relent. "I'm not saying ye lifted yer skirts and showed him a tasty length of leg, but ye were more than indulgent of our host. I saw ye smiling at his compliments, and heard ye laughing at his words like he be the wittiest man alive. Everybody did. And don't be thinking I'm the only one who noticed ye danced with no other."

"I danced with Brendan."

"And who else?"

She was finding it harder and harder to keep up the pretense of uprightness when she knew herself guilty of a far greater indiscretion than those of which Seumas accused her, but still she persisted. "No one else asked."

"And that did not strike ye as odd?"

Meary swallowed hard. "I did not think . . ."

"Ah. Truer words have never sprung from yer lips. Ye were not thinking, that is for certain. If ye're not careful, ye're going to be finding yerself in a situation not to yer liking."

Meary could feel the heat in her cheeks rise sharply, and she prayed the increased heat would not manifest itself in the color of her complexion.

"Meary?" Seumas demanded, his voice thick with authority and apprehension. "Have ye done something else ye should be telling me about?"

Meary pivoted another quarter turn, presenting the full width of her back. She stood as rigid as a statue and equally as mute. She could not bear to speak another lie, but neither could she bring herself to speak the truth.

"Meary?" Seumas repeated.

She shook her head back and forth, but the tears trickling down her cheeks gave a different answer. Her shoulders began to shake uncontrollably, and she wrapped her arms around herself. Slowly, her head began to nod up and down.

"Blessed Mary, Mother of Jesus," Seumas supplicated in a guttural gasp of sweeping comprehension. "Watch over me Meary. I am too late."

Pulling Meary into his arms, he turned her so she faced him and cradled her like a child, stroking her back as he murmured over and over again, "Me poor Meary. Me poor Meary."

"I'm so sorry Seumas." Meary spoke through a torrent of wracking sobs. "I didn't mean to disappoint ye. I didn't mean to hurt ye. I don't know why I am feeling these things I feel for him. I don't know why . . . I tried to stop meself. I tried. Truly, I tried."

"I know ye did. I know," he soothed. There was no reproach in his voice, only pain and loving concern. "Ye need not be fearing I'll think ill of ye. 'Tis as much me fault as yers. I should have been more forceful with ye from the beginning. I should not have given ye the freedom to deal with this burden in yer own way. It was wrong of me to expect so much of ye. Ye look so much like an angel, sometimes I be forgetting ye be a victim of human frailties every bit as much as the rest of us."

"None of this is your fault," Meary protested.

"Aye. I fear it is. I have no real experience being a father to a maiden. I did not do right by ye."

"Please, Seumas, do not compound me guilt by making me responsible for ye losing faith in yourself. Ye are the wisest man on earth. I believe that with every fiber of me being, and I want ye to continue to be believing it too. I lied to ye about me feelings. Over and over, I lied to ye."

Seumas continued to hold her tenderly. "I have never believed meself to be the wisest man on earth, and the day

I do start believing it, I truly will be an unconscionable fool. Do ye think I have not known from the start ye were being less than plainspoken with me? I knew; I just didn't know what to be doing about yer reserve. Ye need not be feeling responsible for me feelings about meself. I alone am responsible for me thoughts."

"But . . ."

"Shh. Ye have enough to think about without conjuring meritless reasons to be worrying about me."

"But I have failed ye."

"Ye have failed no one but yerself," Seumas corrected. His soothing tone suddenly became harsh. "And don't be thinking I have forgotten ye are not alone in this. Lord Colin Garrick be a villainous bastard if ever one crawled upon earth."

"Nay. He is not." Meary stiffened, gently extracting herself from his embrace. Lord Colin might be many things, some less than praiseworthy, but she knew without a shred of doubt he was not evil.

"Has he offered to be giving ye his name?"

"Nay."

"I thought not," Seumas rejoined. "He be a villainous bastard, and I fully intend to demand satisfaction. He must pay for his crime against ye with his life."

An icy cold enveloped Meary, draining her tear-streaked face of all trace of color. Seumas could not be serious; yet, she knew with dreadful certainty that he was. It was in his voice, a timbre she had never heard before but one on a visceral level she recognized as deadly earnest. "Ye must promise me ye will not be demanding any such thing!"

"I cannot."

"Please, Seumas. I beg of ye." She grabbed his hand

and held tight. "Ye are not skilled with a sword. He will kill ye."

"There are many kinds of death, Meary. I could not be living with the shame if I did not defend yer honor."

"And could not be living with your death upon me conscience. It may be his sword that kills ye but 'twill be me hand upon the hilt. There is naught to defend. I freely gave up all claim to me honor. We will leave here just as ye have wanted from the very beginning. I was on me way upstairs to pack when ye called me name. Ye will not do this terrible thing!"

"Mayhap God will bless me with the strength of ten men and I will win the duel. He has been known to work miracles when the cause be just." There was a calmness in his voice that only enlarged Meary's terror.

"But the cause 'tis not just!"

"Ye be mistaken."

"Then Lord Colin will die, and I could not bear to live with that on me soul either!" Meary's voice became more high-pitched and frantic with each word.

"Do ye love the man?" Seumas asked, though his tone clearly evinced her answer, whether it was "aye" or "nay" would not alter his course of action.

"In truth, I know not. I only know I do not want to see him dead. Please, if ye desire me to beg ye on me knees, I will do so without hesitation. Do not be calling tragedy upon our heads by insisting on this madness."

Doggedly prying her hand from his, Seumas offered the only comfort he could. "Meary, I wish I could be giving ye what ye ask, but I cannot. 'Twill be over quickly, I can give ye that. Ye are young. Ye may not believe so now, but ye will survive this and be the stronger for it."

Chapter 13

"Where is Lord Colin?" Meary burst into the kitchen. "Annie are ye here? I must be finding Lord Colin."

"Annie be not here. And as to his lordship, I've no notion where he be," a kitchen maid informed her.

"Oh," Meary wailed. Her face was ashen and her slender body was trembling violently as she stumbled her way through the kitchen and out the door at a run.

"Have ye seen Lord Colin?" she demanded of the first man she bumped into.

"Nay."

"Are ye certain? 'Tis a matter of life and death."

"I be sorry, miss . . ."

She continued to dash across the yard, stopping everyone who crossed her path and demanding to know where his lordship might be. It was not until she reached the stables, that her question was answered.

"He be out riding," the stable master answered her question. "Traveling east when I saw him last."

"How long ago did he leave?"

"Not but a few minutes ago."

"Do ye know when he will be coming back?"

"Nay."

"Is Brendan here?"

"Nay. He be out giving Pansy her exercise. That one has been gone a good long while."

Meary sagged against the post of a stall. "What am I going to do?"

"I've no notion what's worked ye into the state yer in, but might there be something I could be doing for ye?"

Meary forced herself to breathe deeply and focus her thoughts. If she could not convince Seumas to be rational, it was essential she find Lord Colin and convince *him* to refuse to fight. She would not allow this duel. She absolutely would not! A horse whinnied and Meary straightened. "Aye, there is something ye can do. Saddle a horse for the each of us, and take me to Lord Colin."

"Aye, miss."

A short while later the stable master was leading Meary and her horse out of the yard, traveling at a brisk trot in the same easterly direction he had seen his lordship take earlier.

Every few minutes Meary asked, "Do ye see him yet?"

"Nay, miss. Not yet."

His statement was greeted with a frustrated whimper, then silence, until she asked the same question once again.

Lord Colin was feeling especially pleased with his life as he galloped his mount across the heath. And why shouldn't he, he asked himself. Patience had served him well. Meary was his. A summer filled with idyllic pleasure

195

stretched before him like the welcoming arms of a lover.

He would not name the sensation filling his breast happiness; he wasn't even sure such an emotion existed; but if it did, this was the closest he had come to happiness in a long time.

Meary would come to him before the end of her reprieve, he was almost certain of it. For the moment she might be a little reluctant to enthusiastically take up her place in his bed, but he was confident her passionate nature would circumvent her reservations, and she would behave sensibly. If she did not, he would go to her. She would not deny him. She could not. They had loved each other too well for either to resist experiencing the delights of their spirited lovemaking again.

When he had given his horse free rein for over an hour, Lord Colin reined the stallion to a more sedate pace. Glancing up at the sun, he was a little embarrassed he had frittered away so much time. Good-naturedly cautioning himself he could not afford to completely surrender himself to hedonistic pursuits, he decided to drop in on one or two of his more far-flung tenants to justify the long ride.

The sun was a good deal lower in the western sky when Colin rode back into the tower house yard.

The sight that greeted him brought an abrupt halt to his riant mood.

Seumas O'Hanlon stood before the doorway leading to the great hall, a gleaming sword gripped tightly in his gnarled hand. Colin had heard seasoned soldiers talk of blood lust, but he had never seen it with his own two eyes. That Seumas O'Hanlon wanted him dead, there could be no doubt. There was also no doubt in Colin's mind as to the reason behind his sudden display of violent hatred.

Giving his horse over to a groomsman, he charily approached the older man.

"Mr. O'Hanlon," he acknowledged his menacing presence with a formal nod of his head.

"Lord Colin Garrick, ye have dishonored the fairest flower in Ireland. I demand ye give me satisfaction."

Colin stared into his piercing green eyes. O'Hanlon might be bad-mannered, and he most definitely had done his best to be an annoying hindrance to his pursuit of pleasure, but he had no desire to kill him. They were grossly mismatched. A duel between them would be a slaughter. Even if O'Hanlon proved himself to be a far more worthy swordsman than he looked to be, Lord Colin knew his greater size and youth gave him unfair advantage.

"I will not fight you," he stated calmly.

Seumas's expression remained unchanged. "I demand ye give me satisfaction," he repeated.

Keeping one eye on O'Hanlon, Colin surreptitiously glanced around the tower yard. "Where is Meary?"

"I know not. She ran out of the great hall some time ago. Where she be matters not. This be between ye and me." Seumas spat the words at him.

"She told you what happened today on the heath," Colin stated the obvious.

Seumas nodded.

"And she asked you to kill me for it?"

"Nay. Honor demands that I kill ye."

Colin was relieved to learn Meary was not behind this lunacy, but he still had O'Hanlon with whom to deal. Choosing his words carefully and keeping his tone peaceable, he said, "Surely, your sense of honor can be

197

satisfied in some other, less bloody, way. If I agree to fight you, it is you who will die not I. You cannot have overlooked such an obvious fact."

Seumas stood soldier straight. "I know what I be about."

"You cannot hope to win."

"I can be hoping anything I damn well please. Ye may possess superior size and strength, but I possess a pure heart."

Colin did not contest his proclamation of moral superiority but dryly observed, "I have had the misfortune to witness more than one pure-hearted man die at the sword of one less noble."

"If that is what God wills, so be it."

Colin could see there was no arguing with the man, not while the wound to his fatherly sensibilities was so fresh. He was more than a little surprised and irritated with Meary for running to her mentor with the tale of her seduction at first opportunity. From her words on the heath, he had thought her reluctant to spread the news. At the very least, she could have forewarned him of her intention to bring O'Hanlon into her counsel. Unfortunately, ruminating over her motives would have to be postponed till a more convenient time. At present he must find some way to dissuade O'Hanlon from committing suicide. Mayhap a good night's sleep would help him see reason. "We can talk about this again in the morning," Colin stated firmly.

"We will be settling it now."

Colin remained adamant. "Duels are traditionally fought at dawn."

"I made a promise to Meary I would be seeing this done without delay. Draw yer sword."

Meary again. Was she behind this after all? Whether she was or not, made him no less reluctant to engage in an inequitable battle. "I will not fight you," he repeated his original assertion.

"Then I will skewer ye like the pig ye are," Seumas vowed.

"You will hang for the pleasure."

"'Tis a price I'll gladly pay."

Raising his sword, Seumas bellowed a war cry and lunged.

Colin deftly side stepped the maneuver, unsheathing his sword as he turned to face his opponent. The man was plainly committed to orchestrating his own demise, and Lord Colin resigned himself to doing battle. At least he could be grateful O'Hanlon did not possess a pistol, he muttered to himself as he parried the first blow.

The ringing clash of the swords as Colin met Seumas's crude thrusts with expert parries immediately drew a sizable crowd. A footman and a steward stepped forward to offer assistance, but Colin stayed their hand with a firm, "Do not interfere."

When Annie arrived on the scene, he was forced to repeat the warning.

Colin deflected some blows and evaded others. Occasionally, he engaged in a brief riposte just to keep the fight interesting, but O'Hanlon's defensive maneuvers were as crude as his offense, and he had to take great care not to draw blood. He did not want the fight to end too soon. If O'Hanlon demanded vengeance, he would give it to him.

Their blades sang each time their swords clashed as they circled each other, wielding their weapons through a rapid succession of lunges, thrusts, and parries. . . .

The thunder of horse hooves followed by a piercing scream caused Colin to tense, but he did not let himself be distracted.

"Nay!" Meary leapt off her mount, landing in the dust with a dull thud. Scrambling to her feet, she ran toward the sound of clashing swords and threw herself between the two men.

"Somebody be holding her back," Seumas ordered, his face going pale as his blade whished past her wrist. Before anyone could respond, Meary hurled herself against Lord Colin, clutching the fabric of his shirt.

"Ye must stop this! Please, I beg of ye! He won't listen to me. Make him understand I care naught for honor. Make this stop!"

Any doubts Colin had had about Meary vanished with one look at her anguished face. Whatever the reason behind her confession to O'Hanlon, this duel was not a result she supported. She was as out of her mind with panic as O'Hanlon was out of his mind with vengeance. "I tried to put him off. He will not listen to reason."

"Then refuse to fight!"

"Meary! Be getting yerself out of the way so I can be running him through."

Meary ignored Seumas and continued to cling to Colin. "Please."

"If I could do as you ask, I would, but I cannot. You must trust me to settle this as I see fit." Colin signaled for two men to take her from him.

Each grabbed an arm, dragging her kicking and screaming from the field of battle. The clang of metal striking metal echoed in her ears.

"Nay! Nay! Somebody stop them! Do not let them be doing this dreadful thing," Meary beseeched over and over as she strained against the hands shackling her arms.

The soul sickening din of battle raged on unabated. Over and over Meary heard their swords come together with biting force. She writhed with every clangorous blow.

Naked terror caused each breath she drew to congeal in her throat. How could these people stand by and do nothing? How could they let one good man die at the hand of another? It was obscene.

Seumas's roars of vengeance preceded the shrill swish of a blade slicing the air; then, the clash of metal assaulted her ears. He cursed fiercely as blade met blade again and again. He was breathing hard. The shuffle of feet was accompanied by more sword play. Lord Colin's movements were less distinguishable, but his mood was all too palpable. She could feel a grim determination emanating from him as he fought.

The darkness was suffocating her. To hear and not see the battle raging before her was unbearable. Her heart pummeled her ribs. Numbness born in her fingers and toes, prickled up her limbs. "Nay! Nay!" she continued to scream at both the combatants and the immobile crowd, each plea becoming more strident and desperate. She was oblivious to the painful bruises her writhing caused her wrists and upper arms; oblivious to the pain filled grunts of the men she struggled to escape.

"Relax child." Annie's voice was of a sudden beside her. Her hand gently stroked Meary's cheek. "My Colin has the battle well in hand."

"He must not be allowed to kill Seumas."

"He will not kill him," Annie assured her.

"How do ye know?"

"Because he defends himself but does not attack."

"And Seumas?"

"That old fool is doing his best to smite my Colin, but he's no match for him. He swings his sword like a club. He'll soon wear himself out, and this unfortunate business will be over."

It was not Annie's words so much as the calm way she spoke them that gave Meary comfort. That small comfort combined with the encroaching numbness weakening her limbs caused her to strain against her captors a little less vigorously, but she did not give up her efforts to get loose.

"Are ye sure neither will be hurt?"

"Quite certain. Mr. O'Hanlon possesses the will but not the skill to inflict harm. My Colin possesses the skill but not the will. I'm sorry to see them come to blows. I had hoped we could avoid this. But when it is over, you and my Colin will be free to pursue your romance."

If Meary had been less preoccupied with trying to wrest herself free to stop the duel while simultaneously trying to follow the progress of the battle by keenly attending every ring of the swords and every intake of breath, she might have been more conscious of the matter-of-fact tone which Annie used when speaking of the "romance" between herself and Lord Colin. She might have wondered how much Annie knew. But her mind was consumed with more onerous matters, and she gave Annie's last words no consideration.

Annie continued to stroke her cheek and speak to her in soothing tones, sometimes providing her with a running commentary on the scene being played out before them, sometimes reassuring her that neither man would come to harm.

202

"There, you see. It's almost over," Annie announced. "His lordship is about to put an end to it."

Every muscle in Meary's body clenched.

"Do you yield?" Lord Colin's voice resounded over the silent crowd.

"He has him pinned to the wall and his blade to his throat," Annie whispered.

"Nay!" Seumas growled.

There was a pause; then, their swords met again.

"What 'tis happening?" Meary demanded, renewing her efforts to get free.

"He's forcing his lordship to play with him a little while longer. Don't be alarmed. Mr. O'Hanlon is very winded. He'll be obliged to give up his stubbornness and yield soon."

The clashing of swords continued to assault Meary's ears. It helped mitigate her terror to have Annie be her eyes, but what helped far more was Lord Colin's refusal to slay Seumas when he had had the opportunity. She had wanted to believe Annie's assessment of the situation, but until that moment, her faith in it had perished with every fresh clang of their blades.

The panic in Meary's breast gradually began to ebb enough so that, on occasion, she was able to draw in a full breath of air. Her heart still pounded like a cannonball bombarding the walls of her chest, and she had lost all feeling in her limbs, but the whirling chaos of fearful emotions and terrifying thoughts overwhelming her mind began to spin a little slower.

Though Meary measured the time as hours, in truth it was only a matter of minutes before Lord Colin was once again demanding, "Do you yield?"

"Nay!" Seumas wheezed.

The din of battle resumed.

The same scene was played out thrice more—each time Seumas's refusal to yield sounding more ragged but no less determined.

"Old fool," Annie hissed under her breath. "He should not press my Colin's patience too far."

Before Meary could demand the housekeeper explain the extent of the danger to Seumas implied by her statement, Annie let out a shrill gasp.

"What? Has Seumas been wounded? Ye must tell me!" Meary commanded as she frantically landed a series of vicious kicks on the shins of one of the men holding her back. She applied her teeth to the wrist of the other, but they both held fast.

"It's not your Mr. O'Hanlon but my Colin," Annie lamented.

"Lord Colin has been hurt?" Meary cried. "Nay! Let me go! I must go to him!"

The length of time Annie took to answer her caused the alarm in Meary's breast to increase sevenfold.

"His arm is bleeding, but he doesn't look to have lost any of his fight," Annie informed her when she had satisfied herself the wound was superficial.

Meary's anguish and fear for Colin's life shifted to Seumas. If Lord Colin's patience had been nearing its end before, surely receiving the wound would assure its demise. No man, even the most small-minded Irishman, would accuse him of playing foul if he cut Seumas down. Time and time again, Lord Colin had given Seumas the opportunity to yield.

Though the world might rightfully credit Lord Colin with gentlemanly restraint and forgive him for killing Seumas, Meary knew such would not be possible for her.

Neither would she be able to forgive herself. Seumas had been her mentor and faithful friend for too long. She loved him too much. If Seumas died . . .

The black world Meary lived in began to swirl. Her beloved Seumas could not die. She could not accept it, would not accept it. She would break loose and stop this insanity. She had to break loose. She had to break loose. She had to break loose. . . . Frantically, she wrestled in vain to free herself.

The knell of their swords spurred her struggles. She tried to shout but no sound came from her lips. Anything. I will give ye anything if ye will spare Seumas's life, she vowed, willing the words to be heard in Lord Colin's head. Again and again, she repeated the vow, praying to every saint in heaven to carry the message to Lord Colin and praying even harder for him to heed it.

The clash of metal against metal continued to reverberate in her ears. She could hear Seumas laboring for breath. His roars of vengeance were now whispers barely discernible from his wheezing gasps, but still their swords rang out their song of death. Did Seumas yet persist in his attack, or did he now only defend his life?

A sword clattered to the ground. A body hit the earth with a dull thud. The blood in Meary's veins froze.

The air hung heavy with silence. Then, everyone was talking at once.

Chapter 14

"It's all over, my dear," Annie announced. "Oh, my, you're pale as a ghost and your skin feels like ice. Let her go, you two brutes. I'm sure she'll be wanting to go to Mr. O'Hanlon."

"Is he dead?" Meary squeaked.

"Merciful heavens, no. He's merely fainted from exhaustion. Wore himself out just as I said he would. Of course, I didn't think he'd be quite so mule-headed, but now that I consider the man, I suppose I should have guessed it'd not be in him to know when to give up. Lucky he didn't fall on his own sword." Annie clasped Meary's hand. "Come along. I'll take you to him and you can see for yourself."

As Annie pulled Meary in tow, she shouted orders. "You, fetch me a rag and a pitcher of cool water. Niall, I'll be needing you to carry Mr. O'Hanlon to his room. The rest of you, get back to your duties."

When they reached Seumas, Meary dropped to her knees and cradled his head in her lap. Despite Annie's assurances, it was not until Meary had run her hands the length and breadth of him and found him unscathed she truly believed he had not come to some grave harm. His heart raced within his chest and his breathing was heavy, but both were hale. She kissed his sweat stained brow and tenderly stroked the hair at his temples.

"Ah, Seumas, 'tis sorry I am for bringing this misery upon ye. I never meant for any of this to be happening. Never," she whispered to him.

"Let Niall have him. You can say whatever you feel needs to be said after we have him snug in bed," Annie admonished. Gently but firmly, she urged Meary to her feet.

Meary did not resist. Still half numb from trauma, she meekly allowed Annie to lead her into the house and up the stairs. Once they arrived in Seumas's room, she was unceremoniously plopped onto a chair near the side of his bed and left to sit and feel useless.

Listening to Annie bustle about the room, Meary knew Seumas's care was in capable hands. She heard his boots drop to the floor, followed by the softer sound of his garments. The bedding was pulled back. The mattress rustled as Seumas was positioned between the sheets; then, the air stirred as the blankets were tucked back in place.

The maid arrived with the rag and pitcher of water and left again. The trickling of water greeted Meary's ears as Annie dipped the rag and squeezed out the excess moisture. The rag moved from pitcher to Seumas's brow several times as Meary sat silent by his bedside.

After a few minutes, Meary heard Seumas begin to toss and turn on his mattress. A moment later he expelled a groggy groan and called out to her, in a hoarse whisper, "Meary?"

"I'm right here, Seumas." She reached for his hand and laced her fingers with his.

"Did I kill him?"

"Nay."

"I thought not," he lamented.

"Go back to sleep you old fool," Annie scolded him. "You've caused enough trouble for one day."

As if the housekeeper's words carried the force of magic, the room was of a sudden filled with the sound of Seumas's rhythmic snores.

Meary held fast to Seumas's hand, listening to Annie sniff and tsk as she finished tucking her charge into bed. There was something soothing about the housekeeper's workaday manner. So much had happened to Meary in the space of but a few hours, that though she judged Annie's behavior odd, she welcomed its steadying effect on her frayed nerves.

Now that Meary had had time to assure herself of Seumas's healthy condition, her concern turned to Lord Colin. That Annie was tending to Seumas and not to her master was proof enough Lord Colin's wound was not serious, but that he had been injured at all caused Meary's eyes to well with tears. Her head understood Seumas's desire for revenge, but her heart judged herself every bit as blameworthy as Lord Colin. He should not have been called upon to pay the price of their transgression while she received nothing but compassion from her mentor. That Lord Colin had been forced to defend his life and refrained from taking Seumas's weighed heavily with her. It was a debt she could never hope to repay, and she had not forgotten her vow. "Where is Lord Colin?"

"Standing in the yard was where I left him."

Meary started to rise from her chair. "I should thank him for sparing Seumas."

"There'll be time enough for that. Leave him be a little while," Annie advised as she puttered about the room.

"But . . ."

"But nothing. I'm sure he knows you appreciate him sparing your friend here. He needs time to recover himself."

"'Tis his wound worse then ye have told me?" Meary asked in alarm, bolting the rest of her way to her feet.

"No. I'll be tending it just as soon as I finish here, but I doubt it's more than a scratch."

"Then why must he recover himself?"

Annie gently pushed Meary back down on her chair. "Dueling takes a lot out of a man, especially when he cannot allow himself to kill an opponent who sincerely wants him dead."

"I will be eternally grateful he did not kill Seumas, but why do ye say he *could not* kill him?" Meary queried. "He is English; we are Irish. Seumas issued the challenge to him, not he to Seumas. He gave Seumas many chances to yield. No one would have condemned him had he struck him down."

"You would condemn him."

"Aye," Meary acknowledged. "I could not help meself. But I would condemn meself in equal measure."

"I know you would, and I think my Colin knows it as well. He would not want you to think ill of yourself."

"But I am naught to him."

"You're his lover."

Meary blushed, but she made no attempt to deny the truth. "Does the whole world already know?" she asked.

"It don't take a scholar to deduce why Mr. O'Hanlon

209

of a sudden challenged my Colin to a duel."

"By the morrow the whole county *will* know of me shame," Meary morosely predicted.

"Like as not. But don't be too downcast. It'll be old gossip in a fortnight," Annie promised.

It was small comfort to be informed one's life-shattering crises were barely worthy of notice in the wider world, but it did help restore Meary's sense of perspective. Thousands of maidens had been laid low by temptation before her and thousands would follow. Rather than worry about public censure, she would do better to concentrate her energies on dealing with the results of her failings.

"If ye think I should wait to be thanking Lord Colin, I will do as ye wish," she said.

"Very wise." Annie patted her shoulder and removed Meary's hand from Seumas's, placing it on Meary's lap. "Now, what I wish you to do is sit here and rest yourself. To be blunt, my dear, you look in far worse shape than Mr. O'Hanlon and his lordship put together." Before Meary could argue, Annie continued, "I also want you to keep a careful watch over this old man until I get back. We don't want him waking up and trying to dispatch our Colin again."

Our Colin? Meary's stomach tightened at the change of pronoun. She unconsciously rubbed the bruises on her wrists. Annie seemed to accept her change in status from guest to paramour in stride. Meary was uncertain whether to feel comforted or insulted. She was glad she did not have to face Annie's castigation, but the housekeeper's lack of surprise at the recent turn of events was rather off-putting. It had been a long time since Meary had seen her face in a mirror, but she did not remember her countenance to one that advertised a deficiency of moral fortitude.

"Well, I've finished my work here," Annie declared. "I'll be back in a bit. Don't be distressed if I'm gone over long. There was a calamity brewing in the kitchen before the duel began, and if someone else hasn't dealt with it—which I doubt considering the way things go around here—I must tend to it as well as our Colin."

Meary sat erect as she listened to the retreat of Annie's footsteps followed by the bang of the heavy chamber door against its frame. She maintained her stiff posture for several minutes, staring sightless in the direction of the door; then her carriage crumpled, and she hid her face in her hands.

For a long time she sat there, letting the myriad of thoughts roiling in her mind assault her at will. Over and over again the events of the day played themselves out in her aching head. Each thought brought with it a resurgence of the terror or passion or shame or joy that had accompanied the moment. She made no effort to organize her thoughts or pass judgment on her feelings. She was too emotionally spent to attempt such a formidable task.

Seumas continued to evince his deep slumber with a chorus of wooly snores. Meary found the sound of his steady breathing comforting. She envied the temporary oblivion he seemed to have found in sleep.

To escape her thoughts would be heaven on earth, but despite her exhaustion, Meary knew it would be a long time before she was able to find repose. Even when she did, she knew her sleep would be filled with dreams—dreams of Lord Colin.

What she now felt for him, she wasn't certain. She was

no longer certain of anything. She judged by now she ought to be accustomed to living in a constant state of confusion, but she was not. The relentless chaos and contradictions were making her feel physically ill. She couldn't go on living like this. Meary knew she must try to make decisions about how she would deal with her situation or lose the last remnants of her sanity.

At first, when her mind began the intimidating task of trying to sort out her thoughts and feelings, she was prone to grasp at preposterous solutions to her dilemma. If Annie possessed the power to order Seumas to sleep like a babe, mayhap Annie could order Lord Colin out of her head and heart. . . . She could run away and live the rest of her life as a hermit. . . . She could pretend this day never happened.

As late afternoon eased into evening, Meary's turn of thought became more rational. Seumas slept because he had pushed himself to the edge of his endurance. She liked the company of people too much to be a hermit. No matter how hard she might try, she could not pretend the day away. She must face reality whether she liked it or not.

She could not conveniently forget her vow to "give anything." Lord Colin had spared Seumas's life. Whether or not he would have done so regardless of the silent bargain she had made through the powers of heaven, it mattered not. The vow had been made and must be kept.

Meary was grateful to have her thoughts interrupted by a knock at the door. Doreen entered bearing a bowl of soup and thick slices of buttered bread on a tray.

"How be ye?"

Meary managed a wan smile. "Fine."

"Annie bids ye eat. She says to be telling ye she'll be up shortly."

Picking up the spoon, Meary stirred the soup about. The aroma of chicken broth laden with vegetables wafted up from the bowl, tickling her nostrils, but she had little appetite.

Feeling Doreen watching her, she forced herself to take a sip for politeness sake. "Tell Annie 'tis delicious," she said.

The moment Doreen left the room Meary lay the spoon aside.

Lord Colin fingered the bandage on his left arm and scowled so fiercely he sent the maid carrying the bowl of water Annie had used to cleanse his wound scurrying from the room.

"Is it your wound paining you or your conscience?" Annie asked, knowing full well the minor wound she had just bound had nothing to do with his dark look.

"What are you prattling about?" Colin snapped. "I didn't kill the old man. He left the battlefield with nary a scratch unless he contrived to injure himself when he fainted."

"Oh, I wasn't thinking of Mr. O'Hanlon. Your behavior toward him was above reproach," Annie assured him as she planted her feet on the floor before him. "One would not be stretching the truth to say it was noble."

"I doubt Meary will think so," he grumbled, folding his arms across his chest and pouting like a little boy just denied his favorite toy.

"Then you've misjudged her," Annie charged, secretly smiling at his childish posture. "She feels very grateful to you. She told me so herself."

Ignoring Annie's response, he continued to bemoan his bad fortune. "The man is half my size and twice my age. It never occurred to me he would challenge me to a duel."

"Nor to me. But what's done is done."

Colin started to ask Annie why, if she was so understanding about the duel, she would inquire if his conscience was bothering him, but his instinct for self-preservation counseled him to keep quiet on the matter.

Her earlier statement suddenly registered, and he sat a little straighter. Mayhap matters were not as gloomy as they seemed. "She is feeling grateful?"

"Yes, poor dear." Annie's expression was all concern and sympathy. "I think the duel was hardest on her."

"She hasn't made herself sick?" Colin demanded.

"No. All she needs is a little rest. She'll be fine by morning. You must admit, she's had a very trying day."

Colin nodded. "The duel unsettled her, of course."

"The duel and other *unsettling* events," Annie amended, looking Colin directly in the eye to let him know she was fully aware of everything that had happened that day.

"Hmmn," he growled. Annie was not stupid, and Colin assumed she had quickly deduced the reason behind the duel. He also assumed she would not approve of his pursuit of lusty pleasures, but he had not expected her to directly confront him about his behavior.

When it was clear he did not intend to elaborate, Annie prodded him. "Well?"

"My personal behavior is my business and mine alone."

Annie bobbed a curtsy and continued to stare him in the eye. "Yes, *Lord* Colin."

"Do you censure me?"

"On the contrary. I am quite pleased with you."

Colin's irritated expression turned to one of confusion. "Pleased?"

"Yes. Of course, if you want to shut me out of such an important part of your life, I can't stop you. Just because I have loved you since the day you were born is of no consequence."

"Do not play that game with me, Annie. It is beneath you. If you have something to say, say it."

Annie was instantly penitent. "I want you to inform me of your intentions concerning that pretty maiden upstairs."

"I intend to enjoy her company."

"For how long?"

"Until I tire of her."

"And what if she tires of you first? What will you do then?" she demanded.

Colin glowered at her. He had successfully banished that glum possibility from his mind, and he did not appreciate having it brought back to bear. Eager to oust it once again, he gave Annie an answer designed to quiet her. "She is free to leave my home any time she pleases."

"Are you sure?" On that cryptic question, Annie left him sitting alone in the great hall.

"Meddling woman," Colin muttered as he slipped on the fresh shirt she had brought him. He had enough to concern him without wasting time puzzling out what vagaries spun beneath her mop of greying hair.

His chief concern was Meary, but Seumas O'Hanlon was not far behind in his thoughts. He had complete confidence he could defend himself against any new assaults the old man chose to launch against his person, but he had no more wish to expend his energy on him than he did on his meddling housekeeper. He could hope the man would consider the matter settled; he could hope he could depend on O'Hanlon's sense of fair play, but he was not optimistic it would be so. O'Hanlon had been like a rabid wolf out in the yard. He was not convinced he would conveniently come to his senses.

Then there was Brendan. As soon as he returned with Pansy someone was sure to apprise him of the situation. Need he guard against additional attacks from that pup? Meary exercised more control over the younger man than she did over her mentor, but who knew what violence his devotion to her would invoke, especially if O'Hanlon chose to egg him on.

His thoughts circled back to the inspiration for all this fierce devotion. He had seen with his own eyes how distraught Meary had been over the duel. He had never seen such anguish on another human being's face. He knew her primary concern was for his opponent's safety, but he hoped at least a little of that anxiety was for him.

Probably not, he sullenly concluded. She was probably sitting up in O'Hanlon's room thinking him a villain. He was sure she blamed him for this day's events. If he had not seduced her, there would have been no duel. Annie said she was grateful he had spared O'Hanlon, but how grateful? Grateful enough to honor his twenty-four hour injunction? He doubted that very much.

He would most likely have to force the issue, and the thought left a bad taste in his mouth. It would have been so much better if Meary had had the opportunity to accept the inevitable and come to him instead of him going to her. He wanted them to be on friendly terms. He wanted her to be comfortable with his attentions, wanted her to gain pleasure from being his lover.

Even without the complication of the duel, that was probably expecting too much, he chided himself. He was not the sort of man who inspired affection. He had simply been in the right place at the right time and been able to take advantage of the flowering of her physical needs. The best he should hope for was that she would accept the situation without giving him too much trouble.

It would be nice if it could be different. . . .

Colin tightened his hands into fists. Fanciful imaginings were for poets and buffoons, and he was neither. He would have to take what he could get.

For now he would take comfort in the fact, by his own word, he would not be required to act until tomorrow. When her reprieve ended, and still she had not come to him, then he could decide how he wanted to proceed. That he would have her in his arms again, he was determined. He could exercise understanding and patience tonight. That much he would give her. On the morrow he could decide if he was willing to give her more.

"Seumas, ye have been sleeping so long, I was starting to become concerned for ye." Meary laid her hand on his brow and found it cool as he stirred to wakefulness. "Are ye feeling better now?"

He pushed himself to a sitting position. "What time be it?"

"I know not. Past the supper hour," Meary offered what she did know.

"'Tis getting dark outside," he confirmed.

217

"Are ye hungry? I can have Doreen fetch ye some soup. 'Tis quite tasty."

"Ye have barely touched yers."

"I was not hungry."

"Neither am I."

Minutes ticked by.

"I was pleased to see ye'd overcome yer reluctance to sit atop a horse," Seumas commented.

Meary nodded. She had been so intent on preventing the duel that the new fear had overwhelmed the old. She had not even realized the significance behind what she had done until Seumas had mentioned it. It should be cause for celebration, but she was not in a celebratory mood.

More minutes ticked by.

"Brendan came up to see ye," Meary volunteered.

"Does he know?"

"Aye."

Tension hung thick as curdled milk in the air, souring the rapport that had always been the crowning comfort of their relationship. Meary shifted on her chair, trying to think of the right thing to say.

"'Tis sorry I am I failed ye." Seumas was the first to break the heavy silence.

"Ye have not failed me," Meary softly insisted.

"I did not send him to his maker."

"I'm glad of it." Her voice took on more strength. "Though I begged ye not to, ye have had your duel. Honor has been satisfied."

"Nay."

"Aye. The fight has been fought. Ye cannot challenge a man to a second duel for the same offense. The honor that almost took your life, now will be saving of it. Honor

218

demands ye let the matter be."

"It pains me greatly that ye be right," Seumas muttered. "Go to yer room and pack yer trunk. We will leave at first light."

Meary turned her face away from his. "I cannot do as ye ask."

"Why not?" he petitioned. "Ye said yerself, ye were ready to leave."

"That was before the duel."

"And if we stay, what will become of ye?" he demanded.

"I know not."

"Do ye intend to give yerself to him again?" The tone of his voice said the question was posed as a goad to make her think through to the consequences, not to solicit information.

Wrapping her arms around her waist Meary shrugged.

"A sighing of the shoulders be no answer."

She acknowledged his statement with a nod and remained silent a long while before admitting, "I fear ye will despise me for the answer."

"Why Meary?" Seumas beseeched in utter disbelief. He reached for her hand, holding tight, as if the physical connection would somehow provide a conduit for understanding. "What power does the man have over ye to make ye do this thing ye know 'tis wrong?"

In stark contrast to Seumas's emotion charged response, Meary's voice was composed. Her composure was born of many hours of deliberation and a firm belief she was doing what integrity demanded must be done. "I made a promise. If he spared your life, I said I would give him anything. I know not if he still wants me, but if he does, I cannot deny him."

"A man who would be exacting such a promise from a maiden be no man at all but a devil," Seumas fumed.

"He did not exact the promise. I said it in me heart during the heat of the battle."

Seumas's voice lost a little of its sharp edge. "If he does not know of it, he cannot demand ye keep it."

"*I* know of it," Meary argued. "I have already forsaken me personal code of decency once this day. I will not do it again."

"Ye are too good for the likes of him," he protested.

"Nay." The word was spoken as a sigh. "I am no better nor worse."

"He be a viper!"

"He spared your life," she calmly countered. "For that I would pay him any price even if I knew him to be the vilest man on earth."

"There be none viler."

"Nay. He is a good man."

"How can ye be saying that after what he has done to ye?"

"Because 'tis the truth. I am no more happy to be finding meself in this position than ye are, but I will not be assigning Lord Colin all the blame for what happened between us. We must share it equally."

"But ye were an innocent!" Seumas expressed his outrage at her magnanimity, and he held onto her hand even tighter.

"I could have said him nay. He would not have forced himself upon me."

"Ye cannot know that."

"Aye, I can." She made the statement with such conviction that Seumas knew it was futile to argue the point. He tried a different tactic.

220

"Ye say he did not force himself upon ye. Be he absolved of sin because he chose to use a soft voice and trickery rather than brute force against ye?"

Meary shook her head. She wished she knew how to find the words to make Seumas understand. She had made her decision, and she knew this one was a right one. "I never proclaimed him guiltless. Only that I am equally at fault. If ye hate him for what has happened between us, ye must hate me also."

"I could never hate ye," Seumas firmly rejected her conclusion.

"Then, pray, do not hate him. 'Tis unfair to judge us differently for the same sin."

Seumas's next words, spoken after an interminable silence, were a miserable statement of fact rather than a question even though he posed it as such. "So, ye are committed to yer own destruction?"

"I am committed to keeping my word. What will follow, only the saints can say."

Chapter 15

Meary paced the width of her bedchamber, alternately wringing her hands and chewing her fingernails.

Before leaving Seumas in Annie's care she had made him swear he would not attempt to assault Lord Colin's person again. She could not secure his promise he would refrain from interfering altogether, but at least she need no longer fear for either man's safety.

Telling Seumas she intended to give herself to Lord Colin, if it was his wish, had been wrenching. She had known it would be, but she had not realized how difficult the conversation would prove. He had not shaken her resolve, but his words had left her trembling. Meary felt his profound disappointment in her. She shared his disappointment, but her chagrin arose wholly from what she had already done rather than what she was about to do.

In her mind, giving herself to Lord Colin again was a minor transgression when compared to their making love on the heath. Then she had had no worthy reason compelling her to submit. She had been compelled by

222

naught but lust. Now, she owed an enormous debt of gratitude. She could not take back her virginity no matter how much she might want to do so. Having already lost her virtue, she judged becoming Lord Colin's mistress a small price to pay for Seumas's life. And mayhap humbling herself before the world would atone for her sin of pride.

Despite her reasoning, Meary found when faced with the actual task of informing Lord Colin of her decision, she quaked at the thought. If she had found his lovemaking repugnant, it would be easier to do what she felt she must. But she had not been repulsed. She had been pleasured beyond her wildest imaginings. What if the pleasure she found in his arms nullified the penance of humbling herself? What if she was deluding herself and using her promise to give Lord Colin anything he wanted as a convenient excuse to experience again the sensual delights of his lovemaking?

Nay! If not for her promise, she would not feel compelled to go to him. She would ignore his demand she reconcile herself to being his lover by tomorrow afternoon. She would pack her trunk and flee further temptation. She needed to believe such of herself. To do otherwise was to name her whole life before this day a fraud.

Meary told herself there was always the possibility that being forced into a duel because of her had been so annoying to Lord Colin that when she went to him he would no longer want her. The thought comforted not at all. She did not for a moment believe it.

Distraught as she was, when she had made her vow, she had known in her heart what she was offering to give. Deluding herself with false hopes was childish.

Her situation was untenable and an hour more of pacing did not make it any less so.

The household was all abed now. She had not heard anyone stirring for quite some time. She ought to be in bed herself, getting a good night's sleep to fortify herself for the day to come. The trouble was she knew she would not sleep.

Nevertheless, having some course of action was better than having none at all. Meary took a protracted length of time to strip down to her chemise, taking elaborate care to fold each discarded item of clothing neatly and lay it in her trunk.

She exchanged the chemise she wore for a fresh one, folding the soiled chemise as carefully as she had her other garments before laying it aside to be laundered.

She gave equal attention to her hair—combing out every tangle, brushing it until her scalp began to ache, then meticulously plaiting it into a single braid.

When she had exhausted every excuse to delay retiring, she pulled back the covers and climbed into bed.

Tossing and turning for well over an hour, Meary was no closer to falling asleep than when she had first retired. She sat up, hugging her knees to her chest, and sighed loudly. After spending considerable time worrying about the morrow in this position, she lay down again, only to toss and turn some more.

Finally, she gave up, announcing to the empty room as she swung her legs over the side of the bed, " 'Tis impossible."

She had sealed her fate with her desperately made vow, and the sooner she faced it, the sooner she would learn to accept it. The doing of the deed could not be any worse than sitting here dreading it.

Meary was sure Lord Colin would not be pleased to have his sleep interrupted, but she could see no help for it. She would be a madwoman by morning if she did not settle this now.

Padding across her room on her bare feet, she edged her door open and stepped into the gallery. Meary took a deep breath, closed the door behind her, then began the laborious task of forcing one foot in front of the other.

She knew Lord Colin's room lay at the end of a second flight of stairs at the top of the tower. Upon locating the staircase, she began the long climb to what she could only view as an ambivalent future.

By the time she reached Lord Colin's door, Meary's heart was pounding and her breath was coming in shallow gasps. It was not the climb but anxiety that caused her body to respond thusly. Only the knowledge that returning to her room to fret the night away would be worse than facing what lay before her propelled Meary to open the door.

Her ears were immediately greeted with the rustling of a mattress followed by the whish of a sword as it cut through the air.

"Who goes there?" Lord Colin demanded.

"Meary," she said, easing the door closed behind her. "Please, I beg ye, do not speak so loudly."

She heard him lay his sword aside.

"I feared it might be your friend Mr. O'Hanlon come to finish what he could not this afternoon."

"Nay. 'Tis just me," Meary assured him. "And ye need not worry about Seumas. He has given me his word he will not seek to harm ye again."

"Is his word trustworthy in this case?"

"Aye. He would have refused to give it rather than

225

swear falsely to me." Lacing her fingers together, she continued, "I am not saying he will behave civilly toward ye. I fear he will never be able to bring himself to do that. But he will not challenge ye to another duel, and never would he resort to the methods of a common criminal to slay ye. Seumas is a man of honor."

"I am glad to hear it."

The sound of flint striking steel was shortly followed by the odor of melting tallow.

"Please, do not be lighting a candle."

"Why not?"

"I do not wish ye to be seeing me."

Lord Colin did as she asked but not before noting she stood before him in naught but a lace-trimmed lawn chemise. Though the garment hung loose, the candle-light illuminated the sensuous curves of her figure through the sheer fabric. "A beautiful woman should be proud to be seen," he protested.

"I cannot be proud of why I am here."

"Come closer and tell me why you are here."

Meary took two steps only away from the door. She could not discern the color of his mood from the tone of his voice. He did not sound angry, but neither did he sound pleased to see her here. She pressed the palms of her tightly laced hands together and rocked her weight from heel to toe several times before firmly centering her weight. "I have come to tell ye of me decision concerning ye and me," she informed him.

Lord Colin braced himself to hear her tell him she would not be his lover. Her expression was too grim for her decision to be one that would bring him joy. Why she had come in the middle of the night dressed only in a chemise to deliver such a message intrigued him more than a little. That she had yet to find sleep was evinced by the shadows he had seen under her eyes. The furrow in her brow named distress over the day's events the cause. He credited her lack of dress to her blindness. She could not know how revealing the fabric was and was plainly too distraught to be aware of her state of undress.

Lord Colin waited, every muscle tense, not knowing if he was ruthless enough to use any means available to coerce her into changing her mind. There were several avenues he could follow to gain his own ends, but none that he liked. He clenched his jaw. His trouble was, try as he might, he just couldn't think of Meary as nothing but an engaging plaything. He was too aware of her vulnerabilities, too aware of her pain.

Still, he did not want her to leave him *yet*. The time might come when he would willingly let her go, but that time was not now. If he could think of some noble way to win her over, he would use it, but he could not. He was faced with two distasteful options: lose an enchanting lover or resort to emotional extortion.

The silence between them stretched taut as a bowstring. Lord Colin relit the candle. Still, she did not speak.

"You have come here to tell me of a decision," he prompted.

"Aye."

"What is that decision?"

Meary lowered her chin to her chest, then slowly raised it again. Her lips quivered as she carefully formed each word. "I have come to tell ye . . . I am prepared to give ye anything in me command to give. If it is your desire that I keep ye company in your bed I will do so . . . *willingly*." Meary suffered on the last word.

Colin stared at her. Never had he even entertained the

227

hope that this was what she had come to say to him. He told himself it mattered not to him that she had choked on the word "willingly" or that she looked as though she wished to bolt from the room. She had come to him of her own accord. He had not had to coerce her in any way. Only an idiot would take too close a look at the private reasons that had pressured her to make such a decision.

His intellect argued a good case, good enough to override the uncomfortable stirrings in his heart. He had what he wanted, and he fully intended to enjoy his good fortune.

Rising from his bed, he came to Meary. For a long while he simply stood before her, drinking in her shimmering beauty with his gaze. She glowed golden in the candlelight. Every finely carved feature of her face embodied perfection. The gentle slope of her shoulders, the curve of her breasts, the feminine flaring of soft hips—all were without equal in the delight they gave him. When his eyes had drunk their fill, he lifted her hand to his lips and kissed her knuckles.

"Come to bed, sweet lover," he whispered.

Meary meekly followed as he led her to his bed.

Chapter 16

Warm breath wafting across her cheek caressed Meary as she stirred to wakefulness. It was an ethereal sensation, almost imperceptible, but exceedingly soothing.

She stretched against Lord Colin, snuggling closer against his side and pillowing her head on his chest. Her cheek crushed a thick matt of hair. Her hand rose, tracing the bandage encircling his arm. Meary's lips tensed into a weak frown before gradually relaxing again. Trailing her fingers across his chest, she stroked from sternum to naval.

His heart beat strong and steady beneath her ear, and his chest rose and fell in the deep rhythms of contented sleep.

Last night she too had slept well. For the first night since coming here her sleep had not been plagued by troubling dreams. This morning she felt refreshed rather than discomposed. The world felt solid. Coming here last night and humbling herself must have been the right decision. How else could she explain the unexpected peace she had gained? She could think of no other logical reason.

Lying abed with a man who was not one's husband should not be heart-salving. Everything she had ever been taught and everything she had ever believed said it could not.

But there was no denying, when Lord Colin had made love to her last night, she had been engulfed by a sensation of deep contentment. He had held her gently, sheltered her, and worshiped her body with his words and hands and lips. He had nurtured her soul all the while he tantalized her senses. It was an odd transaction—all the more odd that a saturnine man like Lord Colin was its author.

Her brow wrinkled as she was struck by a realization. The feeling Lord Colin's lovemaking evoked within her breast was not unlike the tranquil state she attained when she played her harp. It made no sense. How could two such dissimilar activities produce a similar response?

Meary had no answer to her question.

She felt Lord Colin's muscular form stir beneath her. Stretching, he rolled to his side and pulled her against him.

"Good morning," he greeted heartily.

"Good morning." Meary's salutation was far more tentative.

"What would you like to do today?"

The first reply that materialized in Meary's head caused her cheeks to warm. What she would like to do was make love all day. The tranquility attained from lovemaking was similar to her harp playing in another way also. It was ephemeral. It only kept the world and her worries at bay while she engaged in the activity. Keeping

230

the world at bay held great appeal.

"Can you think of nothing?" Lord Colin queried when she did not respond to his question. He was neither blind to her blush nor ignorant of its cause, but he preferred to hear a request they stay abed from her lips rather than his own.

"We could break our fast then be resuming your language lessons," Meary meekly offered up a conventional agenda.

"We could," Lord Colin acknowledged. "Or we could forego my lesson for today."

Tension lent her voice a little more vigor. "We already neglected your lessons yesterday, and I do not want ye to be getting out of practice."

"You could conduct my lesson right here," he suggested. "For instance, what should I call these?" He brushed his fingertips across her eyelids.

"*Sùil.*"

"And these?" He kissed her lips.

"*Buel.*"

His hand traced the curve of her chin, trailed down the column of her throat, then came to rest on a breast. He lingered there, gently cupping its fullness in his palm before sliding his warm hand to its companion. "And this? What should I call this?"

"*Broilleach.*"

"Broilleach," Lord Colin tested the word as he rubbed her nipples to taut peaks. "Meary O'Byrne you have lovely breasts," he murmured in Gaelic.

She blushed rosy red, and Lord Colin chuckled.

"Lovely scarlet breasts," he amended.

Meary hid her face in the crook of his neck.

"Do you know what I'd like to do today?" he asked,

reverting back to English.

Pretending ignorance with his firm manly appendage jutting against her thigh was impossible. "Aye," she said.

"What say you to satisfying the hungers of the flesh before we feed our bellies?"

"If 'tis what ye desire, I will do as ye desire."

"What do you desire?" he coaxed.

"I desire to be meself again," Meary breathlessly whimpered.

Colin had been hoping to entice her into admitting she desired him every bit as much as he desired her, and he was not pleased with her obscure answer. What did it mean "to be herself again?" She was still herself. He supposed she was trying to tell him she wished she was a virgin still. If she was, he wanted to hear none of it. If by some miracle he could restore her virginity, he would only take it again at first opportunity.

He pulled her more tightly against him. There was nothing to be gained through idle chatter. She was in his bed. She had said she was willing to let him make love to her. If he required more than these fortuitous circum- stances to be satisfied, then he was caviling.

Three weeks had passed, and once again Meary's life had settled in a predictable pattern. More often than not, she and Lord Colin made love before rising. They broke their fast together, and she spent her mornings tutoring him in Gaelic. Afternoons she devoted to her own education and practicing her harp while Lord Colin tended the business of his estate, unless he requested she ride with him. Whatever he asked of her, she gave to him, and she had spent several of her afternoons sitting in the circle of his arms atop his great stallion.

When she did not accompany him, he rejoined her for the evening meal. After, she and Brendan entertained him and members of the household staff with music. Every Saturday evening Lord Colin hosted a dance.

Seumas refused to join them in the making of music, but he exercised his story telling talents with great relish—nightly telling grisly tales of noble Irishmen triumphing over immoral Englishmen, the final scene invariably including a protracted description of the Englishman writhing in hell.

His lack of subtlety made Meary squirm, and she admired Lord Colin for his forbearance. Even when she offered up private apologies, he refused to complain, assuring her Seumas's stories did not bother him and even professing he considered the gruesome tales a healthy way for Seumas to vent his spleen, thus lessening the likelihood of him being overcome by another violent fit of vengeance.

Meary was not so sure, but she didn't argue with him. *Her* relationship with Seumas was precarious at best.

Because of her decision to submit to Lord Colin, there was now a yawning chasm between their once-kindred spirits.

Seumas had made his position abundantly clear. He would respect her decision to stay and submit to Lord Colin's demands upon her person insomuch that he would not interfere, but he would do naught to ease her way. He had told her plainly, he deemed any suffering she brought upon herself as his only hope of saving her. He told her, nightly he prayed she would forsake her vow and her "feelings" and flee this place.

She had thought Seumas of all people would understand why she considered the vow she had made binding. One did not blithely ignore a bargain made with the saints. He knew this, had nurtured her respect for powers unseen, had demonstrated his respect in the conducting of his own life. She could not comprehend why he now wished her to ignore his good counsel and imperil her soul.

Being mistress to Lord Colin might jeopardize her place in heaven, but breaking a hallowed promise would insure that when she departed this earth her soul would be sent straight to hell.

Brendan behaved much as he always did. He spoke little, met her every request without question, and spent as much time as possible in the company of Lord Colin's horses. She had yet to discuss her "change of circumstances" with him. Meary knew some day soon she must. Each day she sensed his confusion growing, and though she assumed Seumas had already explained her situation in full, she knew it was her duty to help Brendan understand the why of it.

Despite the tension her choice to become Lord Colin's lover caused between Meary and her old friends, she could not claim her position as Lord Colin's mistress was without pleasures.

Colin, as he now insisted she call him, was an attentive lover in and out of his bedchamber. When they were alone, he wasted little time on words but instead communicated his enjoyment of her company with his hands and lips and loins. He patiently taught her what pleased him most through deep-throated sighs and growls of gratification, and always no matter how feverish his own need, he took the time to insure she was given pleasure equal to or exceeding his own. She loved the times they were together, locked in intimate embrace. It was the best and most satisfying part of her day.

As Meary had predicted, the entire household and every tenant knew of her change in status within the space of a day. Colin was openly affectionate when they were in the presence of others, though he was always careful to treat her with gentlemanly regard, confining his displays of physical affection to holding her hand and the occasional chaste kiss on the cheek. However, compliments flowed freely from his lips at the slightest provocation. In many men this would go unnoticed, but Lord Colin's wide spread reputation for habitual saturninity gave every softly spoken word of praise the effect of a bugle's blare.

Rather than put the servants off, as she had felt sure her becoming an Englishman's paramour would, if anything they treated her with more respect than before her fall from grace. They catered to her every whim, and when Lord Colin was not about, they came to her for direction as if she was the legitimate mistress of the household.

Annie was especially supportive. Since the day of the duel, she treated her more like a daughter than a houseguest. She was constantly fussing over her comfort. Annie was plainly not the least bit put off by her new role in the household, and at times Meary was almost willing to swear Annie applauded her decision to become Colin's lover.

Then, there were the gifts—one day a broach, two days later a flask of perfume, the next a new silk riband. . . . Colin's gifts brought her both pleasure and pain. No one could ever accuse Lord Colin of a lack of munificence, but the profusion of presents made her uncomfortable. It was not that she didn't appreciate them. She did. It was just a vague impresson he felt he *had* to give her these things or she would not like his company well enough. Every time he gifted her with some new item she assured him it was not necessary to do so, but to no avail.

They had never discussed her concern over his motives directly, but Meary had tried to discern the truth of it indirectly on several occasions. She had only succeeded in annoying him. There was a part of himself her lover kept closely guarded. And whenever she inadvertently drew too near he became surly.

As one day flowed into another, Meary found it increasingly difficult to maintain her debt of gratitude was the only reason she gave herself to Lord Colin. That first night it had been the truth, and the second, and mayhap the third, but now . . . If she was honest with herself, she would admit she was now his lover not only to oblige the demands of a debt of honor, not only to satisfy the demands of the compelling voices in her head, but to oblige the demands of affection as well.

When they conversed, they conversed as intellectual equals. He possessed a sterling sense of responsibility for the welfare of his tenants, a dry wit, and an elusive charm. Despite her dubious position, she enjoyed being the man's lover. She enjoyed giving him pleasure. She enjoyed being pleasured by him. She wanted to stay with him always.

This last thought caused Meary to groan. When Seumas had first asked if she loved Lord Colin, she had been as uncertain of her own heart as she was of Lord Colin's. She was yet uncertain of Lord Colin's feelings for her, but hers for him she could no longer deny. Hers was not a fleeting passion. She loved the man.

Facing the truth brought a precarious form of peace. It was easier to forgive herself for succumbing to the temptations of the flesh if love was the impetus, but it also forced her to acknowledge a new vulnerability. Love could exact a price far more dear than the travail of humbling herself ever could.

When Lord Colin grew tired of her, she would be heartbroken. She was ever cognizant that despite his attentiveness, he had never once indicated he considered their relationship permanent or that he might someday consider asking her to be more than his paramour. He was clearly content with matters just the way they were.

If she had come here for a reason as the voices in her head persisted in telling her she had, could that reason be to give Colin her love? Her heart told her it was; yet, her head, knowing the consequences of that love, could not accept the dictates of her heart.

The pleasure she took in Colin's company was immoral. Only marriage would sanctify their union. Then why did the pleasure they shared feel so right when she knew it was wrong?

The more Meary thought about it, the more melancholy she became.

To her mind, the future held only two possibilities. Lord Colin could keep her indefinitely, and she would live out her life in a state of moral destitution. Or he would grow bored with her, discard her, and she would live out her life in a state of abject loneliness.

Meary could not bring herself to believe he would ever ask her to wed him. She could hope, but she couldn't believe. He was English; she was Irish. He was rich; she was poor. He was sighted; she was blind.

Each objection considered alone made a marriage between them unlikely. Together they carried decisive weight. An Irish wife would bring no honor to an English nobleman. She had no jewels, no land, no dowery to bring to a marriage. And, no matter how well she might compensate for her lack of sight, there were some ways that, regardless of how hard she strived, she could never hope to compete with her sighted sisters. She might make an entertaining lover, but she would make an inconvenient wife. Men made marriages for power, wealth, and convenience.

Meary sternly reminded herself her purpose in becoming Lord Colin's lover was not to attain a beloved mate but to pay for Seumas's life. Pining for a happy ending to the plight caused by her wanton behavior on the heath was a waste of energy and probably sinful as well.

Since her future was doomed to be decidedly grim, Meary deemed taking what cheer she could in the present the only sensible course. It wasn't easy to shut out thoughts of tomorrow, but she was determined to do her best to do just that. She would pay her debt, loving Lord Colin while he let her . . . and face the consequences when they were rudely thrust upon her.

"Meary, why do ye allow Lord Colin to be kissing ye on the cheek whenever he pleases?" Brendan posed the dread question one afternoon as they strolled hand in hand under the warm summer sun. Earlier in the day, he had asked Meary, in a beseeching tone, if she could spare the time to walk with him, and though she had mentally braced herself for this moment, and had suffered considerable guilt over not arranging it herself weeks ago, she still felt unprepared for it.

"We have become very good friends, Brendan," she replied with measured words.

"'Tis that why we still be here?"

"Aye."

"And why ye now sleep in his bed?"

She swallowed the knot in her throat. "Aye."

"We be very good friends and ye never sleep in me bed," he observed.

Whatever Seumas had explained to Brendan about her relationship with Lord Colin, it was clear to Meary he had spared him the unsavory details. Either that or Brendan had not understood what was said to him.

Meary was determined to tell Brendan the truth, but she knew she must be careful to do so in a way that would help him accept what he could not change and bring him the least amount of pain. Too, she did not want Brendan to come to hate Colin as Seumas did. Ever since Colin had given him permission to ride Pansy, Brendan had expressed a guarded liking for his host. Because she loved them both, she wanted them to be friends.

"Lord Colin and I share a different kind of friendship than ye and I share," Meary began. "We are like brother and sister, whereas Lord Colin and I are . . ." She found herself at a loss for the right words. "Lord Colin and I . . . We are a little like a husband and wife only . . . we've not made the necessary vows to each other."

"Do ye like sharing his bed?" Brendan asked softly.

"Aye," Meary admitted.

"But ye be not looking happy. Ye be looking sad when ye say it."

She sighed. "I am a little sad."

"Why?"

The need to share her tender feelings, even if naught could ever come of them, was irresistible. "Because . . . Ye must promise to keep this a secret if I be telling ye . . ."

"I swear."

Meary knew from long experience Brendan could be trusted. "I know 'tis foolish, but sometimes, I wish Lord Colin would be wanting us to be more than special friends. Sometimes, I wish he would be asking me to be his bride."

"Ye should tell him so," Brendan stated without hesitation.

Meary smiled wanly. "'Tis not so simple as it sounds."

"But how can he be doing what ye want if ye do not tell him that ye want it?" As Meary contemplated the answer to that question, he continued. "Lord Colin let me ride Pansy when ye asked, and I know he be liking ye far better than me. If ye ask him to marry ye, I'm sure he'd be more than happy to oblige ye."

"Mayhap he does not think himself in need of a wife—especially a blind one."

"Why would he not? If ye asked me to be marrying ye, I'd sing with joy on me way to the altar. I'd shout me joy for all the world to hear!"

Hugging his arm, Meary laughed with delight. "Brendan, I love ye for your exaggerations. Ye always know just the thing to say to lighten me heart."

"I be not exaggerating. I love ye more than me own life. I've always been in love with ye, ever since we were children," he said with husky earnest.

Meary's tongue floundered. Brendan in love with her?

She had had no notion. She knew he loved her, but . . . Her complexion pinkened and paled several times as she struggled to respond to his revelation. "I . . . I'm sorry, I didn't realize . . . I . . ."

"Ye love me like a brother," he supplied the missing words. "'Tis all right. I've always known ye would never love me the way I love ye. I be not a good enough man for ye."

"Ye are too good a man for me," Meary protested.

"Nay. I be not clever. Many times I don't understand half of what ye and Seumas say when ye talk to each other. Ye need a man who can match yer fine wits. Lord Colin be clever like ye. I understand less than half of what he says."

Meary did not refute Brendan's statement by pointing out that the reason he found Lord Colin so difficult to understand was that most times the man spoke English or that his accent and ofttimes awkward grammar made his Gaelic less than easily understood. There was no purpose to be served by refuting his statement because in essence he was correct. Though she was inclined to call the quality of her own mind into question of late, Lord Colin possessed a solid intelligence. It was one among many of his characteristics that attracted her to him.

Still, she did not assign cleverness the same significance Brendan did. It had naught to do with a man's worth. She had told him so on many occasions, and was tempted to repeat it again, but she feared she might give Brendan false hopes. He might *say* he wished to be more to her than a brother, but she sensed he was comfortable and content with the way things were between them.

As she recovered from the intial shock of discovering Brendan's secret feelings for her, Meary became more and more intrigued by Brendan's endorsement of the notion of her becoming Colin's bride. That he should do so in the same breath he declared himself in love with her was proof of the depth of his affection for her. He valued her happiness above his own. That he should do so repeatedly made her wonder if the blindness of her eyes had extended to her mind as well.

All along she had had a difficult time accepting the idea that the unseen power behind the voices that had brought her to Lord Colin's estate, then urged her to remain here when she sought to run from her weakness for him, had no better purpose than to bring about her ruination. Her voices had always provided good counsel.

Could it be she had missed the obvious? Could it be she was sent here to become Lord Colin's bride? She was good for him. She knew that of a certainty. She could feel it. He was not the same man he was when they had first arrived here. The note of suspicion that used to rarely leave his voice, now only made occasional appearances. He was more relaxed, more giving of his time and himself—not just to her but to others also. He laughed from his belly, not from his throat. Could it be the something she had always felt he needed was her?

The notion was too fanciful for Meary to embrace it with any amount of confidence. In truth, she was more than a little convinced the mere thinking of it indicted her sanity. Still, the possibility, no matter how slim, once planted in her mind, stubbornly stayed there.

Subconsciously, she began to toy with the idea of following Brendan's advice and asking Colin if he would wed her. The worst that could happen was he would confirm her own disheartening assessment of her situation.

Consciously, she chided herself for engaging in wishful whimsy and vowed to give up the singing of love songs if inane flights of fancy were to be the result.

"Meary?"

The sound of her name slowly brought Meary out of her thoughts and back to Brendan. "What, friend to pale all friends?"

"Will ye be asking him to marry ye?"

She hesitated before answering, "Nay . . . Not yet at any rate."

"Would ye be liking me to ask him for ye?"

Coming from Brendan, Meary realized the generosity of his offer. She held fast to his hand and gifted him with a gracious smile. "Nay. When the time comes, if it comes, I can be doing the asking meself."

Brendan sighed in relief. A few moments later Meary heard him suck in a deep breath; then, he began to speak. "There be something else I wanted ye to help me understand. When the servants gossip among themselves, they talk of the duel between Seumas and his lordship. They say 'twas a grand affair. That they both proved their mettle as men. But when I ask Seumas of it, he gets angry and says naught except that he failed ye."

Apparently, Seumas had told Brendan less than she had assumed. Though Meary was sorry for the confusion Brendan had suffered, she was grateful Seumas had kept his own counsel. She doubted he was capable of explaining the reason for the duel to Brendan in fair terms, and she preferred he be given the whole truth.

"Remember. Ye were gone riding Pansy the day of the duel," she began. "Lucky ye were to be so. 'Twas horrible! Seumas did his best to kill Lord Colin, but thank the Lord he collapsed from exhaustion before he

243

managed to do so. Lord Colin spared Seumas's life on many occasions." Meary paused to draw a breath, but she didn't shirk the truth. "The reason Seumas challenged him to a duel in the first place and the reason he thinks he failed me was because while sharing a meal on the heath, his lordship and I engaged in behavior that is only considered proper between married couples. Seumas was very angry with Lord Colin, but what occurred between the two of us was as much me own fault as his lordship's."

There was a long silence before Brendan offered, "Seumas always blames the man when there be improper behavior. When he caught me in Squire Burke's stable loft being improper with one of the squire's dairymaids, he shooed her out with barely a word of rebuke, but he scalded me ears for over an hour. I guess he knew he scared me enough not to ever do *that* again till I'm a married man 'cause he didn't challenge me to no duel." He hesitated and Meary felt his deep blush in the heat of his fingers. ". . . Except I have been wicked twice since with other maids, 'cause it feels so nice. Only Seumas never found out about those times. If he does, do ye think he will be challenging me to a duel also?"

"Nay," Meary mumbled. The disclosure that Brendan, too, had surrendered to the weaknesses of the flesh, and if memory served, their last visit to Squire Burke's estate had been over four years ago, left Meary dumbfounded. Three women? Sweet, innocent Brendan? He knew far more about life than she thought he did.

There certainly was no condemnation in his voice. He accepted the fact she and Lord Colin had succumbed to their passions on the heath as calmly as if she had told him they had gone for a stroll in the sunshine. In truth, when she had told him she and Lord Colin behaved as husband and wife he might have known *exactly* what she was talking about. Meary felt her color rise.

Brendan's tone became worried. "Ye won't be telling Seumas on me?"

"Nay. I am in no position to be telling tales, now am I," she reassured him.

"Are ye angry with me?"

"Nay, just a bit surprised 'tis all." Meary forced her thoughtful frown into a sympathetic smile. "It never occurred to me. . . . Never mind." She held fast to his hand as they continued to walk. "Thank ye for telling me. In a way, 'tis nice to know I'm not the only one to be defeated by temptation. It does not make me any less dissatisfied with meself, but I no longer feel so wretchedly alone in me folly."

Chapter 17

Meary lay in the wide bed listening to the steady march of Colin's boots as he ascended the stairs to his chamber. Her heartbeat quickened as it did every night.

It was Colin's habit to let her retire before him, but he was never far behind. She appreciated the offer of a few moments privacy even if she had given up all claim to modesty with him long ago.

As the door creaked open, she sat up and smiled at him.

"Are you tired?" he asked.

"Nay."

"I am glad." His words teemed with lusty promise.

Meary listened to him move around the room as he shed his clothes and put them away. A few minutes later the mattress sagged under his weight. His warm hands eased her chemise past her thighs, hips, breasts, and over her head.

Meary rolled to her side and nestled herself into his arms.

"I am gratified you are an eager lover," he whispered

against her neck. "It warms my heart to be greeted thusly."

Meary silenced his lips with a long, loving kiss. There was a time for talk and a time when a more earthy form of communication was desirable. Now was not the time for talk.

Pulling Colin deeper into her embrace, she held him tightly to her. He returned her kisses with enthusiasm, sliding his hands up and down her back and massaging the muscles supporting her spine.

Meary sighed with contentment, letting her own hands explore where they willed. She knew every inch of Colin's flesh intimately, but she never tired of renewing her acquaintance.

A serene smile graced her lips as she stroked the sides of his face, the column of his throat, splaying her fingers as she stretched her hands across his chest.

When her hands reached his arms, for a moment she paused to trace the outline of the thin scar marring his once-perfect arm. The reason she was in his bed flashed in her mind. Her smile began to fade, and she quickly moved her hands back to his chest. His flesh quivered beneath her fingertips like the strings of her harp vibrating to her touch.

As she caressed him, her lips nibbled at his neck and shoulders, trailing up to his earlobes where she playfully nipped at his soft flesh, then across his jaw and down the column of his throat.

Meary's hands slowly traveled over his heart, descending the flat of his stomach, and came to rest mere inches from the nest of hair surrounding his manhood. She teased him with her ever-encroaching touch, shivering

247

with delight as his muscles contracted beneath her fingers.

He grabbed her hand and brought it to his lips.

Tumbling her to her back, Colin pinned her to the mattress with his weight. "Now, it is my turn to torment you," he drawled into her ear.

He plunged his tongue into her mouth, stroking the sensitive skin within with hungry relish. Their tongues sparred. Thrusting and parrying, they slid against each other in emulation of the mating act. Their breath came in gasps and their hearts thundered against each other.

Raising himself on his elbows, Colin lowered his mouth to her breasts and showered them with suckling kisses before settling his attention on one of the pair. His hands caressed as his lips kissed the roseate tip to a passion-stiff peak; then, he turned his regard to the other. He groaned with satisfaction as Meary's hips rose up against him, seeking the rapturous consummation of their flesh.

Instead of obliging her, he released her. Propping himself on his knees, he brought her hand to his lips, kissing each fingertip in turn before gently applying his teeth to the perimeters of her palm.

Though she urged him to abandon his game and return to her arms, he persisted to kiss his way down her arm, stroking her with his lips and tongue and teeth.

Meary squirmed beneath his sensuous onslaught. "Please," she begged as she opened her thighs and tried to pull his weight back onto her. " 'Tis too much to bear. Too much . . ."

He ignored her entreaty and continued until he had kissed his way down to her toes. Then, ever so slowly, he began to kiss his way back up to her passion-flushed face.

By the time he reached her lips, Meary was beside herself with need. When at last he filled her, her muscles contracted around his manly organ, pulling it deeper within her.

Straining together, they lavished each other with kisses between breathless pants. Their hips performed the dance of physical love with rhythmic pulsating strokes, heating their bodies hotter and hotter until first Meary, then Colin, exploded in a torrential release of erotic tension.

Sagging against each other, they slept peacefully in each other's arms. When they awoke the next morning, their limbs were still entwined.

The sun shone brightly for at least a part of most every day, and the summer storms came and went with equal regularity. Cattle munched on the plentiful grass. Fields of potatoes grew green and lush. The large plot near the kitchen and smaller plots behind every cottage sprouted turnips, carrots, leeks, and cabbage. The corn crop inched toward the sky.

The growing season marched toward harvest time just as it had every year.

Everything was as it always had been, everything except for Meary. She vacillated between joy and despair despite her vow to live only for the present. She could accomplish the feat when she lay in Lord Colin's arms, but whenever she was alone, the future forever plagued her mind.

She tried to use her harp to soothe her soul, but the more deeply she fell in love with Colin, the less effective was her music when it came to keeping her disquietude about their relationship at bay.

Though Colin treated her with kindness and respect, he had yet to give the slightest indication that the thought of making her more than his kept woman had ever crossed his mind. She knew he enjoyed her company both in and out of his bedchamber. He told her so daily, not with words but through his actions. Despite her protests, he continued to shower her with presents. He consulted her on how they should spend their days and ofttimes asked her on how to best deal with an inept maid or a neglectful tenant. He even went to great lengths to be polite to Seumas, who continued to publicly proclaim his host an unrivaled candidate for hell and mutter curses under his breath despite her fervent pleas for him to have mercy.

Meary's regard for Colin daily multiplied, and she could not think of one complaint to lodge against him except that he was clearly content with matters just the way they were between them, and she could not be.

Though she had once stoically discarded the dream she would ever be any man's bride, she could no longer do so. She wanted to spend the rest of her life with Lord Colin, to stand proudly by his side, to share his bed, to have a family with him.

It mattered not that she was Irish, poor, and blind. She might be a little slower than other women when it came to performing some of the duties of a good wife, and others were beyond her abilities, but in all the ways that really mattered she believed she would make an admirable mate. These past weeks she had been Colin's wife in all ways but in name, and she had proven to her own satisfaction he would sacrifice nothing of import by wedding her rather than another maid.

And, he had much to gain. She had grown to love him with every fiber of her being. What man wouldn't welcome that kind of devotion? Being Irish, she could help him better understand his people. She could indulge his fondness for music. She had a good head on her shoulders in all matters save him. Her manners were impeccable. She would make an excellent mother for his children.

This last item in Meary's list of her qualifications caused her to give pause. Well she knew, the absence of marriage vows did naught to prevent the conception of children. For herself she would welcome a child under any circumstance. Before meeting Colin she had always judged children the chief reward of marriage. But for the child's sake she was glad she had yet to conceive. A bastard child, no matter how well-loved by his parents, was denied the acceptance of society. To wish such a burden upon a tiny innocent was not within her no matter how much she might long to hold a babe of her own in her arms.

The thought that there was a very real probability of such an ill-starred fate befalling her progeny if things remained as they were spurred Meary to seriously consider how and when she should approach Colin and bring up the matter of a marriage between them.

A direct solicitation would be the tidiest. There would be no risk of misunderstanding. But there would be other risks. He might be put off by her boldness or casually brush off her entreaty as if it was a pesky gnat. After all, there was nothing stopping him from bringing up the subject himself if he desired to do so. Meary was ever aware there was much about her lover she did not fathom. There were dark places in his soul she had yet to touch. Mayhap it would be best to test the depth of the water before jumping in with both feet.

More than anything, she wanted his answer to be the one she longed to hear. She wanted to regain the peace her soul had once known. She was paying her debt; she was obeying her voices; she knew she was doing what she must. Still, she could not accept her situation. She could not accept she was destined to live out her life as a whore. She acknowledged the role she had played in her own ruination; yet, she couldn't help but believe she deserved to be loved and honored as she loved and honored the man whose bed she shared.

A full two weeks passed before Meary worked up the courage and method to broach the subject that occupied an ever-increasing space in her thoughts. She and Colin were returning from an idyllic afternoon of lovemaking under the warm summer sun. He had a passion for making love in the shadow of the hawthorn trees where they had shared their first intimacy, and he took her there whenever he could cajole her with handsome pleas and honeyed kisses into indulging his fancy.

The happy squeal of a child as he ran across their path and Lord Colin's satisfied mood provided the conditions Meary deemed favorable to her cause.

"'Tis a lovely sound, the laughter of a child, don't ye think?"

"I suppose it is pleasant enough," he commented without enthusiasm.

Meary's heart began to sink, but she carried on. "Don't ye like children?"

"I hold no opinion of them."

"Ye must have formed some opinion," she pressed.

"They are small, rather noisy, a necessary nuisance,"

he offered, his deep voice evincing his lack of interest in the subject.

Meary fell silent and turned her face from him so he would not see the tears welling in her eyes. Though she had broached the subject of the child as a prelude to a discussion of marriage, she was so taken aback by his view, she had thoughts for nothing else. How could she have fallen in love with a man who disliked children? She adored children. If given the sanctity of marriage, she would happily bring a dozen babies into the world. She could not abide with Lord Colin if he harbored an abhorrence for children in his heart. It mattered naught what the voices in her head told her to do. Some shortcomings were too grave to overlook. She didn't want to believe him possessed of so awful a character flaw. Meary's pace increased with her dismay, and she broke into a run.

Colin caught up with her just as she stumbled over a rock, and he reached out and grabbed her, spinning her to face him as he did so. "Meary? What on earth is wrong?" he demanded as he stared at her tearstained face.

"Everything is wrong."

"If you want me to have the slightest idea how to comfort you, you will have to be a little more specific."

Twisting her shoulders, she tried to wrench herself from his grip. "I don't want ye to be comforting me. I want ye to be leaving me alone."

Colin was totally confused by her sudden change of mood. Was this not the same woman who less than a half hour ago was lying naked in his arms eagerly returning his passion? He knew there were times when despondency overtook her usually cheerful spirit, but never had she gone from joy to woe in such a headlong manner.

"I am not going to leave you alone. I am going to stand here and hold onto you until you have the courtesy to explain yourself."

"The children. I am upset because ye hate children," she cried.

"I do not hate children."

"Ye said ye view them as a nuisance."

"Shaving every morning is a nuisance, but that does not mean I hate my face. And if you will recall, my first statement was that I had no opinion. My experience with children is extremely limited. Who knows what I would think of them if I took the time to find out. It was only when you pressed me, I . . ." He stopped short as what he thought was the light of understanding dawned. "There was a purpose behind your question, was there not?"

Meary drew a snuffly breath and nodded miserably.

"Why didn't you just come out and tell me I have gotten you with child?"

"Because ye haven't."

"I haven't," he repeated, a confounded timbre to his voice.

"Nay."

"Then why are you so distraught?"

Meary worried the fabric of her skirt as she tried to blink back her tears. "Because I have been thinking that ye might."

"True, I might." Colin dabbed her tears with his handkerchief. "In fact, considering our circumstances, the probability is likely quite high eventually it will happen. But it is nothing to distress yourself over. I assure you, I fully intend to see that you and any possible consequences of our liason are well provided for."

"How will ye provide for us?"

"You want me to name a sum in pounds and pences this very moment?"

"Nay. I want none of your money."

"Then what *do* you want?"

"I want to know of a certainty if a child 'tis ever a part of this bargain of ours, that ye would love it," Meary pleaded. "Nay, 'tis more than a want. 'Tis a need."

Colin was silent a long while. ". . . If I father a child on you, I will love it. To do less, would be to become despised in my own eyes," he stated.

Meary's lips curved into a wan smile. Laying her hand on his heart, she said, "Pray, say it again."

"If I father a child on you, I will love it."

Her smile broadened and she sighed with relief. "Ye are speaking the truth," she proclaimed.

"Yes."

. . . Slowly, her smile began to fade.

"What is wrong now?"

"There 'tis something else I would like to know, but I hesitate. 'Tis related to the first, but . . ."

"Ask," he commanded.

Meary squared her shoulders and took a deep breath. "We seem well suited to each other. I am content in your company, and I think ye are content in mine. In all ways but one we are . . . I want to know if ye have ever, even in passing, considered making me your bride?"

"No. I have no intention of burdening myself with a wife."

He hadn't needed a moment to give pause to her question, and the swiftness of his response increased the sting of his succinctly spoken words, but Meary did her best to appear stoic. "Ye think of me as a burden?"

"I think of you as a delightful mistress. As a mistress, I

255

do not consider you a burden."

"But as a wife ye would?"

"Yes."

"Because I am Irish?"

"That matters little to me."

"Because I lack wealth?"

"I have no need of money."

"Because I am blind?"

"That is only a small consideration."

"Then what is your chief objection to me?" Meary inquired.

"I have none. It is the taking of a wife I find objectional, not you personally. From the very beginning I have been honest with you, and it pains me to think you may have been nurturing false hopes. I like you too well to wish to see you hurt, but I will tell you plainly, so there will be no further misunderstanding between us, I am resolved to die a bachelor."

"I appreciate your candor." She managed the right words, but the expression of disappointment on her face could not be masked.

"I am sorry I cannot give you what you ask," Colin stated without emotion as he stroked her arms. "If it consoles you at all, I am sure I would make a poor husband; . . . so in the end, my denial will be what saves you from a lifetime of disappointment."

Chapter 18

"Master Colin, it's past time I sit you down and we have a serious talk," Annie announced, as she circled around the great hall snuffing the wall candles. She left two candles burning, using one to light the candle in the brass candlestick she held in her hand.

It was late, and the rest of the household had already retired. Colin had been taking advantage of the quiet, reviewing his accounts by the firelight. He looked up from his ledger, his eyes gazing longingly in the direction of the stairs. Meary had appeared weary this evening, and he had urged her to retire early. Her sweet, lithe body was warming his bed. If she had fallen asleep, he would not disturb her, but if she had not . . . Nestling in his lover's arms sounded far more appealing than reckoning with some household crisis. He sighed. "Can it not wait until morning?"

"No. I prefer to speak with you privately, and this is the best time for it."

Colin placed a riband between the pages of his account book, closed it, and laid it aside. "If you are sure this discussion cannot be postponed, have a seat." He motioned to a chair near his. "You will note I am already seated."

Annie set her candle on the table, giving her skirt and apron a brisk twist as she crossed the distance between them. Before sitting, she scooted her chair a little closer to his.

"Now, what is it you would like to discuss?"

"Meary."

Colin gave his housekeeper a jaundiced look.

"I would like to know when you intend to ask the girl to wed you."

"You what?"

"You can hear me perfectly well, so there's no need for me to repeat myself. I've been more than patient with you. Now, answer my question."

Colin felt his gut tighten. First Meary and now, not three days later, Annie was dredging up the subject of marriage. Was he the victim of some kind of female conspiracy, or was he merely suffering a bout of bad luck? In either case, he had no wish to continue this discussion. "It is impertinent of you to question the conduct of my private life."

Annie clucked her tongue at him. "Call it anything you like, just answer the question."

"I do not ever intend to wed Meary O'Byrne."

"Why not?" she demanded.

"Because I do not want to marry her."

"Then you're an extremely stupid man."

Colin's face reddened and his jaw dropped. "Stupid? You are calling me stupid?"

"Yes, I am." She raised her chin a notch and looked him straight in the eye. "Meary O'Byrne is in love with you; any fool can see that. And you, if you'd let yourself be, would be in love with her. She's good for you. You've smiled more since she's come here than you have in all the years I've known you put together. You've started to take some time to have a little fun. You've started acting more like the sweet boy I used to know. It took me less than a week to know she was the woman for you. Why do you think I helped you romance her by keeping Mr. O'Hanlon out of your hair? So you could ruin a sweet, young woman? Think again if that's what you believe. I helped you because you need her for your wife."

Colin clenched his hands into fists. "I neither need nor want a wife."

"Yes, you do."

His eyes narrowed. "Did she put you up to this?"

"Ha! You can wipe that suspicious expression off your face. When has anyone ever been able to tell me what to think or say? I hinted to her once, a long time ago, that I thought she would make you a fine wife, but I don't think she caught my meaning. Otherwise, we have never discussed the matter."

"Then why are you bringing this up now?"

"I've told you. You've exhausted my patience."

"Then you better find a well from which you can draw more because I am not going to marry her," he informed her, his voice as tight as the hands on his lap.

"You're just going to sit there like a stone and let her walk out of your life?"

"What makes you think she is going to leave me? Has she said something?" A subtle note of anxiety tainted his voice as he asked the questions, and Colin cursed himself under his breath. Annie acknowledged his plight with a leisurely raised eyebrow and a penetrating gaze.

"She doesn't have to say a word for a body to know how untenable she finds the situation you have put her in. She may be Irish, but she possesses the heart and soul of a fine English gentlewoman. No matter how much she loves you, I believe being forced to live in sin will eventually cause her to flee you."

"She is free to go whenever she wishes," Colin stated. He smiled at the nonchalant timbre of his own voice.

"And you are free to do whatever you wish, but I don't have to like it, and I don't have to sit idly by while you imperil your future," Annie proclaimed as she rose to her feet. She folded her arms across her chest. "I am going to do my best to see you wed the girl as you ought, and this time when Annie Baine sets out to champion your welfare, no one is going to stand in her way."

Meary pulled her shawl more snugly about her shoulders and sighed as she sat alone on a granite boulder facing the sea. The signs of the changing season were in the air. The breeze off the sea was a little cooler. The aroma of fresh-cut hay and ripening corn wafted off the fields. The cries of the sea birds heralded an increase in activity.

Everything was changing—even herself. It had been four weeks since Lord Colin had made it perfectly clear she should expect nothing in the way of a commitment from him. He continued to treat her with tender regard, but she was finding it increasingly difficult to countenance the undignified life she led.

When she was alone with Colin—whether they worked on his Gaelic, discussed matters of the estate, or made love, she felt warm, secure, and rapturously happy.

She wanted to stay by his side forever. But when she was alone, or they were in the presence of others, every thought made her squirm with discomfort. There was nothing secure or gladdening about her position as Lord Colin's paramour. Daily she violated her own moral standard and for what? Sensual pleasure and the promise she would never be anything more than a whore? It was a poor bargain.

And what of Seumas and Brendan? She had told them they could go, but they would not abandon her. She tarnished their lives as well as her own. Brendan only cared for her happiness and was unconcerned with the finer points of ethics, but Seumas . . . She knew how he suffered on her account, and it distressed her greatly. Keeping his promise not to directly interfere was exacting a terrible toll on him. He had ceased to make music even in the privacy of his chambers. He took less and less joy in his storytelling. His voice, to her ears, sounded aged a hundred years.

Whatever debt of gratitude Meary owed Lord Colin for sparing Seumas's life, she judged she had repaid long ago. She had denied him nothing and given him everything. Now, she stayed because . . .

She stayed because she loved him, and would not give up hope that he might someday return her love. She stayed because she believed in her heart her love was somehow essential to his well-being. She stayed because she could not muster the will to ask for permission to depart.

Seumas was growing increasingly restless, and the guilt she felt over the pain she caused her beloved mentor made her want to leave. The sincere belief that by remaining she was consigning her soul to hell in the afterlife was a compelling reason to leave. The remnants of her pride said: go and never never look back. But still she stayed.

And so she continued to agonize, daily praying for the strength to ask to be released from the obligation to stay, only to be engulfed by a wave of panic that her prayer might be answered. She knew she must come to some kind of decision. She must insist Seumas and Brendan leave her here to face alone her fate or pack her harp and trunk in the pony cart and take up the life she had known before coming here. It was unfair to her friends and to herself to procrastinate coming to a firm stand about which way her life was to go, and each day she did so she felt her burden of indecision grow more weighty.

Lord Colin held his reins loosely in his hand, allowing his horse to wander where it willed. He was pleased with the bounty his tenants had harvested from their fields. They would have plenty to eat this winter, and he would make a handsome profit. Everything was going according to the plan he had laid out upon arriving at his estate. He should be content, yet he was not.

Thoughts of Meary continually infringed upon his contentment. It was not that she ever said or did anything to displease him. The opposite was true. She pleased him too well. She saw to his needs with uncanny foresight, and though when she thought the cause worthy, she would make requests on behalf of others, she had never asked for anything for herself—except that once.

He had tried repeatedly to convince himself that Meary was like all others, that she desired him to take her to wife because of his position and wealth, that she had contrived to secure him for a mate from the very first, but both his head and his heart recognized his accusation as the crock it was. He had bluntly told Meary he would not consider wedding her, and she had never mentioned the matter of their marriage again.

Colin frowned. His lover might be gratifyingly mute on the dreaded subject, but Annie was not so reserved. Having once brought up the matter of his wedding Meary, she harangued him about it constantly. No argument or threat would silence her. Her tenacity was most vexing.

He told her he had no use for a wife—especially not a blind, Irish one. He had come to Ireland to escape the commitments of family. To create another family for which he would be responsible was the height of insanity. He willingly had abandoned his native country to rid himself of familial obligation. Why would he want to saddle himself with a wife?

Colin shifted on his saddle. Why, indeed, he asked himself as he repeated the litany of arguments he habitually gave Annie? He knew the answer to his plaintive "why" without a minute's contemplation. Meary might be blind, but she was more resourceful and independent than any sighted woman he had ever met. As to her being Irish, he cared not a whit who her ancestors were. She was nothing like his relatives in England. She deserved better than he was giving her. He was afraid she would fly from him if he did not legally bind her to him.

It was the last of his reasons that gave him the most cause for concern. He had told Annie that Meary was free to go whenever she chose, but every time he tried to imagine his life without her, his rebellious mind refused to conjure scenes of solitary contentment. It drew only dark pictures of a life devoid of laughter and joy. Pictures of a man growing more bitter with each passing year.

Annie had said Meary was in love with him. At first he had refused to believe it, could not believe he could inspire romantic fervor in any woman's heart, but gradually he had come to wonder if Annie might not be correct in her assessment. How else could he explain Meary's actions? Everything she said and did bespoke of loving devotion.

Something else Annie had told him had stuck in his head. She had said that if he would let himself, he would be in love with Meary. He didn't know if she was right, but he was terrified to test her assertion. When you loved someone, you gave them power over you, you opened yourself up to all manner of abuse.

He preferred to keep things just the way they were. It was safer that way.

"I see ye be out walking again," Seumas commented as he came up along side Meary and fell into step.

"Aye," she said.

"Ye be troubled."

Meary did not respond to his second statement, but her brows drew together, and her shoulders hunched a little closer to her ears.

They walked side by side in silence for a space of time before he spoke again.

"How long do ye be planning to keep doing this to yerself?"

Meary was not surprised by his question. Of late, she was finding it more and more difficult to disguise her low spirits. She knew her explanation for her behavior would not satisfy, but she gave him the only answer she could. "I love him, Seumas."

"I know." He patted the pale hand that clenched the head of her cane. "But he does not return yer love else he would have married ye by now."

"He does not want a wife," Meary stated softly.

"And ye be content to be his wh . . . ?" Seumas could not bring himself to finish the word.

"Nay, I am not content."

"Do ye think if ye love him well enough he will be deciding to marry ye after all? If ye do, ye be sadly mistaken. The whole household has been championing yer future welfare, especially that Annie Baine."

"She is a good friend to me."

"Aye. I've never in me life met a more obnoxious, muleheaded, shrew of a woman, but I'll not be denying her heart be a good one."

Meary smiled at his less than flattering compliment. "I'm glad ye like her."

"I do not like her. I tolerate her," he gruffly informed her. "But I be not here to discuss Annie Baine. I only mentioned her to impress upon ye the futility of dreaming Lord Colin will ever do ye the dubious honor making ye his wife. She has called him every name for fool and scorches his ears with her fiery tongue most every day. Ye know they be almost like mother and son. If she cannot be changing his mind, no one can."

Meary was well aware of Annie's tireless efforts on her behalf, and she did not need to be reminded Annie's counsel fell on deaf ears. She also did not need to be told what Colin's refusal to listen to his housekeeper meant. "I do not delude meself. I know me situation 'tis hopeless."

265

"Then, why do ye stay?"

"I made a promise to the saints and . . ."

"I know of yer promise. How long are ye going to use it for an excuse?"

" 'Tis not an excuse."

"Nay?"

"I cannot break me vow," Meary insisted.

"But ye can ask to be released from it."

"Aye," she acknowledged after swallowing the hard lump in her throat.

"Have ye?"

". . . Nay."

"Why not?"

"I . . . have tried, but . . . Me *feelings* tell me I should stay. I am good for him. He needs me. I . . ."

"Meary, I have always had great respect for yer 'feelings.' Ye know that. 'Tis why I have let this go on for as long as I have, all the while every inch of me screaming in protest." His voice remained gentle as it had throughout their conversation. "I could have trussed ye up and carried ye away from this place in spite of yer vow, but I did not. I have let ye honor it as ye believed ye were bound to do even though me heart told me the saints would never be so enamored with the letter of the law they would wish ye to submit yerself to an Englishman. Even though I despise Lord Colin, I prayed ye were right to do as ye have done. For yer sake, I wanted to be wrong about the man. . . . But we both know 'tis ye who be wrong. Yer heart be deceiving ye by conjuring false voices to tell ye what ye wished to hear. 'Tis past time ye accept it."

*　　*　　*

Meary was not so certain as Seumas that her feelings were false, but his words did set her to wondering if they were wholly true. She knew without doubt that giving her love to Colin was right. No matter how steep the price to herself, she would never believe her love a mistake. But as to the other . . . Meary was not so certain staying on indefinitely as his mistress was what she was required to do. If Colin would not release her from her vow, she had to stay, but she was well aware she had never given him the opportunity to tell her she could go.

Meary contemplated her untenable position for several days. She could not see how her love could do either Colin or herself any good if they lived apart, but she also knew unless and until she screwed up her courage and gave Colin the opportunity to tell her to go, she would continue to be plagued by uncertainty. Whether he told her she must stay or go, at least she would know whether she stood on firm moral ground.

That night when Colin came up to his room, Meary was sitting up in the bed, twisting her hands in nervous knots, waiting for him.

"What is wrong?" he asked, his voice full of concern as he came to sit on the side of the bed.

Meary was at a loss how to begin. She had been rehearsing this moment in her head all day, but now that he was here, she couldn't remember a word of what she had planned to say. Abandoning all hope of easing into the subject, she came right to the point. "I would like ye to release me from me promise."

"What promise?" Colin asked, his voice evincing genuine confusion.

Meary forced a deep breath into her lungs and answered him. "The day ye spared Seumas's life I promised the saints I would give ye anything ye desired if ye did not kill him. These many months I have strived to give ye all that ye asked. Now, I am asking if ye will release me?"

"The only reason you share my bed is to fulfill some secret promise to the saints?" he demanded in an angry, injured tone.

Reaching for his hand, Meary cradled it against her cheek and kissed his wrist. "Nay. 'Twas the reason I came to your bed, but love has kept me here as much as me promise."

"You truly love me?"

Meary nodded. "Aye, with all me heart."

His muscles relaxed. "Then, I release you."

Meary's grip upon his hand tightened as his words hit her heart with the force of a musket ball. She had her answer. She could go. To continue to stay now would be an insult to herself and all her ancestors. She hated the knowledge, but her hatred did not change it. She wished she could call back the question, but she could not. Seumas was right. 'T was past time she accept the miserable truth. She dropped her lover's hand.

Rising from the bed, Meary padded on bare feet to the wardrobe, filled her arms with as much of her own clothing as she could readily find, and started for the door.

"Where are you going?"

She heard the mattress rustle as it was deprived of his weight, but he did not pursue her. She blinked back the tears welling in her eyes before she turned to face him. "To me own room to pack me trunk. I'll be back in the morning to retrieve the rest of me things."

"What!"

"I have been your mistress these many months, but now 'tis time I go," Meary whispered.

"No!"

"Aye. I should not have stayed so long."

"I thought you said you loved me. Was it a lie to trick me into releasing you from your promise?"

She winced at the cold suspicion in his voice and took a step toward him. When she spoke, she spoke with passion. "Nay. I have already told ye I love ye with all me heart. You know 'tis true. Me words are but a faint echo of me actions. I have given ye all I have to give. I have held none of meself back from ye." Meary paused, struggling to maintain custody of her composure. When she was confident she could continue without bursting into tears, she did so. "I will always love ye. Even if I am consigned to the deepest pit in hell because of what has occurred between us, I would never wish these past months away."

"Then, why are you leaving?" Colin protested.

"Because I have paid me debt."

"What debt? There was never any debt! I never had any intention of slaying O'Hanlon. I thought you knew me better than that."

Meary smiled wanly. "Now, I do. But at the time I did not know ye as well and was too distraught to be thinking clearly, in any case."

"Then, why have you honored the promise?"

"A promise 'tis a promise, even if 'twas made unnecessarily."

"I don't want you to go."

Meary knew Colin was not a man to beg, and the fact that his statement was a plea tore at her heart. Every word he had said tore at her heart. He sounded so hurt, so

269

bewildered, so lost. She felt like a villain. Though her common sense told her not to do so, she found herself offering him the chance to take back what he had given. "Do ye withdraw your release?"

He was silent a long time. She could hear him pacing back and forth across the room from her. More than once the pacing stopped. She could feel him staring at her, hear his slow deliberate breathing; then, the pacing began again. Finally he spoke. "No. I have no wish to keep you with me against your will. If you do not want to stay, you are free to go."

"Have ye not heard a word I've said?" she cried. "I do not *want* to be going. I love ye. I wish to abide with ye always. I wish to be your helpmate. I wish to bear your children." She stretched her arms toward him . . . then dropped them to her side. "But me conscience will not permit me to stay as your mistress, and ye do not want me for a wife."

"Curse your conscience."

"I have, but still it will not leave me in peace!"

"If you are determined to go, I will not stop you," he began after a long, pregnant pause. There was authority in his voice, but also a note of hollowness. "But I require you to give your decision more thought before you do anything rash. A week or two more of my company will not harm you."

"I would ask ye to let me go now before I lose courage," Meary beseeched.

"I refuse to grant my permission for you to do so. If you love me, you will stay a little while longer," he insisted, refusing to let the panic in his breast manifest itself in his tone. "Now, return your garments to their

270

rightful place in the wardrobe and come back to bed before the floor turns your feet to ice."

He had told her a week or two more of his company would not harm her, but after three days Colin no longer believed his own words.

Meary behaved as she always did, giving of herself to him and others without expectation of recompense. She never complained. She tutored him, oversaw the running of his household, offered her advice on the management of the estate whenever he solicited it. She played and sang for him whenever he asked. She made love to him with a passion that stirred his soul as well as his loins.

. . . But there was a difference in her these past few days, a tangible sadness of spirit in everything she did. She made a valiant effort to hide her unhappiness from him, to appear cheerful and accepting of his will, but she had never been any good at disguising her feelings.

That she loved him, he had no question. He had known it even before she had said the words aloud, though he had done his damnedest not to recognize it. He had not the slightest idea why she should love him. In fact, he could easily name a dozen reasons why she should not. But that did not alter the truth, and the truth was that for some inexplicable reason Meary O'Byrne had given him her tender heart.

And now he was hurting her terribly by his inability to let her go. The ruthlessly logical part of him understood why she could not be happy with things just the way they were between them. His logical self understood how sorely she felt the loss of her mentor's approval. It understood her need to comport herself with dignity, to live a life of which she could be proud, and that by releasing her from her promise, he had deprived her of the reason that allowed her to stay.

Of course, he could marry her. That would satisfy all concerned—*except himself*. He didn't want a wife. He didn't want a family. All he wanted was to keep Meary as his lover.

He had come to Ireland a bachelor, and a bachelor he would stay. He had good reasons for wishing to remain unattached. A smart man did not court disaster.

Colin repeated his long held convictions over and over in his head, vowing to stay on the sensible life's course he had plotted for himself even if it meant losing Meary. But he found every time he was in Meary's gentle and giving presence his resolve to remain a bachelor wavered precariously.

Each morning as she patiently instructed him in the language and culture of his people, he was reminded of how much more difficult the task of running his estate would be when she was gone. He had complete confidence the estate would prosper with or without her by his side but without her, where would be the joy in it?

When he spied her walking alone on the heath, which she did whenever she pleased—against his express instruction, he was impressed by her courage and independence. On one of these "forbidden" walks she had met a little girl, mayhap four or five years of age. From a distance he had watched her. She and the child knelt in the grass for quite some time. When they arose, he saw each had woven a crown of wildflowers. Placing their crowns upon their heads, they danced round and round, spinning with arms stretched out to embrace the sunshine until they dropped. The tinkle of their giggles carried on the wind. He would miss the sound of Meary's laughter if she left him.

At the dinner table, she conversed intelligently no matter what the subject. The opinions she expressed were thoughtful. When she believed she was right, she argued like a barrister, but she was not afraid to admit it when she felt she did not possess sufficient knowledge to form a competent opinion. And she was always willing to listen, even if she refused to agree. If she left him, his meals would return to the silent, solitary affairs they had been before her coming.

In the eventide, when she played her harp for him, her fingers nimbly plucking at the harp strings, her heavenly voice making music that surpassed the glory of her harp's, he was of a sudden acutely aware of the unwelcome quiet that would descend upon his house like a shroud if she was not here to share his evenings.

In the dark of night, after they made love, when she curled against him, he could not help but be mindful of how much warmer his bed was now that she shared it. He had not grown bored with making love to her, as he had predicted he would. In truth, he desired her more now than he had in the beginning. The thrill of conquest had not faded but evolved into some heretofore unknown sensation—an uncommon combination of the comfort of a cozy winter fire, the stimulation of a lightning storm, and the serenity of a hymn. His analogy was crude at best, but it was the closest he could come in the temporal world to describing his ethereal erotic experience. Having once experienced such an exalted form of lovemaking, would the commonplace variety ever again be able to provide him satisfaction?

The more he watched her and listened to her and touched her, the less convinced Colin became of the virtues of bachelorhood. Why shouldn't he take her to wife? She had never done anything but please him. If he had been in the market for a wife, she possessed every quality he deemed necessary and an overabundance of qualities he could only judge as honey to sweeten the marriage cake.

His reasons for desiring to avoid the wedded state had nothing to do with her. They were authored by his past not his present. He had come to Ireland to make a new start. To allow the shackles of his past to prevent him from making the most intriguing, loving, beautiful woman in the world his wife seemed folly at its worst.

Annie, who he trusted above any other human being, thought he should wed Meary. It was true she had developed a strong affection for her, but he knew without a doubt Annie's insistence that Meary was the wife for him was solely motivated by her desire to see to *his* welfare. She had told him as much a thousand times these past weeks, and even if she had not, he would have known it to be true. Her loyalty had never been in question. Annie did not even like Ireland. She would not be badgering him to take an Irish bride unless she was absolutely convinced it was for his good.

None of these thoughts were entirely new to Lord Colin, but until now he had done his best to ignore them. Where before it suited his purpose to believe his housekeeper pushy and addled, it now suited his purpose to judge her determined and wise.

Lord Colin argued the pros and cons of taking Meary to wife until he had exhausted the last remnants of reluctance. The pros far outweighed the cons and one by itself held enough weight to tip the scales in favor of marriage all by itself. He did not want Meary to leave him, and in the dark depths of his heart he knew if he did not offer her marriage, he would force her to deprive him of her presence. He might be able to come up with a host of stratagems to delay her departure, but eventually she would leave him.

Given a choice between marriage and keeping Meary for his mistress, he told himself he would choose the latter. But given the choice of marriage or losing her, marriage was the clear choice.

Besides, his were not the only feelings to be taken into account. Meary had needs and desires, and they deserved consideration. Well he knew how soul-weary she had grown of her role as his mistress. Her heavy heart was evident in her wan smiles. It was evident in her carriage. It was evident in the watery sheen that so often glazed her beautiful, blue eyes.

If marriage was the price he had to pay to keep Meary contentedly by his side, he would gladly pay it, and consider himself the chief beneficiary of the bargain.

Once having come to the decision to ask Meary to be his wife, Lord Colin was rather taken aback by the potency of the sense of relief that washed over him. It left him feeling giddy—so giddy in private moments he was willing to consider the possibility he might be a little bit in love. He preferred to believe he was wedding Meary for pragmatic reasons, but the idea love might play a small part as well did not discomfit him quite as much as it had before.

The more he thought about it, the more the idea of

giving himself permission to fall in love began to appeal to him. When the notion first occurred to him, he judged it fraught with hazard, but two nights later as he lay, his eyes hooded, watching Meary sleep in his arms, he was struck by a realization so powerful it jolted him out of his tranquil state of half-slumber and caused him to stare wide-eyed.

Long ago O'Hanlon had admonished him pity was a dangerous emotion—a double-edged sword that drew the life's blood from both the giver and the receiver. All his life he had been shamelessly guilty of pity. Self-pity. As he gazed at the face of the woman who loved him, Colin knew he had pitied himself for far too long and suffered needless anguish because of it. Worse, he had caused Meary to suffer.

His family may have used him badly, but that did not mean everyone else he ever came to love would do the same. If he let himself love Meary wholeheartedly, she would not of a sudden turn into the opposite of what he knew her to be: a warm, loving, giving woman. She would never use his love against him. He tightened his arms around her.

"'Tis something wrong?" she murmured as she stirred to half wakefulness.

"No. I just of a sudden realized I am the one who is blind not you."

Meary yawned. "Ye are talking nonsense."

"Am I?"

"Aye."

"I am sorry to have disturbed you," he whispered. "Pray, go back to sleep." Nestling deep under the covers, he deliberately made his breathing slow and rhythmic. When he was certain she was again asleep, Colin grinned

276

and began to make his plans.

He did not consider himself by nature of a romantic bend of mind, but Colin was convinced Meary would appreciate any effort he made to make his proposal sentimental. The hawthorns had long ago exchanged their fragrant blossoms for red ripe berries, but he thought the shadow of their spiny branches, where he and Meary had first joined together, a fitting place to ask her to make the union permanent. He would ask Annie to pack a basket with the same foodstuff he had brought there that first day, mayhap substituting some French champagne for the red wine he had ordered before. The smuggling trade along the coast was brisk and conducted in open disregard of English law, and his housekeeper would have no trouble attaining the sparkling French wine. Mayhap he would approach Brendan and request he teach him one of Meary's favorite poems. He considered going to Seumas and asking permission for Meary's hand, but decided not to take the risk.

When he had settled the whimsical details of his planned proposal in his mind, Colin turned to matters less entertaining. The banns must be posted, a license must be obtained, and the matter of their separate religions dealt with. It was illegal for a Protestant and a Catholic to marry, but it was accepted practice in such circumstances for one or the other member of a couple to conveniently "convert." Knowing Meary's views on religion, he did not think she would oppose the idea of pretending to be a Protestant. He shared her view of religion and would willing be the one to "convert" if she preferred he do so, except the present political climate prevented him from granting such a wish. If he legally became a Catholic, he would be stripped of his land and livelihood and would no longer be in a position to provide her with the comforts she deserved. She knew this and he was confident she would agree with the wisdom of his plan without argument. In any case, he would be careful to assure her, once having satisfied the letter of the law, she was free to believe anything she liked and could raise their children, when and if they came, any way she liked.

The next morning Colin rose early and set out to make the necessary arrangements. He did not tell Meary or anyone else where he was going, only that he would be away for the better part of the day. He preferred to keep his own counsel until he was sure all the legalities could be swiftly satisfied and he had the stage perfectly set. Then, and only then, would he be ready to propose.

Chapter 19

A wide, contented grin adorned Lord Colin Garrick's face as he sat tall upon his galloping stallion headed for home. He had accomplished everything he had set out to accomplish, and all that was left to do was make his request for the basket of food and champagne and propose the marriage to Meary. He was certain she would be startled when she learned what he had been up to. He was looking forward to seeing her face alight with surprise. It had been too long since he had seen a untempered smile grace her lips. If all went well, they could be married by the end of the month.

He could not remember ever being in quite so fine a mood and wondered why he had taken so long to come to the decision to marry his pretty, Irish lover. Reasons he once had judged good now seemed meritless. By some stroke of luck, God had gifted him with a warm and beautiful woman to stand by his side. He should have recognized his good fortune long ago and taken the proper steps to secure it.

But there was little point in bemoaning his past

hesitancy to enthusiastically embrace his blessings. He was prepared to do so now. Meary would be his. That was all that really mattered.

His knees squeezed his stallion's flank, urging him to carry him home as swiftly as his powerful legs were able.

Upon arriving at the tower house, the first thing Lord Colin noticed was a strange, heavily laden carriage standing before his door and the grim countenances of the several servants who bustled about it. Two of the men he did not recognize, but the rest of the servants were his own.

His high-spirited grin tightened into a curious frown. His estate was located miles from any thoroughfare. He could not imagine a traveler becoming so lost he would end up this far afield.

After handing his mount over to a groom and giving strict instructions as to his care, Colin approached the carriage with long strides. The interior was empty, but as his eyes surveyed the profusion of luggage strapped to the vehicle, they became black and cold as sleet. An invisible, gelid hand reached up and encircled his heart.

He flinched as a high-pitched, nasal whine screaked through the heavy wooden door leading to the great hall.

Drawing in a deep, angry breath, Colin stepped past the carriage and entered his hall.

"Lady Swanscroft, Lord Swanscroft," he addressed his mother and brother by their formal titles. "To what do I owe this honor?"

"There you are. And it is about time, I say. I cannot believe after all we have suffered being bounced and bruised along what these vile Irish have the audacity to call roads for so long I have lost count of the days my misery was so great, to be greeted by no one but servants, the insult is too monumental to be described in words," his mother returned his greeting.

"Did you write me of your impending arrival?" Colin queried without any show of emotion.

"Of course, I did not. You know how bothersome I find such tasks."

He acknowledged her statement with a leisurely raised brow. "If you did not inform me of your coming, I fail to see how I can be held responsible for my failure to be here to greet you."

"Do not abuse Mother with your damnable logic, Colin. You are clearly at fault here. Give her the apology she deserves," his brother directed, his arm snaking around his mother's shoulders to give her a supportive squeeze.

Colin stared at the two. They were just as he remembered.

His brother, the marquess, was dressed to perfection in a full-skirted, green coat stitched of the finest satin money could buy and embellished with a profusion of silver buttons and braids. He sported a brocade waistcoat, cream-colored satin breeches, silk stockings, and black leather shoes with high red heels and lavish silver buckles. Upon his head he wore a powdered wig with a full dozen fat sausage ringlets reaching down to the middle of his back. His mahogany-colored eyes sparkled even as Edwin rebuked him, and his full lips stretched wide in a roguish grin.

His mother—leaning limply against Edwin—had chosen to bedeck herself in yards of crimson silk and Belgian lace. Her sleeves flared at the elbow into five lace festooned bells, her stomacher and petticoat were embroidered with gold thread, and every finger boasted a jeweled ring. She, too, wore an expensive, heavily powdered wig, but the hair of her wig was pulled up into a high frill and her curls cascaded from the back of her crown. The hat perched atop her frill matched her gown in both its fabric and its excess. Her eyes were dark and hard; her nose remained tilted at a lofty angle; her lips were pursed in a perpetual pout. The bones of her face and stringy frame protruded sharply beneath her skin, and she kept her nails long. He had always thought her resemblance to a bird of prey striking.

"Why are you here?" he asked, ignoring his brother's demand for an apology.

"We are here to fetch you home to England, dear brother," Edwin informed him.

Colin stiffened. "If that is your purpose, you have wasted your time."

"It is not a request, Colin. It is an order," his mother chimed in. "You may have two days to settle your affairs here. It shall take me at least that long to recover from my journey to this godforsaken place, although how I shall ever recover in such crude surroundings is impossible to imagine."

"Mayhap you should not stay at all. We would not want you to put your good health in jeopardy."

Lady Swanscroft brought her hand to her bosom and moaned. "I must. Until I see you home, I shall not know a decent night's sleep."

"Then I fear the circles under your eyes will grow very large indeed," Colin stated.

"What do you mean by that?" she demanded, her tremulous tone instantly strident.

"I am not leaving Ireland."

"Yes, you are. You have thrown your little tantrum long enough. I will tell you plainly, it will be many years before I will be able to bring myself to even think about forgiving you for putting me to such trouble."

"Then I suspect I will be bereft of your goodwill for a very long time, for I will not oblige you in this matter."

"Oh come, Colin, you cannot actually mean to say you like living among the Irish riffraff," Edwin drawled. "Look at the damage it's already done to you. You wear your hair like a peasant, and your garments . . . tsk, tsk, brother. They are months behind the fashion. Why, it pains me to look at you. A few more weeks in this country and you are in danger of being corrupted beyond restoration."

Though he diligently maintained his civil mien and tenor of voice, Colin did not mince words. "I find the company of those I have met in Ireland preferable to that which I left behind in England."

The marquess and Lady Swanscroft snorted in unison, but it was Edwin who spoke. "Well, I suppose there is no accounting for taste. I always suspected your tastes ran toward the base. How else could you be so good at business? In any case, I must side with Mother and insist you come home. Whatever your predilections, duty calls."

"How far in debt have you run the estate this time?"

"Rather far. I am afraid once again we're in peril of losing the estate," Edwin stated without a hint of contrition.

"How did you manage to run through the vast sum I left on account for you so quickly?" Colin queried. There was no note of rebuke in his voice only morbid curiosity.

"A series of unfortunate wagers. I've been having beastly bad luck at the card table. Then there was this little bauble." Edwin raised his cravat to display an elaborately wrought gold and ruby neck pin. "A few trinkets for my mistresses. I added three racing horses to the stables. And of course both Mother and I needed new wardrobes. Living expenses are high in England these days."

"It must be very trying for you," Colin commiserated.

Edwin nodded. "So you see, you simply must return to England and quickly. The creditors will soon be beating down our door."

"Then I suggest you take what money you have left, if there is any, and buy yourself a sturdy door. I told you before I left England that the sum I granted you was the last gift you would see from my purse, and I admonished you to spend it wisely. As you will recall, it was a considerable sum. Enough to finance a comfortable style of living for years. I will be sorry to see you lose the family estate, but as I said before, I will do naught to stop it."

"How can you be so cold?" Lady Swanscroft raised her nose a notch and spat the question at him. "After all we have done for you."

Colin curled his lips into a mirthless grin. "Refresh my memory, dear mother. I seem to have forgotten your many sacrifices."

Lady Swanscroft's dour face went momentarily blank; then, she rallied with a terse, "The list is too long to recite."

"Then name just one," he proposed.

"I brought you into this world at great pain and discomfort to myself! And against my will I might add!"

Though inwardly he recoiled at his mother's ugly tone, outwardly Colin continued to show no more emotion than he would had he been discussing the weather with strangers. His voice remained steady and dust-dry as he contended, "And I have been paying for the gift of life ever since. I consider that debt paid several times over. I am through supporting Edwin and your extravagances. Nothing you say will sway me."

"You would let your own mother starve in the streets like a common peasant?" she screeched.

"Sell a few of your jewels, and you will neither starve nor be forced to live in the streets. Come January and every January after, you will find a living stipend deposited into your accounts just as I promised, but that will be the full extent of my financial contribution. Swanscroft sits on good land and is capable of providing both you and Edwin with an excellent living if you wish to live more luxuriously. Mr. Bartlett is an excellent manager and will serve you well if you will but listen to him."

"But we can't live as we ought without you!"

"You could live quite nicely. All you have to do is persuade Edwin to invest in the estate instead of the gaming tables, his tailor, his jewelers, his whores. A little self-restraint is all that is required."

Genuinely appalled, Lady Swanscroft cried, "How can you ask me to deprive my darling boy of his pleasures?"

Colin shrugged. "I ask you to do no such thing. I merely suggested it as the most obvious way out of your troubles."

Peeling Edwin's hand from her shoulder, she took a step toward her youngest son and impaled him with her icy glare. "The way out of our troubles is for you to do your duty and come home to England. It is your duty to see to our comfort! It is your duty to save the estate! It is your duty to do as I will!" She advanced on him one step for each shrilly spoken demand. "What use are you to us if you do not tend to the dreary obligations of life so we may concentrate on pursuing its pleasures?"

Colin tried to force himself to meet her loveless gaze but found to his discomfort, as always, he could not. He focused his eyes on the trim of her hat. "Of no use at all," he stated.

Lady Swanscroft smiled. "Then you will pack your things and return to England."

"No. I prefer the title 'useless' to that of 'lackey,'" Colin corrected, the ice in his voice matching the cold shards gleaming in his mother's eyes. "I am content, no more than content, I am delighted with my decision to give up the life of family ass and instead live the life of a man here on my own estate in Ireland."

"You are a horrible, hateful son!"

"Believe what you will," he offered, slowly pivoting away from her to warm himself at his hearth.

"Ohhh . . . Ohhh . . . It is too much to bear. My own son turned against me." Lady Swanscroft staggered back from him, collapsing in Edwin's arms. "Edwin, my beloved, I cannot bear to be in *his* presence a moment longer. Carry me to my room. I must rest. I must have rest. I must have rest. . . ." She continued to wail the phrase as Edwin scooped her up into his arms and cradled her against his chest.

The marquess obediently carried her to the stairs. On the third step, he stopped and turned to face his brother. "I hope you are happy, you selfish lout. You can see what you have done to her. I cannot believe you are so changed in such a short time." He turned away and resumed his ascent up the stairs. "Mother and I will pray for your redemption."

Chapter 20

Meary slowly rose to her feet, stretching the crimp from her legs and shoulders. It was getting late and she knew she should be returning to the tower. Before turning her back on the sea, she lingered a moment longer, letting the westerly breeze tickle the hair at her temples and breathing in deep breaths of salty air.

She came here every day now to sit and contemplate her situation. She did not know why she continued to come. She never found the ease of spirit she sought.

By giving her permission to leave him, then adamantly refusing to let her depart at once, Colin had placed her in a position that was even more untenable than the one she had occupied before.

His insistence that she prove her love by staying was cruel; yet, she could not muster any emotion more damning than frustration to lend her the strength to leave him against his will.

And her head continually counseled her to remove herself from Lord Colin's influence. She should consider the shame she brought upon her family name—the shame she brought upon Seumas and Brendan. She should consider herself lucky Lord Colin had yet to plant a child in her. Leave immediately, it told her. There was naught to be gained in staying.

It was good counsel. She fully intended to follow it. But every time she came to the decision to leave without permission or delay, her heart constricted so painfully she lost the will to go.

A future without Lord Colin seemed cold, dark, and bereft of even the most simple of pleasures. How could she leave and never know the touch of his hands again? How could she live without the sound of his voice? The scent of his skin? The taste of his lips?

At times she felt as though there were two beings living inside her skin—one ruled by common sense, the other by raw emotion. Each battled to wholly conquer the other but to no avail.

The war was killing her by inches. Her nights were harrowed by disturbing dreams. She had little appetite. Simple tasks she had once performed with ease now seemed to require a herculean effort to accomplish, leaving her weepy from the strain. Even playing her harp no longer brought her any comfort.

She was caught between two equally repugnant choices. For a long time doing nothing had been the easiest path to follow and so she had, but these past days the pain of living with a self she could not esteem had grown unbearable.

The scales had tipped. As she walked away from the sounds of the crashing sea, Meary realized the pain of staying had come to outweigh the pain of leaving.

She had fulfilled the bargain. There was no honor in staying. Colin had said he required her to ponder her decision to go a week or two. A week had passed. It was enough.

This evening, when he returned from whatever errand had taken him away, she would tell Colin she was leaving him.

He would not be pleased, and he would do his utmost to persuade her to stay. He might even try to command her to stay. But in the end he would offer her naught but more expensive baubles in exchange for her affection. She did not need baubles. She needed his love.

There was a fine line between hope and delusion. She had been deluding herself for a long, long time. What she needed from Lord Colin he would never give her. She must face the fact that her love was destined to be unrequited.

She would always love him. And she wished the very best for him that life had to offer. She wished him a happy future even if she could not be a part of it.

Meary swiped at the tears running down her cheeks, promising herself over and over again she would be strong. She would do what she knew she must.

Colin lay his hands upon the hearth and gripped the stones beneath his fingers, allowing the blank mask he had shrouded himself with while conversing with his mother and brother to fall away.

Cold fury battled with utter dejection for supremacy in his heart, and both emotions graphically manifested themselves in the twisted features of his face. Why had they had to come now? Just when he was putting his life in order. Just when he was starting to feel genuinely content.

He had thought the remote coast of Ireland a safe haven. He had thought he had seen the last he would ever see of them.

He did not hate his mother and brother, but he hated the way they made him feel. Cold and dead inside. They were experts at robbing both his purse and his soul.

He wanted nothing to do with them. He wanted them out of his house. He wanted to be left in peace.

His fingers bit deeper into the stones. Damn them both for coming here. Damn himself for letting their indifference to his needs and desires cut him still. *Damn. Damn. Damn.*

As Meary approached the tower house the sounds of nature were replaced by that of human activity. She had nearly reached the door when she heard rapid footsteps coming toward her and her name being called.

"At last, you've come back! I've been watching for you from the kitchen window for nigh on an hour and was just getting ready to come looking for you," Annie proclaimed, taking her by the hand and leading her away from the house to a quiet corner of the yard. "The most terrible thing has happened!"

"What has happened now?" Meary asked in alarm and dismay. She had managed to compose herself before reaching the yard, but she didn't feel she was capable of facing any more adversity without completely falling to pieces.

"Lady Swanscroft and the marquess arrived while you were out taking your stroll. They're demanding our Colin return to England with them!"

Meary was aware Colin and his family were not close-knit. He habitually refused to discuss them whenever she brought the subject up. In light of this knowledge, she found it hard to comprehend why they would want to come here or why they would want him to come back to England. But she was so relieved Annie's "terrible thing" was naught more than an unexpected visit from Colin's relatives, she heaved a great sigh.

"His mother and brother are here?" she asked to make certain she had understood Annie correctly.

"That they are," Annie confirmed. "Stay away from the soup tonight. I'm thinking of poisoning it."

"Annie!"

"I wouldn't really do it, but the thought has more than a little appeal. They're every bit as vile as I remember them."

"Surely they must have some virtues to be recommending them."

"Not a one!"

Meary knew Annie held a grudge against Colin's English relatives, and she knew Annie was extremely upset. The housekeeper had yet to let loose of her hand. She held it between her own, which she was wringing, causing Meary's fingers considerable distress. There had to be more to the matter than she was saying.

The most obvious reason for the housekeeper's agitation was also the one that caused Meary the most discomfort to contemplate. Logic proclaimed Lord Colin's departure from Ireland a blessing. It would relieve her of the necessity of leaving him. But love did not allow her to feel a whit of enthusiasm at the prospect. "Does Colin plan to be returning with them to England?" she asked, physically bracing herself to hear the answer.

"Of course not! His life is here with you in Ireland."

Upon learning Colin would not be leaving, Meary was awash with equal measures of regret and relief. Still, she appreciated Annie's support, even if she judged it as futile as her own hope. Desiring to soothe the older woman, she said, "If he says he will not be going, I cannot be understanding why ye are so distraught."

"Because they're despicable human beings, and they will make all our lives miserable until we can find a way to purge the house of them."

If all Annie had to offer were disparaging statements for explanations, Meary could not see that the drift of the conversation was leading anywhere useful. She decided to take charge. "Ye said ye wanted me for something?"

"To warn you of their arrival . . . and to ask you to go to our Colin. He's in the great hall now looking as black as a hundred-year-old kettle. He needs you to put a smile back on his face. You're the only one I know can do it."

"I'll see if he's wanting me company," Meary assured her. Though she felt certain Annie's personal dislike was causing her to exaggerate the effect the arrival of his relatives had had upon Colin, if he needed comforting, she would willingly provide it. But before she left Annie, Meary wanted to make sure the housekeeper was under control. "Try to calm yourself, and under no circumstance are ye to do anything foolish. I plan on taking a generous portion of every dish ye serve tonight," she warned.

"I'll not do anything without your approval," Annie reluctantly promised.

"Thank ye."

Quitting Annie, Meary made her way to the door leading to the great hall and stepped over the threshold. The room was silent except for the sound of someone breathing.

Meary crossed the room to where Colin stood near the hearth. She lay her hand on his chest and could feel his heart beating faster than was common.

"I understand your family has come for a visit," she said softly.

"One could call it that."

"Where are they?"

"Upstairs recovering from the shock of my sedition."

"They are angry because ye will not be returning to England?"

"To put it mildly." He removed her hand from his chest. "But how do you know what we discussed? Were you listening at the keyhole?"

The harshness of his tone caused Meary to grimace, but her own voice remained warm and sympathetic as she explained, "Annie overheard ye talking and told me of it, so ye need not sound so suspicious."

"I apologize. I did not mean to take my foul mood out on you. You have done nothing to warrant my ire." Though he said the right words, his tone remained chilly.

"Is there something I can be doing to help ye feel better?"

"No. Run along and prepare yourself for the evening meal. You might consider a nap. You look tired." He turned Meary away from him and toward the stairs.

Meary was not happy to be informed she was neither needed nor wanted, but she had no desire to force her company upon him. She had no claim on him and if he chose to shut her out, it was his right. She started for the stairs.

"Meary." He stopped her halfway across the room.

She waited tensely, listening to his approaching footsteps. When he arrived at her side, she could feel him

293

staring down at her.

Wrapping her in his arms, he pulled her tightly against his chest and kissed her with such force he stole her breath away. He continued to cling to her, kissing her again and again—with less force but equal urgency.

Just as abruptly, he released her and set her traveling back in the direction of the staircase with a firm nudge.

Feeling exceedingly confused, Meary mounted the stairs.

As Colin watched Meary ascend the stairs, his eyes took on a glassy sheen and he exhaled a dispirited sigh.

He had been so eager to surprise her with his proposal. Now, he must postpone it. Rather than weaken his commitment to wed her, seeing his family again had reinforced it. Meary was as unlike his mother and brother in temperament and spirit as emerald is to slate. But now more than ever, he wanted everything to be perfect when he proposed and with his mother and brother here it would be anything but perfect. He would not let them spoil the moment for him or Meary. He would just have to wait until he could get rid of them.

Though ridding himself of his relatives as expeditiously as possible was his paramount goal, Colin's more immediate concern was protecting Meary. His mother was unlikely to be kind to her in any case, but if he presented her as his mistress, he guaranteed Meary would be subjected to the cruelest of barbs.

He could not present her as his betrothed until he proposed, and that could not happen until his family was well on their way back to England.

Finally, he settled on simply referring to Meary as his guest, invited to his home for her musical talents. O'Hanlon and Brendan's presence would lend the title legitimacy. O'Hanlon might despise him, but his affection for Meary should motivate him to have the good sense to keep his mouth shut. Brendan couldn't speak English, so there could be no slips of the tongue from that quarter. While his mother and Edwin were closeted behind closed doors, he would quietly have Meary's clothing moved back to the room she now only occupied during the day. Along with her garments, he would send instructions she should once again sleep there until he said otherwise. To make certain the pretense held, he would instruct Annie to inform the servants anyone caught wagging his or her tongue would be immediately dismissed.

Colin slowly nodded his head in approval as he went over the list twice again in his mind to be certain he had not overlooked some detail.

The deception should be simple enough to foster the few days it would take for his mother to recover herself enough to begin the journey back to England.

Chapter 21

" 'Tis time for ye to be coming down for supper," Doreen called through Meary's chamber door.

"I believe not," Meary replied. "I think Lord Colin would be preferring I take a tray alone in me room."

" 'Tis his lordship himself sent me up to fetch ye."

"He did?"

"Aye."

Curiosity made Meary eager to meet Colin's family, even as embarrassment made her hesitate. Her position in the household almost guaranteed she would not receive a warm reception.

She had thought the arrival of her clothes and his message an unambiguous sign he did not wish to flaunt her residence in his household.

Mothers and mistresses did not dine together. At least they did not in Ireland. She could not imagine what Colin could be about.

Mayhap English custom was different. In any case, he knew his family better than she, and if he desired her presence at the table, she would oblige him.

Meary took a deep breath, squared her shoulders, and checked her appearance with her hands twice before she opened the door.

"Yer looking pretty as can be," Doreen complimented.

"Thank ye." Meary continued to fidget with the hair at her temples. "Ye are absolutely sure his lordship desires I join him at his table?"

"Aye. I am."

"Well, if that be his desire . . . Though it does seem odd," Meary commented before she followed Doreen down the stairs.

She wondered what she would think of this family of his. Annie despised them, and their effect on Colin had not been at all salubrious. His behavior this afternoon was incomprehensible. One moment he was distant and suspicious, the next he was holding onto her as if he feared to let her go. It made her worried. What manner of people were they to rouse such stormy reactions?

Whatever their manner, she was determined to do her best not to be prejudiced against them. They were Colin's family, and as family they deserved to be treated with an extra measure of understanding and respect one would not feel obliged to extend to strangers. She would form her own opinions based on fact not rumor and conjecture. Mayhap as an impartial third party, she could help Colin heal the rift in his family relations. It would please her greatly if she could give him the gift of familial harmony before she left him.

Meary shrunk at the thought of her impending departure, and she thrust it from her mind. This evening she would think of naught but how to bring Colin closer to his family. It was a noble aspiration, and one that was far easier to embrace than the duty of saying fare thee well to the man she loved.

"Ah, here she is. Mother, Edwin, I would like to introduce you to Lady Meary O'Byrne, the third member of this musical trio and the last of my guests. She is an accomplished harper, and I am sure you will enjoy her playing when she entertains us tonight."

Meary slowly approached the occupants of the room. Colin had abandoned calling her "Lady" long ago, even in Seumas's company, and the fact he had introduced her as a "guest" had not gone unnoticed. Neither had the cool, civil tone of his voice. It was now clear to her why he had extended the invitation to dinner. He intended to hide the true nature of their relationship from his family, and if she remained cloistered in her room, questions about her presence were bound to be raised. She applauded his decision to be discreet, not only because it showed concern for his relatives' sensibilities, but because it made her position much less embarrassing and awkward.

"Lady Meary, may I present my mother Lady Swanscroft and my brother, Edwin, the Marquess of Swanscroft."

"I am honored to be making your acquaintance." Meary extended her hand.

"I'm sure you are. I daresay it is not often you Irish have the chance to meet English nobility," Lady Swanscroft replied. When she did not offer her hand, Meary withdrew her own.

Lord Swanscroft was not so remote. Clasping Meary's hand, he brought it to his lips and bestowed upon it a wet and unconscionably overlong kiss, before drawling, "Charming. Very, very charming."

Meary extracted her hand from his the instant she was able to do so and tucked it behind her back.

She smiled as cordially as she was able. Her first impression of Lord and Lady Swanscroft did not bode well for her plan to perform the services of a diplomat. Her skin bristled with distaste. But Meary resolved she would not let herself jump to hasty conclusions. She stretched her smile a little wider.

"I hope you had a comfortable journey," she remarked.

"Comfortable?" Lady Swanscroft cried. "From the moment I stepped foot from England's shores I have not known a moment's comfort. It is a wonder I survived the trip at all."

"I'm sorry."

"And well you should be. You Irish are a primitive lot. Hardly above savages. One would think you would have picked up some understanding of civilized living from the English who rule you."

Meary was finding it harder to maintain a friendly tone than she reckoned, but she persevered. "Traveling does not agree with many people," she consoled.

"It most certainly does not agree with me! And furthermore, *you* do not agree with me. I command you to stop staring at me this instant. I do not appreciate having my person perused with such interest."

"Mother, Lady Meary is not staring at you. She is blind," Colin intervened.

"Oh . . . How dreary."

"Blind, you say," Lord Swanscroft joined in the conversation. "I would not have guessed. How very intriguing."

Meary supposed "intriguing" an improvement over "dreary," but the sly way he said the word made the muscles of her stomach tighten. To her great relief, Colin saved her the necessity of replying.

"Mr. O'Hanlon, if you will guide Lady Meary to the foot of the table, I will seat my mother, and the servants can begin laying our meal."

"You share your table with itinerant musicians?" Lady Swanscroft asked in horror.

"Yes, I do," Colin replied coolly. "If their presence makes you uncomfortable, you are welcome to take a tray in your room."

The lady sniffed but offered no further protest.

"She be a real harridan, that one," Seumas whispered in Meary's ear as he led her to her new place at the table. "Not one agreeable word has passed her lips since we've come into the room."

Meary acknowledged his comment with a subtle nod and what she hoped was a furtive look to communicate her heartfelt desire that he cause no trouble of his own.

As she settled herself on her seat, Meary's ears pricked to the sound of a small commotion directly to her left.

"Edwin, your place is here at my right," Colin instructed. "That is Brendan's place."

"I prefer to sit by Lady Meary," Edwin stated.

A hush fell over the table, and Meary could feel the tension smoldering between the two brothers. "As you wish," Colin gruffly acquiesced. "Brendan, come sit by me," he said in Gaelic.

"Why are you talking like that?" Lady Swanscroft demanded.

"Because we are in Ireland, and I desire to be understood."

"Well, I can't understand you."

"But Brendan does and I was speaking to him. If I used English, *he* would not know what I said."

"Why not? If he wishes to serve an English master, he should learn to speak English. It's demeaning for the rest of us to have to listen to that gibberish you were spouting."

"I am not Brendan's master but his host. I consider it the duty of a host to see to the comfort and convenience of his guests."

"Pah! As if it is not bad enough I have to sit at the same table with blind beggars. Now, you insist I must tolerate their language as well."

"Lady Meary is blind. Brendan and Mr. O'Hanlon are not. And none of them are beggars." Every word he spoke was a little more constrained than the one before it, but he maintained his refined tone. "They are accomplished musicians, and in Ireland members of their class are held in high regard."

"Well, if I must endure them, I must," she fumed. "But I suggest you have your servants bring on the food before I completely lose my appetite."

Lord Colin ordered the meal to be served.

As the servants began serving their supper, Lady Swanscroft kept up her steady litany of complaints, completely dominating the table conversation.

Listening to her querulous monologue, Meary felt her fingers slowly tightening around the stem of her wine goblet. She took a deep breath and forced herself to slack her grip.

"Don't mind her. Mother is always peevish when she's tired, and the journey here has left her dreadfully exhausted, poor dear. Give her a day or two and she shall be her sweet self again," a voice she recognized as Lord Swanscroft's whispered in Meary's ear. She started as she felt a hand grab her knee and shifted her legs as far away

301

as the seating allowed.

"I will do me best to be forgiving of your mother . . . and your wandering hand," she whispered back.

"Pray do. I appreciate beautiful women no matter what their ancestry and would like us to be friends."

For a fleeting moment, Meary wondered if Colin only desired to protect his mother from the knowledge of their affair and had confided in his brother that she was his mistress, thus giving Lord Swanscroft cause to think her receptive to his randy attentions; but almost as soon as it formed, she dismissed the thought as unworthy. Colin would never willfully place her in such an adverse position. His repeated attempts to present them to his family as honored guests was ample evidence of his loyalty if she needed more proof than the conviction of her heart.

She waited until a maidservant finished ladling soup into her bowl and had moved on. "Then I suggest ye appreciate me from afar."

Continuing to keep his urbane voice low enough his mother's high-pitched caviling easily concealed his words from the other diners, he asked, "Do you have another beau?"

"Aye," she stated, thinking the existence of a beau might help put him off.

"Lucky man."

She nodded.

"Does he treat you well?"

"Aye." Meary had no intention of elaborating.

"I would treat you better." He reached for her knee again, but she caught his hand and firmly placed it on his own leg.

"I'm doubting that very much."

"Name your price."

Much of the color drained from her face at his ugly assumption, but she succeeded in keeping her outrage in check. "Me affections are not for sale," she told him plainly.

"A pity. Opportunities like me don't come along every day. Let me know if you change your mind."

Meary turned away from him and faced Seumas. "What tunes do ye think Brendan and I should be playing for his lordship's family tonight?"

"Laments."

"Please, Seumas," she begged under her breath. "If ye have a whit of affection left for me in your heart, help me to be getting through this evening."

"The mother 'tis more vile than her son," he opined in Gaelic.

"At least she is open in her mockery. I fear Lord Colin's brother 'tis a snake." Meary too used Gaelic to disguise her words, but where Seumas spoke at a normal volume, uncaring if Lord Colin heard him, Meary kept her voice low so only her mentor could hear.

"I was referring to Lord Colin, not his brother, though I can't be saying I like him either."

"Lord Colin 'tis a fine man. And compared to the rest of his family, he 'tis a saint," she added vehemently. "If not for me, ye would judge him so yourself."

"Some sins outweigh any virtue a man might possess."

"Can we not be discussing this at another time?" Meary pleaded. "I can feel them all staring at us."

She had barely gotten the words out of her mouth when Lady Swanscroft demanded, "Stop using that guttural language in my presence, and I'll brook no argument from the two of you! I know you can speak English."

Seumas growled then fell silent.

"Many find the Irish langauge rather melodious. I number myself among them," Colin refuted his mother's slight before falling as mute as Seumas.

Meary was left with the formidable task of trying to solicit some sort of civil dinner conversation. She nibbled on a succulent piece of roast squab while she contemplated a prudent course. "How 'tis the weather in England this time of year?" she addressed the question to Lady Swanscroft, deeming the weather and England innocuous subjects.

"It is lovely. Of course I am missing it because my disloyal son has forced me to chase him halfway around the world, so I might bring him home."

Meary ignored most of what she said and concentrated on her first statement. "I'm told the English have delightful flower gardens. Do ye have one at Swanscroft?"

"Flowers make me sneeze."

"I'm sorry. Mayhap ye have some other interest ye could tell me about."

"Why should I tell you of my interests? I have no desire to carry on a conversation with you. My son may enjoy fraternizing with Irish peasants, but I do not."

Meary clamped her jaw shut so hard her teeth clacked.

"I apologize for my mother's rudeness," Colin addressed Meary. "But mayhap it is best you give up all attempts to converse. Considering my past experience with our present company, I cannot see it leading to any pleasant exchange." In Gaelic he added, "I promise I will

304

do my utmost to send them packing as quickly as possible. I beg your patience and understanding."

Lady Swanscroft huffed in indignation and slammed her goblet upon the table. "First you flay me with insults; then, you defy my authority by persisting to speak their nasty language."

"Really, Colin, you *are* being a dreadful bore," Edwin chimed in.

Lowering her head, Meary earnestly applied herself to her meal. She was more than happy to take Colin's advice. There was too much ill will at this table for her to counteract alone. Mayhap when they finished eating and commenced the evening's entertainment everyone would be less cross.

Meary concentrated all her energy on that hope as she endured the rest of the meal in strained silence.

Lady Swanscroft might not want to speak with her, but she was more than willing to address the table at large and Colin in particular with her endless complaints about the quality of the food, the wine, the table services, each and every servant who entered the room, and the room itself. She made certain Colin realized she held him personally responsible for everything she found amiss, and that she judged his behavior deliberate.

Since Meary could find not the least thing wrong with the meal or the service—knew it to be as excellent as always—she could not help but respect Lord Colin for his self-restraint. He never once raised his voice to defend himself against Lady Swanscroft's unwarranted insults. The only time he commented at all was to defend his table companions and staff against her barbs, and he did so not through direct confrontation but by coolly stating the facts.

Someone who knew him less well than she might conclude him indifferent to his mother's disparaging comments, but she discerned the underlying pain and frustration in his dispassionate voice. She knew he was angry and that he was expending great effort to maintain a modicum of gentility at his table.

Meary longed to come to his aid, to say something to comfort him. But she sensed there was nothing she could say without doing more harm than good. So, she fought back the fierce protective instinct roiling up in her and kept her tongue imprisoned behind her teeth. Any consoling she did would have to be done in private.

The marquess was a no less odious dinner companion than his mother. He delighted in making his brother the butt of his cutting wit, and he was forever consoling his mother, in blatant disregard of the fact she had yet to voice one legitimate complaint. He spoke to her in intimate, caressing tones—almost like a lover. Meary found it most unnatural.

When he wasn't twitting his brother or pampering his mother, the marquess amused himself by mounting forays to Meary's knee. Thus far, she had been able to intercept him without calling notice to the battle of hands waging beneath the table, but she didn't know how much longer she could manage the ticklish feat.

As soon as the servants came to clear away the dishes, Meary excused herself from the table and took her place on the stool by her harp. She rubbed her hands along the burnished wood as she waited for the others to take up their places. She was determined to play and sing extra sweetly for Colin tonight as a show of support.

The rearranging of benches and chairs occasioned more acetous grumbling.

Meary sat tensely on her stool, praying they would settle themselves quickly before she forgot her vow to be a peacemaker, threw good manners to the wind, and gave in to the urge to tell Lord and Lady Swanscroft just exactly what she thought of them.

When all was ready, Colin said, "You may begin any time you wish."

"I would like to be dedicating this first tune to our generous host," she announced, smiling warmly in the direction of Colin's chair. A song and a smile seemed a paltry offering, but she hoped he accepted her gift of moral support in the spirit it was given.

Lifting her hands to her harp, Meary plucked out the opening notes of a lighthearted air. She played through the melody once. Then she joined her voice with the harp's the second time through.

Meary played and sang with great skill and feeling, putting her whole heart into the effort. The harp strings hummed, her fingers danced, her voice projected like a clarion. When she had finished the song, she knew she had never performed better.

"Well? Did I not tell you she was very good?" Colin said. She could hear the pride in his voice, and Meary sat a little straighter.

"You did not exaggerate," Edwin agreed. "I can't imagine how *you* contrived to attract such talent to your household. What think you of Colin's little harper, Mother?"

"I suppose if one liked harp music, they might judge her performance tolerable," Lady Swanscroft commented in her usual nasal whine. "For myself, I've never been fond of the instrument. As for her voice, it is as common as any I've heard."

307

An ominous rumbling arose from Colin's throat, and Meary heard him slap his hand down on the arm of his chair. She did not need to see his face to know he had reached his patience's end.

"Brendan and I will now be playing 'The Seas Are Deep,'" she quickly interjected. "Brendan, start playing!"

She and Brendan launched into the song, playing and singing as loudly as they were able. Though Meary appreciated Colin's willingness to defend her talent, she refused to be the cause of his losing his temper after he valiantly had held on to it for so long. As they approached the end of the song, Meary called out the name of another, and they proceeded into it without pause.

Meary kept her senses finely tuned to the emotional atmosphere of the room but found no improvement.

Six songs later, things were little better, but she felt it might be safe to rest their voices a moment or two. To her relief, nobody said a word, and she continued the evening's entertainment at a less frantic pace.

Three ballads and a half score of airs and jigs later, Colin declared, "It is getting late. I think you have played enough for one night. It is time to retire."

The scrape of chair legs against the stone floor indicated to Meary the audience was bowing to his recommendation. She gracefully rose to her feet, slowly stretching the stiffness from her spine, gladdened by the sound of retreating footsteps.

"How come the grisly old man did not play?" Edwin queried. "He eats your food."

Meary was furious with Edwin for trying to stir up more turmoil. Hadn't they all had more than enough turmoil for one night?

"He is very selective of his audience," Colin replied. Meary was relieved to hear the composure back in his voice.

"He insults us. You should throw him out," Lady Swanscroft commanded.

"This is my home and I choose who stays and who goes. Mr. O'Hanlon may stay as long as he likes," Colin informed her.

"But he insults us," the marquess echoed his mother's words.

"You and Mother have insulted *me* and my guests countless times since crossing my threshold. If Mr. O'Hanlon must go, so must you."

"It is hardly the same thing," Edwin protested.

"I agree. Mr. O'Hanlon has the good breeding to quietly express his disfavor; whereas, you and Mother loudly abuse my hospitality." Colin paused significantly before he calmly continued, "So, unless you wish me to reconsider my generosity and throw you out into the dark of night, I suggest you allow me and my household to retire without further delay."

Chapter 22

Rest did not improve Lady Swanscroft's disposition.

She had been at the estate for three days. She slept till noon every morning. When she did arise, she draped herself on the cushioned chair in the great hall and spent the rest of the day shouting orders at the servants. They ran hither and yon, doing their utmost to satisfy her interminable needs but to no avail. All they earned for their efforts was verbal abuse.

If Lady Swanscroft had had her way, they would be beaten as well, but Colin steadfastly refused to bend to her behests he take a whip to his staff.

Avoiding the woman was fast becoming the life's ambition of every servant in the house. Seumas and Brendan had embraced it as well.

It was an ambition for which Meary held great sympathy. Never in her life had she met a more demanding, disagreeable human being. She had earnestly tried to find something she could like about Lady Swanscroft. Heretofore, she had sincerely believed no one was completely devoid of some quality to recommend them. But her efforts to find some good in her had proved fruitless. The longer she spent in the woman's company, the less she liked her.

The marquess was no better. In his own way he was worse. Though he stayed abed as late as his mother, once up he was a moving menace. No maidservant was safe from his roaming hands—though he was always careful to make his untoward advances when there were no witnesses. The maids brought their troubles to her rather than Lord Colin, but there was little Meary could do but counsel them to avoid situations where they might be caught alone with the man and give them permission to use whatever means was necessary to fend off the marquess should their best efforts to evade him fail.

If the randy marquess forced her to, Meary knew she would have to ask Colin to confront his brother about his behavior, but she preferred to save Colin the burden if she could. Happily, Lord Swanscroft also had a passion for horses and was out of the house a good part of the afternoon.

Meary judged Colin already had more than enough troubles of his own with which to deal. His mother and brother would not accept his decision to remain in Ireland, and they were constantly badgering him to change his mind. When that failed, they tried wheedling. Eventually they gave up on that tactic also and descended to belittling him in general. The pattern repeated itself constantly throughout the day.

Not once had she heard them gift him with a word of endearment. The only worth they seemed to find in him was his ability to bring money into the family coffers.

It was hard to accept Annie's opinion of Colin's family had not been grossly exaggerated against their favor, but

311

Meary was rapidly coming to the unwelcome conclusion the housekeeper's assessment of them had been unerringly accurate.

The mother was a lazy, carping, bigot and the brother a self-aggrandizing, lecherous, ne'er-do-well. She might have been able to turn her head the other way to these glaring defects if the Garricks had exhibited a genuine regard for Colin, but she had seen no evidence they harbored a whit of affection for him. Even if they had possessed every other virtue known to man, their lack of feeling for a member of their own family would have condemned them in Meary's heart.

She had given up all hope of playing peacemaker. It took every ounce of her will to just be polite to them.

Not for the first time in the past three days, she wondered what possible life circumstances could have molded them into what they were.

Though Meary had given up hope of reconciling Colin and his family, she had yet to tell Colin she was leaving. She still intended to go, but she couldn't bring herself to abandon him under siege. It would be disloyal—outright ruthless—to leave him now.

Besides, she had not had the opportunity to inform him she was leaving, even if she had been selfish enough to do so.

Every night she heard Colin's feet pause in front of her door as he ascended the stairs, but he quickly moved on. They had not shared the same bed since the arrival of his family. In fact, they had not shared one private moment.

No harm would be done by postponing her departure a few more days. She stayed on as a sympathetic guest not as a lover. Remaining was no longer an immoral act. She

312

was confident as long as she and Colin kept their physical distance, she could linger for as long as she felt he needed her without further sacrifice of her dignity and pride.

Even though Meary missed the time they used to spend together both in and out of bed, she understood why it must be so, and did not think ill of Colin for his sudden lack of attention.

It was her banishment from his bed that allowed her to stay, and if they were to maintain the illusion she was a guest, he couldn't be too attentive in front of his family. Too, with winter fast approaching, there was much on the estate that required his time. She knew he stayed away from the house more than was strictly necessary, but it was the only way he could find a few minutes peace.

She loved him too much to deny him that peace, but she could not help but be concerned by his behavior. She worried as she felt him draw more and more inside himself every day. It was not good for him. Those times he was in the house, there was no emotion in his voice when he spoke, no spark of life. She feared this visit from his family was undoing all the good she had done him.

Staying did naught to change his present situation, but she could watch over him and offer her support should he find himself in need of a good friend.

Dusk followed dawn, marking the passage of each day . . . and still, they did not leave. No one knew what kept them here. Colin was unwavering in his refusal to return to England. He habitually met their slander to Ireland, his estate, and his character with polite yet firm suggestions that they would be happier if they returned to their own home.

313

Meary did not know how he could stand it. Even with her strong beliefs about the importance of kin and the virtues of showing them the greatest of respect, she feared had Lady and Lord Swanscroft been her mother and brother she would have lost her temper days ago and had them forcibly evicted.

She hoped God had a special place reserved in heaven for forbearing sons. Colin deserved to be divinely rewarded for his saintly perseverance.

Combing her fingers through her hair as she rose from her bed, Meary sighed loudly.

"I'm wondering what torments those two English devils have in store for the household today," she commented to the empty chamber as she began laying out her clothes.

A quiet rapping at the door prompted her to call, "Come in, Doreen."

"Who were ye talking to?" Doreen asked as she entered the room and found it empty except for Meary.

"I was muttering to meself," Meary admitted.

"There be lots of muttering going on in this household of late." Doreen finished laying out the clothes, then began helping Meary dress. "Some be saying they're going to look for employment at another house if his lordship's English relatives don't take their leave soon."

"'Twould be hard to blame them," Meary commiserated. "I admire Lord Colin's clemency, but I'd be less than truthful if I did not admit the Irish woman in me would derive great pleasure in seeing him throw them out on their pompous English asses."

"Such language 'tis not seemly for an Irish gentlewoman," Doreen scolded. "But in this case, I cannot help but feel there be no better way to express yer noble

314

sentiment." She pulled the last petticoat over Meary's head. "I can't think why he tolerates them. They're making him as miserable as they make the rest of us."

"He tolerates them because one tolerates one's family. They won't stay forever."

"It already feels twice that long."

Meary nodded her head. "I know."

Doreen smoothed Meary's gown into place, secured the fastenings, then turned her attention to dressing her hair without saying another word on the subject. However, as she wove the final riband through her mistress's plaited hair, she was moved to comment, "'Tis hard to believe the three of them share the same blood. Until ye came here and melted the ice in his heart, I was always a little afraid of his lordship, but he never—even at his worst—came close to them in noxiousness."

"I have had similar thoughts," Meary softly replied. "No matter how I might have judged Lord Colin in the past, after seeing the fountain from whence he sprang, I can only marvel he turned out as well as he did."

"Aye," Doreen wholeheartedly agreed. "'Tis a blessed miracle."

The day proved like every other since the arrival of Colin's family.

Colin was already gone tending the business of running his estate. Meary spent the morning tending to as much household business as time allowed during the reprieve granted by the late-rising Garricks.

She made a special point of spending as much time as possible with Annie. Whereas the other servants expressed their disgust for their vexatious house guests

315

by avoiding them, Annie was openly antagonistic. Meary was half afraid Annie might carry out her threat to poison them despite her promise to the contrary, and she felt compelled to avert such a disaster if she could.

Once Lady Swanscroft and the marquess descended the stairs, Meary reassumed the role of guest, channeling her energies into being charming and relentlessly gracious to Colin's family—for his sake willing to put her personal feelings aside and do what she could to make the atmosphere in his home less hostile.

She prudently followed her own advice, never allowing herself to be caught alone with Lord Swanscroft. Since his prurient interests were indiscriminate and the household was filled with maidservants to divert the course of his unwanted attentions, she managed quite nicely.

Lady Swanscroft presented a different sort of problem. Though she was wise enough to veil her most vicious insults to Meary when in Colin's presence, she exercised no such restraint at any other time. Meary could only stomach so much of her before her incessant grumbling and cruel comments drove her from the room.

Some days she took herself on a brisk stroll to cool her temper. Other times, she retreated to her bedchamber to soothe her ruffled feelings by playing her harp until the supper hour.

Her harp now resided in her room instead of the great hall in consideration of Lady Swanscroft's dislike of harp music. Colin had protested when Meary had had it moved there, but she had convinced him to let her have her own way with the truthful argument that she had no desire to play for an unappreciative audience.

Colin was in attendance at supper. Meary now sat at his

right again, with Seumas flanking her other side. Colin had moved his mother to the opposite end of the table with his brother after that first night. Edwin had protested loud and long, but Meary was more than happy with the arrangement.

The conversation at the table revolved around the needs and desires of Lady Swanscroft and the marquess as it always did. Seumas and Brendan did not speak at all. Lord Colin spoke only to defend others against his family's barbs. Meary spoke only to defend him, being careful to phrase her defense in terms appropriate for the guest she played and to copy Colin's even-tempered tone.

As soon after the meal as politeness allowed, Meary excused herself and retired to her room. Seumas and Brendan followed on her heels.

Meary sat on the edge of her bed, listening for the sound of Colin's boots upon the stairs, knowing he too would be retreating to the privacy of his room momentarily. Just as she had predicted, she heard the sound of his feet. They paused as they always did in front of her door; then, they carried him up the second flight of stairs.

Content that everyone she loved was safely closeted behind closed doors, Meary rose to her feet, crossed the room, and sat down to her harp. She wasn't the least bit sleepy, and playing the harp was the best way she knew to fill the long, solitary evening that stretched before her.

It was several hours later before she heard the familiar commotion that nightly accompanied Lady Swanscroft and the marquess's ascent up the stairs. They cackled and crowed at their own wit, shouting orders to the hapless servants who carried their candles up the stairs, in total disregard of anyone who might already be asleep.

Meary's hands stilled on her harp strings as she waited for them to pass her door. She started to rise, then changed her mind.

Every other night she had ceased her playing when they retired to their rooms, but tonight she was feeling rebellious. Evenings used to be such a pleasant time in this household. These two had reduced them all to virtual prisoners in their separate rooms. They were prisoners by choice, the alternative being an evening spent in the aggravating company of the marquess and his mother, but still they were prisoners. She struck up another tune.

If she had hoped her harp playing would disturb them as much as they disturbed her, Meary was disappointed. The two performed their night time rituals as usual, taking the better part of an hour before they released the servants to find their own beds. Meary ruefully concluded they probably couldn't hear her defiant harp over their own noise.

"'Tis just as well," she counseled herself. "I'm just being mean-spirited." Despite her pronouncement, she continued to play.

The rest of the house had been silent for well over an hour when Meary finally rose from her harp to prepare for bed. She startled as her door creaked.

"Don't stop playing."

Meary instantly relaxed when she recognized Colin's husky voice, though she was bothered that she had not noticed the approach of his footsteps.

She waited until he had eased the door shut behind him before she spoke.

"What if someone comes to complain?"

"They won't. Mother and Edwin make free with my wine every evening. Nothing short of the voice of God will wake them." He crossed the room and gently laid his hands on her shoulders. "Are you angry with me for being here?"

"Nay . . . Just surprised. I did not hear ye coming."

"Bare feet," he offered by way of explanation.

Each breath she drew filled Meary's lungs with his subtle manly scent, and she allowed herself an extra moment to satiate her senses before quietly asking, "What would ye be liking me to play for ye?"

"Something soothing."

Gone was the rigid control from his voice. Gone was the icy edge. Those two words, spoken as a plea, besieged Meary's heart. Even in her darkest hours, she had always been surrounded by love and acceptance—first her parents', then Seumas's and Brendan's. With the exception of Annie, Colin had never had anyone care for him. He needed her. He needed her music. He needed the warmth of her arms. There was no question in her mind what she would do. Gladly, she would give him both. On the morrow, she knew her conscience would exact a heavy price for her decision to give herself to him, but she was willing to pay it even if she could bring him only fleeting comfort.

Lowering herself to her harp, Meary softly plucked a series of ethereal notes. Colin settled himself on the floor at her feet and laid his head on her lap.

Meary played the sweetest songs she knew for him, pausing only briefly between melodies to stroke the hair at her temples or bring his hand to her lips to gift his palm with a gentle kiss. Neither spoke. There was no necessity for words.

She could hear his breathing deepen, become more relaxed with each successive song. It warmed her heart.

She might not have title or land or riches, but she had a wealth of love to give. Love was the only thing he needed tonight.

When he took her hand and led her to the bed, Meary smiled.

They shed their clothes into a heap on the floor, slipping quickly under the covers and into each other's arms.

"I tried to stay away," Colin whispered. "I know I should not be here. But I want you so desperately."

"Shh," Meary soothed, pressing her fingers to his lips. "'Tis all right."

She replaced her fingers with her lips, checking any further speech he might have in mind to make with a warm, loving kiss.

Colin pulled her tighter into his arms as she kissed him again and again.

Meary held nothing of herself back from him as they silently clung together, their hands eagerly renewing their acquaintance with each other's flesh. She caressed his arms, legs, back, buttock—imbuing her touch with all the love she had for him. She pillowed his head on her breasts. Her lips cherished his. She made love to him in the purest sense of the act.

Colin drank in the passion she offered him in great gulps, never slacking his hold on her.

When they merged their bodies into one flesh, it was less a congress of carnality than an infinitely tender communion of an impoverished spirit and a giving soul.

The two lovers slept entwined in each other's arms.

"You are horrible! I demand you cease this abhorrent

behavior at once. I have endured all the rustic living I can bear to endure, I tell you! You are coming home to England, and that is final!" Lady Swanscroft screeched.

Colin stared through her at the unlit candle on the wall. How many times must they repeat this tiresome argument? Would she never admit defeat and go back to England? He didn't know how he could make his position any more clear. Keeping his voice carefully modulated, he stated for at least the hundredth time since his family's unfelicitous arrival, "I am staying in Ireland. This is my home now and I have no intention of ever leaving it."

"What about Swanscroft! Have you no feeling for your ancestral home?"

"Swanscroft is Edwin's home, not mine. I haven't lived there for years."

"But what about all the years you devoted to its upkeep?" she cajoled.

"They were wasted years. As fast as I put money into Swanscroft, Edwin took it out *with your blessing*. I am afraid retaining Swanscroft for the family has been a lost cause since the day Edwin became marquess."

"Edwin is no different than your father."

Lord, the woman had a grating voice. Could she not speak one word at a natural volume and refrain from using that shrill pitch? Adjusting the lace at his sleeve, Colin replied, "Father loved his luxuries but he accepted, albeit reluctantly, the responsibilities of his position and tended the family fortunes enough to finance his pleasures and yours."

"You're just jealous of your brother!"

"There is some truth in your accusation. I have not found being a second son to my liking. But that is neither here nor there. Swanscroft belongs to Edwin, and if he wants to keep it, he will have to do what is necessary to do so."

"That's why we are here," Lady Swanscroft proclaimed. "Don't think we are bringing you back to England because we enjoy your company. We are doing it because it is necessary."

"Rest assured, I have never suffered under the delusion you were asking me to come back because you missed me. It is only my generous purse you have missed."

Lady Swanscroft did not refute his blunt statement. She saw no reason to do so. Instead, as she had done so often it was taking on the qualities of a chant, she said, "It is your duty to keep us in comfort." For added emphasis she asserted, "It is what you were born for."

"I half believed that once, believed it far too long for my own good." Colin shook his head and sighed ruefully, for the first time during the conversation letting his expression reveal a glimpse of what he was feeling. "The trouble is, it is a most unsatisfying way for a man to live his life. In truth, my behavior was not that of a man at all but that of a boy—a boy desperately trying to find favor in the eyes of his kin. In a way you did me a kindness by refusing to appreciate all my efforts on behalf of Edwin and you. You made me grow up and face the truth."

"You're talking nonsense! You are thirty years of age and have been full grown for years. This has nothing to do with your stubborn refusal to return to England and do your duty."

"It has everything to do with it. I left England because I had grown tired of letting myself be used. Ireland has taught me the pleasures of being master of my own world."

"You are master of a barren track of Irish soil and a ruler over a house that is nothing but a cold pile of stones. How can that compete with Swanscroft?"

Colin's emotionless mask slipped firmly back in place. "Because it is mine. If I make a profit, it is mine to keep. And if I fail to prosper, it will be my doing and mine alone."

"You've gone completely mad! I shall have you locked away in Bedlam."

"I fail to see how that will improve your and Edwin's situation."

"You are horrible!"

"And you are starting to repeat yourself, Mother. I suggest we end this conversation." Colin turned to go.

"You are not leaving this room until you agree to return to England!"

He continued to walk away. "Wrong. I am leaving now."

"And where will you go? Back to the arms of your blind little Irish whore?" Lady Swanscroft called after him.

Colin whirled around to face her. Had his mother seen him slip into Meary's room last night or out again this morning? He cursed himself for allowing his own needs to override his responsibility to protect Meary. "Lady Meary is not a whore," he stated tersely.

"Then why do you look so startled? Why look, you're blushing. I've caught you haven't I? And I just said it to bait you. I had not the slightest inkling it was true. Edwin will be so delighted with me." She laughed at her own cunning. "You may call her Lady Meary and pretend she is a guest, but now I know the *real* reason you do not wish to depart Ireland. You've always been such a skinflint with your money. Blind Irish whores must come cheap compared to the sighted English variety."

"I give you fair warning, if you dare use the term 'whore' and Meary's name in the same breath again, I shall personally eject you from my house," Colin growled, casting the veil from his emotions and giving his mother full view of the extent of his wrath. His eyes narrowed to rapier-sharp slits, and his lips stretched taut across his teeth. "Meary is not my whore. She is my betrothed, and you would do well to remember to treat her with the respect due my future wife!"

"You can't be serious," Lady Swanscroft gasped.

"Oh, yes I can," he vowed.

Meary stood at the top of the stairs, not knowing whether she should proceed or retreat back into her room. She had only caught the last of their argument, but what she heard was enough to make her heart pound and her head spin.

Colin had called her his betrothed. Despite his assurance to his mother that he was serious, she could not quite believe her ears. She wanted it to be true, but if it was, why hadn't he said a word to her? It was customary to secure the bride's acceptance before publicly announcing a marriage.

Meary took a step toward the stairs, realized she was trembling violently, and quietly slipped back into her room.

After all this time, if he meant to wed her, why hadn't

he told her so? He had been gone when she awakened this morning and had been out of the house all day, but he had had ample opportunity to do so last night. It didn't make sense.

Mayhap he was only trying to protect her from his mother's vicious tongue by pretending he was going to wed her. She should not let herself be deluded by false hopes.

Still, she could not help but be hopeful.

She had never wanted to leave him; she loved him. If he married her, there would be no reason to go. There would be no need to flee from her weakness for his flesh. If he was willing to marry her, it meant he loved her.

Meary hugged her arms around her waist to steady herself. It was not intended she should hear what Colin had said to his mother. He might be embarrassed if he knew she had. She could not say a word. She would just have to wait for him to come to her; then she would have her answer.

Chapter 23

Lady Swanscroft paced back and forth across her empty bedchamber, wringing her hands and scowling so intensely deep lines etched crow's-feet around her mouth and eyes.

"I cannot believe he would even consider sullying the Garrick name by marrying that little Irish nobody. What could he possibly see in her? She has nothing of worth to offer him. She's not even whole. He has grown not only selfish but stupid," she muttered to herself.

She stopped short. She might not hold her second son in high regard, but she knew he was not stupid. That thought led her to her next. He was lying about his intentions to marry his whore. He had only said what he said to shock her into silence.

A sense of relief washed over her with the realization, but it quickly was supplanted by a cold, calculating fury.

"I have been too indulgent." Lady Swanscroft clawed at the lace trimming her sleeves. "Far too indulgent! I should have never let him leave England in the first place. It's past time I take matters into my own hands and see that justice is done."

She passed before the mirror and snarled at her own reflection. "I am sick unto death of Ireland!"

She had told Colin she believed the real reason he stayed in Ireland was his whore, but even as she spoke the accusation, she knew it to be illogical. She didn't doubt he was enamoured of his little harpist, but he could drag the woman with him back to England if he must have her. He'd probably enjoy doing just that, if for no other reason than to embarrass his family with his boorish tastes. No, Meary O'Byrne could not be the reason he continued to stay . . . but she could be used to help convince him to leave.

She continued to pace and mutter. "I vow I'll make him sorry he put me to all this trouble. He needs to be severely punished for his disloyalty. . . ."

Her eyes hardened with determination as she recalled the countless injuries she had suffered since leaving her home in England. Colin knew how she hated to travel. He knew how boring she found country living. Why if she was back home, she and Edwin could be visiting jewelers and dress shops all day and attending parties every night. Instead, day after day, night after night, they sat in this dreary house.

Justice most definitely wanted to be done, and she was most eager to mete it out. But she needed to do so in a way that would serve her purposes. Colin must be brought back under the family yoke. He must be made so thoroughly disillusioned with life in general and Ireland in particular, he would never have the will to leave them again.

*　　*　　*

"Mother, I came just as soon as I heard you requested my presence." Edwin Garrick bowed low over her hand as he brought it to his lips.

"Such a good, dependable son. I can always rely on you, can't I, my love."

He preened at her words and smiled slyly. "What is it you wanted to see me about?"

"As you know we have been in Ireland far longer than I ever intended," Lady Swanscroft began, her voice crackling with emotion. "I want to go home."

"How can we do that? Colin is being decidedly stubborn about leaving this place. If we return without him, we shall never be able to fend off our creditors."

"I realize that," she said somewhat impatiently.

Edwin hunched his shoulders and turned his back to her. "Has he agreed to come home?"

"Not yet, but he will soon." She lowered her voice to a whisper. "Your mother has a plan . . . but I need your help."

Colin surveyed the long expanse of broken stone wall from atop his horse, then dismounted and inspected the damage more closely. "When did you say you found this?"

"This morning, yer lordship," Fiach O'Conor, the crofter who had reported the destruction, replied.

"It is obviously deliberate."

"Aye."

"Do you have any idea who might have done it?"

Fiach hesitated.

"A disgruntled local?" Colin prompted.

"Could be," Fiach opined. "Or it could be the Houghers have come down from Connaught."

"If they have, it means we're in for more trouble."

"Aye. They'll not be stopping at breaking down fences."

Colin ran his hand over his chin and reset two stones where the wall had been. "Mayhap we are being overly gloomy. There is no evidence this is the work of a gang of marauding cattle killers. When I first came to Ireland, there were several similar incidents. They stopped of their own accord."

"Aye . . ." Fiach did not sound convinced.

"But?" Colin urged him to speak what was on his mind.

"I'm not saying the locals 'twere responsible the first time, but assuming they 'twere, why would they be making this sort of mischief now? Ye may be English, but ye've proved yerself a fair landlord."

Colin acknowledged his statement with a nod. "I have done my best to be equitable; however, as you say, I *am* English. Mayhap that is reason enough for some men to hate me still."

"'Tis true." Fiach shifted his weight from one foot to the other.

"But you have no idea who might carry a grudge?"

"Nay," he stated.

Colin saw no point in interrogating him further. Even if he did know something, O'Conor would keep his lips tightly sealed. Irishmen had an instinctive distrust of the authorities—especially English authorities. They did not tell tales on each other, even when they felt the other in the wrong.

329

"Gather some men to fix the fence, and ask them to keep their eyes alert for any strangers in the area," he instructed.

"Aye, yer lordship."

Mounting his horse, Colin spurred him in the direction of the house.

Though he was concerned about the fence smashing, Colin saw no purpose in becoming unduly distressed. No matter how worthily he acquitted himself, there would always be those who objected to his presence on this land.

If he could find out who was responsible, he intended to see them punished, but all in all the landlord portion of his life was going rather well.

In his first year in Ireland he had turned a tidy profit and established his authority in a firm but friendly manner with most, and the two-story wing he was adding onto the tower house was nearing completion.

If only his private life was going so well. It had been two days since he and his mother had had their last argument about his refusal to return to England. He must have finally convinced her he would not be changing his mind, as she had not broached the subject again, but neither she nor Edwin had given the least sign they had started packing their bags.

He wanted them out of his house.

He could not propose to Meary until they were safely on their way back to England, and he was growing more and more impatient by the day. He had not returned to Meary's room since the night she had played a private concert for him, and he sorely missed the intimate aspect of their relationship. A part of him counselled that since the news was out, there was no point in continuing to maintain the appearance of propriety. But for Meary's sake, he felt such was the wisest course.

His mother may have stumbled upon the knowledge he and Meary were lovers, but thus far she had wisely kept silent on the subject. He didn't want to give her reason to abandon her uncharacteristic restraint.

Of course, if she did, he could then throw both her and Edwin out of his home, but he didn't want Meary to suffer the humiliation.

Colin knew he could throw them out without giving any reason at all, but he was loathe to do so. His mother was behaving herself where Meary was concerned, and in fairness she should be rewarded for her efforts. Besides, much as he might regret the fact, they were his family. He preferred they go of their own accord.

If he thought they meant to move in with him permanently, his position would be different, but as long as this was just a visit, and he could cling to the hope that each day they were here would be their last, he was determined to resist the urge to sink to their level and churlishly pack them into their hired coach and give the horses the whip.

"Ho, brother. Why the grim expression?" Edwin cheerily greeted as he thundered up alongside Colin, barely reining his horse in in time to avoid a collision.

Colin noted with disdain the froth bubbling at the lips of the gelding Edwin rode. "I have told you before, and I will tell you again, Edwin: if you persist in abusing my horses, I will forbid you the use of my stables. This is your last warning."

"It is good to ride them hard. It expands their lungs," Edwin argued.

"An interesting theory, but one I don't embrace. What you do with your own horses is your business. I make the rules concerning mine."

"Oh, stop being so arrogant. That's my prerogative."

"May I say, you do it exceedingly well."

"Thank you. I do try my best to comport myself as befits my title. Keeps the peasants in their place, you know." He chortled at his own wit.

Colin sighed. Edwin's one virtue was that he was not as peevish as their mother, but his brand of humor failed to amuse Colin. There was too much truth beneath his glibly spoken words. Edwin's sincere belief he was innately superior to his fellow man was easy enough to understand. To Colin's knowledge, his brother had never been denied a single desire. To be raised thusly could not help but warp his view of the world. Once grown, his handsome looks and bottomless purse had served Edwin well. Colin realized that, in a way, he had helped make him what he was. Still, understanding did not bring with it respect or a liking for his companionship. He gripped the reins in his hands a little tighter. "Is there a reason you tried to run me down with my own horse?"

"No. I was just out enjoying my afternoon ride when I spied you on the heath. You looked lonely."

"I am perfectly content with my own company," Colin assured him.

"Really? Rumor has it you're quite the Romeo."

Colin pressed his lips together. It did not surprise him in the least his mother had confided in Edwin, but he didn't like it. The more people who knew of his plans, the more likely Meary would find out about them before he was ready for her to do so. It was his own fault for telling his mother in the first place, but he had been provoked beyond reason. In any case, he had no intention of discussing Meary with his brother. He was not so naive he missed the double entendre behind Edwin's goading comment. "The rumor is false," he stated succinctly.

"Then you do not intend to wed your pretty little harpist?" Edwin asked, waggling a knowing brow. "I told mother even *you* would never do something that oafish." He sighed dramatically. "Of course, she agreed with me. She had come to the same conclusion herself and only feigned belief in the union to solicit my unbiased opinion of your intentions. We discussed the matter quite thoroughly and concluded you were only shamming her to punish her for stumbling onto your little secret. A true Garrick would never stoop so low he would consider giving the family name to an Irish peasant no matter how pretty. I'm sure Meary O'Byrne makes a fine lover, but she would never do for a wife."

"If your lengthy discussion with Mother led you to such a conclusion, then I'm afraid you both wasted your breath," Colin informed him. "I fully intend to wed Lady Meary. In fact, the reason I was gone from the estate when you and mother arrived from England was because I was off making the arrangements."

"Then the rumor *is* true? How very droll."

"The rumor I intend to take a bride, yes. The rumor that I possess the romantic spirit of Shakespeare's Romeo is not."

Edwin grinned from ear to ear. "So some rumors are true, and some rumors are not. How very very interesting. I wonder how one judges the difference?"

"A wise man judges all rumors false. It is by far the safest course." Colin made no attempt to veil the threat in his tone.

333

Edwin was not daunted. "If it is true you are engaged to your house guest, why didn't you introduce us to her as your betrothed?"

Colin shifted on his saddle. "I have yet to ask the lady to be my bride," he admitted.

"Really?"

"Your arrival forced me to delay my plans," he murmured through tight lips.

"How very vexatious for you. Let us fly to her side this very moment and inform your bride of her happy fate."

"No," Colin stated adamantly. "I will ask for Lady Meary's hand in my own time and way."

"Tsk, tsk, brother. Still trying to maintain your little deception, aren't you. You no more intend to wed Meary O'Byrne than I do. You've too keen an eye for a bargain to pay for merchandise you can have for naught. You just want to keep her charms all for yourself," Edwin cooed.

"Keep away from Meary," Colin warned.

"This is delightful. My baby brother has fallen in love with his mistress and doesn't want to share. Be careful Colin. I would hate to see her break your heart." Laughing gleefully, he spun his horse on its heels and galloped off in the opposite direction.

"Damn!" Colin cursed his miserable fortune. He should have known this was how Edwin would react. He should caution Meary.

Even as the prudent thought formed in his head, he knew in his heart he would do no such thing.

If Meary's love was true, it wouldn't matter what Edwin did. And if it was not, it was best he find out now . . . before it was too late.

Chapter 24

The next day another section of fence was found destroyed and the day after that ten head of butchered cattle were discovered rotting in the pasture.

Colin was furious at the senseless waste. He spent the day riding from cottage to cottage, talking with his tenants in hopes of learning anything that might help catch whoever was responsible. Everyone he talked to claimed not to have seen a thing.

He went over every encounter he had had with his tenants over the past few months, trying to recall when and where he might have made an enemy. There were three men with whom he recently had exchanged terse words. Two were neglecting their property. The third he had caught beating his wife during a fit of drunkenness.

He called each man to the tower house and questioned him at length. Each proclaimed his innocence and vowed to have no knowledge of who might be behind the attacks. Colin did not dismiss them as suspects, but his instincts told him they were telling the truth.

On the fifth day, nine more head of cattle were found

butchered. Scratched in the earth in Gaelic near the dead cattle were the words: "Get out of Ireland!"

Colin continued to question his tenants. He organized his most trusted servants and crofters into bands to patrol the perimeter of his estate. He enlisted Meary to keep her ears open to the local gossip.

He couldn't understand why this sort of trouble was starting up again. The attacks were much like those he had experienced during his first months in Ireland, but their frequency and the number of animals killed exceeded the hostility he had experienced upon his arrival. He had never caught those responsible for the long ago attacks, and it was possible the same men were involved, but he could think of naught he had done to incite rebellion among his tenants. Unless they resented his relationship with Meary. . . .

It was no secret how O'Hanlon felt about him. Mayhap the man had finally reached the limits of his forbearance and had decided to stir the locals up in hopes of driving him out of Ireland. Though he had no other reason to believe he had anything to do with the recent attacks against his livestock, and such underhanded methods seemed beneath O'Hanlon, he quietly asked Annie to keep an eye on him—just to be sure.

Because he was desperate, Colin even considered his mother and Edwin as suspects, but only fleetingly. His mother never left the tower house, and Edwin did so only to visit the stables. Though they had the most to gain by his leaving Ireland, the pattern of the attacks was too familiar and too Irish in nature to have been authored by them.

Seven days after the first stretch of fence had been toppled, a cloud of thick, black smoke was spotted rising

336

up from the heath shortly after dawn. Colin gathered a band of men and rode out to investigate. What he discovered made his blood boil.

An entire herd of sheep had been slaughtered, doused with lamp oil, and set afire. The culprits responsible for these assaults upon his estate clearly intended to insure nothing could be salvaged from the carcasses.

"Damn them to hell," Colin murmured as he and his men stood helpless, staring at the heap of burning flesh. The stench was horrendous, and the smoke made their eyes water.

After a few moments, he shrugged off his lassitude and began a methodical scrutiny of the ground. The earth was badly churned, but he found fresh tracks leading away from the area. They traveled north for about one hundred yards, then disappeared into the rocky terrain.

He had his men fan out, but further searching discovered no more tracks. The miscreants had planned well their route of escape. The hard earth made their path impossible to follow. Slowly, the searchers returned to their horses.

"Fiach." Colin called the crofter over to his side. He knew him to be trustworthy and had given him the duty of overseeing the various patrols. "I fear you may have been right. It seems we may be dealing with the Houghers or a similar gang of outlaws, after all. I want your patrols doubled at night."

"Aye."

"Also spread word to all my tenants, I want the presence of any and all strangers to the area reported immediately. I don't care how innocent the man might seem. I want to know of his whereabouts and purpose in coming here. Anyone who helps catch those responsible will be given a generous reward. Anyone caught withholding information will face eviction."

Fiach nodded. "I'll be telling them, yer lordship," he said grimly.

"You dislike my use of threat?"

"Aye."

"Do you have a better idea?"

He scratched his head and thought long and hard before replying, "Nay."

"Then I can see no help for it. It is my duty as landlord to see the law upheld, and I must do so by whatever means necessary. They must be made to see whoever is doing this injures them as well as me. There will be empty bellies this winter, if this level of destruction continues unchecked."

"I'll tell them so," Fiach said.

"Good. If you need me for any reason, I'll be back at the house for a short while; then, I intend to ride north and personally inquire of all I meet what if anything they saw last night."

Upon riding into the tower house yard, Colin gave his horse over to the care of a stable boy and strode into the house.

His mood was exceedingly black, but the sight of Meary sitting by the fire brought a tentative smile to his lips.

"Good morning," he greeted.

"Is it after all?" she asked hopefully. "Annie said there's been more trouble."

"There has." Colin pulled up a chair and sagged onto it. He stretched his hands toward the warmth of the fire. "This time they slaughtered a whole herd of sheep, then set the carcasses on fire. In truth, the only thing good

338

about this morning is finding you sitting by my hearth."

"Ye sound weary."

"I am. I feel as though I am being besieged from every direction. Mother and Edwin make my home a hell, and now some invisible band of villains is turning my estate into a battlefield."

"Ye know for certain more than one man is responsible?" she queried.

"We think we found three, mayhap four, different sets of hoof prints this morning. There may have been more, but the ground was so torn up it was difficult to tell for sure. Then we lost the tracks in the rocks."

"'Tis difficult to believe that many tenants would of a sudden turn against ye at the same time, especially when ye have done naught to be stirring up their ire."

"My thoughts exactly. It is possible some sort of rebellion against my rule has been organized, but why now? And who could be responsible? Fiach O'Conor has suggested it might be the work of a group from up north called the Houghers. Even though no strangers have been spotted in the area, I am inclined to agree with him. It is well known the estates of Englishmen are most often the target of their crimes."

She nodded. "I hope ye catch them soon."

"As do I. I wish to return to the tranquil life we once knew. I am tired of watching this year's profits dwindle and having all my time consumed in fruitless pursuit of an enemy I am not even sure I know."

Meary reached for his hand and gently squeezed it. "I wish there was more I could be doing to help."

"You do more than enough. I know it is not easy for you with Mother and Edwin here. Annie tells me how hard you strive to maintain the peace between them and

339

the rest of the household, and I though I have had little opportunity to show it, I appreciate it more than you know. My life would be bereft of pleasure were it not for your presence in my home."

"I'm glad to do what I can."

Colin rose to his feet. "Have you eaten?"

"Nay."

"Nor have I. Mayhap you will join me at the table and share a breakfast? I cannot stay long, but I would be grateful for your company."

Meary eagerly accepted Colin's invitation to breakfast with him before duty called him away from the house again. Once the food arrived, he spoke little, but she didn't mind. Their moments alone together were too rare, and just being with him was enough to make her happy. Well, *almost* enough . . .

If he truly intended to wed her, he had yet to mention the fact to her. She knew he was preoccupied with his problems with the estate, but she could not imagine thoughts of marrying her had been crowded out of his mind completely. Then, again, a marriage proposal was so serious a step mayhap he wanted to wait to tell her of his intentions until he had more time to devote to the matter of their marriage. These past days he had made no secret of the fact he appreciated and had come to depend on her presence in his home. No one could claim it was her services as a mistress to which he referred. Since the arrival of his family, they had shared the same bed only once.

Meary longed to bring up the subject herself, but two things prevented her from abandoning her original decision to let him be the one to bring up the issue. One was a sincere desire not to add to Colin's present burdens if his words to his mother had not been true. The other was the lack of an opportune time. This morning was the first day all week they had had more than ten minutes alone together, and his mood was not favorable. He was too tired and frustrated. It was difficult to be patient when her entire future hung in the balance, but until conditions improved, she had no choice.

There was no question of her leaving now, not before she knew the truth. She would never forgive herself if she allowed impatience to cause her to throw away the chance, no matter how uncertain, to stay with the man she loved on the terms her pride and conscience required. If she thought a marriage between them would benefit only herself, she might not be so willing to continue to deny her mentor's repeated pleas she remove herself from this house without further delay. But she did not believe such was the case. She had always believed she was good for Colin, and now having met his family, she was more convinced than ever that the love she would bring to their marriage was far more important to his well-being than any wealth or prestige some other bride might bring him.

There was no guarantee her staying would result in the happy state of affairs she most desired, but even if it did not, she at least would have the satisfaction of knowing she had not abandoned Colin in his hour of need.

As soon as he finished eating, Colin excused himself and headed back to the stables, leaving Meary to face another day alone.

When Colin had said the presence of his mother and the marquess did not make her life easy, she had been silent on the subject, but truer words were never spoken.

Lady Swanscroft was as she always was. She complained from the moment she arose until she closed her eyes at night. A steady stream of general slurs against the Irish race flowed from her lips. And she had personal insults for those unfortunate enough to come within striking range of her tongue. Nothing and no one, except her son Edwin, was ever good enough for her.

Meary had taken to avoiding direct contact with her with near religious fervor, fearful that without Colin's protective presence, Lady Swanscroft would sling the epithet "whore" in her face with unbridled enthusiasm. If she did call her whore, Meary did not know how she could defend herself. It was, after all, the miserable truth.

As Lady Swanscroft disliked her company as much as Meary disliked hers, it was not that arduous a task to keep her distance.

Lord Swanscroft was proving to be far more difficult to elude. Of late, he seemed to be bored with chasing the maids and be concentrating all his undesirable attention on her.

He was constantly at her elbow, whispering blandishments in her ear and finding excuses to catch hold of her hand, which he had an annoying penchant for kissing. One day he sent a footman to her room with a rose sachet, the next day a tray bearing wine, two days later a bottle of perfume arrived at her door. She refused them all, bidding the footman to return them to the sender along with the message she would not accept gifts from him.

Meary strongly suspected that Lady Swanscroft had recounted her conversation with Colin to her eldest son, and that might have something to do with his increased interest in her. Though she had rebuffed his every overture, well she knew a fallen woman's words and actions carried far less weight than one of virtue. He might now consider her fair game.

But if Lady Swanscroft had told him the former, she must also have told the marquess of his brother's intention to wed her. Meary might harbor her own doubts about Colin's unexpected proclamation, but Lady Swanscroft had no reason not to believe it true. Surely, the marquess would not chase after his own brother's bride.

In the end, Meary decided it didn't much matter what, if anything, the marquess knew of her relationship with Colin. There was no question in her mind he was a scoundrel; the only thing she was unsure of was to what degree.

"Lady Meary. Wait up. I'd like to walk with you," the marquess called.

Meary grit her teeth and cursed under her breath. She had thought she had escaped the house unnoticed. Every day but one this week she had had to forego her afternoon walk because she couldn't elude the marquess. She was loathe to do so again.

Tightening her grip on the head of her cane, Meary kept walking. However, she altered her planned route to one that would not take her too far from the house.

"My, my, what a brisk little walker you are," the marquess commented as he came up alongside of her. "I hope you don't mind if I join you."

I mind very much, Meary answered in her head, but to him she said, "'Tis not anywhere fascinating I am going. Ye would enjoy yourself better if ye stayed in the house."

"I cannot imagine how I could find any enjoyment

343

without your company."

"Mayhap your mother would be interested in joining ye for a game of piquet."

"I would rather be with you."

"I cannot be thinking why."

"Your beauty and charm lures me to your side. You have bewitched me."

Meary did not respond to his flattery.

"I have a present for you." He pressed a small cloth wrapped package into her hand.

"Thank ye for the thought, but 'tis not necessary." Meary tried to give it back, but he kept his hands closed and repeatedly stepped out of reach. Sighing in frustration, she tucked the package into her pocket.

"Aren't you going to open it?"

"Mayhap later."

"And deny me the pleasure of seeing your expression of joy when you find out what it is? You would not be so cruel."

Meary knew she was being blatantly rude, and she decided to acquiesce, though expediency motivated her far more than guilt. She merely wished to avoid further argument and had little care if she insulted the marquess by displaying bad manners. She had no intention of keeping the present, but it could be returned by one of the footmen after it was opened as easily as before which had been her original intention.

Retrieving the package from her pocket, she removed the riband. Her finger explored the contents. Inside lay a pair of filigree earrings with large stones set in the center of each design.

"They're gold and sapphire to match the color of your hair and eyes. Cost me a small fortune, but I was glad to pay it knowing how beautiful they would look on you."

"And where would ye be buying such a thing in these parts?" Meary queried.

"Say what?" he protested in a startled voice.

"No peddler has come to trade that I'm knowing of, and I'm doubting these would be among his wares even if he had."

"Why do you care where I bought them?"

"I don't. I'm merely trying to let ye be knowing as politely as possible that I know ye are lying when ye say ye bought them especially for me."

The pitch of his voice changed from whining to one of wicked delight. "Do I detect a note of jealousy?"

He captured her hand and attempted to bring it to his lips. With the deft execution of a series of strategic twists of the wrist, Meary managed to drop the earrings into his palm and extract her hand.

Smiling triumphantly, she replied, "Nay. Even if ye had purchased them especially for me, I would not be accepting them. I don't know how I can be making myself any more plain. I am not going to be accepting *any* gifts from ye."

"But why not?"

She was tempted to tell him the reason she refused his gifts was because she considered him a lazy, foppish, thoroughly loathsome man, but good breeding prevailed, and she offered a more diplomatic answer. "'Tis improper for a lady to be accepting gifts from a gentleman she has no interest in."

"The other beau you spoke of would not approve?"

"Nay, he would not."

"But I am more handsome than Colin."

Meary grit her teeth. So the marquess *did* know Colin's

345

relationship with her was more than that of a patron of the arts. It made his pursuit of her that much more repugnant. "That matters not to me," she tersely informed him.

"Oh," he exclaimed with annoyance. "I suppose it wouldn't, would it, you being blind and all. But mayhap the fact that you will find me far more generous will hold sway with you."

"Ye are generous with your brother's money."

"He told you that did he. How very droll of him."

"Nay. He said not a word to me. 'Twas your own voice and that of your mother that carried the tale of your greed to me ears."

"Do you often eavesdrop on private conversations?"

"Actually, I do," Meary replied without compunction. "But in this case, 'twas not necessary. When ye speak to Lord Colin, your voices are ofttimes so loud 'tis impossible not to hear what 'tis being said."

"It is amusing you disapprove of me, when you are no better. Is not your hand in his pocket as firmly as mine? Or does Colin require his mistresses to support themselves?"

Meary did not know how to answer his first question. The sarcastic tone of the second made it clear he had only asked it to sharpen his original goad. Though she had never asked Colin for a penny, there was enough truth in the marquess' words to make her squirm inside her skin.

"Well? Where is the difference?" the marquess pressed.

"The difference 'tis I do not ask Lord Colin to support me. He does it of his own free will. And I give back to him something ye do not. I give him me music and I give him me love."

"Are you suggesting I take up singing and engage in unnatural acts with my brother to repay him for his financial contributions to the family coffers?" Lord Swanscroft drawled.

"I was speaking of a passion of the heart not of the flesh!" Meary replied indignantly. "I esteem him for his many fine qualities. . . ."

"Are you claiming you do not share his bed?" he interrupted.

"Nay. But 'twas more than lust that brought me there, and 'tis more than lust that keeps me by his side."

"Don't tell me you have been deceived by the false promise he will someday wed you?" he asked with a mixture of sympathy and disbelief. "It is the oldest ploy in the world and one my brother has used often. Forgive me, but I would have judged you far too intelligent to fall for so unoriginal a lie."

"Your brother has not lied to me," Meary stated.

"You poor, silly thing. I know it is hard but you must face the truth."

Meary knew he had misinterpreted her words, but she didn't care. What purpose would be served if she explained to him the reason she could make her statement with such certainty was because Colin had never promised her anything except that he would provide financially for any offspring that might result from their illicit union? What purpose in claiming she gave herself to his brother out of love? None that she could think of. She doubted the marquess was capable of understanding such noble concepts as debts of gratitude, genuine affection, and loyalty. They would be as incomprehensible to him as his lack of brotherly love was to her.

"I would like to be returning to the house now," Meary said.

"Of course, you would." He sounded the epitome of compassion. "You need time alone to accept the magnitude of your folly and to decide what you shall do. Just remember, I am the one who saved you with the truth, and you can depend on me to save you from a life on the streets. I shall be eagerly waiting to show you how a true gentleman treats his lover."

Chapter 25

Everyone was tense.

Not a day went by without the discovery of some new outrage against the estate. Some days it was only a toppled length of fence, but more often it was slaughtered livestock, a wagon set afire, or a field destroyed.

Colin was obsessed with finding out who was responsible for the crimes to his property. Meary worried about Colin, the estate, and what to do about the marquess, who was becoming increasingly impatient with her for failing to prefer his charms to his brother's. Lady Swanscroft spent her days wringing her hands and wailing piteously that any day now they would all be murdered in their sleep. Seumas continued to urge Meary to leave her English lover, his efforts enhanced by his intense dislike of Lord Colin's family. Brendan was afraid something might happen to the horses. Annie was convinced the arrival of Lord and Lady Swanscroft had called a curse upon the house and was incensed that neither Colin nor Meary would let her throw them out. The servants and tenants were fretful Lord Colin might tire of his troubles and decided to become an absentee landlord, replacing his fair rule with a manager of the same ilk as the one his uncle had imposed upon them.

Meary sat at the table in the great hall toying with the lump of porridge in the bottom of her bowl and frowning fiercely.

Any minute now the marquess might be heard coming down the stairs. He had taken to rising earlier these days, so he could have more time with her.

His pursuit of her was getting out of hand. She had not a moment she could call her own. She had tried reasoning with him, rebuking him, ignoring him, and twice she had chased him off with her cane; but nothing seemed to penetrate his thick, lecherous skull.

The man was clearly so enamored of himself he couldn't grasp the concept that she did not welcome his attentions. He laughed when she told him she preferred his brother's company to his. No matter how many times or how sternly she rebuffed him, he behaved as though she was merely confused and would recover her senses if only she spent more time in his company.

Adding to Meary's misery was the certain knowledge Colin had observed his brother's pursuit of her on more than one occasion, and he had said not a word. Whether he intended to wed her or not, surely his brother's trespass should elicit some reaction. She understood how upset he was about his estate and how busy he was, but it would go a long way toward soothing her ruffled feelings if he would say or do something to discourage his brother. It might not do any good, but he ought to at least try to do something.

The dread sound of the marquess descending the stairs assailed Meary's ears.

"Good morning, my dearest Meary. What shall we do to amuse ourselves today?" Lord Swanscroft greeted in syrupy tones.

Meary gritted her teeth at his uninvited familiarity. When he had requested she call him Edwin, she had refused, but he had seen fit to drop the title "Lady" from her name. Neither would he call her Miss O'Byrne. "I plan to be spending me day in the kitchen with Annie," she informed him.

"Then you must change your plans. I am ordering a basket packed and the carriage readied. We are going on a drive."

"A drive sounds like a lovely thing for *ye* to be doing, and I hope ye have a pleasant time." She rose to her feet. "*I* am spending the day in the kitchen."

"But you can't." Grabbing her arm, he pulled her toward him. "I shall be devastated if you do not go."

"Unhand me this instant or I shall be forced to use violent means to be securing me release." Meary wedged her cane between them and poked the head into his stomach.

Edwin instantly released her and took a step back. "It's lucky you're so beautiful, or I daresay I might start to find you tiresome. I like the thrill of the chase as well as the next man, but you carry the game too far."

Wielding her cane like a sword, Meary suffused her voice with icy authority. "I do not play a game."

The marquess ignored her words and peevishly proclaimed, "If you poke me with it again, I'm going to burn that grotesque stick before you do me some grave injury."

Meary's grip tightened on her cane. "Ye will be doing no such thing. 'Twas a gift and one I value highly."

His voice promptly lost its edge and became thick and cajoling. "Give me a kiss and I may reconsider."

"The only thing I'll be giving ye 'tis a swift whack on the head if ye do not leave me be!"

She heard him suck in his breath, then exhale it as a sigh. "If you show half the spirit in bed as you do out of it, I am going to be well rewarded when you join me there."

"I will roast in hell before I succumb to the likes of ye!"

"If it is heat you seek, I am more than willing to provide it," he drawled, ignoring the substance of her words. "I will set you afire with the flames of my passion and leave you begging for more of my fiery touch."

Meary groaned. These unromantic encounters with Lord Swanscroft were monotonous to the point of tedium. Since there was no hope of communicating with him, why endure his execrable company a moment longer?

Navigating a wide berth around him, she strode toward the kitchen door. "Good day, Lord Swanscroft. Please feel free to be taking the whole day for your drive. I promise ye, ye shall not be missed."

Meary knew she must do something. Every aspect of her life was awry, and it showed no sign of improving.

Her relationship with Seumas was in tatters. Lady Swanscroft treated her with contempt. The marquess tormented her. Annie was unbearably irritable. Colin was gone all day and sometimes half the night. When he was in the house, he was short-tempered and so exhausted his presence afforded her more pain than pleasure.

She had all but abandoned hope in the possibility Colin's statement to his mother concerning their marriage had any truth in it. If it had, he should have said *something* to her by now.

He had not visited her room once since she had overheard his conversation with his mother. Since both his mother and his brother now knew of their relationship, she could think of no good reason for his neglect. She knew it was sinful of her to crave his lovemaking, but as long as she was here and must bear the stigma of being his mistress anyway, why shouldn't she enjoy the benefit of his tender touch?

Because she was in the mood to feel thoroughly sorry for herself, she neglected to remember her own determination not to engage in physical relations with Colin again without the sanctity of marriage.

As if his neglect of her physical needs was not enough, he had withdrawn from her in other ways as well. Though he always inquired after her health and comfort when they were together, he said little else. He had never been loquacious, but since they had become lovers, he had always included her in the day to day affairs of the estate and his life. She missed the soothing sound of his voice.

She hadn't seriously reconsidered her decision to stand loyally by his side until his life was back in order and she had no positive proof a marriage between Colin and herself was never going to come to pass, but it was difficult to persevere under such adverse conditions day after day without some reassurance her presence was important to him.

After closeting herself in her room and wallowing in a trough of melancholy for half a day, Meary picked herself up and decided if she wanted life on the estate to improve, she best do something more than sit around bemoaning the situation and face the task head on.

What to do seemed obvious. There was nothing she could do about Lord and Lady Swanscroft. Colin must deal with them. But the attacks against the estate were a different matter. Colin had not requested her assistance, and she had been reluctant to interfere without invitation, but now he was going to get her help. If he didn't like it, he could order her to stop.

Most of the tenants might respect Colin as a man, but he was still an *English*man. She was Irish. Mayhap they would be more willing to confide in her than him. It was possible those involved possessed the cunning of the devil himself, but she found it difficult to believe someone somewhere hadn't seen something. It was more likely they couldn't bring themselves to tell tales on a fellow Irishman to an English landlord, even if remaining silent hurt them as well as him.

Annie was more than capable of running the household without her help. Meary had never suffered from the delusion that Colin's housekeeper required her guiding hand. Deferring to her as mistress of the household was just one of the many ways Annie employed in hopes of influencing Colin to wed her.

Meary was a little concerned that freed from her restraining hand, Annie's bad behavior toward Lord and Lady Swanscroft would become even more splenetic than it already was, but in the end she admitted to herself if Annie succeeded in driving the Garricks out, she would be inclined to applaud her rather than scold her. Besides, Annie was not her responsibility. She was Colin's. If he didn't want her abusing his family, he would have to deal with her himself.

Meary knew the estate was no more her responsibility than Annie was, but directing her energies there suited her purposes better. She was primarily motivated by a sincere desire to help Colin uncover the villains who were damaging the estate and urge loyalty to him, but she was also influenced by a strong desire to escape the house, or more specifically the marquess.

She knew he would try to follow her, but she planned to thwart him by never leaving the house alone. Brendan could be depended on to serve as her guard and guide most times, and when he could not, she would enlist one of the footmen.

She doubted the marquess would want to tag along if there was no hope he could ensnare her in a compromising situation, but if he did insist, she would ask Annie to slip a dose of laudanum in his evening wine to ensure he would sleep late enough into the morning she could be well on her way before he arose. Meary was certain Annie would be more than happy to accommodate her. She hated to resort to Machiavellian tactics, but it would be a waste of time to try to talk to the tenants if Lord Swanscroft was by her side. They would be less inclined to speak freely in front of him than they were to Colin.

Having thus settled everything in her mind, Meary set out to accomplish what she could.

Reining his horse to an abrupt halt at the edge of the yard, Lord Colin sat atop his horse and stared at his home.

He ran his hand across his sweat-stained brow. Another long, frustrating day of chasing nonexistent clues to nowhere. How many more would there be? He knew there were three men involved. He knew after committing their crimes, they rode north into the Burrens. There their trail disappeared into the rocky earth and was never found again. No one ever saw them come or go. It was as though he was dealing with ghosts.

It was possible some of his tenants were lying, but he had no idea which ones, and he could not punish them all for the iniquity of a few. It would only stir up more rebellion. He had known before he came to Ireland this sort of sabotage against the estates of Englishmen was not uncommon, but he had thought this business done with many months ago.

The only suspect with a strong motive he had was O'Hanlon, and Colin was loathe to believe he was responsible. It would complicate his relationship with Meary immeasurably. Too, he might not like O'Hanlon but he had come to respect him. There was an undeniable nobility about the way he refused to abandon Meary *or* his convictions. He would be extremely disappointed if he discovered the old man had resorted to villainy as a means to his ends. The evidence against O'Hanlon would have to be irrefutable before he would believe it.

Though he realized the thought was born of extreme mental as well as physical fatigue, Colin was beginning to wonder if there was some law written in the book of fate decreeing he should forever live his life in a state of wretchedness.

It seemed to him from the moment he had decided to wed Meary, the moment he had accepted his decision with joy, his life had become a series of misfortunes. Before he had even had a chance to ask Meary to be his bride, his mother and Edwin had arrived. Now, his livelihood was threatened.

Neither trial showed any sign of coming to an end any time soon.

Of a sudden, he realized what a fool he was being. His mother and Edwin would decide to leave eventually. If not, he could throw them out. Either he would catch those responsible for attacks on the estate or he would not. His fortunes did not depend on a profitable season. He had more than enough capital to see him through several years without eking a penny from the land. His whole future stretched out before him, and only one person held the power to determine whether it would be a future filled with contentment or empty of promise. His future depended on Meary.

How easily he had fallen back into his old bad habit of self-pity. He had thought he had cleansed himself of the stain his family had visited upon his soul, but he had not. Since the minute they had arrived, he had let them influence his thinking.

He had gone from a man on the verge of discovering himself in love to a shell of a man in the space of a heartbeat.

He thought himself not influenced because he refused to return to England with them, but he was still letting them control his thoughts and behavior. He had postponed his proposal. He had completely disrupted his normal schedule, in effect becoming a refugee from his own house. He couldn't remember the last time he had smiled, let alone laughed. He had shut himself off from his own feelings and the feelings of others.

He *knew* Meary loved him. The very fact she had stayed with him under the most adverse of circumstances, long after the two week deadline he had forced upon her had passed, evinced beyond a shadow of a doubt how very much she loved him. Yet he had been willing to stand by and do nothing while Edwin tried to steal her away from him. Why? Because of his unwavering faith in her? No. That reason would have made some sense. He had done nothing because he desired to test her. He ought to be horsewhipped!

What she must think of him he could only guess, but he knew he had a lot of explaining to do.

He wanted Meary by his side always. He would never find another woman like her. He should not have waited this long to realize the monumental error of his ways.

He hoped Meary would forgive him for his stupidity. He hoped many things. But mostly he hoped he would one day prove himself worthy of her love.

"There you are. I've been waiting for you for hours. I have something very urgent I wish to discuss with you," Lady Swanscroft greeted Colin as he entered the hall.

"Yes?"

"Edwin and I are homesick. We shall perish if we don't return to civilization immediately. Our trunks are already packed."

"I will have a carriage ready for you at first light," Colin promised, trying hard to repress the joyous grin that threatened to erupt on his stoic countenance. Mayhap his luck was finally turning. The departure of his family would not solve all his problems, but it would greatly improve the atmosphere of his home.

"You will be coming with us, of course," she stated.

His high spirits plummeted as he realized he had hoped for too much too soon. "No."

"But surely you see that you must."

"No," Colin repeated. "I thought we had settled this argument."

"I have held my tongue on the subject for as long as I am able. I will not pretend I ever liked the idea of you living in Ireland. Coming here was a selfish thing to do. It showed a great lack of loyalty to your family and your country. Still, I was doing my best to accept your decision." She dabbed at her eyes with a scented handkerchief. "But that was before these horrible attacks began. You may hold title to this land, but your people hate you. They are doing all they can to destroy you. It is clear they will never accept a foreign master."

"Why should that concern you? You hold no great affection for me yourself."

"I know in the past we have not been as close as we might have been . . . but whatever our differences, you are my son and I do not wish to see you dead."

It was a fine speech his mother made. Her voice held just the right note of penitence, but Colin was not going to be taken in. The game was too familiar to work. Though he believed his mother when she said she did not wish him dead, he did not believe the sentiment was motivated by maternal feelings. If he was dead, from where would her money come? "I grant you these attacks are not pleasant, but no human lives have been threatened," he reminded.

"Yet," his mother said. "I believe it is only a matter of time. It may not be today or tomorrow, but if you stay here, you will find an early grave. I know it as surely as I know the quality of diamonds. Come home where you will be safe."

"I am home," Colin stated, meeting his mother's gaze.

"You can't mean to say you are still considering

staying in this wretched land?"

"Ireland is my home, and Ireland is where I will stay," Colin confirmed. He continued to look his mother directly in the eye and was suffused with a soul-satisfying sense of accomplishment that he could do so. It was she who began to squirm and averted her gaze.

"But it is not reasonable," Lady Swanscroft protested.

"It is what I want."

She fell silent and her brow wrinkled in consternation. Colin watched her pace in a tight circle for a long minute; then, she came to an abrupt halt and faced him squarely. "I have steadfastly refused to believe it true of you. I can hardly bear even to think a son of mine might sink so low." Her gaze hardened. "But it must be true. It is her, isn't it? You don't want to leave your little Irish wh . . . *friend*."

" I believe the term you are looking for is: betrothed."

She appeared genuinely startled. Recovering herself, she twisted her grimace into a sympathetic frown and reached for his hand, stopping just short of touching him. "I would not be too quick to marry the wench. I tell you this as a kindness, and because I do not wish to see you make a dreadful mistake. The woman you say you plan to marry has taken advantage of the distraction your trouble on the estate has provided and has freely been bestowing her favors upon your brother Edwin. He has done his best to discourage her, but to no avail. I fear she is too fickle to make you a good wife."

"Lady Meary has been pursuing Edwin?" Colin calmly queried.

"I'm afraid it's true."

"How very interesting. From my observations I would

360

have said it was the other way around."

She forced fresh tears into her eyes. "You have not been here enough to observe them as I have."

"That is true; however, I have seen all I need to see to convince me Lady Meary is pure of heart."

"Then you are a fool."

Colin shrugged and smiled.

Lady Swanscroft took a step back and began to wring her hands. Her lips stretched tight over her teeth. Though she pretended to concentrate on the large ruby ring adorning her finger, she kept throwing furtive glances in his direction. At length, her shoulders sagged and she said, "I suppose, if you are determined to behave like a lovesick pup, you can bring her to England with you. Edwin and I will just have to bear the shame. Mind you, I am talking of your keeping her as a mistress. Marriage is out of the question."

"Thank you for your generous offer," Colin replied, "but I must decline."

"Why? I am giving you what you want!"

"I'm afraid you are suffering from the misconception that Lady Meary is what is keeping me in Ireland. She has naught to do with my decision. It is true I love her, but a woman is a portable creature. She could be *my bride* in England as well as Ireland." He paused, waiting for his mother to balk at his words. When her only response was a further tightening of her pursed lips, he continued, "What keeps me in Ireland is not love for a woman, but a love of possessing my own property. Edwin has Swanscroft. I have this piece of Irish soil. I am master here. In England I am nothing."

"Is being master so important you prefer to be the

master of a bunch of savage foreigners and a tract of worthless land to helping your brother keep Swanscroft?"

"Yes."

"Even if it means your death?"

"Yes."

"How can you behave like such a brute? I do not understand you at all!" she cried.

"I know you don't," Colin agreed. Where once he would have retreated behind a wall of self-pity at such words, now he only felt mild pity for her. He stood a little taller. "Fortunately, it is not necessary for you to understand. You only need accept I am never returning to England."

"But Edwin is incapable of running Swanscroft without you. He has no head for finance."

"I am not convinced Edwin is incapable—he is only unwilling to shoulder the responsibility that comes with the honor of the title marquess. All he need do is listen to Mr. Bartlett and all will be well for you. Edwin is capable of that."

"You are wrong."

"Then it is a shame he was your firstborn."

As she argued her strident voice rose and fell in pitch in direct connection with her ability and desire to disguise her true feelings in hopes of fostering a favorable outcome, but the underlying note of desperation had risen steadily. It continued to do so. "All this over a title? How can you be so selfish and coldhearted? I could not help he was born first!"

"It is not the title, but the privilege to be the master of one's own property and the fate that goes with it. That is what I would lose if I returned to Swanscroft."

"But what about the attacks?" she demanded.

"I will handle them."

Her face was now so florid even the thick, white layer of face powder she wore could not conceal the ruddiness of her complexion. She grabbed the front of his coat in her fists and twisted the fabric into hard knots. "Must I suffer for your brother's inadequacies?"

One by one, Colin disengaged her fingers from his coat. "I fear you must, for it is your pampering that molded him into the man he is today. But you need not despair. You will always have each other *and* the yearly allowance I promised to send. . . . Now, if you will excuse me, I have an important matter to which I need to attend."

"But we have settled nothing!" she wailed as he walked away.

Colin did not turn nor slow his stride. "The matter we discuss was settled long ago before you ever set foot in my house. I am sorry things have not turned out as you had planned, Mother, but we all must suffer some disappointments in this life."

Oddly, the conversation with his mother left Colin feeling light of heart rather than drained and depressed as their conversations usually did. He had stated his position plainly, without rancor. Of a sudden, he realized the underlying bitterness that had tied his gut in knots during all their previous encounters was absent. He regretted the absence of love between his family and himself, but for the first time in his life he accepted it. He did not feel compelled to try to win their affection by subjugating himself to their endless desires as he once had, nor did he feel a need to punish them for their lack of feeling.

He could not think what would make the difference except that he was determined to propose to Meary without delay. Mayhap in forming a new family he would purge the heartache of the old from his soul.

"Annie, where is Meary?" Colin demanded as he strolled into the kitchen, a triumphant smile on his face.

"Up in her room, the last I saw her," she replied charily as she stared in bewilderment at the grin on his face.

"Good." He turned to leave, but stopped before he left the room. "Arrange for a dance in the hall tonight. It has been too long since this house was filled with music."

Without further explanation, he quit the room.

A forceful knocking at her chamber door caused Meary to jump in alarm. She rapidly crossed the floor between her and the door. "Who is there?" she asked, half afraid it was the marquess trying to break down her door.

"Colin. Fetch a wrap. I would like you to come somewhere with me."

"Aye. I'll be right there." Meary responded to the urgency in his voice with an urgency of her own. She retrieved her wrap and presented herself at the door almost before she finished her sentence.

"Have I told you how beautiful you are today?"

"Nay." She disregarded the compliment, deeming it a mere politeness, and concentrated on discovering the reason he had sought her out. "Tell me what has happened. Has there been another attack? Is someone hurt? Have ye found out something about who has been killing your cattle?"

"No, no, and no," he systematically answered her

364

questions. "I am not here on business of the estate. Another matter brings me to your door."

When he did not elaborate, Meary asked, "Are ye going to be telling me what it is?"

"Not here. I will tell you when we get to where we are going."

"And where is that?"

He hesitated. "Forgive me, but I do not wish to say."

Meary was not sure what to make of his answer, nor was she sure what to make of the strange inflection in his voice. He was most definitely excited about something, but she wasn't sure if the cause of his excitement was good or bad fortune. "If ye do not wish to say, ye don't have to," she cautiously replied.

"Come on then." He took her hand and led her toward the stairs. He did not let loose of her until they had reached the stables.

Mounting his stallion, he gently lifted her up after him and settled her in the cradle of his arms.

"If anyone wants me, they will have to wait until we get back. I do not want to be disturbed for any reason. Is that clear?" Colin instructed the stable master.

"Aye, milord."

"Good. If there is any more trouble on the estate, have the men report it to Ann . . . Mr. O'Hanlon," he abruptly changed his mind. "Take your orders from him." It was a bold move Colin knew, but it was past time he and the old man learned to come to terms with each other. Mayhap this gesture of trust could be the beginning.

"Ye are leaving Seumas in charge?" Meary mumbled in disbelief as they galloped out of the yard.

"Yes."

Meary could only conclude that something startling

had happened this afternoon while she had been about the business of trying to discover who was responsible for the attacks on the estate. She longed to ask Colin to tell her what it was, but she forced herself to be patient. If it didn't concern the estate, it must concern his family. His reluctance to discuss the matter in the house gave credence to her surmise. But what could it possibly be, and how did it concern Seumas or herself?

Meary went over every word Colin had spoken since she had answered the knock at her door, but found herself becoming more curious and confused, not less.

Several times, she opened her mouth to ask him to enlighten her, but she always closed it again without uttering a word. His family was such a stormy subject, she thought it wisest to let him handle this matter in his own time and way.

"We have arrived," Colin announced as he reined his horse to a halt.

Meary instantly recognized the sound and scent of the place. "Why have ye brought me here?" she asked as he lifted her to the ground.

"Because it is where we first made love."

Chapter 26

"All this secrecy 'tis because ye have been seized by a sudden urge to be making love?" Meary asked, her voice raising half an octave.

"With you as a lover the urge is never sudden; it is constant. However, that is not why I have brought you here." He carried her hand to his lips and kissed her fingers. "I have brought you here to ask you to be my bride."

Meary stood stock still. How long had she waited to hear those words? So long her ears were now playing cruel tricks on her? The hope she had nearly abandoned surged through her veins, warming her from head to toe, at the same time fear her mind had snapped under the strain her life had become filled every sinew of her being, resulting in a state of bewilderment and paralysis.

"Well?" Colin prodded.

"I am not sure I heard ye clearly," she barely managed to choke out.

Falling to his knees at her feet, Colin rephrased his words as a question. "Meary O'Byrne will you do me the honor of becoming my bride?"

She had heard him correctly. Her heart began to dance with joy within her breast. Everything would be all right now. The voices in her head had not led her astray. After all his proclamations against the possibility of their marriage and waiting so long, it was too wonderful to be true. Her last thought sobered her, and she found herself voicing her uncertainty. "I don't fathom ye at all."

"Meary O'Byrne will . . ."

"Nay. I did not mean I needed ye to be repeating yourself. I just cannot understand why ye are asking me to wed ye . . . now."

"Because I was not wise enough to do it long ago."

"Are ye sure ye want to be doing this?" She forced herself to ask the question.

"Very sure."

"I thought ye were committed to bachelorhood. What has happened to be changing your mind?"

"I will explain everything to you, I promise. But first I beg you to give me an answer. I know I don't deserve you, but I pray you will be generous and say aye."

This *was* truly happening. The knowledge flooded over Meary, washing away the last remnants of doubts and she gave herself up to the bliss of the moment without further timidity.

"Aye." Smiling, Meary pulled him back to his feet. "I have loved ye for a very long time. Naught would make me happier than to be your wife."

"Thank you."

Enfolding her in his arms, Colin showered her face with kisses; then, his lips settled on hers, and he expressed his gratitude in a way far more poignant than words.

Meary basked in the joy of his touch, returning his kisses with unrestrained enthusiasm. They clung to each other, celebrating their love. The world outside the circle of their arms did not exist, nor did the past or future.

It was a long time before Colin released her. He did so reluctantly and only allowed a hand's breadth of space to come between them.

"Now, my sweet bride-to-be, I will answer your questions."

She stroked his smooth cheeks, tracing his lips with her fingertips before admitting, "I have so many, I'm not sure with which one to begin."

Meary felt him grin. "Mayhap I can help you. My decision to propose, though it may seem of a sudden to you, is far from it. I have been planning to ask you to wed me for quite some time. You will remember the day my mother and Edwin arrived, I was gone? I was off seeing to the necessary details of arranging a marriage between us. Because of the difference in our religion and nationalities I'm sure you know there are certain conditions we must satisfy, but I will explain those later."

"Ye decided to marry me *that* long ago? Now that I know 'tis true we are to be married, I can confess I overheard ye tell your mother I was your betrothed many weeks ago. But ye spoke the words in the heat of the moment, and knowing I was not meant to hear your words, I feared they were only a ruse to protect me from your mother's tongue. I waited patiently for ye to come to me, but ye did not. I had come close to giving up all hope. . . . And now ye say ye had decided to wed me even before they came? Why did ye not tell me?"

"I'm coming to that. Before I proposed I considered it prudent to determine the exact nature of the legal

369

obstacles we must face and the quickest course to overcome them. I did not wish to appear an ignorant bridegroom." He paused to clear his throat and catch hold of her hand. "I was going to propose the next day, in this very spot. I thought to pack a blanket and a basket of wine and bread and make my proposal as romantic as the love songs you like to sing. But the unexpected arrival of my family spoiled my plans. I need not tell you, they would have snatched the joy from the day. After you have been so patient with me, I wanted everything to be perfect for you."

Smiling at his princely explanation, Meary nodded. "But they are still here, and I am not so naive to think they will be welcoming me into the family."

"They *are* still here." He hugged her tightly as he continued. "And you are right, they will not be happy for us. However, today I realized I was being a fool. I love you. I need you, and I want you by my side always. I am sorry I couldn't give you your perfect day, but I am confident I am doing the right thing by refusing to postpone our wedding any longer."

"Ye love me." Meary sighed in contentment as she reveled in that one short sentence. "I knew ye must or ye would not propose, but I adore the sound of the words. 'Tis manna to me soul."

Colin leaned forward and passionately kissed her upturned lips. "I will say them as often as you like."

"Then I fear ye will soon grow hoarse."

"For you I would gladly bear the pain."

Meary grinned mischievously as she sternly admonished, "Careful, ye are starting to sound like your brother, Edwin."

"Him," Colin growled.

"Aye, him. Now that he has come up in the conversation, I would like ye . . ."

"To explain why I let him pursue you." Colin finished the sentence for her. "I'm afraid you are not going to like what you hear. Before I tell you, you must promise me, no matter how angry you get, you will forgive and marry me still."

"I promise," Meary assured him without a moment's hesitation.

Her answer satisfied, but he did not loosen his hold on her. "I know what Edwin is," he began. "I knew once he had discovered I had feelings for you, he would try to take you away from me."

"But he is your brother," Meary protested.

"Taking is what Edwin does best," he continued. "It is a game with him. All of life is a game. I don't think it ever occurs to him that his actions might cause others pain. Anyway, I decided not to interfere because . . . because even though you said you loved me, I wanted to see if your love was true. I didn't want to marry you if you did not love me as much as I love you." He blurted the last out in one breath.

For a moment Meary was mute. Then she began to laugh. Hers was not the delicate twitter of a lady but robust, intractable belly laughter.

"Why are you laughing?" Colin demanded, taken aback by her reaction.

Meary struggled to regain control of herself with limited success. "Because," she gasped. "That 'tis the sweetest, most pathetic, heart-warming excuse for leaving me on me own to fend off your wolfish brother, I could ever hope to be hearing." She dissolved into another fit of gleeful giggles.

371

"You're not angry?" he asked in disbelief.

Between chuckles Meary replied, "I should be, shouldn't I. I should take me cane and give ye a sound beating on your thick head."

"It is no more than I deserve."

"'Tis true, but I did promise to be forgiving ye, and I've no desire to be kneeling at the altar with a man with lumps decorating his head." She continued to chuckle.

"I am glad you are taking my lack of faith in you so well."

Meary sobered. "'Tis not a lack of faith in me ye were expressing, but a lack of faith in yourself. No woman, even a faithless one, would prefer your brother to ye."

"He seemed to have no trouble winning away the affections of the ladies in England," he countered.

"Irish women have more sense."

It was Colin's turn to laugh. "You'll get no argument from me. I know when to keep my mouth shut and count my blessings."

Meary kissed his cheek. "Very wise. So when can we be announcing our betrothal?" she asked.

"You sound eager to do so," Colin commented cheerily.

"Aye. I am not patient by nature, and ye have made me wait long enough."

"I am planning on making a public announcement tonight. Annie should be making the preparations for a celebration at this very moment."

Meary was momentarily dumbfounded. Did everyone in the household know of her pending nuptials except herself? "How long has *she* known ye planned to wed me?" she asked.

"She doesn't. I want it to be a surprise. She only knows

she has orders to arrange for a dance in the great hall."

The stiffness went out of Meary's carriage. She was too happy to feel truly angry with anyone, but she was relieved to know Annie had not let her suffer needlessly. Smiling brightly, she said, "Annie 'tis going to be very pleased with ye."

"Yes, she is."

Far less jocundly she asked, "Do ye think your mother and the marquess will behave?"

"I doubt it," Colin responded to her question honestly. "What about O'Hanlon?"

"I'm not certain. I hope he will be pleased, but . . ." She abandoned the thought and embraced a more cheerful one. "Brendan will be glad at the news, and I think we can depend on the well wishes of most of the staff and tenants."

"Then I say, if my family and your Mr. O'Hanlon try to dampen the festivities, we lock them in the root cellar for the evening," Colin quipped.

" 'Tis likely we'd find naught but shredded clothes and tufts of hair by the morning. I do not think it wise we force our families to abide each other's company."

He let loose an exaggerated sigh and kissed the top of her head. "I know you are right, but it was a pleasant fantasy to think, at least for one night, we could be surrounded by naught but goodwill."

Neither Colin nor Meary was eager to return to the house. They had so much to say to each other, so many plans to make.

Colin told Meary of his life in England. He told her how since childhood he had devoted himself to his family, how desperately he had tried to please them by doing all

373

they asked and making himself exactly what they desired him to be—until the day came when he realized he was wasting his life in the vain pursuit of the love of a family he neither liked nor respected. He explained how bitterness had poisoned his mind against the very idea of family—how even though he found himself happier in her company than he had ever been with anyone in his life, he was afraid to love her lest he end up being badly used again.

He talked a long time about his life in England, painting in vivid detail his struggles as a child and then a man. He trusted her with his pain and fear, telling her things he had not had the courage to admit even to himself. He begged her to forgive him for using her as he had been used and for all the sorrow his reluctance to love had caused her. He prayed for her to have patience with him if in the future his behavior fell short of what she deserved in a mate, between promises he would do everything in his power never to disappoint her again.

One by one, the walls around his heart came crashing down. Meary listened to all he said with quiet compassion. She treasured his willingness to share the secret parts of him with her. Knew his trust was a priceless gift. Knew it to be irrefutable proof of the depth of his love for her.

As she listened to the story of his life before she had come into it, the light of understanding slowly descended upon Meary. The path her voices had led her on had been a convoluted one, but they had not led her astray as she had so often feared. All the troubles she had endured had had a purpose. It was not enough for her to fall in love with Colin. That had been easy. It was not enough for her to become his bride. It was necessary that her love be tested again and again or Colin would never have been able to accept it.

She who had always been blessed with an abundance of love had come here to share it with a man who had been given none. It was fitting.

Meary smiled serenely with the certain knowledge she at last had found the elusive answer to the question that had haunted her for so long: *Why?*

When Colin finished purging his soul of old wounds, he and Meary made love to celebrate the new lives they were about to begin with each other.

After, they stood facing the sea. Colin wrapped Meary in his arms as they discussed the details they must attend before the wedding. Both agreed, they wished to be wed as soon as the law allowed.

Dusk was falling when Colin and Meary returned to the house. Meary retired to her room to prepare herself for supper and the dance. Colin stepped into the kitchen in search of Annie.

Meary had a difficult time sitting at the table and consuming her supper as if nothing momentous had occurred that afternoon. She was fairly bursting with happiness, and it required every bit of her pertinacity not to say or do something to give away her joyful secret.

She allowed Colin to lead the conversation and pretended to concentrate on her food.

"What's this I hear about a dance tonight?" Edwin asked from his end of the table.

"I am hosting a dance in the hall for my servants and tenants," Colin confirmed.

"You would invite the enemy into your home?" Lady Swanscroft protested.

"My people are not my enemy."

"But they hate you."

"Someone hates me. That I will grant as true. But the majority of my people are loyal. In the past, it was my habit to host dances on a regular basis. They were much appreciated."

"I hope you don't expect me to socialize with peasants," she whined.

"If you do not wish to attend, you are welcome to spend the evening in your room. I will not be offended by your absence."

Under the table Meary and Colin covertly clasped hands, each giving the other a heartening squeeze.

"I suppose she will be playing that infernal harp," Lady Swanscroft dully opined after several minutes of piteous sighs and loud sniffing netted her no response.

Colin's voice remained relentlessly pleasant. "I hope Lady Meary will consent to bless this house with a song or two, but most of her time will be spent on the dance floor. I don't believe I have mentioned it before, but Lady Meary is quite fond of dancing."

"Is she?" Edwin cooed. "How very lovely."

As soon as the meal was finished, the servants cleared the table, moved it to the far wall, and invited the tenants who had been gathering outside to come through the door.

Meary stood where she would not be in the way. She could hear Lady Swanscroft grumbling across the room and knew she had decided to remain. Though her dour presence was bound to dampen the spirits of those with whom she came in contact, Meary was glad she had stayed. She preferred both her and the marquess hear Colin's public announcement of their betrothal with their own ears so there would be no further speculation about the truth of his intentions.

Her ears pricked to the plink of a fiddle string. Though Seumas was unwilling to play for Lord Colin or his family, apparently Annie had persuaded him to play for the benefit of the tenants. The sweet sound of him tuning his fiddle further lightened Meary's happy heart. He had remained mute during the conversation at the table, and until now she had no way to judge his mood. A moment later Annie confirmed her assumption.

"Well, I've worked a miracle," she stated with satisfaction. "I wasn't sure the stubborn old goat would cooperate, but it looks like he couldn't resist my persuasive powers."

"What *did* ye say to him?" Meary asked in admiration.

"I merely expressed the opinion that Lady Swanscroft was bound to be annoyed by the evening's festivities and by playing his fiddle he could prolong her suffering."

"That 'twas very bad of ye," Meary chided, grinning her approval as she did so.

"Thank you. And since I have divulged the secret of my success with Mr. O'Hanlon, perhaps you will tell me what Colin is up to, if he has confided the information to you. His behavior this afternoon has been decidedly odd."

"No, she will not," Colin answered the question for Meary. Placing himself between Meary and his housekeeper, he bowed low over Meary's hand. "Will you do me the honor of sharing the first dance?" he asked with a twinkle in his voice.

"Aye. I would be most pleased to be doing so," she replied.

As Colin led Meary onto the dance floor, he whispered in her ear, "I plan to make the announcement after the first set if that is agreeable to you."

"Do ye think Annie can bear the suspense that long?"

"I suspect she will survive. I think it best we give our guests a chance to get in a festive mood. There are too many long faces in this room."

"Everyone has been tense of late."

"Yes. And with good reason. But tonight we will think naught but pleasant thoughts. This is our evening, and the estate can go to hell for all I care."

The first dance was a reel, and Meary obediently pushed all displeasing thoughts out of her head as Colin guided her through the cross-steps, promenades, and turns. She smiled and laughed and murmured warm comments meant only for her partner's ears.

He responded in kind, interspersing fervent promises to do everything in his power to make her happy between his equally warm replies.

By the time the dance ended, Meary was glowing.

"You will dance with me now," the marquess's voice intruded upon Meary's jubilant mood. Her expression immediately lost its luster.

"The lady declines," Colin informed him, holding tight when his brother would extract Meary's hand from his.

"The lady has her own tongue. Let her give her own answer. . . . Or are you afraid to do so?"

"I have perfect faith in Lady Meary's good taste. Lady Meary, would you like to dance with my brother?"

"Nay."

"She is reluctant to face the consequences of speaking the truth in front of you. I'm beginning to suspect you beat her in private."

"Lady Meary, you need have no fear of reprisal. If you would like to dance with my brother, you may. I grant you permission to dance with whomever you like as often as you like. Would you like to dance with my brother?"

Meary faced the marquess squarely, raised her chin to a lofty angle, and crisply replied, "Nay, I would not. There be only one man with whom I desire to be dancing, and that 'tis ye, Lord Colin."

"You have your answer, Edwin."

"Hrmph! I still say she is afraid of you."

"Lord Swanscroft," Meary addressed him in her most authoritative tone. "I am afraid of no man. If I desired to dance with ye, I would do so. I do *not* desire to dance with ye, as ye well know. And I will not stand mute while ye wrongfully accuse your brother of committing violence against me. Lord Colin is a gentleman. He does not need to be using anything but his natural charm to make me prefer his company over yours."

Taking the lead, Meary pulled Colin into the circle of dancing couples. He spun them away from his brother, and they immediately dismissed him from their minds, giving their attention only to each other.

Much to their vexation, when the second dance ended, the marquess was once again at their side.

"This dance surely is mine," he announced gregariously, latching on to her hand.

Meary yanked her hand free. "Nay, 'tis not. Nor will be the next or the next or a thousand dances hence."

"But . . ."

"The lady has given you her answer. She has made it

abundantly clear she does not wish to dance with you."
Colin stepped between Meary and his brother. His tone
was excessively polite and all the more menacing because
of it. "If you persist in annoying her, as a gentleman, I
shall be forced to punch you in the nose. I would hate to
spoil your pretty face, but if you desire to go through life
with a crooked nose, I will oblige you."

"You threaten me?" Edwin bristled with indignation.

"No. I am merely dispensing a little friendly advice.
Stay away from Meary or there will be the devil to pay
and I, dear brother, shall be that devil. It is not a threat; it
is a promise."

They left Edwin sputtering in outrage.

Colin and Meary danced through the rest of the set
without interruption. When the music stopped, he
leaned close and whispered, "Ready?"

"Ready," she confirmed, then drew a deep nerve-
steadying breath.

Colin led Meary over to where the musicians stood and
borrowed Brendan's *bodhrán*.

He clapped his hand against it several times to gain
everyone's attention. "Friends, there is a reason I have
invited you here tonight besides a long overdue need for
merrymaking."

A murmur ran through the crowd; then, there was
absolute silence except for the shuffle of Brendan's feet
and a nervous cough from the back of the room.
Everyone waited tensely to hear what he might say, in
light of the attacks against the estate, bracing themselves
for the worst.

"Ireland is my home now. I have become attached to
the land and the people." He took Meary's hand in his.
"There is one person to whom I have become extremely

380

attached. Today, I have asked Lady Meary O'Byrne to be my wife, and she has graciously consented." Grinning broadly, he raised their clasped hands over their heads as he announced, "You are all invited to the wedding."

The crowd erupted into spontaneous cheers; then, Meary could hear and feel a wave of humanity surging toward them. Annie was the first to reach their side.

"Well, it's about time, I say." She kissed first Meary, then Colin on the cheek. Her next words she addressed directly to Colin. "I'd about given up hope of ever seeing this day, but I forgive you now that you have come to your senses."

"I appreciate your good counsel," Colin replied in friendly tones, "and I humbly apologize for not taking your advice sooner."

"Better late than never; isn't that what they say," she proclaimed with glee; then, taking each of their hands in hers, she declared, "It's going to be a fine wedding. The best this county has ever seen. You can depend on me to see to that."

"Thank ye, Annie," Meary said.

"Don't thank me. It's me who should be thanking you. You've exhibited the patience of a saint. But it all turned out in the end, didn't it," she warbled. "There's going to be more joy under this roof than one house can hold, mark my words." Reluctantly Annie relinquished her place to the other well-wishers.

Meary and Colin greeted them and one by one accepted their congratulations.

It was some time before Brendan managed to steal a moment of Meary's attention. "I be glad for ye, Meary," he said. "More than glad. I know ye have been wanting this for a long time."

"Thank ye, Brendan."

"I'll take good care of her," Colin promised in Gaelic. "And you are welcome to stay and live with us, if you so choose."

More well-wishers demanded Colin's and Meary's attention. To be surrounded by so much goodwill warmed Meary's heart. It boded well for the success of their marriage.

As happy as she was, Meary could not ignore the fact that three people had yet to offer their congratulations. She had not really expected them to do so, but that didn't prevent her from wishing they would.

Hearty congratulations continued to pour forth from crofters and house servants, groomsmen and dairymaids.

Most of their guests had departed to other parts of the room, when Meary recognized the approach of Lord Swanscroft by the strong scent of the jessamine perfume in which he habitually drenched himself. She sidled closer to Colin.

"I am here to add my congratulations to the others," Lord Swanscroft announced with tight-lipped cool. "Though I must say I find the lady's choice of men inexplicable and extremely provoking. She must be daft as well as blind to choose . . ."

Colin loudly cleared his throat, and though Meary could not see his face, she assumed it wore an expression of warning, as the marquess left the rest of what he was about to say unsaid and quickly moved on.

A few moments later, Lady Swanscroft stood before them. "I see you are going to go through with it," she addressed her son.

"Yes, I am."

"Well . . . good luck."

"Thank ye, Lady Swanscroft." Meary smiled brightly, pretending she did not hear the dripping sarcasm in her words. "'Tis kind of ye to make the effort to welcome me into your family. I will do me best to be giving your son all the love he deserves."

"How sweet. Excuse me, but I feel a headache coming on."

"I am sorry my family was not more gracious." Colin stroked her hand.

"'Tis not as bad as we expected," Meary consoled.

A few more tenants came up to offer their good wishes.

When it became apparent no one else was going to come forward, Meary released her hold on Colin's hand. Slowly, she turned to face the man standing a few feet behind her. Colin turned with her and stood stalwartly by her side. "Seumas, have ye naught to say to us?"

"What would ye have me say?" he gruffly asked.

"That ye give us your blessing."

Meary stood soldier stiff as she listened to her mentor deeply draw in each breath with measured effort. She could feel the tension in him, feel his penetrating gaze as he studied them.

When at last he spoke, his voice was heavy with regret. "I cannot do that. I accept that this be what ye want, and I'll not stand in yer way. I will pray for yer good health and happiness. But I cannot in good conscience give me blessing to a union I oppose."

Meary's shoulders sagged. "Will ye never forgive me?"

"Ye I have forgiven long ago. 'Tis him I can't forgive."

"But in marrying me does he not make amends for past sins?" she quietly pleaded.

"Nay. In marrying ye, he be getting himself a fine wife. Penitence requires sacrifice and suffering."

"I agree I am not worthy of the love of a woman as precious as Meary, and that I will get far more benefit than she from this marriage." Colin soberly entered the conversation. "However, despite my many shortcomings, I hope you will take into consideration how very much I love her. I am not asking for my sake but for Meary's. You are like a father to her. Pray, reconsider your refusal to bless our marriage."

Seumas turned and walked away.

The next few weeks passed in a whirlwind of activity. Meary barely had time to think about the people who were not happy about her upcoming marriage, and for that she was grateful.

Seumas's lack of enthusiasm bothered her far more than others, but she would not believe him a lost cause. His innate goodness would prevail over his stubbornness. This rift between them had endured too long. She could carry on with his mere acceptance, but to be unreservedly happy, she needed his blessing.

More than once she had tried to make him understand how utterly certain she was that a marriage between herself and Lord Colin was what was always meant to be. She tried to explain why she felt the many months of anguish had been necessary steps on the path to an enduring love. He listened to her arguments, but they did not convince him. The best he would give her was assurances of his love and a solemn promise to come to her aid should she discover her heart had led her astray. No matter what she said, she could not convince him Colin possessed the virtues of a worthy mate.

Despite her lack of success, Meary refused to give up

hope that as the day of their marriage approached Seumas would give the blessing she sought.

The situation might seem hopeless, but she had ample proof even the blackest future could turn bright. A few weeks ago no one, including herself, would have been willing to argue she would now be preparing to become Colin's bride. Seumas would not deny them forever.

Lord and Lady Swanscroft were a different matter. Despite the fact they seemed determined to stay for the wedding, Meary held out no hope they would ever like the idea of a marriage between herself and Colin.

They were not openly antagonistic.

When it appeared they would be so, Colin had taken them aside and let them know in unmistakable terms the next disparaging word to pass their lips would see them summarily evicted. To be certain they understood his words were a promise and not a threat, he called in Annie and repeated them in front of her, instructing her to immediately report any misbehavior to him and to order their trunks packed and the carriage readied. The Garricks were wise enough to realize with Annie in charge, they would get no second chance.

Lord Swanscroft pouted and whenever the subject of the pending marriage came up, his tone of voice became decidedly morose, but he was always careful not to step over the line Colin had drawn.

Lady Swanscroft was equally vigilant, but being forced to hold her tongue seemed to Meary to be taking a terrible toll on the lady. Her mood was so black it was palpable whenever she entered a room, and it grew blacker every day. She spoke only when spoken to, and her answers rarely extended beyond a single clipped syllable. Only when Edwin spoke to her did she expand her vocabulary, and these conversations invariably ended in an exchange of terse words between the two.

Meary could not understand why they continued to stay when both were clearly so miserable. It made no sense for them to wish to stay to attend a wedding they opposed, but then, Meary had to admit, fathoming the whys and wherefores of Colin's family was beyond her capabilities. Colin was equally mystified by their failure to depart, but having set up the conditions they must meet to stay, he did not feel comfortable violating his own word and packing them off before the wedding.

Meary's days were consumed with filling the demands of Annie as she orchestrated the preparations for the wedding and studying the Protestant faith to satisfy the demands of the law.

Annie had marshalled her considerable influence and in four days time rounded up material and lace enough not only for a wedding gown but several other gowns as well plus all the necessary underpinnings and three seamstresses to do the work. Meary protested the extravagance, but neither Annie nor Colin would listen to reason. She resigned herself to spending half her day with her arms outstretched, being draped and pinned and clucked over.

Because of the other demands on her time, Meary was obliged to temporarily abandon her efforts to help ferret out the culprits who warred against the estate. She had met with no success anyway.

The attacks continued, but they were becoming less frequent than before. No one was sure why, but all were grateful.

Colin of necessity had to spend a goodly amount of his time dealing with matters concerning his property, but he always made certain he spent some part of his day with her.

He was like a different man since the night he had announced their marriage. The things she loved about him hadn't changed, but there was a buoyancy to his spirit she had never thought to feel from him. It was in his voice when he spoke, in his step when he walked into a room, and in the new command he had of himself in his dealings with his family.

Meary was delighted to see him so confident and happy with his decision to wed her.

By mutual agreement, they remained in their separate bedrooms. Neither Meary nor Colin were happy to spend their nights apart, but common sense dictated they do so. Seumas's blessing would never be secured if they openly flaunted their lust for each other. Added to that strong incentive were the facts that a clergyman now resided under their roof, Annie's sudden affinity for observing every tradition concerning a bride and bridegroom, and an unspoken wish on both their parts to erase the memory of their unconventional courtship from the minds of the community.

What moments of passion they could steal—and they were unsatisfyingly few—were snatched in shadowed passageways or when they had the good fortune to find themselves in the hall with no one present. These encounters were perforce limited to fervid embraces and hungry kisses, a circumstance that went a long way toward making them both desperately desirous for the day of their wedding to arrive.

When the day finally did arrive, it dawned crisp and cold.

Meary took her breakfast in her room, and as soon as the tray was cleared away she found her chambers the center of activity.

Annie assumed command with Doreen as her second. A bath was brought up, followed by a small army of men carrying buckets of steaming water.

When the bath was readied and the men shooed out the door, Meary was stripped to the skin and unceremoniously plopped into the tub where, despite her protests that she could manage the task herself, she was scrubbed from head to toe.

On another day, Meary might have refused to be treated like a helpless doll, but today she was too euphoric to let anything annoy her. She and Colin were to be wed. That was the only thought that filled her head. She knew their future would hold trials and tribulations as well as joy, but they loved each other. They would face the world together. They would make a good life.

After her bath, Meary was wrapped in a towel, then sat down upon a chair so Doreen could tend her hair.

"This is the happiest day of my life," Annie announced as she bustled about the room, laying out the wedding clothes.

Meary laughed. "Aren't those words supposed to be coming from the bride's lips?"

"Yes. But I'm sure you'll not mind if I share them." Annie stopped flitting about the room long enough to kiss Meary's cheek. "I've worked very hard to bring about this wedding, and ofttimes despaired it would ever come. When you have children of your own, you'll understand."

"Both Colin and I are blessed to have ye."

"Thank you, dear. Doreen! Let's not dawdle. We have

mere hours before the wedding, and I want Meary to look perfect."

"Aye, ma'am, but I be working as fast as I can," Doreen insisted.

Meary had more sense than to intervene. Annie was an unstoppable force this morning, and Meary knew no one, including the bride, would be allowed to thwart her. She submitted herself to Annie's fussing with good grace, whispering a word of encouragement and like advice to Doreen when Annie retreated across the room to fetch some other item of clothing.

When she had fluffed it dry, Doreen tied Meary's hair at her crown with a white satin riband, then began the painstaking task of coaxing the flaxen tresses into a waterfall of spiral curls, adding more ribands as she worked. When at last her hair was dressed to Annie's satisfaction, the two women turned to dressing Meary's person.

Every stitch of clothing Meary was to wear was new, from her chemise to her white silk slippers with silver fringe.

Doreen presented her with a pair of garters. "I embroidered the motto on them meself," she proudly proclaimed as she pulled the first one up Meary's right leg.

"What do they say?"

"True of heart."

Meary smiled.

"Most appropriate," Annie clucked her approval.

Meary's wedding gown was made of the smoothest satin. She loved the feel of it. Annie had earlier described it as white with silver flowers, the traditional bridal colors. Every edge was trimmed in silver, as was her petticoat. Her train was made of yards of white lace with silver fringe and tassels at the bottom edge.

As they dressed her, Meary could not prevent herself from continually stroking the fabric and drinking in the image of her gown through her fingers. Even Annie's frequent scoldings to hold still did not deter her.

"You are a vision of loveliness, my dear," Annie announced. "You've always reminded me of an angel, but today . . ." Her voice cracked and she quietly sniffed.

"If I am lovely, 'tis thanks to both ye and Doreen," Meary replied as she continued to smooth her hands over the skirt of her gown.

Regaining control of her emotions, Annie stated, "We couldn't have done it without the natural beauty you possess. My Colin will be hard pressed to contain himself when he sees you."

"Do ye think they will be coming for us soon?"

"I suspect it'll be any minute now."

A knock at the door confirmed her prediction.

Meary felt her cheeks warm as Annie took her hand. "This is the moment we've been waiting for. Are you ready?"

"Aye."

"Every happiness to ye," Doreen said.

"Thank ye."

Meary descend the stairs at a regal pace, Annie and Doreen trailing behind her. She could hear the appreciative murmurs of the crowd gathered below, and she smiled brightly, holding her head a little higher.

Colin was somewhere down there, standing at the head of the crowd, waiting for her. She had so many hopes for their future, it was difficult to contain them all. This day was theirs. Together they would face the world, hand in hand and of one heart. She felt like a princess in a fairy tale. She felt intoxicated by her love for Colin.

Upon reaching the floor of the hall, Meary was hard pressed not to run to her bridegroom's side and throw her arms around him, but she continued to advance at a sedate pace.

When she arrived at the altar especially constructed for their wedding, Colin took her hand.

"You are beautiful," he whispered in her ear as they lowered themselves to their knees.

"My God! No!" A high pitched scream rent the air. "My Edwin! My dear sweet, Edwin!"

Meary cringed.

The wedding guests turned in mass toward the voice at the top of the stairs.

Meary felt Colin stiffen and slowly rise to his feet. She started to follow him, but he gently pressed her back to her knees with a hand on her shoulder.

"Mother, this is neither the time nor the place for one of your little scenes," he sternly rebuked. "I will not allow you to ruin my wedding day."

When she spoke again, his mother's voice was a tortured whisper. "Edwin is dead."

Chapter 27

"What?" Colin demanded in disbelief.

"Edwin is dead," she repeated. "Someone has murdered him." Having expended the last of her strength, Lady Swanscroft let out a wail and crumpled to the floor.

"Somebody carry her to her room. You and you come with me," Colin began shouting orders as he raced toward the stairs.

Meary knelt alone at the altar, listening to the pandemonium around her. Her disappointment was so great, there were no words adequate to express it. This couldn't be happening. Not after she had waited so long. Not at the very moment she and Colin had knelt together at the altar.

She prayed this was just a cruel trick Lady Swanscroft played on them. Much as she despised the marquess she could never wish him dead, and especially not at the hand of a murderer. Who would do such a thing? And why? She could think of no one who would profit from his death.

Slowly, she rose to her feet. The crowd was as anxious as she for the truth. She could barely hear her own thoughts over the ramble, but she continued to pray Lady Swanscroft's words would prove false.

The minister enfolded her trembling hands in his. "Have strength, my dear. There seems to be some question as to the truth of this matter. Mayhap the lady exaggerates."

"Pray with me that it is so," Meary whispered, but even as she said the words a sinking feeling in the pit of her stomach made her fear it was too late for any of their prayers.

Upstairs, Colin burst into his brother's room and stopped cold. On the bed, in a pool of his own blood, lay Edwin. His skin was gray, and when Colin touched his hand, it was cold and stiff.

"Who would do this?" he asked more of himself than the two men with him as he pulled back the blanket. Edwin had been stabbed once in the chest. From the location of the wound, Colin knew it was a mortal wound, but his assailant had gone on to slit both his neck and his wrist, just to be sure the job was complete. A bloodstained knife lay on the mattress. It was Irish in design.

Gritting his teeth, Colin covered the body.

"I want guards posted at every entrance to the house. Nobody comes or goes without my permission. I will get to the bottom of this if it is the last thing I do."

After taking a moment to see his mother was being well taken care of, Colin returned to the great hall. He went directly to Meary's side.

"I'm afraid it is true," he told her grimly.

She reached for his hand. "Colin, I am so sorry. Are ye all right?"

"I am fine," he replied in a measured voice.

"And your mother?"

"She's been given some laudanum. Cathleen is with her."

"When? How? Why?" Meary asked the questions that were foremost on everyone's thoughts.

"It could have happened anytime from early morning to a few hours ago. As to how, someone must have sneaked into his room as he slept and stabbed him. There has been a steady stream of people coming in and out of the house in preparation for the wedding. Someone from outside the house could easily have slipped in and out unnoticed, or it could be someone from inside the house. As to why Edwin and not another one of us, I have no idea."

Meary knew she needed to be strong for Colin's sake, and she was determined not to disappoint him. Holding fast to his hand, she imbued her voice with a steadiness she did not feel. "'Tis there anything I can do?"

"Ask all the questions you can."

"Aye, I will. I'll also be telling the minister we'll be needing him to officiate over a funeral not a wedding."

"Are you sure you wish to postpone our wedding? I have already made you wait too long for this day. A celebration is out of the question, but we could proceed with a private ceremony."

It was tempting to say "aye," but she resisted her initial impulse. "'Tis kind of ye to offer, but 'twould not be right. We should wait."

"I don't want to wait."

"Nor do I," Meary softly consoled. "But we both know 'tis what we must do."

Colin pulled her into his arms and held tight. "I love you."

"And I love ye. Our love will endure no matter how long we must wait to sanctify it with marriage."

He fingered the hair at her temples. "I promise you, the wait will not be long. I will not let you suffer endlessly."

"Ye are not to worry about me," Meary admonished. "The only thing ye need concern yourself with is finding out who would do this evil thing."

The rest of the day and half the night was taken up with interrogating every guest and servant in the hall.

The first two people Meary spoke with were Annie and Seumas.

"Annie, if ye knew anything about the marquess's murder, ye would tell me, would ye not?" Meary began.

"There's no need to look so embarrassed," Annie comforted. "I know everyone must be interrogated. It's no secret how I felt about the marquess, and I'll not pretend to feel grief, but I would not protect his murderer. And no, it wasn't me."

"I never for a moment thought it was."

"I have threatened to poison him on numerous occasions," Annie reminded.

"He was not poisoned. He was stabbed."

"Nevertheless, I wanted to make it clear I had naught to do with it."

"Annie, ye are not a suspect," Meary repeated. "I was merely hoping ye might have seen something that could help us apprehend the real criminal. A stranger on the stairs who had no reason to be there or mayhap a servant acting oddly?"

"I saw nothing," Annie lamented. "I know it's my duty to be aware of all that transpires in this household, but I was so preoccupied with the wedding, I neglected all else."

"I fear we all have been preoccupied."

"We'll catch whoever did this," Annie assured her. "I may not grieve the marquess's death, but murder is not to be tolerated. And I'll not forgive the ruination of your wedding. Never will I forgive that! Whoever is responsible will pay and pay dearly for his deed."

Meary's conversation with Seumas proceeded in a similar vein.

Meary was as sure of his innocence as she was of Annie's, and like Annie though he frankly admitted the marquess's death did not grieve him, he assured her he had naught to do with his demise. He had seen nothing suspicious, but he promised to keep his eyes and ears open and report any information he gleaned. He was no more approving of murder as a means to an end than Annie.

Meary questioned Brendan next, then a long succession of tenants and servants. No one was allowed to go on their way until both Colin and Meary were satisfied they had naught to do with the murder and could offer no clue to who did.

Despite the lengthy questioning, they came up with not one person who they deemed even slightly suspicious. No one had seen anything or anyone unusual in the house, but as Colin had said there were so many coming and going and so much activity in the tower, a stranger could have easily lost himself in the crowd.

That night, Colin had guards posted at every bedroom door.

The next day provided no further clues nor did the next. Edwin was laid to rest. The minister who was to have married them presided over the funeral.

Lady Swanscroft spent all of her time in her room. She emerged briefly for the burial but after, retired directly to her bed.

A week after Edwin's murder, Colin sat alone in the great hall, raking his fingers through his hair as he tried to think what possible stone he could have left unturned.

More and more Edwin's murder was looking like the work of one or more strangers. Probably the same culprits who had been destroying the estate. If it was, the villains were most likely out of the county by now. The fact that the attacks against the estate had suddenly ceased, supported his theory.

Would they be back? It was a question he couldn't begin to answer, but he did not think the timing of the murder a coincidence. It was possible Edwin's murder was a final attempt to frighten him into leaving Ireland and they would now be left in peace. It also was possible the killers had mistaken Edwin for him, and when they discovered their mistake, they would return to rectify the mistake.

In either case, Colin knew he would not rest easy until he had apprehended those responsible. His brother deserved justice. All men did.

"Colin."

He immediately rose to his feet and crossed the room.

397

"Mother, you look pale. Are you sure you feel up to being out of your room?"

"We must speak," Lady Swanscroft rasped.

Colin led her over to a chair. He knew how much his mother loved Edwin, and it was impossible not to feel sympathetic toward her. "What is it you would like to discuss?" he quietly asked.

"I'm sure you have thought about this a considerable amount already . . . but with your brother's death you became the marquess of Swanscroft," she said wanly.

"Actually, I hadn't thought of it at all," Colin confessed, rather amazed that he had not.

"Don't play coy with me," she snapped. "I am not up to it." Before Colin could respond, she continued, "I hold you responsible for your brother's death. I begged you to come home. I warned you something like this would happen, but you would not listen." She shuddered. "You cannot undo your past mistakes, but the future stretches out before us. You are marquess now. It is time we go home."

Colin sighed. He had no desire to increase his mother's misery, but he could see no help for it. She needed to face the truth. "Mother, I am home," he stated firmly.

"No, Swanscroft is your home. You are its master now. It is what you wanted."

He shook his head. "If you think I wished Edwin dead, you are mistaken."

"Did you not say you wanted to be master of Swanscroft?" she demanded.

"No. I said I wished to be master of my own property and fate," he gently corrected. "It is not the same. My life is here, not at Swanscroft."

"Are you mad? You would chose this stone tower over Swanscroft?"

"I made my choice long ago. Edwin's death has not changed it. If anything, it has given me another compelling reason to stay. I am determined to catch his murderer."

"But you are the marquess. You must come home to Swanscroft!" she shrieked.

Her complexion had been pale when she entered the room, but as they spoke, it had become increasingly florid and her voice more shrill with each word. By contrast, Colin continued to conduct himself with polite calm.

"The title will remain with me no matter where I chose to live," he said. "My memories of Swanscroft are not fond, and I have no inclination to take up residence there."

"But what about me? How shall I survive?"

"In light of Edwin's death, I will see the yearly allowance I had promised you both deposited immediately rather than wait for the year to expire. I have already prepared letters for Mr. Bartlett giving him full authority in all matters pertaining to the running of Swanscroft. In addition I have written my solicitor in London. He will confer with Mr. Bartlett, and the two will set up a schedule to repay your debts out of the profits of the estate. He will also see to it that no merchant in England extends you further credit, so you will never have to worry about finding yourself in debt again. You may live in the house at Swanscroft for as long as you like, so you need never worry you will be without shelter. You will no longer be able to live like a queen, but yours will be a comfortable life."

"I cannot believe I am hearing this!" She covered her ears. "It is impossible to bear! You cannot defy me!"

"Mother, I do not wish to add to your pain, which I know is great, but neither will I allow it to rule my life. Edwin's death saddens me, and as I have already said, I intend to do all I can to catch whoever is responsible. Meary and I have postponed our wedding out of respect. These things we do for you and for Edwin." He paused, looking her directly in the eye. "But my sympathy does not extend to abandoning the life I have made here. This is where I will live my life, with Meary by my side. Nothing you do or say will make me change my mind."

Meary was fairly successful at disguising her pensive state of mind from those around her, but when she was alone with herself, she dropped the pretense.

At first the shock of Edwin's death had overwhelmed all other feelings, but now her heart and mind were constantly agitated by worrisome thoughts.

It seemed centuries had passed since she had stood in the great hall, bedecked in her wedding finery, eager to marry the man she loved. In truth it had been less than two weeks.

They were no closer to finding the marquess's murderer now than they were the day his lifeless body had been discovered, and until they did no one would sleep soundly. Everyone was determined to see the murderer apprehended, from the lowest servant to Seumas himself, but their vigilance went unrewarded. She and Colin went over every clue again and again. They made lists of the possible suspects, then methodically eliminated each name one by one until none were left.

They took turns posing hypothetical questions to each other in hopes of stimulating some fresh insight. All to no avail. There was only one question they left unasked. What if Colin was the assassin's next target?

Meary knew Lady Swanscroft had renewed her efforts to get him to return to England. All the lady talked about was his position as the new marquess and how his presence was required at Swanscroft.

Colin repeatedly said he would not go, but Meary feared once he became accustomed to the idea of his new title, he might rethink his decision to stay, and life in England would be far different than the one they knew in Ireland.

In Ireland their marriage was acceptable because the Irish people ranked her an equal of Lord Colin. Her family name and profession as a harpist had value. There would always be those who prejudged Colin because he was an Englishman, but she had had occasion to speak to almost everyone for miles around, and his fairmindedness and genuine concern for the welfare of his tenants had won him the good will and respect of nearly all in the county.

She could not imagine that such would be the case with her in England. Not if Lord and Lady Swanscroft were representative of the prevailing English attitude toward the Irish. She would forever be an outsider, and Colin would be ridiculed for marrying beneath his station.

Living under the constant censure of others would be good for neither Colin nor her. Colin's faith in people was too new to be strong enough to survive the disparagement, and she was too proud. It would only be a matter of time before she lost her temper, loosed her tongue, and really made a disaster of their place in English society.

Colin was an intelligent man. If she had thought of thes
things, then he must have also.

She held onto the hope he would remain in Irelan
but between the enticement of his ancestral lands and th
problems he was having here, she thought the cas
against staying very strong. She loved him enough t
follow him to the ends of the earth if he asked it of he
but it was not something she was eager to do.

If the thought of leaving Ireland was distressful, th
thought that by staying Colin might be putting his life a
risk was even more so. She would prefer to live in he
with him than in heaven without him. The trouble on th
estate had suddenly ceased with Edwin's death, but sh
was realistic enough to realize there was no guarantee th
danger had passed.

Because Meary felt guilty for spending time worryin
how the marquess's death might effect Colin and he
when Lady Swanscroft's loss was so great, she personall
took charge of seeing to it that every effort was made t
see Colin's mother's needs were met.

When Lady Swanscroft had been prostrate with grie
and had kept to her bed, the task had been simple
Now that she was up and about, it was much mor
difficult.

She did not seem to be recovering from her son's death
as time passed but to become more and more distraught.
All night long she paced the floor of her room. She rarely
ate and when she spoke, the pitch of her voice fluctuated
erratically. Whenever Meary was in her presence, she
sensed something was very wrong with her, but as yet she
could not quite put her finger on it. She knew grief did
strange things to people, but it made it hard to know what
to do to help the poor lady.

She and Colin had discussed the matter at length, but he was at as much a loss as she.

Lady Swanscroft lifted her candle to the mirror and stared at her reflection. The eyes staring back at her were cold and empty. She shuddered, turning away from the glass.

She hated Colin. Hated him with every fiber of her being. He had what he wanted. He was marquess now, master of Swanscroft. He no longer had the excuse of Edwin to prevent him from coming home and taking care of her.

Dear, sweet, Edwin. Her beloved son. They understood each other well. Edwin understood that life was meant to provide pleasure for the privileged. Rank and riches, they were what really mattered in this world.

She raked her fingers up her temples. The gesture dislodged her wig, and she yanked it off, flinging it across the room. Edwin was perfect in all ways but one. He was not a dependable source of income, and rank was nothing without money. Much as she hated him, Colin was a necessary evil in their lives. She could not survive without him.

That Colin still refused to return to England ate at her soul. He'd lied to her. He was not staying in Ireland out of love for his own estate. He was staying because of *her*.

All this trouble was *her* doing. She had put a spell on Colin, made him forget his duty to his mother. He had always been such a faithful son, willing to do her bidding.

Meary O'Byrne must be destroyed before she destroyed her.

How dare she steal Colin away from her? She was no

more than an Irish peasant and a blind one at that. She was a nobody. She must not be allowed to spoil the life of a noble woman like herself.

With his Meary gone, Colin would be eager to return to England. She would make him eager to escape the horrible memories of this place.

Oh, she knew he would suffer, and that was the beauty of the plan. He deserved to suffer. All of this would never have happened if he had stayed in England where he belonged. She would kill him, too, if she did not need him. But, alas, she needed him alive or he could do her no good.

Chapter 28

"Meary, come here, please," Lady Swanscroft summoned.

The word "please" was not a natural part of Lady Swanscroft's vocabulary, and her use of it caused Meary's brow to wrinkle in concern as she hurried to her side. "What is it ye desire?"

"A walk in the fresh air."

"A walk?" Meary questioned. Lady Swanscroft never ventured out of doors unless absolutely necessary.

"Yes. I was thinking a little fresh air might help me. I have tried everything else I can think of . . ."

"I'll be getting one of the footmen to escort ye."

"No. I want to walk with you."

The request for her company was even more odd than Lady Swanscroft's polite tenor, and Meary felt compelled to ask, "Are ye sure?"

Lady Swanscroft sniffed loudly. "I know my treatment of you in the past has been . . . less than friendly . . . but a sudden death makes one think, does it not? You are to be my only living son's wife. It is time I got to know you better."

"If ye would be liking me to walk with ye, I'd be more than happy to oblige ye," Meary responded. It seemed too much to hope for that Edwin's death might bring any good, but perhaps it might. Lady Swanscroft's tone was as close to amiable as she had ever heard it.

"Good. Let's go." Lady Swanscroft clasped her hand.

"We will be needing our wraps," Meary reminded. "I'll have one of the maids fetch them."

"The servants here are so slow, it will be dark before they bring them. Could you not fetch them for us? Mine is hanging on a peg near the door. I'm sure you can find it."

"Aye," Meary agreed without argument. She might disagree with Lady Swanscroft's assessment of the servants, but she wasn't about to spoil this chance to foster a better relationship between them. She nurtured no illusions they would ever be close friends, or any kind of friends at all, but even a scant mitigating of the tension between them would be a great improvement. If Lady Swanscroft was willing to offer up the olive branch, Meary was more than a little eager to cooperate.

It took but a moment to fetch their cloaks, and they stepped outside. There was a brisk breeze, but the sun shone brightly, its warmth only intermittently obscured by a puff of cloud.

Meary let Lady Swanscroft lead the way.

"My son is very much in love with you," Lady Swanscroft opened the conversation.

Meary smiled and nodded. "Aye. I am very lucky."

"Yes, you are."

"He is a good man," Meary said not knowing how else to answer her statement.

"Of course, he is. He is my son. Unfortunately, he is also very stubborn. Once he gets a notion in his head, it is ifficult to dislodge it."

"Aye. I have personal knowledge of the truth of that. But sometimes stubbornness 'tis a good thing. It keeps a person from giving up when others see a situation as impossible."

"I suppose a person could look at it that way, though I'm not sure I would. Why don't you tell me about your family," Lady Swanscroft abruptly changed their topic.

"Once me family was great in this land, but politics with its wars, disease, famine, and a host of other misfortunes dwindled our fortunes and our numbers. I lived with me parents in Connacht until their death. They died of the fever the same year I went blind. Since then, I have travelled with Brendan and Seumas, playing and singing for those who invite us into their homes."

"A very sad story."

Sympathy from Lady Swanscroft? Meary could not believe her ears, but the tenuous hope that the trial of Edwin's death might have softened the edges of the woman's hard soul began to grow. "Nay. For the most part, I have lived a happy life," she assured her.

"Did you not dream of luxuries?"

"Nay."

"Then why do you want to marry my son?"

The old, familiar bite was back in her ladyship's voice, but Meary did not take offense. It was one thing to hope for a miracle, quite another to expect it. "Because I love him," she answered simply.

"Love is highly overrated. It makes people behave stupidly. Take my advice: never let love stand in the way of getting what you want."

"But if what I am wanting is love, your advice will not serve me."

"Then don't take it! It really doesn't matter anyway!"

Lady Swanscroft's teeth clacked as she snapped her mouth shut.

They continued to walk, but her ladyship said naught more. Meary was silent as well.

Quiet companionship was what Colin's mother now seemed to prefer, and Meary had no quarrel with providing it. If Lady Swanscroft was not in the mood for further conversation, trying to draw her out of herself would likely be a mistake. Rather than dwell on her ladyship's present lack of congeniality, Meary celebrated the fact they had maintained a civil conversation for as long as they had.

After they had gone quite some distance, Meary cautiously ventured, "I think we should be stopping now. The winds on these cliffs can get quite fierce this time of year."

"Really? Is it dangerous?" Lady Swanscroft asked with a trill in her voice.

The hair on the back of Meary's neck bristled. "It can be if a person 'tis not careful."

"How very convenient."

"What?"

"Surely you didn't think I asked you to walk with me because I delight in your company?"

"I . . ."

"Obviously you did," Lady Swanscroft sneered. "You are a very stupid peasant girl, and the world will be well rid of you."

"Lady Swanscroft?" Meary began backing away. "I hope I am misunderstanding the meaning of your words."

"I have to kill you, you know. He's forcing me to do it," she stated matter-of-factly.

Meary had become accustomed to Colin's mother's wild

mood swings, but naught had prepared her to hear what she heard. A wave of cold dread washed over her. She struggled to keep her wits about her. "Who is forcing you?"

"Colin. As you well know he still refuses to come home to England. He fooled me once with his lies, but he will not do so again."

"What lies?"

"He lied about wanting to be master of Swanscroft. I made him master, and still he refuses me!"

The implication of what she said made Meary's heart stop and her breath freeze in her throat. The lady was distraught. Confused. She couldn't know what she was saying. "What do ye mean, ye made him master?" Meary begged for a comforting explanation.

"I suppose there's no harm in telling you since you are going to die shortly. It was I who killed Edwin."

"Nay. Ye could not have. Ye loved Edwin."

"Edwin was standing between me and my comforts." Lady Swanscroft steadily advanced as Meary retreated. Her voice was as steady as her encroaching footsteps. It was too calm. "I grant you, it was a mistake. A dreadful mistake. But how was I to know Colin was deceiving me with his filthy lies? I thought with Edwin out of the way, he would come home. I had already tried everything else I could think of. I wheedled. I cajoled. I appealed to his sense of duty. I enlisted Edwin to hire thugs to destroy the estate and seduce you. Nothing worked."

"But ye loved Edwin," Meary repeated numbly.

"Did I not just tell you never to let love stand in the way of getting what you want? I want money. Lots of it. Edwin couldn't get it for me." She drew in an exasperated breath. "Besides, he failed miserably in his efforts to seduce you away from Colin. I don't tolerate failure.

Much as I adored him, he had become a liability."

"But killing Edwin gained ye nothing," Meary protested.

"That is why I must kill you." She sounded almost cheerful. "It was you I should have killed in the beginning. I could have spared my Edwin."

"Ye do not need to kill me," Meary spoke the words slowly and with authority.

"Yes, I do," Lady Swanscroft responded with equal force. "It is the only thing that will make Colin come home to Swanscroft and do my bidding again. You've bewitched him. You've made him believe Ireland is his home. He lied to me, you know. He said it wasn't you, but it *was* you all along. He tricked me into murdering Edwin."

"Nay!"

"Yes, he did! And don't you dare argue with me! I know the truth now. It's too late to save my Edwin, but it's not too late to set things to right." Lady Swanscroft lunged forward.

Spinning on her heels, Meary broke into a run. Lady Swanscroft was clearly without conscience and quite likely mad. But she couldn't allow her mind to dwell on Lady Swanscroft's mental state. It would sap her strength, and she needed every bit of it she could muster. Meary knew if she did not escape her, she would share the same fate as Edwin.

Running disoriented her, and she had no idea what direction she took. She ran away from the cliffs and the roaring of the sea, but otherwise she was totally lost.

Her heart pounded in her ears, drowning out the sound of Lady Swanscroft's pursuit.

Of a sudden, she found her path blocked. She tried to change course but was felled to the ground, stunned by a fierce slap across her cheek, then immediately yanked to her feet by clawlike hands which dragged her back toward the sea.

"Nay!" Meary screamed as she struggled against her captor. "Nay!"

Lady Swanscroft laughed in reply.

Meary pulled with all her might as she continued to scream. Though she used every ounce of her strength, she could feel herself losing ground.

Lady Swanscroft was a large woman. Meary was no match for her. Nothing she did seemed to have the least effect. She writhed, bit, kicked, but still Lady Swanscroft held on.

As they inched ever closer to the sound of the crashing waves, Meary realized she was about to die. It was a horrible, paralyzing feeling, and for a second she lost heart; then, the image of Colin filled her head and she rebelled, finding a new reserve of strength and regaining for herself a few inches of safety.

Lady Swanscroft quickly won it back.

For a few moments Meary managed to hold her ground; then, she could feel her feet slipping again.

The pounding of horse hooves reached Meary's ears. At first she feared it was only her own heartbeat, but as the pounding grew louder, the thunder of hooves became unmistakable.

"No! Get away from us!" Lady Swanscroft screeched. "Meary!"

Meary recognized Brendan's voice. "Brendan, help me, please!" she gasped.

With a mighty yank, Lady Swanscroft pulled her so close to the cliff's edge that Meary felt as though they were atop the waves. Brendan caught onto her arm and held fast.

"No!" Lady Swanscroft screamed again.

It was now a battle of three.

Brendan hauled her one way; then, Lady Swanscroft tugged her back toward the cliffs. Over and over they repeated the steps of the macabre dance.

The hope that had swelled in Meary's breast at the sound of Brendan's voice was slowly fading as she was dragged back and forth. It was unthinkable that two could not prevail over one. It must be madness lending Lady Swanscroft her inhuman strength. Madness or the devil. How else could she gain ground against both her and Brendan?

Meary fought for her life with all her might, but she was becoming increasingly dizzy from the pain in her joints, exhaustion, and the precarious closeness of the cliff's edge.

She felt as though she was being strangled in a mass of writhing limbs. She ceased to feel pain. The only sensations she felt were the incessant pressure of being tugged first this way and that, a burning in her lungs, and *fear*.

Brendan gave a stalwart yank. Lady Swanscroft instantly countered it with another, causing them to lurch sharply in one direction.

Then, there was nothing but air beneath Meary's feet.

The arms binding her were suddenly gone.

Three piercing screams rent the air.

One of them was her own.

Chapter 29

Meary was aware of a sharp pain in her back. She gingerly rolled to her side, found nothing but air before her, gasped, and quickly rolled back. She lay perfectly still, gripping the ground beneath her with rigid fingers.

"Where am I?" she asked in terror.

Slowly, her mind became less dazed and the memory of falling from the cliff rushed in upon her. Her already taut body became so stiff she couldn't breathe.

Her first thought was for Brendan, her second for Lady Swanscroft. Where were they? Were they alive? Or dead? If she had had the breath, she would have cried out but she did not.

It took considerable effort to convince her lungs to begin functioning again. When they did, Meary took a few minutes to try to calm herself before concentrating on the sounds, scents and feel of her surroundings. Fear made it difficult to think clearly, but the instinct for survival gave her the strength of will to take command of herself.

The answer to the question of where she was, Meary

concluded, was on a ledge overhanging the sea somewhere on the face of the cliffs. By listening to the crash of the waves on the rocks below, she knew she was high enough she need not worry about the incoming tide, but how close she was to the top of the cliffs she had no idea.

She took inventory of her person. She was badly bruised, but no bones were broken. The persistent pain in her back, she realized was caused not by some injury but by a small rock she lay upon.

With the greatest of care, Meary pushed herself to a sitting position, then paused to catch her breath. Using her fingers to measure the distance, she inched backward until her back was firmly pressed against the face of the cliff.

The ledge on which she had fallen was less than four feet wide where she sat. It took considerable time to work up the courage for further exploration, but eventually she impelled herself. Keeping her back to the cliff wall, she determined the ledge to be no longer than a tall man. Ever so slowly, she crawled on her hands and knees, never moving more than an inch at a time, until she had measured the width of the ledge at several points along its length. It never exceeded four feet and on the ends tapered to less than three.

She returned to the relative security of the center point at the same painstaking crawl, leaned back against the face of the cliff, and curled her legs beneath her.

Meary knew the next thing she must do was rise to her feet and measure the distance upward, but her heart was pounding too rapidly for her to dare to do so just yet.

Now that she knew she was the only one on the ledge, she was forced to confront another horror. Had Brendan been as lucky as she? Was he lying on some other ledge safe from harm? Two miracles seemed too much to hope for, and a cloud of gloom descended upon her. Still, she refused to let logic convince her to abandon hope without a fight.

Mustering a deep breath, she called, "Brendan?"

There was no answer.

Meary swallowed the lump in her throat. It was too soon to despair. If she had survived the fall, he might have also. He was too good to die. She called again, this time a little louder.

There was still no answer.

Taking another deep breath, she shouted his name again and again until her voice was spent and tears choked off her breath. It was possible he could not hear her, but the hollow feeling in Meary's heart made her all but certain he had not survived the fall.

She wept bitter tears. He should not have died like this, Brendan who had never harmed anyone, who had been a loyal friend to her all her life, who loved her so much he urged her to follow her heart and marry Colin. She did not want him to have given his life in exchange for hers. It was too steep a price.

Meary knew not how long she lost herself to her grief, but eventually there were no more tears left to cry. Though she would gladly give her life if it would restore Brendan's, she understood giving in to despair would not bring him back if he was gone. She must survive or the sacrifice of his life would be for naught. She would not dishonor his memory with faintheartedness.

Thus shored, Meary turned her attention to the cause of this baleful situation. Never in her life had she wished anyone dead, but in that moment she prayed Lady Swanscroft had not survived the fall. If she was still alive, the lives of all Meary knew and loved were in jeopardy until she could warn Colin of his mother's treachery.

She shuddered. And what then? Lady Swanscroft must hang for her crimes. Colin should not be faced with the task of turning his own mother over to the authorities to be tried and executed. Meary felt great pools of fresh tears welling in her eyes at the thought. Nay. It would be better for all concerned if Lady Swanscroft had not survived.

Knowing that if she allowed herself to surrender to tears again she would risk hysterics, Meary bridled her emotions. She must think with a clear head, plan what she should do. A miracle might have saved her from instant death, but all danger had not passed.

The first thing she must do was the least pleasant. Squaring her shoulders, Meary made herself call, "Lady Swanscroft?"

When there was no answer, she called again, then again until she was satisfied there would be no answer. She knew the lack of response was no guarantee that Colin and the world were now safe from Lady Swanscroft, but it was a comforting sign.

To pray for the lady's soul was beyond Meary's grace. Someday she might be able to summon the Christian charity necessary to perform such a task, but at present she could not.

With a dint of will she pushed thoughts of Lady Swanscroft from her mind and filled it with thoughts of those she loved and who loved her. They would give her the strength she needed to survive until she was rescued.

She had yet to determine how far she had fallen, and Meary knew it was something she needed do. The fact that her injuries were limited to bruises gave her hope she might be able to reach the top of the cliff and either pull herself up or leave some kind of marker to help those who came looking for her. She used that hope to contain the terror she had of standing up.

Sliding her back up the wall of the cliff, Meary paused to catch her breath when she had reached her full height. Deliberately, she turned so she faced the cliff, then held on tight. Never loosening the iron grip of one hand before the other had a secure hold, she gradually raised her arms above her head. The top of the cliff remained out of reach. Gritting her teeth, she stretched as high as she could. Naught but a solid rock wall greeted her.

Lowering herself back to her heels, Meary waited until her heartbeat slowed to an acceptable level before sidling first to the left and then the right, repeating the process. She sighed with a mixture of disappointment—nowhere had she been able to reach the top of the cliff—and relief that she was able to return to her place in the center of the ledge and sit on firm ground.

If she could see, she would know whether she was inches or feet from reaching the top. At no time in her life had her blindness been more frustrating. All her other senses were useless in measuring the distance.

There was naught she could do but sit and wait for someone to come to the rescue. Though every movement she made caused her heart to beat wildly within her chest, knowing she could do nothing to help herself put even more fear in her heart.

No one had the slightest idea where she was. In her excitement at being asked to walk with Lady Swanscroft, she had forgotten to tell anyone she was leaving the house. Since his brother's death, Colin had left strict

orders that she must never go out alone and to always te
someone where she was going. It was a sensibl
precaution. He did the same, so she would not worr
when he was gone. How could she have behaved s
stupidly? Colin would be furious with her—and just
fiably so.

How she would love to hear the sound of his voic
berating her at this very moment. She wondered ho
long it would be before someone discovered her missing
Minutes? Hours? Had some sweet soul already notice
her absence?

As she contemplated the possibilities, Meary realize
someone could be near the cliff's edge at this ver
moment and there was a very real possibility she woul
not be able to hear them over the roar of the sea.

Immediately, she started to shout. The wind blew he
voice back in her face, but Meary kept up a steady choru
of calls for help until she was hoarse. It seemed sh
shouted for hours, but she wasn't sure. With the breez
blowing off the sea it was impossible to judge the sun'
position in the sky by feeling the warmth of its rays. Sh
rubbed the column of the throat, swallowing over an
over again, until she could coax more sound from it.

A ruckus in the yard caused Colin to quicken his pac
as he strolled out of the stables. Three men stood in
circle around a fourth who kicked at the dust in which h
lay. His hands and feet were bound, and he was swearin
profusely in Gaelic, having obviously just been pulle
from the back of his nag by one or more of hi
companions.

Colin recognized the three standing men as tenant

who farmed the northern most acres of his estate. The man on the ground, he did not know.

"What is going on?" he questioned as he approached the foursome.

"Ye recognize this?" one man asked as he reached in his pocket and pulled out a gold and ruby neck pin.

"It was my brother's," Colin grimly replied.

"We found him trying to bury it along with these." He reached into his pocket again and pulled out several more pieces of less expensive jewelry and a tortoiseshell snuff box.

Yanking the man on the ground up by his collar, Colin pulled him so close they stood nose to nose. His nostrils flared as they were assaulted by the strong odor of rum, and he impaled him with his gaze. "What's your name?"

"Skerett, Rory Skerett," he squeaked.

"Rory Skerett, you are going to hang for the murder of my brother," he stated coldly.

"Nay! I never killed a soul!" the fellow cried.

"Then how do you explain the jewels?"

"He gave them to us."

"Us?"

"Aye."

"And who is 'us?'"

When he refused to respond, Colin twisted his collar until his eyes bulged and his ruddy cheeks began to turn blue. Skerett bobbed his head, indicating he was ready to talk, and Colin loosened his grip just enough so he could breathe.

"Me and me cousins," he croaked out.

"And why would he give you jewels?"

"As payment."

"For what?"

Colin's grip on the man's collar tightened again when no answer was forthcoming. This time Skerett remained mute so long he began to lose consciousness. Colin released his hold on him, dropping him to the ground. "Payment for what?" he repeated.

Skerett ducked his head between his shoulders and continued to refuse to answer.

"I was going to allow you the benefit of a trial, but if you will not answer me, I will string you up here and now."

He whimpered but did not answer the question.

Colin stared down at him in disgust; then, he turned to one of the men in the circle. "O'Kelly, isn't it?"

"Aye."

"Go into the stables and fetch a rope."

"Aye." O'Kelly started for the stable door.

"Wait! I'll talk if ye be promising I won't hang," Skerett meekly offered.

Colin smiled mirthlessly. "I will make no such promise. If you cooperate, I promise I will turn you over to the authorities unharmed. What they decide to do with you is their business."

Given the choice of immediate death or postponing his demise, Skerett chose the latter. "He was paying us to tear down fences, burn yer fields, kill yer cattle, and the like."

Edwin had solicited the attacks? Colin didn't like what he was hearing. He did have motive, and Edwin had been guilty of many misdeeds during his life, but . . .

"Where did he meet you? You are not from my estate." Before he considered whether or not he believed him, Colin wanted the facts.

"In a tavern," Skerett replied morosely.

"And how did he approach you?"

"Just pranced up to our table with his mincing little steps and said how he be looking for some fellas to do him favor in exchange for a real generous fee."

"What was he wearing?"

Skerett's relief at the nature of the questions was apparent on his face, but he still had the look of a rat cornered by a dog. "Fancy clothes. A bright green coat, silk breeches, a shirt with lots of ruffles. And he smelled like an expensive harlot. That's what stands out in me mind most. He like to give me sneezing fits every time I had to talk to him."

"You met him more than once?"

"Aye. We told him we wouldn't do nothing less he paid in advance."

Colin continued to question him, garnering dates of payment, time of attacks, and what was paid until there was no longer any doubt in his mind. The truth sat like a stone in his gut. And if Edwin was involved, it was impossible to believe his mother innocent. One never made a move without the knowledge of the other. There was a very real possibility, she had concocted the scheme.

Giving his full attention back to the man at his feet, Colin stated, "So, my brother was paying you to destroy my property."

"We didn't know he be yer brother till after someone had killed him," Skerett assured him. "We just thought he be a fellow with a grudge and money to spend."

"I see."

"Did he say what grudge he bore?"

"Nay. He only said he be willing to pay us to help him run ye out of Ireland."

Colin rubbed his chin. "Your lack of curiosity is amazing. One would think before you agreed to help

421

drive a man off his property and out of the country you would want to know the reason."

Skerett shrugged. "We be in need of the money, and the country can always be using one less Englishman."

"So, when you failed to rid it of me, you decided to kill my brother."

"Nay! I told ye, I had naught to do with his death! They may hang me, but I'll be damned if I'll be hanged for murdering an Englishman without me having the pleasure of doing the deed."

Colin believed the man. There was genuine indignation in his voice. Even more convincing was the fact Skerett was a dead man and Skerett knew it. Lying about his involvement in Edwin's death would not save his neck. A man could only hang once, and he had already admitted guilt to crimes enough to see himself hang. If he was inclined to lie, it made more sense he would falsely claim responsibility for the murder in hopes of gaining stature in the eyes of his countrymen. Being put to death for a radical patriot was bound to be more satisfying than being hung for a common thief.

Despite his conviction, Colin wanted Meary to talk to the man. He trusted her intuition far more than his own.

"Find out the names of the men who rode with him . . . using what ever form of persuasion is necessary to convince him to talk," Colin instructed, giving menacing emphasis to the last phrase. "When you find out what you need to know, I want one man to take the information to the authorities, so they can begin the search for his accomplices. I want him kept here under close guard. I'll send for him shortly."

"Aye, milord."

"Also, I wish to reward you for capturing him. No

422

ents will be charged you for the next three years, and for
s long as your families choose to live on my property
our rent will never be raised."

"Thank ye, milord," they answered in unison.

"It is I who thanks you." Tipping his head, Colin
rode toward the house.

"Annie, can you tell me where I might find Meary?"
olin asked his housekeeper as she emerged from the
tchen, wiping her hands on her apron.

She glanced around the great hall. "The last I saw her,
e was in here with your mother. I suspect she's retired
 her room for a bit of peace and quiet."

"I already looked there."

"Oh. Well, she must be about somewhere. I'll send a
ouple of maids to hunt her up for you."

"Thank you. Ask her to come to the hall when she is
ound."

Colin stood by the fire, warming his hands while he
aited for Meary's arrival. He was eager to tell her the
ews of Skerett's capture and solicit her opinion of his
ory. He would be happier if he could believe Edwin's
urderer had been found, but capturing one of the gang
f thugs who had been plaguing the estate was no small
ictory.

His thoughts turned to his mother and he grimaced. It
as not as if his family's duplicity was a surprise, but that
ey would sink so low to get him to return to England
mazed even him. He now understood why the attacks
ad of a sudden stopped with Edwin's death.

Colin was angry at both Edwin and his mother, but his
nger was tempered by the knowledge they had both paid

a high price for their crime—Edwin his life and hi
mother the loss of her favorite son. He would demand hi
mother leave his home, but he would pursue no othe
punishment.

He drummed his fingers against his thigh. But havin,
solved one mystery, he was faced with another. If Skeret
was telling the truth about Edwin's death, and he coul
not shake the feeling he was, who had murdered Edwir
and why? Mayhap Meary would have some ideas.

Colin's hands were agreeably warm, and he turned t
face the room and warm his backside.

"I wonder what is keeping her?" he mused as the wai
stretched to the point of tedium. Annie would have
known if she had gone out, so she couldn't be far.

He pulled his watch from his pocket and checked the
time. Mayhap his eagerness to share his news was makin;
him overanxious. Fifteen minutes ticked by and still she
did not come.

Colin decided to go in search of her himself. He me
Annie at the top of the stairs.

"We can't find her anywhere," she told him, her brow
pleating with concern. "No one has seen her for hours.'

"You have spoken to Mr. O'Hanlon?"

"She has." Seumas stepped out of his room, garbed i
his camlet cloak. "I'm going out to be checking the
grounds. I don't like her out after dark and sometime;
she misjudges the time."

"Mayhap she is with Brendan," Colin offered the
explanation, making no attempt to disguise the worry ir
his voice, despite his logical mind telling him it was fai
too early to be concerned by her absence. "She knows
better than to go out alone."

"Brendan be riding Pansy," Seumas informed him.

Colin started down the hall. "I'll ask Mother if she has any idea where she might have gone."

"Lady Swanscroft isn't in her room either," Annie said.

Colin stopped. "Both of them are missing?"

Annie nodded.

"Let's keep calm," he advised. "There is probably no cause for alarm." He had no idea if he had convinced the others to be calm, but he failed miserably to convince himself. With Edwin's death fresh on his mind, it was not possible to shrug off this new enigma without fearful thoughts flashing through his head. He continued to counsel himself that some reasonable explanation for both their absences would be forthcoming, but he wasn't going to take any chances. "Search every inch of the house again. I am going out to organize a search of the estate." Turning on his heels, he left Annie and Seumas at the top of the stairs.

Upon reaching the yard, he bellowed out, "I am looking for Lady Meary. Has anyone seen her?"

Everyone within hearing distance gathered round. Colin repeated his question, "Has anyone seen Lady Meary?"

His ears were assailed with a chorus of "Nays" as heads shook back and forth.

Colin frowned. "Stay here and organize yourselves into groups of three or four. You," he pointed at the blacksmith, "round up every man you can find."

His stable master stepped forward. "I don't know if one has anything to be doing with the other, but Pansy just came wandering in without a rider," he informed Colin. "I was on me way to the house to tell ye when ye called us together."

Seumas had joined Colin on the steps, and Colin turned to him. His expression was grim. "A coincidence?"

"Nay, I think not."

"Nor do I." Colin had been making some effort to hide his disquiet from the crowd, and now he abandoned the cause altogether. There were three people missing, Meary, his mother, and Brendan. Much as he wanted to do so, he couldn't convince himself naught was amiss.

The most comforting explanation he could conjure was that Meary and Brendan had gone out together, and one or both had been thrown from the horse; however, that didn't explain his mother's absence.

"Was Lady Meary with Brendan when he took Pansy out?" Colin asked his stable master.

"Nay, he went alone."

"I feared you would say that." He pressed his lips together, squared his shoulders, and forced himself to face another possibility.

"There is a man being held prisoner in the stables," Colin addressed O'Hanlon. "He has already admitted he and his kin are responsible for the crimes against my property, but he claims to have no knowledge of who was responsible for the murder of my brother. I was inclined to believe him, but now . . . I want you to come with me to see if you can find out anything more from him than I have."

Seumas nodded and started for the stables.

"We'll be right back," Colin called over his shoulder as he followed him.

As they strode to the stables, Colin filled him in on all he knew.

Skerett lay curled in a ball on the floor of a stall. His

lip was bleeding and he sported a black eye. "The name of his cousins be Hugh and Turlough. He says they be heading for the mountains of Connemara," the man guarding him informed Colin.

"Get him on his feet. We have three people missing from the house. I want to know what he knows about it."

"I don't know nothing about it," Skerett protested from his spot on the ground.

O'Hanlon addressed a stream of angry words to him in Gaelic. Skerett responded. Words flew back and forth between the two for several minutes. Colin was able to translate almost all of what they said. O'Hanlon repeatedly demanded answers from the man, and when he didn't answer fast enough or thoroughly enough for his liking, he called curses down upon the fellow, his family, his ancestors, and those yet unborn. When O'Hanlon had finished with him, Skerett was shaking so hard he could no longer speak.

"He hasn't done anything to them. He was caught long before they turned up missing," Seumas announced what Colin already knew to be true. "As to his cousins, he swears they'd never be laying a finger on an Irishman or any woman no matter what the price, but he admits he hasn't seen them since early morning," Seumas announced. "He claims they be as scared as he when they heard a murderer was on the loose."

"Do you believe him?"

"Aye." Seumas reverted back to Gaelic. "But if ever I discover I be wrong and any harm has been done to Meary by his kin, I'll personally be cutting out his heart with me thumbnail and feeding it to the crows."

"I be telling the truth," Skerett whimpered.

"For your sake I hope you are," Colin replied.

427

"Because before I gift Mr. O'Hanlon with your heart, I will vent my ire on you, and if you think the wrath of a poet cause to quake, you will soil your breeches at the wrath of an Englishman."

As Colin and Seumas marched out of the stables, Annie hurried up to them. "We didn't find the either of them, but both their wraps are missing. I can't imagine why Meary would leave without telling me, and Lady Swanscroft never leaves the house, but mayhap they went on a stroll?"

"I have thought of that. We know they must have left the house of their own free will or someone would have heard a commotion. But if that is true, why are they not back by now? My mother is neither fond of exercise nor Meary. Even if Meary convinced her a little fresh air would do her good—a circumstance that seems highly unlikely—they would not have gone far. Besides, Meary would have told you they were going."

"I know," Annie fretted. "I just want to keep hoping for the best."

"And you should." Colin squeezed her hand and tried to smile convincingly. "We will probably find the three of them without a scratch."

"Three?"

"Brendan's horse came back without him," Seumas said.

Annie went pale.

Despite his assurances to Annie, Colin could feel his concern for Meary and the others edging toward panic. There were too many unanswered questions. And one question kept coming back to haunt him. If Skerett and his cousins didn't kill Edwin, who did and why? All along he had assumed the murder was a part of the plot to drive

428

him from his estate. But since he now believed Edwin and his mother to be behind those misdeeds, where was the motive?

The brutality of the murder led him to the unwelcome hypothesis a crazed killer might very well be living in their midst. Someone who killed for pleasure, not gain. If it was true, anyone could be a victim at any time. He banished the thought from his mind before he succumbed to full-blown panic. He would find Meary and Brendan and his mother, and they would all be fine. Any moment now Brendan would come walking into the yard, blushing from head to toe from the mortification of being thrown from his horse. He wasn't even sure Meary and his mother had left the house together. They too would return, each with a perfectly reasonable explanation for her absence.

Colin glanced at the sky. Dusk was falling in earnest. They should be back.

"I am leaving immediately to start seraching for Meary," he abruptly announced. "The two of you take charge of assigning the men sections to search. Annie, you know where I keep my pistols. If there is any word of them, fire three shots in the air."

Before either could reply, Colin was halfway to his horse.

It was past midnight when Colin rode into the yard. He had been back twice before to check if there was any news. He knew Annie would fire the pistol if there was any, but he could not help but hope he had missed hearing the shots.

He wearily stomped into the hall. Annie greeted him

with a tear-stained face and a dejected shake of her head. Hours ago everyone had given up the pretense that all would be well. They would have been back long ago if something dreadful hadn't happened.

"Stand by the fire and warm yourself. I'll bring you a cup of tea," Annie said.

"Where is O'Hanlon?"

"Out searching with the others. I told him I could handle matters here. He couldn't bear to sit and wait for news any longer." She dabbed at the tears streaming down her face. "I fear if something has happened to those children, he'll die of a broken heart."

"They will be found unharmed," Colin stated without conviction. More forcefully he added, "They have to be."

"I can't believe someone would . . ." she could not bring herself to speak the word, ". . . all three of them in one day. There must be some other reason for them being gone."

"We will keep searching until we find them," he promised.

Annie shook her head. "You need to rest a little while."

"No," Colin rejected her advice. Speaking more to himself than to her, he said in a voice barely above a whisper, "There is a full moon tonight. It is a great help. I am glad Meary has her shawl. It is chilly tonight, and I would not want her to be cold."

"Meary has a fine head on her shoulders. I'm sure she's taking good care of herself."

"Yes. I am sure she is," Colin tried to reply, but his voice cracked halfway through his statement. "I'll have

430

that cup of tea now," he brusquely informed her before he was forced to turn away.

Colin listened to Annie's rapidly retreating footsteps as visions of Meary floated in his head. He was worried about them all, truly he was, but he could not pretend his anxiety for Meary was not far greater than his concern for the others. If something had happened to her, O'Hanlon would not be the only one to die of a broken heart. He refused to imagine his life without her. He had no use for such a life. Meary had to be all right. She was too full of life and love and gentle wisdom. A spirit as strong as hers could not be extinguished.

It was far too late and she had been gone far too long for him to convince himself there was some good reason for her absence, but he could still believe she was alive. Edwin had not been lured out of the house to be killed. He had been murdered where he lay. Mayhap, unbeknownst to him, Skerett's cousins had decided to try their hand at kidnapping. They were holding Meary and his mother somewhere safe and would return them in exchange for a ransom.

Abduction did not explain how they had managed to get them out of the house without causing a commotion or why Brendan was missing as well, and to think of Meary in the hands of some villain was not comforting, but it was far more palatable to contemplate than the possibility she was dead.

He vigorously rubbed his arms and sidled a little closer to the fire, trying to dispel the sudden chill that crept up his frame.

Annie returned with his tea. Colin gulped it down in three swallows, uncaring that the liquid scalded his throat, then handed the cup back to her and started for the door. "Don't forget: three shots the moment you hear a word."

"The very moment," Annie vowed.

Meary huddled against the face of the cliff, her knees drawn up close to her body and her arms tucked within the folds of her skirt.

The sun had gone down long ago, and the temperature had been slowly dropping ever since. The breeze coming off the ocean continued to blow, and the fog had risen. She was cold, hungry, and so thirsty her tongue felt chapped. Her physical miseries steadily undermined the little of her emotional reserves she had managed to retain.

Meary had lost count of the times she had thought she had heard the sound of hoofbeats or the neigh of a horse and shouted for help until her voice was spent, only to realize the hoof beats were the pounding of her own heart or the neigh the cry of a sea bird.

She knew she could not afford to waste her energy, but at least the surges of false hopes provided a distraction from her thoughts.

Brendan constantly filled her mind. She tried to conjure happy memories to sustain her, but grief always overwhelmed her, and she could do naught but cling to the ground and sob like a child.

Thoughts of Brendan inevitably brought thoughts of the woman who had caused his death. Though she tried to shut it out, she could still hear the echo of Lady Swanscroft's harsh voice calmly explaining how she had killed her own son because she loved money better and

432

romising Meary her own death. Meary could not comprehend such evil. How had Colin endured under her influence?

Meary consoled herself with the belief that even if she died on this ledge, Colin would at least be safe from the clutches of his grasping mother. Annie would take care of him for her.

Now that she had broken the chains binding his heart, he would be able to trust and love another woman if she did not survive to be his bride.

Despite the comfort of these thoughts, Meary very much intended to survive. She did not want Colin to suffer the grief of her death. She did not want some other woman to marry him in her place. She wanted to be the one to lavish him with the love he deserved.

She nestled deeper into the folds of her skirt. Darkness surely had forced them to give up the search for her hours ago. She should try to get some sleep. It would make the time go faster and restore her strength so she could face tomorrow with more courage.

Meary slept fitfully, awaking every few minutes during the night. When she did sleep, her rest was marred by nightmares of Lady Swanscroft and of falling off the ledge into the cold, merciless sea. It was dawn before exhaustion subjugated fear and forced a few hours of unbroken sleep upon her.

Chapter 30

Colin stood on the beach, staring out to sea as he clutched Meary's sea-soaked shawl in his hands. At his feet lay the corpses of his mother and Brendan, washed ashore by the morning tide. Meary's shawl had been found entangled about his mother's arms.

Seumas O'Hanlon stood by his side. Every few minutes a shudder wracked his frame, and his breathing was labored, but he said nothing. The men who stood around them were equally mute.

There was nothing that could be said. After thirty-eight hours the search was over.

Colin kept fingering the shawl in his hands. She was out there . . . somewhere. His Meary. Her beautiful body being battered by the waves. It might never wash ashore. He would never see her smile again, hear her angelic voice, hold her in his arms.

He knew her body was but a shell, that her sweet spirit had left its earthly shroud, but he couldn't bear to think of her flesh being torn by the rocks and the hungry creatures of the sea.

He felt the scream welling up in his throat, but he could do naught to stop it. It exploded in a terrible roar. "No! You can't have her! Give her back to me!" he cursed the heavens and the sea. "Give her back!"

He dropped to his knees, his roar fading into an anguished whimper, "Give her back."

Seumas put a hand on his shoulder. "She can't be coming back," he stated quietly.

Colin shook his head as if to deny his words.

Seumas continued to speak in a low, soothing voice. "I know ye love her. There's no one who could have tried harder to save her. Ye've barely been off yer horse. Ye've neither slept nor eaten. I also know she's been looking down on ye from her place in heaven and be pleased with ye. She sees how much ye cared."

"It would have been better for her if she had never met me," Colin bitterly proclaimed.

"There was a time I would have agreed with ye . . . but now I do not. Meary loved ye with all her heart. Ye gave her sorrow, but ye also gave her joy." He abruptly fell silent, gripping Colin's shoulder until he had composed himself to go on. "She always feared because of her blindness she would never know the love of a man. She pretended it mattered naught to her, but I knew in me heart it did. Ye brought passion to her life. It was a great gift."

"I should have treated her better."

"As should I. How cruelly we have been reminded that the time we share with those we love 'tis but a brief moment."

Seumus was still and did not speak again for several minutes. "We should be taking the bodies back to the house," he said solemnly.

435

"Would you ask Annie to begin making the necessary preparations?"

"Ye should be coming with us back to the house."

"Not yet," Colin protested. "I cannot go yet. I need to stay here a little while longer to see if . . ."

"I understand."

The men needed no direction from Seumas to do what needed to be done.

When he was alone, Colin raised his head and through tear-hot eyes watched the waves crash, bubble up on the shore, then recede. The day was fair, the water clear. The sun shone brightly overhead in a cloudless sky. No breeze stirred the air. To him it seemed the balmy weather mocked his grief.

He did not have O'Hanlon's strength of character to see him through this loss. O'Hanlon had lost two people he loved, and yet he was able to do what must be done.

He had lost his mother in addition to Meary, but the loss of an unloving mother could not be counted the same as O'Hanlon's loss of Brendan. Colin did not know how O'Hanlon could be so strong in the face of so much pain. He wished he had shared the secret of his strength before he had gone. He needed to know how to go on being a man without Meary. It seemed an unbearable burden.

If Meary was watching down on them from heaven, he wondered if she was grimacing at the irony of life. After all her efforts to get O'Hanlon to accept him, she had finally achieved her aim through her death. Colin was only vaguely aware of what had caused the change in O'Hanlon's attitude, and he was too exhausted and distraught to ponder the matter, but he knew it had occurred. A pity it had occurred too late.

It was a very long time before he could marshall the

ill to stir himself. He rose to his feet reluctantly. The
de was ebbing. Nothing new would be washed ashore
ntil the next high tide. He would be back to watch and
ait for her.

With painstaking care, he folded Meary's shawl in half
vice and lay it over his arm.

Colin intended to go back to the house, but instead he
ook the reins of his horse in hand and led him on foot in
nother direction. He needed to be alone a little longer, to
ort out his thoughts and feelings before he was forced to
ace the world.

"See, I am still running from that which frightens
1e," he whispered to his departed lover. "You should
ot have left me so soon. I still need you to be my tutor."

He stood stock still, as if waiting for the reply, before
esuming his slow, heavy pace.

After a space of time Colin found himself standing atop
1e cliffs, staring out to sea. It was a scene he had enjoyed
ountless times. It had soothed him. Now he hated the
ea. It had Meary and he had nothing.

When he had first met her, he had been afraid to love,
fraid of the abuse he would suffer. And allowing himself
o love had brought him suffering, but not in the way he
ad reckoned. Meary had melted his heart, filled it with
ove, and now he felt pain so excruciating it was a struggle
o draw in his next breath.

He did not blame her for this agony of his soul. He
vould never wish himself the way he had been before he
1et her. But he did wish someone somewhere would tell
1im how to survive her loss without going mad.

He raked his fingers through his hair, and his eyes took
n a tormented sheen as his ears picked up the sound of a
nelody on the still air. Oh, God, he was going mad. The

437

voice was Meary's. She was singing a Gaelic love song. H
could not hear the words clearly, but he recognized th
melody. It was one of her favorites. She had sung it fo
him that night he had come to her room for comfort.

He stood, rooted to the spot, listening. The voice wa
hers and yet, it was not. There was a raspiness to th
notes, a warbling unsteady quality of a diffident singer
He knew he should cover his ears, try to fight off th
madness, but he couldn't do it. He wanted to hear he
voice. To heed its call.

The sound seemed to be coming from the sea, and h
dropped the reins of his horse and began to follow it. Th
voice was barely discernible above the roar of th
crashing waves, but it grew louder as he approache
the edge of the cliffs.

He recognized it was a siren's song he heard, luring
him to his death. Rather than frighten him, the thought
calmed him.

He continued to walk steadily toward the sea. He could
be with Meary again. He would not have to feel this pain.
Death was preferable to madness. A foot from the edge he
stopped.

"God forgive me. I know it is the coward's way, but I
hear her calling me. I cannot deny her," he shouted.
Heaving a shuddering sigh, he lifted his foot to take his
last step.

"Colin!" the voice cried, jolting him out of his haze of
grief.

He took a step back, startled by the sudden strength of
the voice and by the unclouded realization of the fatal
course he had been about to take.

"Colin!" It came again.

"Meary?" he called.

438

"Thank God ye have found me!"

"Meary?" he whispered hoarsely, unable to believe his
~~rs~~. Then, he called her name a little louder, "Meary?"

"Aye, 'tis me. I'm here on a ledge. I had given up hope
~~:~~ would ever find me. But now ye are here!" She began
~~~~ laugh and cry at the same time.

Cautiously Colin again approached the edge of the
~~iff~~, still half convinced the voice was a trick of his grief-
~~:ricken~~ mind. His eyes scanned the face of the cliff but a
~~:ond~~ before they lighted upon her.

There she sat, a bedraggled vision of pallid skin and
~~ack~~ and blue bruises, on a narrow ledge not more than
~~venty~~ feet from the top.

"Meary! You are not dead!" he shouted.

"Nay!"

"I heard you singing!"

"I was trying to keep me spirits up!"

"How badly are you injured?"

"I fear I'm bruised from head to toe, but otherwise I
~~:n~~ sound." Her voice undulated as she yelled back her
~~:iswer~~, but he caught its meaning.

"How did you ever . . . ? Never mind. I cannot be-
~~:eve~~ you are alive!" Colin fell silent as he rapidly took
~~:irvey~~ of the situation. When he spoke again, concern
~~:nged~~ his voice. "I cannot get to you from here. I am
~~:ring~~ to need a rope and a few men to help!"

Meary recovered enough strength of voice to call up,
~~:~~How far did I fall?"

"About twenty feet!"

There was a long pause before she shouted her next
~~:uestion~~. "Can ye see Brendan or your mother?"

Colin flinched. He did not want to answer her, not
~~:ntil~~ he could hold her in his arms and console her

sorrow. "It is too difficult to carry on a conversation this way. We can talk when I get you up. Will you be all right alone for a few minutes while I ride for help?"

"Aye."

"Good. I'll be back as fast as I can. I love you! And don't move an inch!"

Meary leaned back against the rock wall at her back and hugged herself. A few minutes ago she had judged her death a foregone conclusion. After two nights and a day she had given up all hope of rescue.

Meary said a prayer of thanks and basked in the joy of her unexpected good fortune.

The euphoria of being given back the life she had thought she had lost kept her warm while she awaited Colin's return, but it was tempered with a note of sadness. Colin had avoided answering her question about Brendan and Lady Swanscroft, and his refusal to reply confirmed her belief they were both dead. Lady Swanscroft's death was a blessing, but Brendan's loss was a tragedy she would mourn the rest of her life.

She vowed not to let a day pass she did not thank him for giving his life for hers and promised to keep his memory alive.

A pensive smile slowly spread across her face. She had already shed far more tears for him than Brendan could ever countenance. Meary knew in her heart the way he would wish her to honor his sacrifice was by living her life to its fullest. Brendan would never approve of her wearing black and walking about with a solemn expression on her face for years on end. He liked her to wear bright colors and smiles.

Rather than mourn his loss, Brendan would want her to celebrate his life. And that was what she was determined to do. No one would ever cross their threshold without hearing the tale of the hero Brendan Bodkin, and if God saw fit to bless her with a son, he would bear his noble name.

"I found her!" Colin shouted as he thundered into the yard. "Annie, O'Hanlon, she is alive and well! Meary is alive!" His shouts brought everyone running. "I need two stout ropes, blankets, and three or four strong men! Annie, put every pot we own on the fire. I want a hot bath waiting for her when we get back! O'Hanlon, you come with me!"

Seumas was already halfway to the stables before Colin shouted his last order. Half a dozen men were at his heels.

Colin wheeled his horse around.

"Where is she?" Annie demanded, tears of joy streaming down her cheeks.

"On the cliffs. She fell on a ledge. We must have ridden over that acre of ground a score of times but it never occurred to me to look over the edge." A maid thrust an armload of blankets into his waiting hands. His men were in their saddles. "I will explain everything later." He left the yard as swiftly as he had entered it.

The moment he arrived back at the cliff, he shouted to Meary. "I'm back! I will be with you in no time!"

"What 'tis it ye plan to do?"

"I am going to have my men lower me to the ledge! Once I have you, they can pull us both up!"

"'Tis too dangerous!" she protested. "Can ye not just lower the rope to me?"

"Meary, do as he says! He knows what he is about!" It was Seumas's voice.

"Seumas, are ye sure?"

"Aye!"

She could hear men shouting encouragement to each other. A fine shower of dirt fell upon her head, and Meary knew it was pointless to protest further. She held her breath as she listened to Colin's descent. A moment later he was by her side, crushing her in his arms and covering her face with rapturous kisses.

"I thought I'd lost you," he cried as they clung to each other. "I am never going to let you out of my sight again. Never, do you understand!"

Meary laughed as she bestowed her own grateful kisses on every part of his person she could reach, too happy to care that his enthusiastic embrace abraded her many bruises. "'Twill be a long time before I get the urge to go wandering near these cliffs again, that I can promise ye."

"Did you fall?"

She instantly sobered. Swallowing her dread, she quietly answered, "Nay, I was pushed."

"Do you know who did it? I swear, when I find the bastard, I'll make him sorry he was ever born!" He pulled her even closer to him, but instead of pursuing his question, he firmly stated, "We will talk of this later, after we get you warm. Your skin is like ice."

Meary didn't argue. She knew she must tell Colin the truth, but she could not help but be glad she was given a temporary reprieve.

"I am going to slip a rope over your head. Pull it under your arms," he told her as he did as he said. When the rope was in place, he double-checked it to be sure it was snug enough to be secure and the knot was tied so it would not slip and become a noose. "Are you ready to have them pull us up?"

442

She nodded.

Colin checked his own rope, then helped her to her feet. Wrapping his arms tightly about her, he shouted to the men overhead. "We're all set. Have the horses start pulling."

As her feet left solid ground, Meary clung to Colin with all her might. He used his feet to try to keep them far enough away from the wall of the cliff that they would not be scraped on the way up. The security of his arms made the sensation of dangling in midair less daunting. Soon hands were on her arms, dragging her up and away from the edge of the cliffs amidst a masculine chorus of cheers.

Someone pulled the rope over her head, and another man began wrapping her in blankets. Colin finished the task, lifting her to her feet and adding the warmth of his arms to that of the blankets. Seumas did likewise.

"'Tis good to have ye back," he choked out through his tears.

"'Tis good to be back."

The blankets were a comfort, but standing within the circle of the arms of the two men she loved warmed Meary from the inside out. She could think of nowhere on earth she would rather be. They apparently were as content as she because neither budged for the longest time.

Finally, it was Colin who spoke. "We ought to get her to the house."

"Aye," Seumas responded.

Colin scooped Meary up in his arms.

Before they went back to the house, there was a question Meary needed to ask, for her own safety as well as that of the others. She was almost certain of the answer, but she needed to be absolutely sure. "Colin?"

"Yes."

"Ye did not answer me question about Brendan and your mother before, but I think I know the answer. Ye know for sure they are dead, don't ye?"

"Yes, their bodies washed ashore this morning along with your shawl. That is why I was so certain you were dead. I am sorry, Meary. I know how much you loved Brendan."

"He died bravely," she addressed both men. "He died trying to save me."

"Who did this to ye?" Seumas demanded.

When Meary did not answer immediately, Colin prodded, "We have a man in the stables. He has admitted he and his cousins were paid to make the attacks on the estate, but he swears he had nothing to . . ."

"He and his kin had naught to do with it," Meary confirmed, wriggling out of his arms and back onto her own two feet.

"How can you be sure when I have not even told you their names?"

"Because 'twas not a man." She paused to gather her courage to face what must be said. "I would give the world not to have to be saying this, but . . ."

"Who?" Colin gently stroked her cheek, encouraging her to go on.

"'Twas your mother, Colin," Meary said softly. "She asked me to be walking with her, but 'twas only a ruse. She thought if she killed me, ye would return to England with her. She was trying to push me off the cliffs; then, Brendan came. As we battled, we lost our balance and all three went over the edge."

"Mother tried to kill you to get me to go back to

ngland," Colin numbly repeated Meary's words.

She held tightly onto his hand. "Aye. I am sorry Colin. wish 'twas not true."

"I knew she was desperate . . . but murder? Even nowing . . . I never dreamed she would go so far to gain er ends."

"There is more," Meary quietly continued. "She illed Edwin as well."

"But why?" His question was a sincere plea for nderstanding and in no way challenged the veracity of er statement.

"She said she did it so ye would be marquess. She kept aying ye had lied to her. I know ye did not, but she said e tricked her into murdering your brother. I fear she ad gone mad and none of us knew it."

"It was greed, not madness. Mother has always had to ave her own way. She could not bear to be thwarted," Colin said with contempt. "It is possible being faced with lefeat for the first time in her life drove her mad, but nadness does not forgive what she did to Edwin and Brendan and tried to do to you."

Meary lay her fingers on his lips. "'Tis up to God to udge her."

"It is well for her it is."

"'Tis best remembered as a lesson on the evil of varice and otherwise forgotten," Seumas advised him. 'Try to be thinking of the joy of this day rather than be rooding on what cannot be changed. By some miracle of God, the woman ye love be standing by yer side. Miracles e rare, and should be celebrated."

Shaking off the shock of Meary's revelation, Colin collected his thoughts. It would be a long time before he was able to come fully to terms with his mother's

treachery, but he would not let her ghost have pow
over his future. His mother had caused them all enoug
harm.

Turning to Seumas, he said, "You are right, and
know exactly how I wish to celebrate this miracle. Wi
your permission, Mr. O'Hanlon, I'd like to make Mea
my bride this very day."

"I give ye me permission and me blessing."

"Ye give us your blessing?" Meary questioned
wonderment.

"Ye still want to be marrying him, don't ye?" l
asked gruffly.

"Aye."

"Well, then, I guess me mind 'tis settled. I wouldn
feel right letting ye marry a man without me blessing.
He squeezed her hand. "Mind, I'll be watching him t
make sure he treats ye right, and if I ever find he hasn"
he'll be on his knees begging for mercy before I'
through with him. But since ye love him . . . and he ha
proved to me satisfaction he truly loves ye . . . I hav
decided I can give me blessing to yer union with a clea
conscience."

Meary was too joyful to waste words asking what ha
happened between her mentor and Colin to make hir
change his mind about her bridegroom. She threw he
arms around him and kissed his weathered cheek. "Oh
Seumas, thank ye."

"Yes, thank you." Colin heartily shook his hand
before turning to the man nearest them. "You," h
shouted. "My horse is the swiftest I own. Take it and rid
to the church without delay. If the minister is not there
check his house. I want him back here before nightfal
He has a wedding to perform!"

446

Epilogue

Lord Collin Garrick, the marquess of Swanscroft and proud owner of the most prosperous estate in Ireland, looked up from his ledgers and smiled broadly.

His wife Meary sat but a few feet from him, nursing their firstborn and singing a Gaelic lullaby. It was difficult to concentrate on practical matters with her sitting so near, but he had no intention of asking them to leave. Meary and their son bathed in golden firelight was a sight not to be missed.

Besides, Little Brendan was not the only one who was fond of lullabies. He could listen to Meary sing from dawn until dusk and never grow tired of the sound.

Brendan cooed and reached for a strand of his mother's flaxen hair, wrapping it around his tiny fist as she shifted him from one breast to the other. As soon as he latched on to the nipple, he sighed in contentment, gave his mother a rapturous gaze and closed his eyes. Colin grinned his approval. Brendan was a wise lad. He knew wherein the true pleasures of life lay.

Their son was nearly a year old, and every day
surprised them with some new skill. Colin found he d
not mind sharing Meary with his son as he had feared
might. He had discovered in himself a great liking fo
children. They were fascinating creatures.

Of late, he had been thinking it would be nice to ad
another member to their little family.

Colin could easily guess Meary's reaction if he share
his thought with her. She adored being a mother, an
never on this earth could there have been a more lovin
devoted parent. If he told her he wanted another chil
she would squeal with delight and drag him up the stai
to their bed to start on the project immediately.

His blood warmed at the thought. Making childre
with Meary was every bit as delightful as holding th
product of their love in his arms. As soon as Brendan wa
asleep, he would have to suggest just that—not that the
needed the excuse of procreation to share their passio
Any excuse would do, or none at all.

He didn't know why God had blessed him with a wife a
fine as Meary, but not a day went by he did not thank Hi
for his generosity.

She was everything a man could wish for and mor
Comely, intelligent, loyal, loving . . . The list would g
on forever if he sought to chronicle all her virtues.

He had come to Ireland seeking solitude and instea
had found love in the form of a beautiful Irish harpis

He was a most fortunate man.